Karin Baine lives in Northern Ireland, with her husband, two sons, and her out-of-control notebook collection. Her mother and her grandmother's vast collection of books inspired her love of reading and her dream of becoming a Mills & Boon author. Now she can tell people she has a *proper* job! You can follow Karin on Twitter, @karinbaine1, or visit her website for the latest news—karinbaine.com.

Julie Danvers grew up in a rural community surrounded by farmland. Although her town was small, it offered plenty of scope for imagination, as well as an excellent library. Books allowed Julie to have many adventures from her own home, and her love affair with reading has never ended. She loves to write about heroes and heroines who are adventurous, passionate about a cause, and looking for the best in themselves and others. Julie's website is juliedanvers.wordpress.com.

ONE NIGHT WITH HER ITALIAN DOC

KARIN BAINE

FALLING AGAIN IN EL SALVADOR

JULIE DANVERS

MILLS & BOON

First Published in Great Britain 2020
by Mills & Boon, an imprint of HarperCollins*Publishers*
1 London Bridge Street, London, SE1 9GF

One Night with Her Italian Doc © 2020 by Karin Baine

Falling Again in El Salvador © 2020 by Alexis Silas

ISBN: 978-0-263-28448-5

MIX
Paper from
responsible sources
FSC **FSC® C007454**

ONE NIGHT WITH HER ITALIAN DOC

KARIN BAINE

MILLS & BOON

For D xx

CHAPTER ONE

SOPHIE BLYTHE WAS a terrible, horrible person. Why else would the woman she'd agreed to care for on the cruise of a lifetime currently be on a drip in the on-board medical centre?

'I'm so sorry, Edith. It's my fault you're in this state. I should've been keeping a closer eye on you.'

'Nonsense. I'm seventy-eight years old. I'm responsible for my own actions,' she insisted, albeit weakly, from her hospital bed.

'You brought me with you on this trip to look after you.' So far, she hadn't done a very good job. They'd only boarded the cruise ship at Barcelona three days ago and they were already having a medical emergency.

Working full time in a care home, it was literally Sophie's job to look after the elderly and infirm. She had only taken time out because her neighbour had asked her to accompany her on this trip. With her mobility issues, Edith needed someone to help her get around and Sophie had been keen to escape from the aftermath of her break-up with Ryan. A cruise around the Mediterranean was supposed to be doing them both a world of good. But they were off to a dubious start.

Edith slid her hand over the crisp white sheets

to clasp Sophie's. 'You've been a blessing to me. I wouldn't have seen half of the things so far if it hadn't been for you taking care of me and organising transportation. It's not your fault this silly old woman fell asleep on her balcony in the sun. Stop worrying.'

The reminder of those adventures they'd enjoyed before her travel companion had become ill raised a smile on Sophie's lips. They'd been overawed by the sheer volume of noise and number of people in Barcelona as they'd explored the sprawling stalls of Las Ramblas, looking for souvenirs.

Later, the hop-on-hop-off bus they'd taken at their leisure had driven past all manner of designer stores and the fantasy-scape of Gaudi's architecture. She'd found joy in the chatter of the parakeets high up in the trees and the sight of decorative water imps playing in the majestic fountains before they'd even embarked on the ship.

'Pompeii was certainly an experience, wasn't it?' They'd wandered the sprawling ruins of Pompeii together, both amazed at the mosaics and painting still visible in some of the buildings, and solemn when they'd seen the body casts of those frozen in time by the eruption of Vesuvius.

'It was. Naples wasn't at all what I expected either. So many colourful scooters and those Italian policemen… phew.' Edith's sense of humour had helped make this trip so much fun and had taken Sophie's mind off matters at home in England.

Waking up in the mornings in her state room, opening the curtains to find herself in a different port every day was exactly the kind of adventure Sophie thought she needed to re-centre herself.

This Bohemian lifestyle suited her. She'd lived it in her twenties. Once she'd got her nursing qualifications, she'd travelled the world, using her skills to take placements where she could. It was a legacy from her parents that she hadn't been able to stay still for long. Her father had been a wannabe rock star who'd had no intention of giving up touring pubs and clubs simply because he'd got someone pregnant.

He hadn't put her mother off unsuitable men either. He was only one in a line of eternal bachelors she'd followed from town to town, hopping from one relationship to the next in the hope of finding love. They were hardly the foundations for a stable childhood. Or role models. Sophie had no experience of settled family life. She didn't even know where either of them were at this moment in time.

If it hadn't been for Ryan she might still be flitting from one city to the next, but she'd fallen head over heels for him when they'd met in Thailand. He'd convinced her to go back with him to England and settle down. It was everything you were supposed to do for someone you loved. Yet it was a decision she'd come to regret. Domestic life had squashed her free spirit and left her trapped in a semi-detached in Kent. Perhaps she was more like her father with the wandering feet than she'd thought.

Ryan had simply wanted a normal life and she'd tried to be the partner to share it with him. They had loved each other back then. She simply hadn't realised that the adventurous spirit she'd seen in him in Phuket had been a one-time deal. It had meant giving up travelling in exchange for a mortgage and a permanent job in the countryside, too far from London and the city life she'd grown up in for her restless spirit.

After three years together she'd told him how trapped she felt and had pushed for something to inject some excitement into their relationship. When he'd agreed that their relationship had grown stale, she'd imagined swapping suburbia for a trek in the Himalayas or kayaking in Patagonia.

Ryan had taken it to mean he should run off with his co-worker at the bank, to get married in Las Vegas, leaving Sophie with a life she'd never wanted. He was being 'true to his heart,' apparently. She had no idea how long Ryan had been sleeping with his colleague before he'd decided he wanted to be with her for ever, but it had been less time than Sophie had wasted being with him. Now, with her spirit crushed, she didn't know what to do or where to go.

Thank goodness Edith had taken pity on her and flung her a lifeline. She'd suspected the generous offer had been more for her benefit than her dear neighbour's when she'd been so miserable. It was a shame this was how she'd repaid her kindness.

'I'll be back on my feet in no time,' she reassured Sophie.

'You'd better be. It's Rome next on the itinerary. We've still got to tick the Colosseum and the Trevi Fountain off your…list.' Sophie stopped before the word 'bucket' inserted itself in there. This was supposed to be Edith's 'last hurrah before she croaked.' Her words, not Sophie's.

She'd wanted to see Italy and France one final time before she was no longer able to travel at all. Now those plans were in jeopardy and Sophie couldn't help but shower herself in blame.

'I'll still be able to do all that, won't I, Doctor?' Edith addressed the medic overseeing her treatment.

Sophie had been in so much of a panic when they'd first entered the clinic she hadn't given her attention to anyone other than Edith. Her friend had been whisked off for a series of tests, leaving Sophie to marinate in worry out at Reception. Now she could see why the other staff members had a twinkle in their eyes every time someone mentioned his name.

Dr Luciano Montavano was Italian, according to the flag on the badge pinned to his natty uniform. It was the only way she would have known he was a doctor at all. Dressed in his whites he looked like every other officer she'd seen on board. Only much more appealing to the eye than all the rest.

Sophie didn't have a particular type, finding herself more drawn to the soul within the outer shell of a man. Although her judgement clearly needed some work in that department, none of that meant she couldn't appreciate a handsome face or a to-die-for body.

At five foot nine she was no slouch in the height stakes, but he towered over her. He was lean and tanned and his hair was the same almost-black as his eyes, save for the few strands of silver streaking his temples. It was as if the cruise company had drafted him in especially so the passengers had something good to look at whilst they were at sea.

Sophie tutted, disgusted with herself for being so easily distracted by such a shallow thing as someone's appearance and focused back on Edith, who was enduring the ship's nurse's repeated attempts to insert a cannula into her arm.

'Would you like me to do that? I'm a qualified nurse.' She grimaced at the harsh tone of her own voice but Edith had been through so much already it didn't seem fair to keep pricking her with needles.

'So am I. Thank you,' the nurse with the American twang said through a forced smile and gritted teeth.

'Mrs Fields is very dehydrated after the vomiting. It makes it difficult to find a suitable vein,' the Italian distraction informed her.

She knew that, of course she did, but she wanted to do something useful. After all, she hadn't been there during the night when Edith had needed her most. If only she'd knocked on the wall or shouted for her, Sophie could have done something or gone for help sooner. Instead, Edith had decided not to bother anyone and had been ill all through the night alone, until Sophie had called to take her to breakfast.

'There we are.' The American in blue scrubs eventually managed to get a line in and shot her a triumphant look.

'I want a saline drip and we'll do some more scans when she's rehydrated.' Dr Montavano consulted his next in command quietly with Sophie straining to hear the conversation. She didn't appreciate being shut out when she'd told them she was a fellow professional, along with being Edith's carer.

'Have you checked her blood sugar?' Her question was directed at the doctor himself. She knew the standard protocols and wanted to make sure they were following them here. They might be on a ship in the middle of the sea but she still expected Edith to have the same healthcare she would receive anywhere else.

'Yes.' He sounded exasperated with her. Tough. She would make a nuisance of herself until she was sure Edith was in better hands than hers.

'What about her sodium, electrolytes and kidney function? Do you even have the lab facilities to do all that here?'

'We're monitoring Mrs Fields as best we can.'

'I'm not sure that's good enough.' Not that they had any other choice at present but at least by making her professional status known they wouldn't be able to fob Edith off with anything less than the best treatment available.

'Sophie, everyone has been very attentive. Please, don't worry.' Edith tried to put her mind at rest but it was only natural to be concerned when they were so far from home and the medical services they took for granted.

'As long as you're okay, that's all that matters.' She didn't want to upset Edith, so she'd simply have to bite her tongue and let the others get on with their work. It didn't mean she wouldn't be keeping a close eye on things, though.

'Will I have to stay here overnight, Doctor?'

'I'm afraid so, Mrs Fields.' That accent was too much. Surely he was over-egging it? He probably did this with all the female tourists to give them a thrill.

'We want to watch you.'

Sophie snorted. 'I'll stay with you, Edith, while you're here under *observation*,' she said, correcting the doctor's unfortunate phrasing.

'I'm afraid that won't be possible Ms…' He stood

with his hands clasped behind his back, waiting for her to introduce herself.

'Blythe. Sophie Blythe.'

'Sophie.' He tested her name on his lips and gave her a cheek-reddening smile.

This was ridiculous.

'I'm afraid we do not have the space to accommodate you.'

'I'll just stay here.' She plonked herself into the unyielding plastic chair by the bed. It wasn't as though she would take up too much room.

A frown marked the doctor's otherwise perfect features. 'We can only let you come here during visiting hours. As you can see, we are a small facility. We might need this room to accommodate emergencies.'

'I would've thought this constituted an emergency.'

A bell rang out down the corridor.

'That's the end of visiting, I'm afraid.' The nurse didn't bother turning around to glance at Sophie and carried on hooking up Edith's drip. She didn't have to when Sophie knew she'd be sporting a look of relief, glad to get rid of her. If their roles were reversed she wouldn't be happy with someone trying to tell her how to do her job either.

'When can I come back?' She didn't want to whine or appear petulant but Edith had paid a lot of money for Sophie to be with her. If only they hadn't had separate cabins she might have been saved from all of this. As it was, all Sophie could do was keep her company during her treatment.

'Next visiting is from three p.m. to six p.m.' He positioned his hand in the small of her back and gently tried to guide her out the door.

Sophie dug her heels in. 'Wait. Are you actually throwing me out?'

His grin tempted her to stamp hard on his foot. 'Visiting is at three p.m.'

'What am I supposed to do until then?'

'Lie by the pool, drink cocktails, go dancing and do all the things I wish I could do. You're young. Go and enjoy yourself.' Edith waved a hand at her as she ganged up with the others and dismissed her from her duties.

'Your grandmother is right.'

Sophie rolled her eyes as her medical credentials were sidelined for a narrative that suited him better.

'Edith is not my grandmother.'

'Go, enjoy your vacation.'

'I'm not on vacation,' she protested as he propelled her out the door and down the corridor.

'Miss…Sophie, your…friend needs lots of rest. You, however, seem as though you need to cut loose for a while. There is free food and free drink available. You could take in a show while you wait. There is no need to worry. Mrs Fields is in good hands.' Those same hands guided her through Reception, leaving Sophie spluttering with indignation as he closed the door on her.

'I'll be back,' she shouted through the closed door before she realised it sounded like a threat. 'For visiting. Later.'

There was no reply. She tried the door one last time but they'd closed up shop. The note taped to the wall advised that visitors were required to phone ahead to gain access outside the approved hours, something she didn't think the officious doctor would be in a hurry to do.

The long corridor was empty apart from the vending machine that dispensed basic medical necessities such as sticking plasters and antiseptic for those unfortunate enough to hurt themselves out of hours. It struck her how quiet it was at this end of the ship. A conscious design decision, she supposed, for the patients to find some peace away from the partying. However, it meant there was simply nothing for her to do here until she was able to check on Edith again. There wasn't even a seat to sit on.

She walked farther into the belly of the ship, exchanging greetings with the stewards scurrying in and out of the cabins, who were getting them spotless again before the guests returned from their leisure pursuits.

The lifts were busy transporting guests to the many decks, so Sophie took the stairs instead. Happy families and couples dressed for the pool or a spot of sunbathing stepped in time beside her and she followed them out onto the top deck.

She blinked as she emerged into the sunlight, feeling the heat immediately kissing her bare skin. Her senses kicked in all at once, assaulted by the noise of the loud music, the sight of the crowds dancing and the smell of chlorine, sun cream and food. She hadn't realised there was an all-day buffet provided. It reminded her of a school cafeteria, only with better quality food. Edith preferred to sit in one of the more civilised restaurants downstairs. Sophie's stomach rumbled, letting her know it wasn't fussy and she was yet to have lunch.

Perhaps she'd avail herself of one of the sun loungers lining the deck and enjoy an al fresco snack with everyone else. She might even indulge in one of those delicious-looking frozen cocktails in plentiful supply. It was just the thing to take the edge off the day's drama and it might even help her forget Deliciano Luciano, who'd managed to get her adrenaline pumping without even trying.

Luciano watched as the door rattled with Miss Blythe still ranting on the other side of it, a smirk playing on his lips. But it was soon followed by a frown. He shouldn't be amused or find this Sophie person intriguing. For eight months at sea, in his new role as cruise doctor, he'd managed to keep that professional line drawn between him and the passengers and he preferred to keep it that way.

He turned away, hotfooting it back to his patient and the safety of the treatment rooms.

'Sorry about that, Mrs Fields. Now, we will let the drip do its work and take another look at you later.'

'Yes, Doctor.'

That was what he liked. A compliant patient. Sometimes they had to deal with people who'd overindulged in the unlimited alcohol, but if they were too raucous, Security got involved. In extreme cases they'd be ejected from the ship, holiday over. He didn't get a lot of dissension in his own little kingdom here. Certainly, he wasn't used to fellow medical professionals challenging him or his authority. As a result, he was finding it difficult to shift thoughts of the rebellious Sophie out of his head.

'I'm sure you're glad to see the back of her. Wowee,' Patrice, the nurse who'd witnessed most of their exchange, whispered as they left the room.

'She's clearly very concerned.' He didn't want to make excuses for her but neither did he wish to bad-mouth her in her absence. In the past, he too had demanded the right to be included in a loved one's treatment. Many times, in fact.

Each time Renata had lost one of their precious babies, and finally when she'd contracted sepsis, he'd been there, taking out his pain on the very people trying to help his wife. He should have known better and had always apologised after the fact but it helped him understand Sophie's frustrations. What he was struggling to figure out was his reaction to her. Since Renata, he hadn't so much as looked at another woman, never mind given anyone a second thought. Much to his mother's despair.

'You're my handsome boy, Luciano. I know you loved Renata very much. We all did. But you deserve to be happy again,' she'd said to him before he'd left. What she'd meant was that he deserved to have another chance at having a family. Her desire for more grandchildren was no doubt behind the determination to see him married again.

He felt the pressure to meet someone new, despite it being only two years since he'd lost his wife, because his parents' marriage was held up as a template for the rest of the family. They'd been childhood sweethearts, had married young and raised four children—all whilst tending their own vineyard. It was a recipe for a good life that he and his siblings had all wanted to replicate.

He was the only one to have failed so far. Even his kid brother had got engaged and now the expectation weighing down on Luciano had become suffocating. It was even more painful because his own house had become so lonely and empty without Renata waiting for him there. She'd been stolen away from him too soon, along with the dream of having a family of their own.

That was why he'd given up his role as a family practitioner and signed on for the life of a cruise doctor—where relationships amongst the crew were frowned on and he was able to hide out in the medical centre. Working and sleeping was how he spent his days and nights, and he'd been content to do so, foregoing the crew social scene and excursions ashore. He was simply trundling along, existing without having to deal with real life outside. He didn't want anyone else. Not when it meant suffering that same crushing pain when they vanished from existence. He'd barely survived losing the wife and babies who'd been everything to him. There wouldn't be a second time.

It suited him to drift along with the tide, not under any pressure to find another significant other. Something he'd done happily for the entirety of his contract so far. So why, after a brief, emotionally charged introduction to one particular guest, could he remember every single detail of it? And her? Her long dark hair, her sparkling blue eyes and the freckles on her bare shoulders where the sun had been lucky enough to touch her skin.

It was unsettling to be jolted out of this safe space he'd created for himself onboard the ship. Therefore, Mrs Fields and her companion would become his top priority. Then he could discharge them both and let them get back to their holiday whilst he returned to his usual, solitary routine.

CHAPTER TWO

IN THE GOOD old days, Sophie wouldn't have thought twice about lying by the pool, knocking back luminous alcoholic drinks.

That had been pre-Ryan. Since then she'd realised the importance of responsibility and the consequences of people shirking. It made her think twice about taking off into the great unknown again, unprepared with no back-up plan if things fell through. He'd been a valuable lesson to someone who'd thought she'd achieved what her parents couldn't by settling down with one person for the rest of her life. Not so useful to a person trying to relax. Thanks to him, she was no longer able to switch off that part of her brain that worried about poor Edith lying in a hospital bed.

'Your drink, ma'am.' A waiter—Carlo, according to his name badge—appeared by her side and extended a tray towards her.

'Oh, thank you.' Despite her reticence, Sophie had decided to take Edith's advice and at least try to enjoy herself. And she was starting by taking advantage of the all-inclusive drinks package.

'You know we have a singles club for passengers travelling on their own. I think they're hosting a getting-to-know-each-other disco tonight. There's no need to sit up here on your own. There are plenty of other singletons on board you could meet up with.' The earnest waiter was being so super-friendly she was trying not to take offence, despite the fact that he was only a few years younger than she was and clearly thought she was some charity case desperately in need of friends.

'That's okay. I'm not—'

'No need to be ashamed. Everyone's a bit nervous at first but, believe me, by the end of this cruise you'll be having the time of your life.'

What could she do but smile sweetly and sip her drink, hoping it would extinguish the indignant fire burning in her belly. It wasn't Carlo's fault he'd touched on an exposed nerve. Even she hadn't realised the break-up was still affecting her. It wasn't that she was missing Ryan, but seeing everyone else coupled up and enjoying their holiday was a constant reminder that she was on her own. In her early twenties she'd had the world at her feet. She'd been unafraid to go it alone. She wished she could get that person back.

'Is there anything else I can get for you?'

An invisibility cloak?

The attentive Carlo was waiting for further instruction and she wondered how many lonely women propositioned him during their holiday. More to the point, how many he actually obliged.

'No, thank you. I have everything I need.' She raised her glass, which was full of Irish liqueur, vodka, ice cream and chocolate sauce. It was more dessert than drink but calling it a cocktail apparently lessened its calorific content.

Once she was on her own again she was able to

relax more. There was a fiesta vibe as the DJ cranked up the music and people were strutting their stuff on the open-air dance floor.

Sophie unfastened her halter-neck top and slid her shorts off to take in the sun's rays along with everyone else, grateful she had packed a couple of bikinis at the last minute. She popped on her sunglasses, lowered the back on her lounger and stretched out. With her ice-cream cocktail and the plate of food she'd helped herself to from the buffet, she was all set for the afternoon. It wasn't long before her earlier stress began to ebb away and the encounter with Dr Montavano seemed like a bad dream.

'Ahem.'

Sophie was woken up some time later by someone clearing their throat nearby. It was easy to see how Edith had dozed off in the heat, with the gentle motion of the ship rocking her to sleep like a baby in a crib. Thankfully Sophie had had the foresight to put on sunscreen before getting dressed this morning to avoid suffering as Edith had.

She stretched her arms out over the top of the sun bed with a yawn. Apparently, she was capable of chilling out after all. Perhaps it was a muscle memory left over from her more selfish, less responsible travelling years.

'Ahem.'

The throat-clearing sounded closer now as a large shadow settled over her, blocking out the sun. She took off her shades to get a better look at whoever was trying to get her attention. It was possible the ever-attentive Carlo was already trying to matchmake between his sad, lonely customers. She was going to have to be more forceful about not participating in any group activities. She wasn't on some booze cruise, where being on her own for five minutes was an invitation to any predatory males who happened by.

'I'm sorry but I would really appreciate being left alone. I've just got out of a soul-destroying relationship and the only love affair I'm interested in is one with myself.' It might sound egotistical, or like she was oversharing, to someone she didn't know very well, but in her experience being polite in these situations didn't get the point across.

'That's good to know and I'm sorry to disturb your…self-love but I need to speak to you.'

She recognised that heavily accented voice and clumsy choice of words.

Once he stepped directly out of the sun, she could see it was the dishy Italian doctor she'd sparred with earlier.

'Sorry. I didn't realise it was you, Doctor. I had an attentive waiter trying to make me join the lonely hearts club.' Every word she'd uttered came back to haunt her. What must he think of her? Whatever it was had clearly amused him as she witnessed his attempt to hide a smirk.

'We did try to reach you in your cabin.'

'Everyone kept telling me to go and relax, so I did.' As she tried to justify her actions she began to pull on her shorts, aware she was lying here with only a few scraps of canary-yellow fabric to cover her modesty.

'Mrs Fields is experiencing some complications.' His face was deadly serious now, making Sophie's heart pound so hard in her ears it was deafening.

'What's happened? Is Edith okay?' She tugged her top on over her head, ready to move at a moment's notice.

'She's fine but I'd appreciate it if you'd could come with me back to the clinic to discuss her treatment.' He looked as uncomfortable as she felt fumbling with the straps of her halter-neck.

'Let me.'

Before she could protest, his warm hands brushed the sensitive skin of her neck to tie the ends of the coral-coloured straps securely.

'Thanks,' she croaked, her throat suddenly dry and her skin burning where his fingers had briefly made contact.

'It's not too tight?'

'No. Thank you.' She couldn't look at him. At least not until she'd stopped blushing.

Gathering up her belongings, she kept her back to him until she could trust herself not to make eye contact with the owner of those strong, confident hands.

Her thoughts were on Edith and what on earth had happened, but there was a small place taken up by reflecting on the effect the doctor was having on her. Perhaps Carlo was right and she'd been on her own too long.

Luciano was feeling the heat and not solely because he was standing in the sun in full uniform. He almost never ventured up on deck, especially not with the passengers. Neither did he usually volunteer to personally locate a family member. They could have made a public announcement over the loudspeaker to find her but, no, he'd insisted on breaking the news himself. Goodness knew why. She wasn't going to take it well. In fact, she'd probably vent her ire at him when he was the one who'd forced her out of the medical centre.

He was accepting responsibility for that decision and whatever Ms Sophie had to say on the matter.

If that was the sole truth he wouldn't be sweating now at the sight of her teeny-weeny two-piece. Neither would he have jumped at the chance to help cover her up, making skin-to-skin contact in the process.

He was at a loss to explain why he was acting like a nervous suitor around this particular passenger, who was a burst of sunshine yellow in his otherwise cloudy morning. Not only was he a doctor with considerable experience of dealing with the human body but pretty women of all ages and sizes came through the clinic and he'd barely noticed them beyond their ailments. Sophie had clearly rattled him by not falling into line earlier and this was him battling to regain some sort of control of the situation.

He watched and waited as she rolled up her towel, popped it into her bag and slipped her feet into her sandals. 'Okay, let's go.'

With a brief nod he took his cue to leave, heading towards the lift with Sophie falling in behind him.

'*Buenos días.*'

'*Bonjour, Capitaine.*'

'Hello, there.'

As they waited for the lift, Luciano was greeted by guests of all nationalities. He offered them all a '*Buongiorno*' in return.

'*Capitaine?*' Sophie mocked with a raised eyebrow.

He kept his eyes on the electronic display, watching the numbers rise steadily towards their deck. Too slowly for his liking.

'It's the uniform. Happens all the time.'

'And, of course, you don't correct them.'

He jabbed the button again, even though it wasn't going to make the lift come any faster.

'I did for a while. The uniform confuses people and I don't like to embarrass them by correcting them when they're simply saying hello.' She didn't need to know about the selfies passengers demanded. They didn't care. All they wanted was a souvenir snap of a man in uniform and it was part of the reason he tried to avoid coming up here.

As soon as the lift door opened and the new batch of sun worshippers trooped out, Luciano stepped in. He only waited long enough for Sophie to join him before punching in the number for the clinic deck, hopefully before anyone else jumped in with them and forced small talk.

'What's happened to Edith? It must've been serious for *you* to come all this way to find me.' There was nowhere in this steel box to escape Sophie's scrutiny, or her temper if it got the better of her again.

It didn't matter about their personality clash to this point, it was his duty to be professional. He had hoped she'd wait until they got back to the clinic before he the news. At least there he had a sense of authority.

'I wanted to apologise for being so abrupt with you earlier. I understand you have a personal and professional investment in the patient.'

'Edith.'

'Edith. Although we were able to give her fluids and rehydrate her, her blood pressure remains high.'

'That's not unusual after being dehydrated, is it?'

Again, Sophie displayed her medical knowledge of the situation. With cases of dehydration the hormone vasopressin could be secreted into the bloodstream if sodium levels dropped as a result of losing too much fluid. Excess vasopressin could cause the blood vessels to constrict, thereby increasing blood pressure. He'd seen a lot of it over these past months. That was why he'd known something wasn't quite right here.

'No, but with her age I don't want to take any chances. We'll continue to monitor her.'

'But if you can't get it under control there's a chance it could lead to something more serious, such as a heart attack or stroke. This is exactly what I was worried about. I knew I should've stayed with her but, oh, no, you knew best...' Unlike every other tourist he encountered, she wasn't impressed by his uniform or intimidated by his position. She drew herself up to her full height. Tall enough to be a model but still some way from his six-foot-two frame. She made for a worthy opponent, even though they were supposed to be on the same team.

'You can't do any more for her than we already have.'

'I should've stayed with her instead of swanning about the ship like I'm on holiday.' Beyond the anger as she squared up to him, Luciano could see guilty tears welling in her eyes. It was understandable. He'd experienced that same sense of injustice and frustration when he'd been shut out of Renata's treatment. It was impossible not to get emotional, even knowing that made you more of a hindrance in the treatment of a loved one.

'I'm sure she's going to be all right. I just wanted to keep you informed.' Certain parts of his anatomy might've been in danger if he'd kept anything from her and something serious had happened.

The lift arrived with a 'ding,' signalling a timeout as they stopped to let new passengers in. They travelled the remaining floors in silence, though he could feel Sophie's rage emanating from the other side of the lift.

He let Sophie lead the way back to the clinic, although it was down to him to get them on the other side of the locked doors and into the treatment room.

'She's in here, resting.' He wanted her to know this wasn't the time for finger pointing. It wasn't going to do Mrs Fields any good to be caught in the midst of their feud.

'Oh, Edith. Are you feeling okay? I'm a terrible friend for leaving you.' Sophie's guilty plea when she saw her frail companion struck Luciano square in the chest. She was blaming herself, even though it had been his decision to send her away.

'I'll survive. Besides, if the doctor hadn't chucked you out I would've done it myself. There's no point in both of us being cooped up in here.' She was pale and weak but Edith hadn't lost her sense of humour. It went some way to easing the tension in the room and Luciano was grateful for it.

He stepped up to the bedside. 'Obviously we want to take every precaution where Mrs Fields is concerned. In case her condition worsens, or she requires long-term treatment, I'd prefer we put her ashore in the nearest hospital. I'm going to need you to pack your bags and disembark at the next port. Unfortunately, Mrs Fields won't be able to continue this trip.'

Luciano had already discussed it with his patient, the news coming as nothing of a shock under the circumstances. She'd even gone as far as joking that this was the reason she'd taken out such extensive travel insurance—a necessity for someone of her age with such numerous health conditions. The medical bills at sea could be enough to bankrupt any unfortunate individual who hadn't had the foresight to take out health coverage. He didn't think it was going to be as easy a conversation with her companion.

Sophie rounded on him, hands on hips, those flecks around her irises blazing like green fire in her otherwise blue eyes. 'You're actually throwing us off the ship now? You really get off on this power trip of yours, don't you?'

Luciano was agog at the vitriol launched at him. 'It's standard protocol. Not a personal decision or a display of any megalomania. We're not equipped to have passengers receive long-term treatment on the ship.'

Sophie didn't back down, maintaining eye contact and managing to sneer at him simultaneously. 'Obviously I'm going to accompany Edith to the hospital but I'd appreciate a second opinion on whether or not she's able to continue her trip.'

'You're well within your rights to do so but it will mean waiting until another doctor is available.' Strictly speaking, the buck stopped with him. He made the medical decisions and reported them back to the captain. It wasn't going to help relations if he confirmed her idea that he was running a dictatorship here.

'That won't be necessary.'

Sophie stood down once Edith spoke, all that spine-strengthening indignation seeping away until she physically wilted into the chair by Edith's bed. 'Whatever you want. We need to get you back on your feet, Edie. That's the most important thing.'

She clasped the woman's hand between both of hers, abandoning the battle with Luciano to focus on her friend.

'Oh, don't worry. I'll have a few days' rest and I'm sure I'll be as right as rain. There's no need for second opinions or to ruin your holiday.'

'But, Edith—'

It appeared Sophie had met her match in this woman, who raised her hand and cut her off in mid-protest.

Perhaps he should ask Edith later for tips on how best to manage riled passengers.

'"But, Edith" nothing. You need this trip more than I do. Why did you think I asked you to come?'

'To—to take care of you?' Sophie stuttered, no longer sounding so sure of herself.

Edith shook her head. 'For you. You've been so despondent lately and I know you hate that job in the care home. The only time I see you come to life is when you talk about the travels you used to have when you were younger. Or when you and Dr Montavano start bickering over me.'

'I do not!'

As she teased Sophie, the mischievous Edith displayed the fighting spirit Luciano was sure wouldn't let her down in her fight back to full health.

He supressed the urge to smile. Any sign of smugness on his part would undoubtedly come under fire from the subject of Edith's well-meaning affection.

'Nonsense. That Ryan clipped your wings and you

are someone who needs to fly, or in this case *sail*. You are staying here.'

Sophie scoffed at the suggestion. 'There's no way I'm abandoning you in a foreign hospital while I lounge around a pool.'

'Why not? You can't do anything for me. Besides, I've spoken to John.'

'Your son? Doesn't he live in Spain?'

'Yes, and he's flying in to be with me. Once I'm up and about again I'm going home with him to spend some time with the lovely grandchildren and great-grandchildren I rarely get to see. I'll be going to Seville to recuperate and you're not invited.'

'Edith, it's a very kind offer but I don't want to take advantage of your generosity.'

'Not at all. The cruise is all paid for. One of us may as well get the benefit of it and I think a few days away will do you the world of good. Although I will need you to pack my things for me.'

Sophie looked at him as though expecting him to back her up. This definitely wasn't his jurisdiction. 'It sounds as though Mrs Fields has it all planned out.'

'It certainly does.'

Not only did it mean Edith would be in the best place for after-care but Sophie would have no reason to venture into his domain and upset the status quo. He wasn't going to argue and he wouldn't advise Sophie to either.

'Can I at least accompany her when she's transferred to the hospital to make sure she's settled in?' She deferred to him, her whole demeanour changing as she asked him for the favour.

'If you'd like. The ship won't be sailing until later

tonight. I'll let the captain know what's happening. I'll be travelling to the hospital too to oversee the transfer of Edith's care.' If anything was going to put her off the idea, he was sure it would be the thought of spending more time with him.

'As the attending physician I'd expect nothing less.' She batted her eyelashes. No doubt an attempt to lull him into a false sense of security before she launched another verbal attack on him.

'Chief Physician,' he added, in the hope his status would give him more authority in her eyes. All he received in response was a raised eyebrow.

As long as they made it back on board before the ship set sail and they weren't stranded together for the night, he supposed they'd survive. At least they'd have Edith and the paramedics as a barrier between them until then.

It was odd that two people who barely knew each other should immediately clash the way they had. Especially when, or perhaps it was because, they worked in the same field. Usually the nurses deferred to him in matters of treatment and, likewise, he respected their position and input. For some reason there was friction, a spark between them where there ought not to be one. Whatever was causing that flash of passionate temper, he hoped to avoid it in the future.

With any luck, once Edith was settled and they were back on board, they'd go their separate ways. Sophie clearly needed the holiday her friend wanted for her, chilling out by the pool. Leaving him free to return to the sanctity of his clinic, where they needn't run into each other again for the duration of her vacation.

His place of work on board was supposed to help

him escape thoughts of his late wife and the idea everyone had that he should find someone new.

So how had one woman managed to barge her way in and upend those plans?

CHAPTER THREE

KICKING BACK AND emptying your head of all thoughts except your own enjoyment wasn't as easy as Sophie remembered. She and Dr Montavano had waited until Edith had a bed at the hospital and they were up to date with her medical notes before leaving her. They'd travelled back to the ship in a taxi together, making polite small talk whilst avoiding another clash.

That should've ended all contact between them. Unfortunately, as she was unable to get a phone signal out on the high seas, she had to rely on updates from the good doctor to catch up on Edith's condition.

'Are you back again?' It was Patrice, the nurse who'd first attended to Edith, who spotted her in Reception.

'I wondered if you'd heard anything from the hospital today about my friend, Edith Fields?' She walked over to the desk, bypassing the receptionist to speak directly to the nurse, cutting out the anticipated conversation about how everyone was too busy to speak to her.

Sophie had since apologised to her fellow nursing colleague for her behaviour, which Patrice had graciously accepted, meaning there was only one other person left onboard for her to be awkward around.

'Dr Montavano was in contact with them earlier. Let me go and get him and he can tell you himself.'

'That's really not necessary. I don't want to disturb him.' Sophie's plea fell into the void left by Patrice's departure.

She let out a sigh, resigned to the fact that she'd be forced to see the doctor again. It was difficult enough to get him out of her head without seeing him first thing in the morning. She didn't need a refresher of how good he looked in his whites.

Okay, she sounded as shallow as all those other women swooning over him as he passed by. Deep down, she knew it was more than the physical attraction she was trying to swerve. There was something between them masquerading as a personality clash that was threatening to get in the way of her own self-discovery.

As well as serving as a companion to Edith, she'd hoped this trip would help her rediscover the woman she'd once been. Once upon a time if a guy had taken her fancy she wouldn't have thought twice about acting on that impulse. She hadn't worried about the conse-quences of asking a man out or what their future held. Back then she'd lived in the moment. These days she was a much more cautious character. Her time with Ryan had made her think more carefully about get-ting involved with anyone. Especially when the per-son who'd caught her eye couldn't seem to get rid of her fast enough.

'Ms Blythe?'

There was that whoosh of blood in her veins again at the sound of his silky Italian voice. Until now she'd associated it with their disagreement over Edith's treat-ment. Watching him striding towards her, she wondered if the increase in her blood pressure was for an entirely different reason.

The dark hair, tanned skin and that dreamy doctor façade had the same effect on most people. It was possible her attraction towards him, unwanted and ill-timed though it was, had manifested in an outburst of temper instead.

She realised she'd been staring at him wordlessly since he'd said her name. 'I, er, just wanted to find out if there'd been an update on Edith's condition. I didn't mean to disturb you.'

'It's fine.' He smiled, doing his best to put her at ease instead of making her feel she was wasting his time.

Her stomach flipflopped in the same manner as those pancakes she'd watched the chef tossing at breakfast.

'She's comfortable and had a good night's sleep. I hope you did too.'

She cocked an eyebrow at that. That sounded more personal than their usual conversation about their mutual pensioner patient.

'I mean, I hope you weren't up all night worrying.' He went to lean a hand on the edge of the desk but missed, almost resulting in a comedy prat fall. For a moment she wondered if he'd become equally as flustered around her as she had around him. Then he straightened up, looking as smooth and in control as ever, making her believe she had imagined the whole thing.

'I managed a few hours' sleep. Thank you.'

'Good. Well, I should…' He pointed down the corridor, indicating his need to get back to work.

'Yes. Sorry. If it's easier for you I'll ask at Reception for updates from now on.'

'It's not a problem at all. *Ciao.*' He was walking backwards down the hallway, giving her one last smile before turning away.

Sophie watched until his tight white trousers disappeared around the corner out of sight before letting out a long breath. She wouldn't admit to it being a sigh. The whole exchange had been odd. A completely different atmosphere from the one when they were around Edith. An awkward dance between two people afraid of what might be happening despite outward appearances. She wasn't sure what to make of it but one thing was certain, it was the most excitement she'd had in a very long time.

Sophie chose one of the blue plastic loungers around the main pool. Not so close she'd get splashed every time someone dived in but near enough to jump in herself without having to parade around in her bikini if she decided on a swim. She wasn't used to all this spare time and unless she wanted to join the class making origami animals out of towels on the mezzanine deck, this was the best place to be.

There were the party people here for drinks, music and a good time, children chasing each other round the pool and helping themselves to cookies and ice cream from the all-day buffet. Then there were the people like her, here to soak it all in. She laid her towel down and settled back with her holiday read, making the most of the opportunity Edith had given her for a rest.

Although she was scanning the words and turning the pages of her book, she wasn't really taking it in. It wasn't the sound of children shrieking or the loud music disturbing her enjoyment, it was the noise going on in her own head. There was too much to think about to let her concentrate. Apart from her worry about Edith's health and the crush she'd apparently developed on the ship's doctor, she was thinking about the changes she wanted to make back home. Moving away, changing her job were things she used to do all the time but she was afraid of making the wrong decision. Again.

Ryan's betrayal made her question her own judgement, the choices she'd made and the person she'd become. She'd spent so long as part of a couple she'd lost an important part of herself: her independence. Never would she leave herself so vulnerable again by letting someone dominate her life.

She was about to give up all pretence of reading when a flash of something in the pool caught her eye. Putting her book down, she stood up to get a closer look. There it was again, a splash in the furthest corner of the pool. The deep end was empty with everyone else messing around in the shallows with inflatables, more concerned with showing off than actually swimming. Even the lifeguard was posing for selfies.

She peered down over the edge of the pool and saw a dark shadow shimmering underwater. That was when it hit her. The small splashes and flash of colour had been someone in trouble. Their last gasp for air before they'd sunk to the bottom of the pool.

Sophie didn't think twice about diving in. She held her breath, swimming down and down until she reached the dark mass. With her hands hooked under the arms of whoever was down there, she hauled the dead weight back to the surface with her, gasping for air with the effort. It was a child, not more than seven or eight, but she didn't have the energy left to get him out of the pool, her lungs burning as she fought for breath.

'It's about time,' she snapped at the lifeguard who suddenly appeared, helping to haul the boy out.

'I didn't see—'

'No, you didn't.' She was furious he hadn't been doing his job properly but his negligence wasn't uppermost in her mind.

'He's not breathing.'

The now fully alert lifeguard felt for the child's pulse while Sophie got herself out of the pool. She was sure he had to have first-aid training to get this job but right now she wasn't convinced about any of his credentials so she checked the boy herself. No pulse. His chest wasn't moving, there was no sound of breathing, and he was unresponsive to her attempts to rouse him.

'Go and get help,' she shouted to anyone listening.

They'd attracted something of a crowd as people gathered around, watching the drama of a life-or-death situation as though it was part of the onboard entertainment. If they hadn't the decency to help or turn away, that was down to their own consciences. She couldn't be distracted from saving this child. There was bound to be a defibrillator somewhere on board, as well as the medical staff. Until either became available it was down to her to get this boy breathing again.

She brushed her wet hair away from her face before tilting his head back. With no visible obstructions to his airways, she pinched his nose closed and started CPR. Forming a seal over his open mouth with hers, she blew until she saw his chest rising. It fell as she took her mouth away and she repeated the process another four times.

'Joshua? Let me see him. That's my son.' There was a kerfuffle somewhere to the side but Sophie let the lifeguard handle the fraught parent as she started chest compressions. With her fingers interlocked, the heel of her hand placed in the middle of his chest, she pressed down hard. She kept her arms locked out straight, pushing up and down, doing her best to keep his heart pumping.

'Come on.' She urged him to pull through, blocking out everyone and everything else around them.

Working with elderly patients she should have been used to dealing with death but it didn't make it any easier. This was a child, someone who had his whole life in front of him. He was on holiday, for goodness' sake. She wasn't going to let him die.

After several rounds of rescue breaths and chest compressions, she felt movement. He spluttered, coughing up the water lodged in his lungs, his lips slowly losing that deathly blue tinge. Before she breathed her own sigh of relief, she quickly moved him into the recovery position, rolling him onto his side to keep his airway clear.

'Excuse me.' The crowd parted as Luciano appeared with his medical bag. He paid no attention to the water pooled all around as he knelt down beside her.

'He was non-responsive when I pulled him from the bottom of the deep end but I kept on with the rescue breaths and chest compressions until he came around. He's coughed up a lot of water but I think he's okay.'

'Good job, Sophie. I'm glad *you* were paying attention.' Luciano shot the lifeguard a filthy look that would have him fearing for his job, and rightly so. With so many passengers, many of them children, someone in his position had to be vigilant at all times.

'I only saw him because it happened right in front of me. Anyone would've done the same.'

'Are his parents here?' Luciano stood up and addressed those standing around. Once the boy's mother and father made themselves known, he dismissed everyone else with that air of authority that came so easily to him. 'We'll get him down to the medical centre and check him over. What's his name?'

'Joshua.'

'Okay, Joshua, we're going to move you, but Mum and Dad are going to come with you.'

Sophie pulled a towel from the nearest sunbed and covered their little patient until they could get him to the medical centre.

'You too,' Luciano said, grabbing another towel to drape it around her shoulders. It was only then she realised she was shaking, her teeth chattering as the shock of what she'd just done set in. He bundled up her clothes into his arms before they left the scene. This time there was no argument as she let him lead her back into the belly of the ship.

'Something for the shock.' Luciano set a glass of coloured liquid on the desk in front of her.

'Thanks.' She cradled the glass in her hands for a while before she took a sip. The strong alcohol burned on its way down her throat but it did manage to warm her up. Since Luciano had taken over the medical treatment, she didn't think she'd stopped shaking.

'Joshua is fine, thanks to your quick actions. I'm sorry if I've been dismissive of your medical expertise up until now. I know how hard you must have worked to save Joshua and all I can do is apologise.'

She could tell he wasn't a man to say such a thing without complete sincerity, and was grateful for his acknowledgement of her abilities.

'It's all right. I know I was a bit of a handful at first, showing up here telling everyone how to do their job.' If he could admit to his failings, so could she. It might help reduce some of that tension that seemed to accompany their interactions.

'I would've done exactly the same in the circumstances. Now, is there anything else I can get for you?' He got up off the desk where he'd been sitting and Sophie realised she was being dismissed. It had been a long afternoon, he had patients to tend to, and she'd taken up enough of his time. He'd lent her his office to get changed into the clothes she'd retrieved from her sun lounger before they'd come down here. The chat and the drink had been his way of making sure she was all right and wasn't actually going into clinical shock. She appreciated the concern, even if she was put out it wasn't more than a professional interest in her welfare he was showing.

'No. I'll let you get back to work.' She tossed back the rest of the brandy, ignoring the fiery trail it was leaving in its wake, and set the empty glass back on his desk. 'Thanks for that.'

'No problem. I'm sure we'll see each other around.' He had the door open now, seeing her out.

'I'm sure we will.' The prospect set her mind conjuring up ways of avoiding him in the future. She was concerned about what another meeting would do to her equilibrium when she couldn't get control of her emotions around him. Worryingly, there was also a part of her looking forward to it.

'Room for one more?' Luciano managed to bounce onto the excursion bus as the driver was about to close the doors.

'There might be a seat left at the back, Doc.'

'Thanks.' He slapped a hand on Giovanni's back. The twenty-something tour guide worked for the travel company that was contracted to the cruise liner. They transported passengers from the ship to the local tourist attractions and brought them back before the ship set sail for the next destination.

He'd crossed paths with Giovanni and a few of his colleagues before, on the occasions the heat and exertion during the tours had taken their toll on some of the holidaymakers.

As the driver started the engine, Luciano made his way down the aisle.

'We don't usually see you out and about, Doctor.' The cheery rep revealed his identity to the others on board the bus who might not have recognised him otherwise. He'd dressed casually today in the hope of blending in so he could remain incognito. Now his cover had been blown he braced himself for the onslaught of conversations based around the ailments of his fellow passengers. So much for his time off.

'I needed some fresh air.' He didn't intend sharing his thought processes about why he needed to get out and clear his head.

'I'm not sure you'll find it here.' Giovanni guffawed as the bus revved and the smell of diesel filled the interior.

In truth, since Sophie had made herself known to him on board, Luciano had begun to find the clinic as claustrophobic as home. It was laughable: eight months on board a ship and he'd barely ventured out into daylight.

Before he'd broken the news to her about Edith's health the other day, Sophie had looked so carefree lying on the deck, enjoying the sun. Before the ensuing drama around the pool yesterday, he'd envied her that peace he'd yet to find on board. Today he'd decided to try to find his own. Perhaps a walk on solid ground, enjoying the sights like every other tourist, would do him some good.

He staggered down the bus as it jolted to life, passed all the seats occupied by chattering couples anticipating their next great adventure. He spotted one empty aisle seat and swung into it as the bus rounded a corner.

'Missing me already?' The voice of his co-passenger was unmistakable.

'Sophie? What are you doing here?'

'I was minding my own business until you practically landed in my lap. What are you doing here?'

'The same as everyone else. Sightseeing. It's my day off.' He didn't know whether to be pleased or annoyed that he'd found himself sitting next to Sophie. She appeared to be the only other person travelling solo.

'I would've thought you'd have seen everything a million times over by now.'

'Not recently. I thought it was about time I took advantage of everything the cruise life has to offer.' He was beginning to realise that staying locked away below decks wasn't helping him. He was simply avoiding real life. Although he hadn't anticipated seeing the object of his recent distraction again so soon.

'That includes gatecrashing a bus full of tourists, does it? Admit it, you're stalking me. You just wanted another day in my scintillating company.'

'Naturally.' Teasing he could live with. It was preferable to the fiery exchanges they'd had previously and the confused emotions aroused in him as a result.

Sophie moved her bag from between their seats, allowing him some extra room, and set it in her lap. 'I'm flattered but I can't promise any more thrilling ambulance rides or near-death experiences.'

'Good. I'm off duty. I'd like a quiet day for a change.'

Sophie smiled at him. The worried frown had gone from her brow after yesterday's drama and her eyes were back to that calm grey-blue of the ocean.

Mrs Fields would be pleased that they were beginning to get on.

They sat in silence for a while, taking in the view as the speakers played some cheesy Italian music he supposed was intended to provide a local atmosphere.

'You know, I forget how beautiful this country is sometimes. *Bellissima*.' He watched the muted colours of the green rolling hills pass by the window. They reminded him of home. Of his *mamma* and *papà* out there in the Italian countryside. Likely cooking up a feast for whoever happened to stop by the villa today.

For the first time since leaving his old life behind, he experienced a pang of longing to be back in the bosom of his family. Perhaps it was time to stop running and go back and face life without Renata. By all accounts, Sophie had experienced her fair share of heartache too and she'd survived. According to Edith, she was only just getting back to being herself. He needed to do the same instead of hiding away in the shadows, letting life carry on without him.

'Where is home to you?' Sophie's curiosity pierced his self-reflection, reminding him he'd spoken those first thoughts aloud.

'Barolo. It's vineyard country in the Piedmont region in the northwest. Far from the madness of the city. It's quiet, peaceful.'

'Boring?' Sophie laughed.

'Hmm, more insular, I'd say.' His life had been far from dull. It was ironic he should find more peace aboard a busy cruise liner but along with that came a sense of loneliness. He was missing the family he'd once accused of being too suffocating.

'So you ran away to sea?'

'Something like that.' His laugh rang hollow. That was exactly what he'd done. The trouble was he didn't know what to do next. He'd had his timeout and he knew he wasn't going to sail the oceans for the rest of his days.

'Live in the moment. That's what I want to do too.' Sophie was right. He'd spent too long wallowing in the past, worrying about a future without his wife. For once he should try testing that theory for himself and see if it made him any happier, or life any more bearable.

'Where do we start?' It sounded as though Sophie had more experience in this living-in-the-moment stuff, so he was prepared to follow her lead. If she'd let him.

The bus pulled into the side of the road and the passengers began to file off.

Sophie stood up and slung her bag over her shoulder. 'Right here. Let's just see where our feet take us.'

It was a dangerous game but he was thankful he had Sophie to play it with.

CHAPTER FOUR

Sophie's day wasn't exactly going to plan. Instead of joining the throng of passengers going to the larger cities to check out the tourist traps, she'd chosen to visit Civitavecchia, the town closest to where they'd docked.

She hadn't wanted to fight her way through layer upon layer of sightseers in Rome to bag a five-second glance at something that could never live up to the hype. Especially without Edith. She'd traded their coach trip to see the major landmarks for a more laid-back tour, opting for the slower pace of the local town and certainly never expecting the doctor to turn up as her travel companion.

She'd disembarked without a map or any real plan of where she was going or what she was doing for the day. Luciano, as he'd insisted she call him as this was his day off, had fallen into step beside her as they followed the slow-moving herd into the town centre.

'There's something exhilarating about not knowing where you're going.' They weren't living to any schedule, other than being back before the ship set sail again. Exploring. Her first taste of adventure in a very long time.

'It's not as though we are going to get lost. You can

probably see the ship from any part of the town.' He was making fun of her excitement at being let loose but he couldn't possibly understand when he'd been travelling the world, taking it all for granted.

'I'm going to pretend I'm living the dream. Like you.'

That stopped his speed-walking in its tracks. Their fellow explorers carried on ahead, gravitating towards the first souvenir shop they came across. She might take something back for Edith but, personally, she'd rather have a trove of fabulous memories than tacky fridge magnets.

Luciano's scoff drew her attention.

'Hmm?' Her eyes left the contents of the shop window to meet the doctor's scowl.

'What makes you think I'm living the dream?'

She couldn't imagine why her casual remark would upset him. If anything, she should be the one to feel hard done by. They were both working in the same field, yet she was languishing away in a care home with residents who had a busier social life than she did while Luciano was sailing around the sunny Med.

'Sun, sea and whatever else you get up to, in or out of working hours. As much as I love my residents in the nursing home, staring at the same beige walls, day in, day out, can't compare to this.' She only had to glance out at the turquoise sea, sun glittering on the gentle waves, to make her point.

'I suppose it looks like that from the outside but the reality isn't quite so glamorous.' The furrowed lines on his brow smoothed out but his smile only managed to lift the corners of his mouth.

She considered the possible downsides to life on the

sea for a few moments but she reckoned that dealing with a few sick or inebriated passengers was worth the constant change of scenery. 'Nice try but my heart is point-blank refusing to bleed for you.'

There was no way she was going to let him feel sorry for himself and spoil today, whatever the reason behind it. As far as she could tell, this was the life she'd always wanted and she hadn't heard anything to change her mind. He should be grateful for the advantages of his position. Some people weren't lucky enough to experience the same opportunities or had given them up in pursuit of an altogether different foolish dream.

At least her apparent lack of compassion managed to draw his mouth into a less mournful smile. Whatever his issue was with his job as ship doctor, it couldn't have been too bad for him to dismiss the subject so easily.

'Where shall we go first?' Fortunately, Luciano didn't come across as someone to navel-gaze too long, leaving his past in favour of their immediate future.

Sophie didn't know how or when they'd become a 'we.' She supposed they'd organically gravitated towards one another as the only solo travellers—not that she was complaining. Excluding Edith, she'd been on her own since Ryan had left and she much preferred company.

Although she'd backpacked alone after university and had enjoyed the freedom, her adventures had always been improved by the people she'd met along the way. Friends, lovers, employers had all been part of her story and now were consigned to the past along with the experience—even Ryan. Luciano was simply a character in her latest tale. Someone she'd mention in passing when recounting her time on this cruise. There was absolutely nothing for her to worry about in spending time with him as long as she remembered that.

Meanwhile, Luciano was waiting for an answer.

'You probably know the area better than I do. Any recommendations?'

He gave a sheepish shrug of his shoulders. 'I told you. I don't get out much.'

There was a lot to unpack from that statement. Given today's surprise it was obvious he could leave the ship if he chose to. He wasn't a prisoner. So why didn't he visit the many ports and cities available to him? More importantly, why had he chosen today and why with her? All these questions—and their answers—would move him from the role of secondary character to something more substantial. She wasn't ready for that.

'Then we need to get away from enclosed spaces and head for the great outdoors.' They continued along the covered walkway until they reached the end of the row of shops. Without the shade provided overhead it was akin to stepping into an oven. A brightly lit oven turned up to maximum heat.

She'd forgotten the sky could be that beautiful shade of azure blue. The sight was only interrupted by the occasional burst of fluffy white cloud. For the last couple of years she'd been convinced the world only came in various shades of sludgy grey.

They broke free from the main thoroughfare and ventured out to the parallel walkway free from people or buildings inhibiting the view of blue on blue.

Sophie rested her hands on the low wall that she supposed was to prevent people from tumbling into the harbour below. She closed her eyes and took a deep breath, inhaling the fresh, salty air of the sea and everything she associated with freedom.

'Anyone would think you'd just been let out of prison.' She sensed Luciano's presence beside her before his laughter reached her ears, and she shivered despite the powerful heat.

'You should be kissing the ground in relief or running through the town naked after escaping your recent incarceration.' It was glib perhaps, but it was her defence against the way he was staring at her so intently. She didn't want to get involved in the minutiae of his life any more than she wished him to be privy to hers. Ignoring the awful pun, they shouldn't be anything more than ships that passed in the night. Not if she was expecting to go home and carry on as though this cruise was nothing more than another experience to cross off her list.

Another hearty chuckle. 'Maybe I will.'

His hands moved to his shirt, undoing his top buttons. Sophie's temperature rocketed. She was mesmerised by the action, watching as he revealed more of his tanned skin and the dark hair nestled there.

'I'm not sure this sleepy town is ready for that.' Neither was she. 'Actually, you look quite at home as you are. International playboy in the playground of the rich and famous.'

She stood up and snapped a quick picture with her camera phone.

'You don't have a very high opinion of me.' He folded his arms across his chest, his short sleeves showing off his nicely rounded muscles. On the contrary, her opinion of him was increasing so much by the second that he'd be in danger of getting a big head if he knew.

'With your clothes and colouring against the backdrop of luxurious yachts you could be easily mistaken for a billionaire businessman. I don't think my pale, freckly skin would fool anyone into thinking I was anything other than English working class.'

'May I?' Luciano held out his hand for her phone, probably wanting to check out the evidence himself. She wasn't expecting to have the camera turned back on her.

'Say *formaggio*.'

'Formaggio!' she said with a flourish of her hands as he snapped away.

'See?' He turned the screen so she could see the result of his photography skills.

'Yes, thanks.' It made a change from the selfies she used to take, which had never quite done justice to the scenery she was supposed to have been documenting. He'd managed to capture the soul-restoring essence of the moment with one click.

'You misunderstand. I need you to see yourself as I see you. You look just as at home as I do.'

Reluctantly she studied the picture, concentrating on herself rather than the billion-pound property floating in the harbour.

'I look…happy.' It was a stunning revelation. She couldn't remember the last time her smile had reached beyond her face until her whole body was radiating contentment. Free from the shackles she'd attached when she'd hooked up with Ryan, her true spirit was allowed to soar once again.

'Sì. Bellissima.' The compliment warmed her skin as much as the overhead sun but she didn't shy away from it. She felt good so it made sense it should trans-

late to her outward appearance. It was simply nice to hear it from someone else. Unless…

'Is this how you woo all your ladies?' She turned her phone off and shoved it back in her pocket.

'All what ladies? I'm simply telling you that you look beautiful.' He appeared genuinely hurt by her insinuation but pre-Ryan she'd been more streetwise. A lot of British tourists were easily seduced by the romance of a foreign holiday and the handsome locals. In his uniform, surrounded by thousands of women escaping their humdrum lives, it had to be a smorgasbord of vulnerable hearts.

'I'm not naive, Luciano. Women must throw themselves at you. I wouldn't blame you for giving in to temptation. Most men would.' She hopped down off the wall and began walking, the conversation making her irrationally angry. Not least because she'd noticed the gold band glinting on his ring finger for the first time. He hadn't done anything to personally offend her but she resented him on behalf of his absent wife and any easily duped women he might have seduced with that accent and flattering charm.

He wasn't following her any more and when she looked back he'd collapsed onto the wall as though she'd cut him open and removed his entire skeleton. 'I'm not most men.'

She wanted to believe that but it was the type of thing a practised lothario would use to fool a woman into bed. Of course, that wasn't an option now she knew he was married.

'How long have you been working on board? Six months? A year? In all that time you've never succumbed to temptation?'

'Eight months and, no, I haven't been involved with anyone. The cruise company doesn't approve of relationships on board.'

'Oh, so it's not because you're married then?' She nodded at the telltale ring, wondering why she was bothered. He wasn't her husband or her responsibility. Neither was she his conscience.

He lifted his left hand and stared at it as though he'd forgotten he was even wearing a wedding ring.

'No.' He closed the subject down, unwilling to give her any more information on his love life and why should he? Why did she want it? It was none of her business.

Perhaps he was one of the good guys who didn't cheat. It made her feel safer with him knowing he wouldn't try it on with her and make her even more confused about her feelings towards him. He was off-limits.

Unfortunately, that disappointed her as much as finding out he had a wife. She didn't want a relationship or more complications in her life but spending time with Luciano was making her realise she did want something more. If only she knew what.

Luciano should have just told her he was a widower but it wasn't something he shared readily with strangers. For those women who did think he was a candidate for a fling, he flashed his wedding ring in the hope of staving off any further romantic notions. It was his security blanket, his force field to deflect attention about how he came to be here. That wasn't going to work with Sophie. But by voluntarily spending the day with her he was still betraying Renata.

He hadn't so much as looked at another woman since he'd lost her. Now here he was, practically walking arm in arm with Sophie thinking only of how beautiful she'd looked by the harbour. How the sun highlighted the hidden strands of copper and gold in her hair.

It was better if he let them both believe he was still married. There was less of a threat of anything else developing, which would destroy his current peace of mind.

Thankfully she didn't push the subject any further. He hadn't divulged the tragic circumstances of Renata's death to anyone since leaving home and, to be honest, he couldn't be sure how his grief would manifest if he did. It would be mortifying if he broke down crying in the street.

They drifted towards the more populated main boulevard in awkward silence. If they carried on in this vein the day wasn't going to be much fun for either of them.

'The church seems to be something of an attraction. Would you like to go and see inside it?' Anything to relieve the tension, and the silence wouldn't seem so out of place in there.

'Can we just walk in?' He could see Sophie's curiosity was piqued about what so many people were finding fascinating beyond the plain stone façade.

'It's a church. Everyone is welcome.' Seeing her hesitation, Luciano stepped inside first.

'Wow.' Sophie stood beside him, gazing up at the vaulted ceiling then around at the kaleidoscopic colours the sun was making through the stained-glass windows, touching everything with rainbows of light.

It was breathtaking but he felt very much at home

here. The religious icons and candles were as familiar as the smell of his mother's perfume.

Sophie, on the other hand, looked every inch the tourist awed by all she surveyed and trying to take it all in.

'You don't go to church?'

'Not really. I'm not going to go up in flames, am I?' Her attempt at a joke at least broke the frosty ground between them again, letting them move on from their previous difficult conversation.

'I hope not. I don't have a first-aid kit or a fire extinguisher with me.'

'Ha, ha.' Sophie gave him an eye roll and took a seat on one of the wooden pews, shuffling along to make room for him too. 'I suppose you're a good Catholic boy?'

'Not recently. I mean, I haven't gone to church as much as my devoted *mamma* would expect.' He hadn't been at all since the funeral. Sailing the Mediterranean was a good excuse, if he disregarded the fact that there was a Sunday service every week. Church was a place for contemplation as well as worship and he didn't need any more time for self-reflection. As it was, sitting here, he was already considering the conversation he'd have to have in the confessional.

Forgive me, Father, for I have sinned...it's been two years since my last confession. Since then I've taken the Lord's name in vain, abandoned my family and my faith, and been unfaithful to my late wife in my thoughts.

'Penny for them...or is it a euro here?'

Sophie broke through his imaginary soul-cleansing. 'Sorry?'

'You're lost in thought. Is everything okay?'

'*Sì. Grazie.* I'm thinking about home.'

'Would you prefer if I gave you some privacy?'

This was an opportunity for them to part ways and put an end to whatever was going on between them. If he stayed here he knew he'd end up walking into that confessional and unburdening his soul. The trouble was, he was afraid he'd hear those words he'd been running away from. That there was nothing wrong with wanting to move on from his grief.

'That's not necessary. Actually, I fancy a drink. Why don't we make our way to the town square and find somewhere to sit in the shade?' He was enjoying the cool interior of the church compared to the heat outside, even if being here beside her was beginning to make him sweat.

'You don't have to ask me twice. I've never drunk so much in my life, trying to stay hydrated.'

Before they left, he made sure to light a candle for Renata, and the babies who had never lived to grow up, silently begging for her forgiveness for any actions that could be construed as inappropriate.

Sophie hovered nearby, giving him the space he needed, though she could have no idea of the turmoil going on his head. She asked nothing from him and backed off when she sensed he needed it, something no one else in his life had managed to do so far.

There was a slight incline up towards the main square. Far enough in the heat that by the time they reached the first al fresco café in the *piazza*, Sophie was ready to collapse.

'Will this table do?' Luciano pulled out a chair for her under the shade of a free-standing canvas parasol.

'Anywhere will do. I need *acqua*.' Then she spotted the cocktail menu propped up in the middle of the table. 'Ooh!'

'What would you like to drink?' Luciano must've been feeling the increase in temperature too as he loosened another button and exposed more of his manly chest.

'Hmm, something blue.'

That made him laugh. 'That's the only requirement you're looking for in a drink?'

'Yeah. Why not? Let's live dangerously. What about you? What's your drink of choice?'

'I don't mind the odd glass of red wine with my dinner. Otherwise I don't drink in case I get called out.'

'You're not on duty. Someone else is covering today, aren't they?'

'Yes, but—'

'Technically you're on your holiday today too. Besides, I'd look like a lush sitting here drinking on my own.' She didn't really mind. Everyone else here was sitting back and chilling with their assorted alcoholic beverages, too deep in conversation with one another to care what she was doing. It wouldn't do Luciano any harm to relax too. Especially after their tense exchange over his relationship status. She didn't want him to think she cared.

'I'll have the green one,' he said, closing the menu.

'Good man.' It wouldn't be long before the whole cheating accusation she'd thrown at him would soon be forgotten.

He ordered their drinks from the harried waitress

who appeared at their table and seemed relieved to have someone to converse with in her native language.

Sophie managed a feeble *'Grazie...'* and wished she'd learned a few phrases before travelling.

Italian was such a sexy-sounding language. Although, by the way the doe-eyed waitress was fawning over Luciano it wasn't only the language causing a ripple in the female staff.

Their drinks arrived with a dish of roasted nuts to snack on. They sipped at their colourful cocktails, trying not to let the decorative umbrellas and paper parrots perched on the glasses get stuck up their noses. Across the square a young woman set up a microphone stand and amplifier in a shop doorway. Soon they were being serenaded by the haunting sounds of opera, making it a perfect moment that Sophie wanted to remember for ever.

'This is the life I should've had.' She leaned back in her chair, sipping her bright blue drink, soaking up the atmosphere.

'What's stopping you from having it now?'

When she looked at Luciano rocking back on two legs of his chair she wondered that herself. It had been a while since Ryan had left so the only person stopping her from doing what she wanted now was her.

'Responsibilities, bills, financial stability. All of that boring adult stuff.'

He set his chair back onto solid ground and put his drink on the table. 'Correct me if I'm wrong, but that doesn't sound like you at all.'

'I'm not sure if I should be offended by that.'

'Not at all. You seem strong-willed and I can't picture you not following your heart, that's all.'

Sophie tutted. 'That's what caused all the trouble in the first place.'

One glance at his puzzled face and she knew she had to explain. She was sure Edith had blabbed about her troubled love life since, given half the chance, she had been trying to matchmake Sophie with every attractive man she met.

'I was happy living wherever I laid my sun hat. Until I met Ryan, fell head over heels and followed him back to England. I was convinced he was the one I was going to spend the rest of my life with, raising babies.'

'It didn't turn out that way?'

'Does it ever?'

'I guess not.' He swirled the luminescent liquid in his glass, his mind flitting somewhere else that obviously wasn't happy terrain.

'I got bored and made the mistake of telling him so. That prompted him into running off to Las Vegas to marry his work colleague. He's off living it up in America somewhere and I'm left with a mortgage and a job I'm only doing to pay the bills.'

'That must've hurt…but it means he wasn't the one for you.'

'I'm not convinced there is a "one" any more and only a fool would believe that a single person in this whole universe is able to make your life complete.'

'You've had a bad experience, that's all. If you're so unhappy with what you're doing, why don't you quit? Take that leap and do something that excites you?'

'Once upon a time I wouldn't have thought twice about doing that and I never imagined I'd say this, but I'm scared it wouldn't work out. Not all of us are guaranteed to land the job of our dreams.' Call it experience or maturity but she no longer had that throw-caution-to-the-wind attitude she'd once lived by. Not when the consequences could strip away your very being.

'What's the worst that could happen?'

'Um, I could end up broke and homeless.' She had no ties but neither did she have any support around her if she lost everything on a whim.

'Well, it's definitely the best decision I've made recently.' He tossed a handful of nuts into his mouth before raising his glass in a toast to his seemingly perfect life, but there was something about the gesture that didn't sit comfortably. As though he was as miserable as she was deep down.

'How is your wife okay with you working away so far and so long from home?' She knew people had all sorts of modern marriages these days and sometimes you had to go where the money was, but it would take a great deal of trust to let Luciano loose without a chaperon. Surely one would eventually wonder what he was getting up to for the best part of a year?

Luciano gave a heavy sigh before he tossed back the rest of his drink. It seemed for ever before he finally spoke. 'My wife, Renata, died two years ago.'

'Oh.'

'Oh.' The pain he must've suffered and which she'd likely made him relive struck her with force in the chest.

'I'm so sorry. I had no idea or I would never have brought the subject up.' She'd more than put her foot in it, she'd kicked him right in the gut because of her suspicious mind.

'You didn't know. I don't talk about it. I should. That's what they tell you to do, right? Talk it out, express your feelings instead of bottling everything up. It's easier for the heart to go along with people's assumptions than put them straight.'

'I can understand that.' Every time she spoke about her relationship with Ryan it ripped open a wound, although in Luciano's case it was over the loss of his wife, not because he felt sorry for himself.

He had been married. She'd died. Sophie couldn't begin to fathom that kind of loss. Everyone who'd left her had done so voluntarily and, though difficult, she'd come to accept it. To have someone you'd loved enough to marry, expected to spend the rest of your life with, only for them to be taken away must've been devastating. It was no wonder he'd been so defensive, so reluctant to open up. Yet she'd forced this out of him to satisfy her own curiosity and need to know more about him. Now she was responsible for ripping that painful wound open again with no way of closing it.

'We were only married for three years. Together for four but a short, tragic marriage nevertheless. We lost two babies during that time.'

Ugh. This was painful to watch as he stared into the depths of his empty glass. Even the parrot was wilting with the heavy weight of the conversation.

'That's awful. I'm so sorry.' She didn't know what else to say without it being a cliché.

She was so young.

I didn't know her but I feel your loss.

There are plenty more fish in the sea.

That last one was the worst. Something trotted out after every break-up, but it certainly wasn't appropriate in these circumstances. In Luciano's case there probably weren't any more fish in the sea. Not one he wanted anyway. That explained how he'd avoided any romantic entanglement so far. His heart had been broken beyond all repair. Then there were the babies. This was a man who'd had hope of a family, only to have it cruelly snatched away from him. And he'd been left on his own. It was too much to comprehend.

'Not your fault. After her second miscarriage she developed sepsis. No one realised, not even me, until it was too late.' As a medical professional, Sophie knew it wouldn't have been as easy as that to accept her fate. Luciano was a good doctor and as such would've beaten himself up over not spotting or treating the problem himself in time to save her. The guilt was there in the slump of his broad shoulders, much as he might deny it.

'The cruise life was a new start for you?' She had wondered why a well-established doctor would abandon everything he knew and had worked for to live such a transient life. His position would've suited someone with no family or ties to any one place. Someone like her before she'd made the mistake of falling in love. Love ruined your life when it didn't last for ever, like they told you it would in all the fairy tales.

'I'm not sure it was about making a new start. More like avoiding one.' He winced at the admission but she appreciated the honesty. Perhaps that was what she'd been doing in her twenties. She hadn't simply been a free spirit, just a lonely child afraid to return home where there was no one waiting for her.

'How so?' Sophie picked at the corner of a cardboard coaster lying on the table, slightly soggy from the condensation dripping from her glass. She didn't want to appear eager to know all the gory details of what had brought Luciano to this point in his career, even if it was true.

'I know they mean well but my family is pushing me to find someone else.'

'You're clearly not ready for that.' Her acknowledgement opened a chasm deep in her chest, which she chose to interpret as empathy for his loss.

It took him longer to respond to that than she expected. 'I didn't want to think about life without Renata but my family were making it impossible. We're such an Italian stereotype. Lots of siblings, always a new baby to celebrate with vast amounts of pasta and wine.'

'Sounds heavenly to me.' Especially to a woman who'd been way too long on her own and whose idea of a home-cooked meal was something reheated in a plastic container.

'I suppose it was for a while but it's difficult when you need time to yourself and space to breathe.'

'I wouldn't know. Can't say I ever knew my father well. He was a musician. A wandering spirit, apparently. My mother, well, she goes wherever her heart takes her. One wrong 'un after another. I don't see my parents enough for them to suffocate me.' It was incomparable to whatever Luciano had been dealing with but it was her truth. She wanted to find some way of relating to him so he wouldn't regret sharing any of this with her. If he'd run away to sea after losing his wife, chances were he needed someone to talk to. She wasn't a counsellor by any means but everyone needed to vent. Poor Edith had been the closest thing she'd had to a sounding board and look where she'd ended up.

'Swap? I'm sure my *mamma* and *papà* would love to shower you with affection and food.'

'Mine would happily ignore you and give you all the space you want.' Sad but true. 'Be honest now, aren't you missing your family a little bit?'

It was only when Ryan had gone and she'd been on her own in their house that she'd realised how alone she was in the world. Little wonder that Edith had felt sorry for her to the point of booking her onto a cruise.

She really had to get herself out there and get a life again. This trip, today with Luciano, was the most she'd socialised in months. It was beginning to look as though the same was true for him. Perhaps this was the nudge they both needed to make some changes.

'Hmm…' He contemplated her question for so long she could almost visualise the list of pros and cons he was drawing up about his family in his head. 'A little homesick but I'm not ready to return.'

Sophie's heart gave a hop, skip and a jump. Goodness knew why when she was the one going home in a few days' time. They weren't about to sail off into the sunset together. The best she could hope for was to live her travelling dream vicariously through him.

'I know the feeling. I mean, without the homesick part. If I never went back it would be too soon.' It wasn't so much the place, or even the weather. No, it was the memories. Such dreams she'd had when they'd settled down. Now England represented the end of them. The idea of going back to an empty home and the daily grind of her job filled her with even more dread now she'd experienced something infinitely more thrilling.

'Everybody thinks that when they're on holiday. Perhaps you could extend yours for a week or two?' Was it her imagination or was there a hint of hope in his suggestion? Wishful thinking on her part or not, it wasn't an option.

'Even if I could get the time off work I couldn't afford it. I'm here due to the kindness of Edith's heart, bless her.' The only reason she could enjoy herself now was the knowledge that her friend was recuperating at her son's home in Spain and being spoiled as much as she deserved.

'I know you're a nurse but you didn't say where you worked.'

'In a care home for the elderly. Don't get me wrong, I love them all but I don't think I was made to stay in one place too long.'

'You should see if there are any vacancies with the cruise company in that case.' He grinned, as though daring her to prove she had the guts to actually make the same life-changing decision he had. It made her want to call his bluff, prove to him, and Ryan—and more importantly to herself—that she wasn't simply all talk.

'Maybe I will. I'm willing to sign on as a cleaner, dishwasher or barmaid at this stage.'

'Don't sell yourself short. We'd be lucky to have someone like you in the medical bay.' From anyone else it would've sounded nothing more than professional courtesy. It was the look in his eyes as he held her gaze across the table that made it more personal.

The sincerity of his comment was heightened by the fact that the opera singer had taken a break and his was the only voice to be heard in the sudden hush. The second Luciano realised it his cheeks flushed the same colour Sophie imagined hers were.

'Oh, I don't know. We seemed to clash a little bit

when we met. It's probably not conducive to a good working relationship.'

'It shows we're both passionate. I mean, about our work and patients.' Before Sophie had a chance to consider what other ways they could get passionate together he scraped his chair back along the ground and was on his feet.

'I should go and get the bill.' He disappeared into the shadowy recess of the café where she couldn't see him or scrutinise his expression.

For someone who'd gone to the lengths of leaving his family rather than entertain the idea of getting involved with anyone else, he was becoming increasingly flustered at the idea of them spending more time together.

Luciano wanted to get back to the ship and the sanctity of his medical centre as soon as he could. It hadn't occurred to him that disembarking at the nearest port would take him so far out of his comfort zone.

'Let me pay half.' Sophie pulled out her purse when he returned to the table.

'Not necessary. You have the all-inclusive drinks package. Remember?' The joke as they left was supposed to diffuse some of the tension and confusion he'd created with his effusive praise. Instead, as he caught her appreciative smile, his emotions were jumbled all over again.

She was everything he was supposed to be getting away from in this vagabond life. Yet he couldn't stay away and didn't want to. They could have gone their separate ways at any time—when they'd got off the coach, or after their argument at the harbour—but he continued to push his personal boundary, waiting and wondering what their next moments together would bring.

He never imagined he'd open up about Renata, but Sophie was a compassionate person. Enough that he could trust her not to create any drama or tears over his secrets. Just simple understanding.

There was the possibility he'd told her in the hope of creating more distance between them. A widower came with more emotional baggage than the average person. Plus, bringing Renata into existence here should've blocked those developing feelings he was having towards Sophie with guilt.

He didn't understand what was in her genetic make-up that made her so different from all the other women he'd encountered or how she'd made him see that the comments from his family, which had once angered him, came from a place of love.

He didn't have to settle down any time soon. They'd simply wanted him to move on from mourning and at least date again. To think about someone other than his dead wife. He was certainly doing that now but it wasn't bringing him any more peace. Sophie would be leaving soon, on her way back home and out of his life for good. If he ventured back into the world of dating or seeing anyone as more than a friend or colleague, it should be with a free spirit such as Sophie. At least then he wouldn't be torn in two by the idea of permanently replacing Renata in his heart.

Sophie had made it clear that life as a couple wasn't for her—along with staying in one place for too long. He enjoyed her company, was attracted to her, and he was sure after their initial personality clash she felt the same. He simply wasn't sure how far out of his comfort zone he was prepared to go. Perhaps he'd take her advice and see where his feet, his head and his heart took him. Live dangerously for once.

CHAPTER FIVE

'THERE'S A BEACH. Do you think we have time to take a paddle? Just so I can say I've been in the Med?'

'Sure.' The slight detour meant it was going to take them longer to return to the ship but it was impossible to refuse the simple request when her eyes were sparkling like the sea at the prospect.

'It's beautiful down here. I thought it would've been packed out with sun-worshipping tourists.'

It was an impressive panoramic view. The palm trees provided intermittent shade along the broad promenade stretching along the vast extent of the golden sands. Other than themselves, the only souls experiencing the beauty were skateboarders, who were more interested in the smooth lines of concrete available.

'They'll all be fighting for breathing room at the more popular tourist sights but there's a lot to be said for the less well-known parts of the country. You have time to appreciate everything unspoiled by the tourist market.'

'Like your home town?'

'Yes. We have some of the most beautiful countryside you could ever hope to see.'

'Maybe I will someday.' Sophie's big eyes searched

his face for an answer he wasn't willing to give. But promising her a visit, issuing an invitation that suggested a continued acquaintance beyond this week, went against everything he was trying to establish.

'It's off the beaten track.' He knew she would love exploring the vineyards, seeing the colourful wildflowers growing by the side of the country lanes near his parents' home. Funny how he still thought of that as his home. The one he'd shared with Renata, where they'd pictured having a family and growing old together, had been lying empty and unloved since he'd left. Not unlike his heart.

It would be too painful to go back there but going home to see his family might be bearable if he had Sophie there with him. He was relaxed around her, their conversation easy, the mood light. The opposite of everything he'd left behind.

'That's what I was kind of hoping for, but I was angling for an invitation or, you know, directions.' She nudged him playfully with her arm.

'Angling? You want to go fishing? I'm sorry we don't have any rivers near where we live.' If it was a particular hobby she enjoyed he would have to investigate the nearest access. His father would know. It was a long time since Luciano had fished or gone camping as they had done when he was little.

Sophie turned away but not before he saw the grin spreading across her face.

'What? What is it?' He was doing his best to be sincere and honest with himself. Her amusement at his offer struck him like a bullet fired at point-blank range. He was putting himself out there for her. Something he hadn't managed to do for anyone else and she was mocking him? Clearly, he'd read the signs wrong.

'Nothing. Something got lost in translation, that's all. Angling in this case means I was fishing for an invitation.'

'Ah. I see.' The pain gradually decreased. A misunderstanding on his part was much easier to stomach than utter humiliation.

'Sorry. Your English is excellent. My Italian is nonexistent. I shouldn't tease.' She reached out and gave his arm a squeeze—an apology, a show of solidarity and the closest he'd come to physical intimacy since Renata's death. Rather than shrink away from Sophie's touch, he welcomed it. It reminded him he was flesh and blood, more than a medical automaton.

There was heat in her touch. Meaning. More than he experienced from merely treating patients. It reminded him he was alive and hadn't died along with Renata. Even if it had felt that way for some time.

He couldn't take his eyes off the slender fingers wrapped around his forearm that provided that connection between them.

The fingers that travelled slowly down his arm to link with his. Hand in hand, Luciano and Sophie stood by the shore as the crystal clear waves lapped gently nearby.

'I've had a lovely day, Luciano.' Sophie's tender voice drew his gaze from their intertwined fingers to her soft lips.

'Me too.' Standing here with her, nothing else existed. It was a memory no one else would ever share. There was only one more thing that would make it perfect. Something he'd thought he'd never want to do again. Yet the adoration he saw in her eyes, and the slight tilt of her chin, was everything he needed to be sure what he was feeling was right and real.

With a dip of his head he was able to meet her lips with his. He closed his eyes, sighing into the blissful sensation of the kiss—soft and tender, yet filled with so much potential for more. Kissing Sophie was a release from the tension he'd been holding inside for days, trying not to act on his natural instinct to do this. He'd found the peace for which his soul had been searching for so long.

With that, his whole body opened up to the possibility of loving again. She'd awakened the passion inside him he'd thought had died long ago.

He wanted her closer and placed his free hand at her waist, drawing her deeper into the kiss.

Sophie wrapped her arms around his neck, pulling their bodies close enough that her body heat was burning him up. Her mouth was scorching against his. That desire they'd mistaken for battling egos was burning fiercely. The need to immerse himself in her and block out the pain that had tormented him for so long was stronger than the need to breathe.

He slid his hands under the thin fabric of her top, relishing the smooth plane of her skin under his fingertips. It would be easy to lose himself with her and forget who he was and why he'd come here. Sophie flicked her tongue against his and he growled. Too easy.

A slow trickle of cold water splashed over his feet and brought him back to earth. The tide had slowly been making its way in as they'd made out. They'd been carried away by the romance of the setting. This wasn't right. He began to withdraw from Sophie as doubt crept back in. It was a betrayal of his late wife's memory, their relationship and everything he'd ever felt for her.

He saw the confusion on Sophie's face, the daze of passion in her eyes as she stepped back. His feet were well and truly soaked through but it was a small price to pay for the return of some common sense.

'We should get back to the bus in case they leave without us. The ship won't wait, not even for me.' He could barely muster a fake smile to accompany the feeble attempt at levity.

'Luciano?' Heart-breaking bewilderment furrowed her forehead. None of this was her fault. He was the one messed up and in the wrong. The one who continued to sin when he continued to lust after her. He still wanted to reach out to those kiss-swollen lips begging for attention and claim them again.

It was only his thumbs he let trace over her tempting mouth before stroking her cheek, knowing he couldn't go back there. His conscience wouldn't let him, despite every other inch of him begging for mercy.

'Sophie… I just can't.' He pleaded with her for understanding. She knew his background and why this was wrong even if it didn't explain why he'd initiated the kiss or why he was walking away now. He couldn't give his heart to anyone else. Especially someone he knew he was getting too close to and who was walking out of his life again in a matter of days. Sophie had made it clear she was no longer the kind of woman who would stick around and he couldn't risk his heart on anything less.

He daren't look back as he made his way across the beach without her. There was a danger that was all it would take to grab her again and give in to that primal need to possess her. Playing out some erotic movie scene as waves crashed over their feverish bodies writhing on the sand wasn't going to make their lives any easier.

They were both in pain and an entanglement between two people who lived completely different lives wasn't going to heal broken and bruised hearts.

This was for the best, no matter how physically painful it was at this very moment.

Sophie would have kissed everyone on board if she'd thought there was a chance of it lessening the impact one man's lips had had on her.

It wasn't as though she'd asked Luciano to kiss her. At least, not in so many words. It had simply…happened. She didn't regret it but the consequences made her wonder if it was worth the hangover. It wasn't the tender bruising of her lips keeping her awake but the sheer force of desire that had caused it. Goodness knew the last time she'd been kissed like that. If ever. Certainly not by Ryan. He'd been safe and predictable, or so she'd thought. Luciano had been pure, raw passion.

The memory rekindled those little shivers of desire zinging along her spine. She slid the balcony doors open and stepped into the night in bare feet. The man was impossible to get out of her head. Even today, walking around the town of Lavorno on her own, she'd thought of him. The cathedral she'd visited alone had made her think about him. Even strolling along the canals, which had once been a gateway for transporting goods to the local markets, had sparked the memory of that private moment with him on the shore.

They hadn't spoken since that breath-stealing scene. Luciano had sat in brooding silence on the short bus journey back to the ship. He'd also been the first one to alight, without waiting for her. She hadn't seen him since. Unfortunately, out of sight didn't equate with out of mind.

It was obvious why he'd pushed her away and she hadn't forced him into conversation or an explanation. His grief was stronger than her feeling of rejection in the pain stakes. He'd told her he was mourning his late wife, to the extent that he'd left home to work anywhere else. Neither of them was in the right head space for a serious commitment, but she would have settled for short term after sharing *that* kiss.

A holiday romance would have done her confidence and libido the world of good but this wasn't the time to be selfish. Luciano was a man in pain and she couldn't take advantage of that vulnerability. Falling for someone mourning his wife and unborn children was a complication she didn't need. Whatever had passed between them was over after that hot, blistering start.

She should think about making more connections on board to prevent her from obsessing over the one person consuming her thoughts. Now Ryan was nothing more than a distant memory she'd chalked up to experience. A day in Luciano's company was all it had taken to bring her back to the woman she'd once been. Passionate, free and living in the moment.

There was a certain kind of calm to be found, standing out her on the balcony with only the stars piercing the darkness. The rush of the waves against the hull below sped them towards a different destination and the change of scenery she needed.

Somewhere far out at sea an orange pulsating light lit up hidden clouds in the sky. The dull rumble of thunder disrupted the soothing swoosh of the waves followed by a whip of lightning cracking open the world above.

The charge of electricity in the atmosphere couldn't compare to what had flashed between her and Luciano yesterday. Yet as the storm grew closer, Sophie knew there was a change coming in the air.

She shivered and the cold blast of air across her skin made her draw her robe tighter around her body. Watching the drama unfold was exciting and beautiful, something she might never experience again in her lifetime. Up close it would be dangerous and destructive and she couldn't help but compare it to her unfurling feelings towards Luciano. She considered herself fortunate to be on the outside looking in rather than caught in the eye of the storm.

Sophie was woken some time later by the rolling motion of the ship and the phone ringing somewhere near her head. With the curtains closed she had no concept of time or place but a quick glimpse at the clock confirmed she'd slept later than intended.

The shrill ringing continued until she picked up the receiver. As far as she was aware, the lines were inter-cabin only so she had no idea who would be ringing her. Her heart fluttered with hope that it would be Luciano, wanting to meet up.

'Hello?' Her voice was husky from sleep and a desire to see him again.

'Sophie? Is that you?' The line crackled with interference but Sophie could just about make out the voice on the other end of the line.

'Edith? Oh, my goodness. How are you?' She sat up, wide awake now and eager for news.

'I'm fine. Hypertension, apparently, which they've given me medication for. A whole lot of fuss over nothing. The family won't let me lift so much as a finger.'

'Good. That's how it should be. You deserve a rest.' At least someone had managed to get her to take a break and it was nice to know she had family around taking care of her—something Sophie was sadly lacking in her own life. There was no one to whom she could unburden herself, no one to put an arm around her and offer support. Apart from Edith, the only one who'd offered her that had been Luciano.

'A rest? I'll have forgotten how to use my arms and legs by the time I go home.' Edith gave a cackle and it was easy to tell she was content in the arms of her family.

'I'm glad you're doing well. How did you get through on the phone? It must be costing an absolute fortune.' She had no idea how technology worked out here but she did know it was expensive trying to get any sort of contact with the outside world.

'That nice young doctor sorted it out. He called to see how I was and thought you might like to hear for yourself.'

Sophie swallowed the shock at the mention of their mutual acquaintance. 'He was right.'

'Such a lovely man.' Edith's dreamy voice suggested she might be harbouring a crush of her own on the handsome Italian.

'What's the weather like where you are? Things are

a tad bumpy out here today.' She changed the subject so she didn't have to talk about the man who'd orchestrated a much-needed catch-up between friends—something he hadn't *had* to do either professionally or out of courtesy. He knew she needed it and had gone above and beyond the call of duty to contact Edith for her. Unless he was doing whatever it took to keep her out of the clinic, on the hunt for news herself…

'Awful. Sun, sun and more sun.' Another laugh.

'Make sure you're wearing sunscreen and drink plenty.'

'Don't worry. I'm safely ensconced in the shade with a gaggle of attentive waiters tending to my every need.'

'Sounds as though you're enjoying yourself.' It was a weird thing to say to someone who'd had a serious health scare but Edith did come across as happy and that was all Sophie wanted for her.

'I am but what about you? Are you taking advantage of everything on board?'

Flickering images of her passionate tryst with Luciano as waves lapped around their feet popped into her head, making her blush. 'Er…yeah. I've gone out on a couple of excursions and sampled some of the local life out here.'

'Where are you today? What exciting adventures lie in store?'

Sophie stretched across the bed to jerk the curtain to one side but they were still out at sea in choppier waters than usual.

'I have no idea. I haven't left the cabin yet.'

'What? That's not the deal we had, missy. Now, you get yourself out there and see what life has waiting for you.'

'Yes, ma'am.' Sophie saluted, even though Edith couldn't see her.

'Please thank that delicious doctor of yours again. Such a lovely man.'

'He's not *my*—'

'Go, get yourself out there and I'll see you when I get home.' The phone clicked as Edith hung up, refusing to hear Sophie's denial.

Sophie continued to cradle the receiver in her hand long after Edith ended the call, the dawning truth leaving her in a trance.

No matter how much she tried to deny it, someone hundreds of miles away could tell Luciano was playing a significant role in her latest adventure. In defiance of all inner protests otherwise, Sophie was missing him... all signs she was heading towards disaster. She'd become too dependent on his company being part of her journey. He was in mourning and she was still carrying wounds from her last relationship. She didn't need to add any new ones.

No, she'd thank him for putting her in touch with Edith and discharge the debt she owed him. After that she'd get back to being her.

CHAPTER SIX

'COME BACK TOMORROW and we'll change the dressing for you. In the meantime, I'll give you some painkillers and antihistamines to ease any pain or itching.'

'Thanks, Doctor.' Luciano's young patient eased himself off the bed and gingerly pulled his football shirt back over his head, grimacing as the fabric slid over his burned shoulders.

'Remember to keep covered up, stay in the shade and keep hydrated.'

'Yes, Doc.' The twenty-something English passenger hung his head as he left the clinic but Luciano knew from experience he was fighting a losing battle.

'They never learn their lesson.' Patrice tutted, hands on hips at the latest in a long line of swimmers who had forgotten to reapply sun cream after being in the pool.

'Despite it being a painful, blistered one.' It never failed to amaze Luciano how much damage people put their bodies through in the space of a week or two. His latest casualty had done it accidentally but there were plenty who purposely went out with little or no sun protection in the name of a tan.

His thoughts immediately turned to Sophie, who was comfortable enough in her own skin not to worry about such vanity. She didn't need to, beautiful as she was with her porcelain skin dusted with sprinkles of freckles. She was such a contrast against his dark, Mediterranean complexion. He was earthy, hardwearing terracotta against the finest English bone china. Exquisite. Elegant. Too delicate to treat carelessly yet too pretty to hide from view.

He was guilty of attempting to do both. It had been a mistake to kiss her, to lead her on the way he had when it could amount to nothing. Trying to pretend she didn't exist either wasn't working. He was aware of her presence even if he couldn't see her.

That was what had led him to contact Edith through the number she'd left for her son. He'd considered it the next best thing to speaking to Sophie herself. They hadn't spoken since the trip but that didn't mean he hadn't been thinking about her, the taste of her or the sensation of having her in his arms.

The abrupt end of that moment had been entirely down to him and the spectre of betrayal haunting his conscience. None of it was fair on Sophie and he hoped the small act of putting her in contact with her friend would go some way to her forgiving him.

When the rap on his office door sounded he hadn't expected to see the woman herself standing next to Patrice.

'There's someone here to see you,' his favourite staff nurse said with a knowing look as she showed Sophie inside then quickly disappeared out of sight. Was it that obvious something had happened between them? He'd hear whatever Sophie had come to say then put an end to whatever was happening between them. It wasn't going anywhere, therefore he wasn't willing to put his job or reputation at risk for one little kiss. Except if that was all it had been, his pulse wouldn't be so frantic at the mere sight of her again.

'Sophie? I wasn't expecting to see you here. Are you unwell?' He rose from his seat to close the door behind her so gossip wouldn't spread beyond the office walls.

'No, nothing like that.' She had one arm wrapped around the other, defensive and ill at ease. It did nothing to alleviate the guilt when not so long ago they'd been able to talk so openly to one another.

'I'm glad.' In more than one way… He was happy she was well and also secretly delighted she'd come to see him. Despite his insistence to the contrary, he'd wanted to see her. This way he could deny it was his doing. Fate had intervened—or perhaps it was Sophie's desire for closure.

'I…er…just wanted to say thank you. For the phone call. With Edith.' The short, clipped explanation for her visit wasn't in keeping with her usual chatty manner. It was difficult to tell if she was being abrupt with him—understandably so—or if she was only here out of courtesy. On the other hand, she could be experiencing the same awkwardness he was.

'She's my patient. I wanted to make sure she was okay and it was only a matter of connecting her to your room afterwards. It wasn't a big deal. There really was no need to come and thank me in person.' He was trying to downplay his part but he could see by the sudden hurt clouding her eyes he'd gone about it the wrong way. It sounded as though he didn't want her here when nothing could be further from the truth.

'Right…well, thank you anyway.' She glanced at the door, clearly regretting having come.

He was going to let her go and end their mutual misery when the ship suddenly lurched, unbalancing Sophie and pushing her towards him. She reached out a hand to steady herself against his chest. Instinctively he took hold of her, anchoring his hands at her waist to steady her, their position a re-enactment of their time in the shallows.

'Are you okay?' There was no disguising the thick sound of desire in his voice. He could almost taste the salt on her lips from that day. What would they taste of today? he wondered. They looked sweet and pink like plump strawberries.

'I'm—I'm fine,' she stammered, staring up at him but not breaking contact.

'The sea is rough today. Usually I forget we're even on a ship.' He was rambling, keeping his mouth busy to stop him doing the only thing he wanted it to do. Kiss her.

'I'll have to get my sea legs or I'll be stumbling into people all day.' Her laugh was as shaky as his breathing.

'It's no problem.' As long as it was his arms she kept falling into he wouldn't mind.

There was another jolt, a shudder as the ship forged through more rough water. The sudden, sharp incline of the motion sent them both stumbling back, still caught up in each other's arms.

Luciano let go of her waist to brace his hands on the back of the door before the force of the waves left her crushed between him and the walls.

'Wow.' Despite his efforts to save her from injury, she sounded winded.

'Are you all right, Sophie?' He scanned her face for

signs of distress but all he could see was her waiting for something he was afraid to give.

'No.' To his horror he saw tears pooling in her beseeching eyes and he didn't think it had anything to do with any physical injury she'd sustained.

'What can I do to make things right between us?' He brushed his knuckles down her cheek, knowing he shouldn't be touching her but unable to stop himself. It had never been his intention to hurt her but it was a consequence of letting himself believe he could act on their chemistry.

She closed her eyes and shook her head. 'Nothing.'

The pain in her choked response and the hurt she was trying to hide behind closed lids was worse than if she'd called him out on his behaviour. If she'd slapped him, yelled at him for blowing hot and cold, it would have been punishment he'd be willing to take. Now that she knew as well as he did why this couldn't happen, maybe she'd think twice about coming to see him in future.

Sophie scrabbled to find the door handle. It had been a mistake to come here but she'd wanted to find out for herself if his call to Edith had been his way of putting her off visiting. Now she knew for sure the reason wasn't because he didn't want to see her. Quite the opposite and with good reason. Within a few moments they were back to the place that had caused all the trouble.

'I don't know what's happening, Sophie.' Guilt was there in every confused word he uttered. Since she was the one who'd sought him out, she had to be the one to walk away this time and save them both from further torment.

She steeled herself against the door and hardened her heart as much as she could. 'Chemistry, Luciano. I'm sure you've experienced it before, during and after your marriage, with women other than your wife. As you're also aware, you don't have to act on it. It's there between us, there's no point in pretending otherwise, but I don't want to make this into something it's not. We aren't about to embark on some great love affair when I'm only on board for another few days. You're clearly not on the market for a holiday fling, which, if we're being honest, is all I'd be interested in. So let's just go our separate ways.'

With a push against Luciano's chest first, she yanked the handle down and let herself out. She wasn't sure how much of that speech *she* believed but someone had to do something. The situation was becoming intolerable, waiting for Luciano to decide if she was worth risking his conscience on.

Her steps quickened as she made her way back down the corridor. There was a fear she would run into a member of staff and give herself away by bursting into tears. She liked him and he liked her but this was still so damn hard.

A thud sounded back from where she'd just come from but she daren't look back. Instead she nodded goodbye to the receptionist and waited impatiently for her to buzz the door open for her to leave.

She wasn't going to attempt to wait for the lift. It was so claustrophobic on this level and she was wondering if a cruise had been the best holiday idea for her after all.

Taking the steps two at a time, she raced up towards the top deck and the illusion of space. Every now and then she imagined Luciano calling her name. Wishful thinking.

She was out of breath by the time she reached her destination but instead of heading towards refreshments or seating she made for the open deck. A sudden surge sent her wobbling across the lobby into the wall.

'Sophie!'

This time she knew it wasn't her imagination. Luciano was standing at the top of the staircase, calling her name. He was only making this harder for both of them. She cursed herself for bringing out this fresh wave of torture.

She released a sigh of frustration that they were going to keep rehashing this. Before she could engage in another battle of emotions with him, there was a deafening roar followed by the sound of glass shattering all around.

The deck was literally pulled from under her as she was swept off her feet by a tidal wave of water. The shock and cold stole her breath away, leaving her splashing around, swallowing mouthfuls of water as she tried to work out what was happening.

As the ship listed, she was carried along at speed beside pieces of broken furniture and crockery. She was hurtling towards Luciano, who was still clinging to the handrail at the side of the steps.

'Grab hold of me!' he yelled over the roaring noise in her ears. Although he was no more than knee deep in the water, she knew once she hit those steps she'd be battered and bruised and goodness only knew if she'd be able to fight her way back onto her feet. All those terrible disaster movies she'd watched as an impressionable youngster came back to haunt her.

As she contemplated her watery grave, her body floating tragically towards the ceiling, there was a tight band of pressure around her chest. She looked down to see Luciano's arm wrapped around her torso.

'Hold on.' Unable to hear anything now bar the rush of water, she had to lip-read his muffled words, but he'd hooked her under the arms and she grabbed his thick forearm like a lifeline. Together they fought against the current until they managed to get her back on her feet.

Luciano manoeuvred her around until she was able to cling to the rail as he shielded her with his body.

Sirens began to blare around the ship to let them know too late that they were in danger, along with an announcement for all passengers to return immediately to their cabins and remain there until further notification.

'Wh-what's g-going on?' Her teeth were chattering as she coughed and spluttered, trying to catch her breath again.

'I think we've been hit by a rogue wave. Hopefully that's the worst of it over.'

The violent movement was subsiding and the water level, though sloshing around her middle, wasn't rising any faster.

'Where did that come from?' Still winded, she was draped over the handrail like a soggy ragdoll.

'That's why they call it a rogue wave. Sometimes they happen out of the blue when rough seas are nowhere to be seen. They can be anything up to a hundred feet high. I haven't seen one before but I've heard about them.'

'I thought I was a goner.' Her life had actually flashed before her eyes when she'd thought she was about to be whisked off into the dark depths of the ocean or drowned on the lower decks—not in a montage of cinema-slick highlights, rather those past few wasted years and all the things she should have done.

What if she had died? There was so much she hadn't lived or experienced. Regardless of how minor this event might turn out to be, it had only fuelled her desire to grab onto life with both hands the way she'd done to Luciano's arm.

'You're here. You're here.' Luciano rubbed her back with the same solid reassurance she had come to expect from him. He'd be there whenever she needed him. She'd have done the same for him if circumstances had dictated or if she'd been strong enough to hold him up against the current. She'd have done anything to keep him alive, even if it had meant risking herself.

'I'm wet.' Despite everything, she managed a laugh. Luciano was right. Thanks to him there was no real harm done. She'd hug him if she weren't soaked through.

'Let's get you back to your cabin. You need to get warmed up and change your clothes.' He prised her fingers from around the cold steel bar and curled his hand around hers.

'You need to go and tend to your real patients. Although it might be an idea for you to get changed too. We don't want any old ladies fainting at the sight of your entry into the wet T-shirt competition.' His entire outfit was leaving little to the imagination.

It wasn't her intention to make him feel self-conscious but accepting all his attention seemed selfish. Besides, he was only making her want him more when he was being so protective towards her.

'Will it be safe? We don't know what's happened down there.' She couldn't be sure the clothes in her cabin were any drier than the ones she was wearing. For all she knew, they might be safer up here.

'Look at your feet. The water is only ankle-deep now. It was one wave.'

'Rogue.'

A single goodness-knew-how-high wave that had swamped the ship. She'd simply been standing in the wrong place at the wrong time, had got caught in it. They'd hit a pocket of turbulence at sea, which they'd hopefully now passed through. If there were no further incoming swells, they'd only have to mop up the mess this one had left behind.

'A bit like you,' he said with a grin. 'It struck out of nowhere and caused chaos in the brief time it was on board.'

'Charming.' She wasn't sure the comparison was complimentary but she was intrigued by the thought that he found her troubling. Perhaps his feelings about her weren't entirely dealt with just yet.

'One of nature's fun surprises.' Luciano charmed her back onside with a wink. 'Now, let me escort you back to your cabin.'

He took her arm and helped her wobbly legs make it down the puddled steps.

'I'm sure I wasn't the only one hurt. There was a lot of smashing and crashing going on there.'

'Are you hurt? I could carry you back to your cabin.'

'No! Only my pride was wounded. I can walk on my own, thank you.' Being swept up in his arms as he carried her back to her suite wasn't going to help put an end to her fantasies about him. Especially when she was jealous of the way his wet uniform was clinging to his body.

'If you're sure. I want to be certain you're safe.' He was entirely too chivalrous for his own good.

The ship was no longer lurching and now that the danger seemed to have passed the whole place sparked back to life. The sudden sights and loud sounds were overwhelming as she was trying to get to grips with her own trauma. Horns were blaring, followed by further announcements for passengers to return to their cabins and a call for the crew to muster echoed around the hull.

'At least we don't have to go port side with our life jackets on.' If she took Luciano's word for it, the ship wasn't going to sink to the bottom of the ocean regardless of how it sounded.

'Trust me, if that was the case I'd have you deposited in the first available lifeboat by now,' he muttered.

'Doctor, I think you're needed over here.' A blur of uniform paused long enough to inform Luciano before hurtling away again.

'If you're sure you're okay, I'm going to have to go.' He dropped a light kiss on Sophie's cheek and hurried off to don his Super Doc cape for whoever needed him next, leaving her daydreaming about turning her head to meet his lips for another bone-melting kiss.

CHAPTER SEVEN

THE CREW WERE running around, splashing across the decks with buckets and mops on what seemed like an impossible clean-up operation.

He knew there was another doctor on duty today along with the nurses who could take care of any incoming casualties to the clinic. It was those who couldn't make it there on their own he was concerned about. Both he and Sophie had been lucky to avoid serious injury but not everyone had necessarily been as fortunate.

His skin was clammy and not merely because of the soaking he'd endured but at Sophie's near-miss as she'd almost been carried away by the wave right in front of his eyes. His only thought had been to save her. He hadn't cared if he put himself in jeopardy, and he knew that if she'd gone overboard rather than down the stairwell, he'd have gone after her. Putting his own life on the line wasn't something he'd do for just anyone. If he could have sacrificed himself to save Renata he would have, and the same was true for Sophie. Someone he'd only recently met.

Driven by a need to remind himself that she'd survived intact, he'd kissed her again—only a peck on the cheek but he'd *needed* that physical contact, no matter how brief. He didn't know if any of what had happened would change things between them. She was still going back to England in a matter of days. It already felt like a bereavement of sorts, knowing he might not see her ever again.

Whatever lies his conscience had been telling him that putting her in touch with Edith would somehow remove him from the equation, the opposite was true. He'd known deep down that Sophie would seek him out to thank him, absolving him of the responsibility of seeking her out first.

It was selfish, and he was hurting them both by continuing to deny his feelings towards her. Sophie was the one being honest. They both knew what this was between them and he couldn't run away from it for ever. Probably not even for the few days left of her trip. Every moment he spent in her company brought them closer and closer to temptation.

Luciano was beginning to find life on board stifling. He wasn't any more in control of his life here than he had been back on dry land. The only place he felt confident was at work.

'We need some help over here, Doctor.' He was beckoned over to the restaurant, Sophie following close behind, ignoring his instructions to go back to her cabin, ignoring her own bad experience and current discomfort.

'Where do you think you're going?'

'You need all hands on deck. Pardon the pun.' She gave an apologetic shrug for the ill-timed joke but he couldn't deny any help would be gratefully received in the circumstances.

He frowned, unwilling to put upon her but ultimately aware he had to for the good of any injured people.

'I know you're not going to take no for an answer.' Even if he did reject her offer, he knew he'd be wasting his time.

'Correct.' Any potential argument was over before it began.

As they walked back up across the deck, he couldn't help but be aware of the utter devastation caused during that short demonstration of Mother Nature's power. The crew were doing their best to sweep up broken glass, which was ebbing and flowing at the will of the remaining water. The smell of alcohol around the outdoor bar was strong. The bottles had been whipped from the shelves and dashed to the deck in the melee. Sun loungers were strewn around, some broken and some floating in the overflowing pool.

At least there didn't appear to have been anyone swimming at the time of impact, given the lack of abandoned towels around the area. A squad of crew were like worker bees, stacking up damaged furniture at the side like a soggy bonfire. When they walked into the restaurant, he could see areas of the ceiling tiles had been broken or shifted out of place. It was going to take a great deal of work to get the ship back the way it had been but it could have been so much worse.

'I need you and whoever else you can get to help. Go down to the medical bay and get wheelchairs for us to transport anyone seriously injured.' He sequestered the assistance of a porter he recognised and issued his orders, remembering at the last second to add, 'Please. I'll need whatever medical supplies you have

available.' One of the chefs who appeared through the
galley double doors was promptly despatched back inside by Luciano. It was the area most likely to have a
first-aid kit for emergencies. Kitchens were notorious
places for all manner of accidents and injury.

Officially, he wasn't the man in charge. That was
the captain. But in this instance he felt equally responsible for the souls on board and therefore jus-
tified in organising help for the casualties. After
all, the captain would be onto him if he thought he
wasn't doing his job well enough by putting passengers' safety first.

Whilst he'd been issuing orders, Sophie had set up a
triage system using the tables and chairs usually occupied by hungry diners. Those who'd been caught up in
the carnage or been hit by falling debris were marked
by scarlet stains on their usually pristine uniforms.

'What's the initial impression of casualties?'

'Mostly abrasions and lacerations. A few possible broken limbs in those knocked off their feet or
slammed against the wall with the force but we'll need
X-rays to confirm.'

Again, Luciano was reminded how fortunate he and
Sophie had been not to have suffered more than a few
knocks.

The chef returned with the medical supplies that
would be needed to patch up the walking wounded.
Sophie flipped open the first-aid kit and set to work
cleaning and dressing the most serious injuries.

'If you could point out the possible fractures, I'll
have them transported down to the clinic for further
assessment.'

She separated the casualties into priority groups

so Luciano attended those who were most critically injured.

He assessed the injuries himself, coming to the same conclusions as his colleague. Once the wheelchairs arrived, he delegated transportation to the clinic by the more able-bodied among them.

'Careful not to jolt that leg,' he said, helping a porter to lift a young female attendant into a wheelchair, kicking out the stand so she could keep the limb straight. 'Tell them to X-ray that and I'll be down as soon as I can.'

'What do need me to do?'

'You're supposed to be resting.' Her hair still hung damply around her shoulders. He could tell she was one of those selfless people who never thought of themselves. It didn't matter what adventure she craved, she deserved to have someone to look after her too. She didn't seem to have that loving support from family that he'd found overwhelming but was now beginning to appreciate. If he didn't have a clinic full of patients to treat, he'd be tempted to do it himself.

For a start, he'd dry her hair for her. It would be uncomfortable soaking into her supposedly dry clothes. He'd make sure she was tucked up in bed for some much-needed rest after her ordeal and he'd stay to keep an eye on her.

However, any pampering would have to wait until they'd finished with the emergency cases. That had to take priority over his concern for Sophie.

'What I would like to do is take a further look below decks to see if there's anyone else in need of assistance.'

'Lead the way.' Sophie stood aside to let him pass just as the captain made his presence known. Immediately the rest of the crew stood to attention, ready to receive any further orders.

'Doctor, I'd like a full report on casualties, please.' Usually an affable presence on board, the captain's face was stony, no doubt anticipating the bad news he would have to report back to the company and the coastguard regarding the incident. It was the sort of freak event that, although no one's fault, would bring negative publicity and a stack of paperwork. If that was the extent of their worries, Luciano would be grateful.

Luciano gave him a briefing of what he'd seen so far. 'I'll know more once I get down to the medical centre.'

'I'm going down there now myself if you have everything in hand here.' The captain was going to have his work cut out for him on all levels and Luciano didn't want to hold him back.

'We have. Sophie, one of our passengers and a qualified nurse, has already triaged casualties here.'

It wasn't a favourable look the captain shot at Sophie. More as though she was an added complication he could do without, but he couldn't deny that they needed her.

He took Luciano aside where Sophie couldn't hear. 'Can we get a temporary work contract sorted out? I don't want us getting sued for medical negligence on top of everything else.'

'Of course. I'll get it sorted with head office as soon as I have some free time.' He was keeping his tone courteous, professional. All the while Luciano's jaw was like a steel trap, ready to snap. They were lucky to have Sophie here in a professional capacity. Not everyone would be stepping up like this during their holiday. Sadly, there weren't enough Sophies in the world.

Even if she hadn't been medically qualified, he could see she was the sort of person to volunteer her help in a crisis. Captain Superior wouldn't be reluctant to let her get her hands dirty if she'd grabbed a mop to assist with the general clean-up.

There was an abrupt nod before the captain took his leave, apparently not entirely satisfied by what he'd found.

'What was all that about?' Sophie waited until he strode off before enquiring.

'The neurosis of a man who knows he has serious paperwork to fill out. Speaking of which, he wants you to sign something official if you're going to be working in a professional capacity with us for a while. Everyone needs to cover their backs in the world of liability claims.'

'Understandable. I'll provide references and copies of my qualifications too if you need to check them out. You shouldn't just take my word for it that I'm a nurse.'

'Yet I do.' Although, it was more than that. He'd seen that caring nature of hers enough to know the empathy and kindness that was clearly in the marrow of her bones. What she was capable of could never be adequately expressed on a mere slip of paper.

'Doc, I don't feel so good.' Pavel, the chef who'd supplied the first-aid kit, was leaning heavily on Luciano's shoulder and clutching his side.

'Here, sit down.' Sophie was on the other side of the hefty cook, escorting him towards a seat before his full weight crushed Luciano.

Once Pavel was seated, Luciano knelt beside him on the wet carpet, checking his pulse, whilst Sophie opened the top button on his chef's whites. His pulse was rapid and Luciano could see sweat forming on the man's skin. Luciano held his hand to his forehead and could feel fever burning through his body.

'I need you to tell me exactly where it hurts.'

'Here,' he gasped, and pointed to his lower right-hand side.

Sophie unbuttoned the rest of his shirt to uncover his torso, letting Luciano get a clearer look at his abdomen.

'Did you fall or get hit by anything during the storm?' Luciano pictured solid steel industrial appliances in the kitchen and the force with which Pavel could have been flung against any of it.

'I was ill before the wave hit. I thought perhaps it was too much drink.' He gave Luciano a sheepish look as though he didn't know the crew sometimes partied too much below decks after hours.

It was unsurprising that they let their hair down when they worked so hard with scant free time. Luciano was the exception to the rule.

'When did the pain start?' Luciano applied pressure to the area Pavel had pointed out, causing him to draw a sharp intake of breath.

'Couple of days ago.'

'Do you have any other pre-existing medical conditions I should know about?'

'No.'

'Why on earth didn't you visit the medical centre?' They were there to treat the crew as well as the passengers. Any sign of illness was important to address, especially in someone who worked in the kitchens. He would've been treated straightaway. With so many people in an enclosed space, good hygiene was the only way to prevent illness spreading throughout the ship. Pavel really should've known better than to leave his health to chance.

'I was going to, once we'd prepped for lunch. I thought it was too much drink but it hurts.' With that, he doubled over and vomited.

'Appendix?' Sophie suggested.

'Entirely possible. We need to get him down for tests right away.' The location of the pain, the fever and vomiting all pointed towards appendicitis, something that couldn't be left to chance. They would have to test his blood for signs of infection and X-ray his abdomen to confirm his diagnosis but he was certain that was what they were dealing with here.

Sophie commandeered one of the returning wheelchairs on his behalf and between them and the porter they got Pavel transferred into the chair.

'The crew lift is still working.' The porter pointed them in the right direction otherwise Luciano would have faced the prospect of carrying Pavel sedan chair–style down to the clinic.

'Thanks. We'll take him from here.' He didn't even have to ask Sophie if she was coming too.

Appendicitis often started with a dull cramping sensation. It was possible that the pain Pavel was experiencing meant the appendix was inflamed because it had been left too long without treatment. Usually they'd treat the condition with antibiotics until they reached the nearest port. Only blood tests and X-rays could tell him if his hunch was right and they were fast running out of time.

Despite being run off her feet with patients vying for her attention, Patrice provided a set of scrubs for Sophie to change into. 'Welcome on board.'

They mightn't have hit it off at the start when Sophie had questioned every aspect of Edith's treatment but she certainly looked relieved to have the extra help now. No wonder. The waiting room and corridors were chock-a-block with injured passengers. Thankfully the lower decks had suffered minimal, superficial damage and there had been no major injuries reported so far. Hopefully those waiting would be patched up quickly and able to continue their holiday without too much disruption.

Luciano had already informed her that they needed to jump the X-ray queue as a matter of urgency, so he'd gone ahead, leaving Sophie to change in his office. Their earlier almost-kiss seemed like a lifetime ago now. Those fevered bodies entwined in this very room a short time ago had been doused with cold water even before the wave had hit.

Yet he'd gone after her. Why? When Luciano had been the one saying it was wrong and there was no future for them? He'd saved her too. He'd caught her with so much conviction he could've broken a rib. Now wasn't the time to get into it but when the ship was calm again, she intended to stir the waters with him. She wasn't going to drift away without a fight.

As soon as she'd changed and pulled her damp hair into a more manageable ponytail, she sought her place beside Luciano in one of the treatment rooms.

'Do you want the bad news or the worse news?' He pulled her to one side, with Pavel's X-rays to hand.

Her stomach plummeted. She had hoped the tests would prove them wrong and he'd simply been suffering from an easily treated urinary tract infection. Appendicitis on a ship in bad weather wasn't as straightforward as it might have been in a hospital.

'His appendix?'

'Ruptured.' He was right, that was the worst possible scenario. Life-threatening. A ruptured appendix could spread the infection into the bloodstream and could be fatal if emergency surgery wasn't performed to remove it and clean the abdominal cavity.

'We need to get him to hospital for surgery at the next port, then?' The hospital would be better equipped to perform the procedure than the medical centre, which was essentially an infirmary, not a hospital.

'We do but we don't know when that's going to take place due to the weather. According to the captain, we're too far out to have Pavel evacuated by helicopter and the weather is too bad to make it into port any time soon. I need to move now.'

'You're going to operate?'

'I don't see that we have any choice. We can't wait for sepsis to set in.'

'You're sure you're not rushing into this?' It wasn't that she doubted his medical opinion but this sounded too close to home. He'd told her he'd lost his wife to sepsis and was still reeling from the consequences of that. If he had another patient succumb he might never recover from it. She would go along with whatever decision he made but in this case she wanted him to be doubly sure he was doing the right thing.

'You think I'd put a patient's life at risk simply to justify my own existence? To prove I could've saved my wife if I'd acted sooner? I already know that, Sophie. Trust me, that's something my conscience won't let me forget. Oh, and to put your mind further at ease, the captain is in agreement that this is the best course of action in such life-threatening circumstances.' He was trying and failing to control the volume of his voice, every inch of him as tense as a coiled cobra ready to strike.

It was understandable when she'd insulted his capacity as a medic and an honourable man.

'I had to ask, Luciano,' she mumbled, wondering if that was true or if she'd simply wanted to know for herself if he was truly over the manner in which his wife had passed. It was becoming more and more difficult for her to keep her distance from him, emotionally as well as physically. She didn't want to cross that line with him if he was still confused about what he wanted. It would only cause him more heartache in the long run and she didn't want to put him through that simply because she fancied him.

'It's a question I've already asked myself but I always put my patients first. He can't, *we* can't, wait any longer. The coastguard and closest hospital are on standby but this is an emergency. Believe it or not, we're equipped to deal with those.'

'I understand that. I wasn't trying to undermine you or the facilities here.'

'I should hope not. Along with speaking English, cruise doctors have to be able to perform advanced life-support practices, emergency cardiovascular care and minor surgical procedures.'

'I worked as a theatre nurse for a while. I can assist.' His eyebrows shot up. 'What? You're not the only one who had a working life outside this ship.'

He shook his head. 'You're always surprising me, Sophie, that's all.'

She didn't know what that meant other than that he'd never asked about her previous work experience and vice versa. All they really knew about each other was based on their time together during this trip. It had proved enough for her to let Luciano close but she wasn't sure he was ready to let her in.

With the anaesthetic administered, it was time to do what Luciano did best: work under pressure. In contrast to his time working in the hospital, he hadn't been tested too often during his time at sea. Usually the priority was keeping the patient stabilised until they could reach land. However, they weren't unused to dealing with emergencies. Getting the coastguard out to evacuate a patient by helicopter was rare. Not only did it put vulnerable patients at risk, it could be dangerous for the crew and everyone on board. It was strictly limited to emergencies and better weather.

They had a small operating room with the equipment to carry out one of the most common emergency abdominal surgeries. But Luciano was finding it difficult not to consider the implications of the appendix having already burst, especially when he'd lost his own wife to a blood infection.

'Scalpel.'

Sophie handed him the instrument and he made the first incision into Pavel's stomach, cold sweat beginning to form all over his body.

It had been some time since he'd done anything like this and there was a lot riding on the outcome—not least his burden of guilt. He couldn't lose anyone else this way. Certainly not if Sophie believed he was doing this to somehow make up for his wife's death. It was precisely the opposite. His growing feelings towards Sophie led him to believe he was finally moving out of his mourning period. He'd never forget Renata or what had happened but life had to continue without her. That was what scared him. Not knowing what the future held or if he'd lose someone else.

Death could happen in an instant. If they hadn't acted so quickly with Pavel he could've died. He still might. Life was a fragile thing. But so was Luciano's heart. He wasn't sure it would withstand losing someone else he loved. It was that fear that kept him from getting too involved with anyone else.

'Dr Montavano? Luciano?' Sophie registered his hesitation but he was confident in his medical skills. It was fate that unnerved him. All the expertise in the world couldn't help if events like this were predetermined. Perhaps the wave had happened so they would come to Pavel's aid in time. Perhaps Renata was always going to die, no matter what he did or didn't do. In which case, it made a mockery of his attempts to avoid any emotional entanglements. There was no way to outrun destiny and only a fool would try. Sophie standing here beside him was proof. They kept being thrown together—sometimes literally. These were all signs he should stop fighting his feelings and just let fate take its course.

'I…er…I am just going to divide the fat and underlying tissue to expose the site.'

'Yes, Doctor.' Sophie helped with the positioning of the self-retaining retractors to hold the tissue out of the way so he could work freely.

He did a finger sweep to locate the appendix before carefully tying off both ends. With precise movements he dissected it and disposed of it into the tray Sophie held out to him.

'I need to irrigate the abdomen.' It was necessary to

eliminate any bacterial contamination to prevent septicaemia by flushing out the area with saline. Once it was all drained away again, and he had checked the gall bladder and liver to make sure they hadn't been affected during the procedure, he was able to begin closing the wound.

To Luciano, suturing was a signal that he'd completed his task and he could begin to relax. It was something he had plenty of experience doing on board. There was no shortage of gashed knees around the pool or drunken passengers cut by broken glasses they'd dropped.

'We'll leave the drainage tube in to make sure all infection is clear and keep him on antibiotics and pain-killers for a few days.'

'How long do you think it will take for him to recover?'

'It will probably take a few weeks to get back to full health. Hopefully most of that will be done in a hospital.'

When the crisis had been averted and Pavel had been sewn up again, Luciano breathed a bigger sigh of relief than he'd ever done in a hospital emergency department.

'Thanks for your assistance, Nurse Blythe.' She'd been a quiet, calming presence beside him, assisting his progress with her physical support and a quiet confidence in his abilities.

'Any time, Dr Montavano. It was my privilege to work with you. You saved his life. You should be proud of yourself.' Only Sophie's eyes were visible above her face mask but they expressed genuine respect for him.

'No, *we* did and I think we deserve a drink after

that.' Today had been a wake-up call. Life was too
short and, as he knew all too well, could be snuffed
out at any time. He couldn't spend the rest of his life
worrying and grieving when every second was too precious to waste. Instead of trying to quash his feelings
towards Sophie, he should be celebrating the fact that
he'd met someone who'd resurrected the side of him
he'd thought had died with Renata.

'Are you allowed to socialise with the riff-raff? Isn't
there a danger you'll get mobbed? You're the closest
thing to a celebrity around here.' She was mocking him
but he didn't care when she made him laugh so easily.
Even if nothing happened between them, he enjoyed
being around her. He didn't need to keep punishing
himself by remaining in isolation.

'I was thinking about the crew bar. You're a member of staff now.'

'Ah, so it's just a drink between two work colleagues
after a difficult day?'

'What else would it be?' He didn't see any reason
to label it as something else in case it didn't work out
or scared her off. She knew about his past and his current confusion. It would be understandable if she didn't
want to get involved in his mess when all she was looking for was a bit of fun on holiday.

'You're right. It'll be nothing more than two people
meeting at the same time in the same place, socialising
outside work.' Her teasing made it evident she didn't
believe it any more than he did and there was a chink
of hope that it wasn't too late to act.

'I trust I'll have to go and get changed. Unless it's
some sort of fancy-dress theme we're going for?'

'I'll come by your cabin at about eight.' He had no

choice but to accompany her when he'd have to practically smuggle her in. It was a risk taking her into crew quarters, even if she was a temporary recruit, but he was willing to do it if it meant he could spend more time with her.

'All right. It's a date,' she said blowing him a kiss as she left and almost sending him into cardiac arrest.

CHAPTER EIGHT

'Not a date,' Sophie reminded herself in the full-length mirror at the end of the bed. Luciano had told her exactly that when they'd made the arrangement.

It didn't matter that her body was burning for more or that his vocal protest hadn't matched his body language. He was still in mourning and therefore it didn't make any sense to keep a candle burning for him. She'd only get burned. Besides, after-work drinks with a colleague was still more of a social life than she'd had in a long time.

There was a rap on the door.

'Not a date,' she reiterated. Yeah, right. That was why she'd showered, blow-dried her hair, put make-up on and dressed to impress.

On her way to answer the door her heart gave an unprompted leap, trying to escape the confines of her chest. Why did the prospect of spending the night with Luciano seem more intimidating than assisting him with emergency surgery?

She forced herself into an I'm-not-bothered-at-all casual stance as she opened the door...until she saw him leaning against the door frame in his black turtleneck and dark grey chinos. Cartoon-style *Arooga!*

signs went off in her head and she imagined her eyes had popped out on stalks. He'd shaved and his hair had that fluffy, just-washed look, and he smelled divine—of citrus and the sea. Forbidden fruit and freedom.

'Hey.' She suddenly felt very shy.

It might've had something to do with the way he was looking at her. As though the royal blue silk jumpsuit Edith had talked her into buying 'for one of those fancy dinners they do with the captain' was the disposable wrapper on a sweet he was about to devour. It was not an unwanted reaction and perhaps exactly what she'd been hoping for when she'd chosen the outfit tonight.

'Too much? Not enough?'

The longer he took to reply the more room there was for the doubt crows to set up roost.

It was way too many rapid heartbeats until he answered, 'Just right.'

'Just call me Goldilocks.' She flicked her hair off her shoulder with the sass of a woman who knew she could have anything she wanted—including the sexy man at her door.

'I thought you might like to go for dinner first. Have you eaten?'

'Not yet.' Her stomach had been in too much turmoil at the prospect of spending the evening with Luciano to contemplate eating a meal. Now she was glad she'd waited. It would line her stomach before they went for drinks but it would also give them more time together.

'Dinner it is, then.' He offered her his arm and she hooked her own through it as they made their way through the corridors into the glitz of the atrium, where the awe-inspiring chandelier hanging from the ceiling seemed to illuminate every deck and the glass staircase glittered with encrusted crystals.

'Wait, doesn't dinner lead us into date territory?' There could be little doubt about what was happening now but she liked teasing him. He'd told her he hadn't as much as looked at anyone whilst in mourning so taking someone out for dinner wouldn't be an everyday occurrence for him. Or her.

'We don't have to label this as anything. Let's just go with the flow, Sophie.' He seemed much more at ease about going out as he adopted her recent philosophy; it brought a smile to both of their faces.

'Are we going to one of those posh restaurants? I suppose you can get a table any time you choose. The rest of us mere mortals have to join a waiting list before we can gain admittance.'

As they strolled arm in arm past the queues of people outside the Japanese and French restaurants, she admitted to feeling smug. She'd had her time as a solo diner and not only was she in the company of the most handsome man on board but one of the most important. Even out of uniform he drew nods of respect from those around him. He took it all in his stride but Sophie took it as the measure of the man as much as the doctor that he was appreciated and liked by all. Including her.

'I thought we'd go somewhere more exclusive.' Bypassing all the other guests, he took her towards the lift and pressed the 'up' button. They were the only ones in the lift but the atmosphere between them was buzzing with expectation for the evening that lay ahead.

Perhaps the crew had a separate restaurant and he had a chef friend who was going to cook specially for them.

When they arrived on the now-familiar deck and walked towards the all-day buffet, that fizz of excitement suddenly went flat. She was aware that everyone else who was walking around, plates in hand, helping themselves to the array of food, were dressed very casually. Shorts, T-shirts and sundresses were the uniform here, and she was distinctly out of place. The eyes assessing her outfit told her so.

'I think I'm a tad overdressed. I wish you'd told me this was what you had in mind.' It didn't matter to her where they went when Luciano's company was the main attraction but by building her hopes for something fabulous he'd left room for disappointment.

'We're not there yet. Don't worry. You look amazing.' He gave her a squeeze but she was only reassured when they carried on past the main dining area and down a flight of stairs.

The restaurant below was small, intimate, with a distinctly French theme. The decor was cream and black with paintings of fruit and old wine caskets dotted around to give it some colour and texture. It would've been perfect if not for the fact that it was empty and the chairs were stacked on the tables.

'You did tell them we were coming, didn't you? Or are we too early?' There weren't even any staff about so goodness knew when dinner was going to be served.

'I called in a favour. Come with me.' He took her by the hand and led her past the closed bar and serving area towards the door marked *Staff Only*. With a flick of a light switch he revealed a spotless kitchen.

'Ta-da!'

Sophie looked at the empty stainless-steel surfaces

then back at him. 'Ta-da, what? I don't understand what I'm supposed to be looking at.'

'We have free rein to make our own dinner here. This is ours for the night. They only use this as an overflow during lunchtimes.'

She got why this might be a big deal for him when he'd spent the last eight months having meals made for him. It was a novelty. To her, though, not cooking every night was a bonus of this holiday.

'Great. What are we doing? Reheating leftovers?' She couldn't muster a whole lot of enthusiasm with a rumbling stomach. Perhaps they should've grabbed a plate on the way through the buffet and come down here to eat in peace instead.

Luciano cocked his head to one side and watched her with amusement. 'No. I'm going to cook for you.'

Now, that changed things. Made it more intimate. Special. He wanted to cook for her and this was as close as she'd get to him taking her back to his place. The equivalent to a fourth or fifth date in her mind. What else would you call leaving the public arena, letting her into his inner sanctum, and trying to impress her with his culinary skills?

'What are we having?'

'Pasta.'

'Oh.' Her anticipation of watching him show off in the kitchen as expertly as he'd done in the operating room was quashed as quickly as it had sprung up. Even she could throw a bag of pasta into some boiling water. She tried to look on the bright side. Whatever the meal, they were getting to spend some time together.

He pulled out a stool and rolled up his sleeves. 'If you want to sit there, I'll get started.'

She sat down while he flitted about the kitchen, gathering ingredients. He opened the fridge and loaded his arms with fresh produce. Which, frankly, she thought was overkill when he could easily open a jar. Then he dropped an onion on the floor and bent down to retrieve it, giving her the opportunity to ogle...and she was definitely grateful for the view.

'Do you do this often? Take over the kitchen?'

He set the food on the counter before reaching for two wine glasses out of the dishwasher. 'Never. I cook at home, or I used to. This is the first time I've commandeered the galley.'

'The first time? I'm privileged.'

'I've been saving this too.' He uncorked a bottle of wine. 'It's from the family vineyard. I had to smuggle this on board with me.'

'Are you sure you want to waste that on me?' She was honoured he deemed her special enough to crack open the bottle after all this time but she wasn't sure she deserved it.

'It's not a waste when I'm sharing it in good company.' He poured two glasses and handed one to her.

'I suppose it beats drinking it by yourself in your room. To good company.' She clinked her glass to his in a toast then took a sip of the mellow red liquid. It tasted of summer and carefree afternoons in the sun somewhere she wished they were able to visit together.

'Tastes as good as I remember. Like home.' For someone who claimed he had been desperate to escape the place he appeared wistful at the reminder.

'It's really nice but I imagine we shouldn't drink too much of it on an empty stomach.'

'Is that a hint to get on with cooking your dinner?'

'Not at all. I'm simply saying if we don't eat soon I might end up dancing on the tables and singing like a scalded cat.'

'Okay, okay. I'll get started.' He opened more cupboards until he found the dry ingredients he was looking for. 'Although, I wouldn't mind seeing that.'

'Cook,' she said, rapping her knuckles on the work surface.

'Si, signorina.'

Sophie watched as he poured out some flour, made a well in the centre and cracked eggs into the middle of it. 'I thought we were having pasta?'

'We are. I'm making it now. No self-respecting Italian would ever use that dried rubbish. We only use fresh, home-made pasta.' He started mixing the concoction with a fork and added a dash of salt.

'You're making your own pasta? Right now?' The idea was incomprehensible to her when to most people it was a convenience food made in minutes. Still, she appreciated the effort.

'It's not a big deal.' He was kneading the dough, bringing it together into a ball with a smooth action. The few times she'd tried to make dough it had been a sticky mess, clinging to her hands, the work surfaces and the rolling pin, bearing no resemblance to the pictures in the recipe book.

'It is to me. I can't remember the last time I cooked a proper meal. There doesn't seem any point for one person. Usually I make do with some beans on toast. Sometimes I change it up with some cheese too. I suppose all Italians learn to cook at their mamma's knee?'

'Something like that. Everything was centred around our kitchen at home. It's the most important room in the house.' After he'd stretched the dough out a few times, he flattened it on the counter with the rolling pin.

'I need to let that rest for a while,' he said, then set to work chopping and frying off the vegetables in a little olive oil. Once the sauce was simmering away on the stove, he pulled out some sort of steel trap.

'What's that? Some kind of torture device?'

'It's to make the pasta. Have you never used one?'

'I've never even seen one before.' She got up to inspect this strange toy he was completely at ease with.

'Would you like to try?'

'I don't want to ruin anything.'

'You can't. It's fine. Hold this and I'll fetch you an apron. I wouldn't want you to ruin your outfit.' He left her in charge of his creation to get something to cover her clothes. In hindsight, silk wasn't the best choice for working in the kitchen.

He hung the apron around her neck then leaned in to double tie it around her waist. He was so close she could feel his breath at her neck and all the way down to her toes. 'Thanks.'

'We feed the dough in here and wind the handle to flatten it out. See?' With his head at her shoulder, his chest to her back, he guided her hands with his to make the dough into a smooth sheet.

'Uh huh?' She wasn't paying any attention to what he was showing her, only what he was doing to her by being so close.

'Your turn,' he said, testing her. She'd have done a better job of telling him what aftershave he was wearing or what toothpaste he'd used because she'd paid more attention to those details.

As a result, she was all fingers and thumbs, her composure in tatters from having him touch her. His lovely pasta dough got caught up in the machine and fell out in lumps instead of the smooth sheet he'd shown her.

'Sorry. I should've left it to the professional.' She stood back, leaving him to clear up her mess and try to rectify it.

'Honestly, I haven't done this in ages. I think the last time I did this was for… It doesn't matter. It's all done now anyway.' He expertly whizzed it back through the steel mangle a few times before producing freshly cut spaghetti.

'It's all right. You can say her name. We've both been as churned up as my attempt at using the pasta machine because of our pasts. You don't have to hide it and there's no point in pretending the worst parts of our lives didn't happen.' Sophie took her seat again, content to let him chop the vegetables in case she lost a finger too.

It didn't bother her that he'd done this for his wife. On the contrary, she was glad he was sharing this side of himself with her. Clearly, he was comfortable enough with her to revisit something that meant a lot to him and held lots of memories—something of the life he'd run away from.

He kept winding the dough through until it was a long, silky ribbon. With the last pass through the machine, he cut it into thin strips. 'Renata. Cooking for her is one of the good memories I have. Sometimes they get lost in amongst the bad. The majority of our lives at the end revolved around tragedy. Now, do you want to set one of the tables in there or shall we eat here?'

Whilst a candlelit dinner in an otherwise empty restaurant would've been the traditionally more romantic option, she was content to be here, talking and getting him to open up to her.

'I'm happy to stay here.' She pulled a stool over for Luciano and once he'd cooked the pasta, he plated up the meals so they could eat together off the counter-top he'd just cleaned.

'It's not quite the evening I had planned,' he said as he topped up their wine glasses.

'I'm still enjoying it, though, and this is delicious. You can definitely taste the difference with it being home-made.' Sophie did her best to twirl her spaghetti without splashing sauce over everything and completely showing herself up. Thank goodness for the giant bib she was wearing.

'*Buono.*'

'I don't think Ryan ever cooked for me. Not like this. He wined and dined me when we first got together but soon it was takeaways and comfortable nights in. By the end of the relationship we weren't eating together at all. He was always working late. Allegedly. He was probably out wooing his future wife. He left me with a few trust issues and called my judgement into question. I think that's why I was so defensive when we first met.'

'I'm not surprised. Although I think he's the one with the problem if he didn't appreciate what he already had at home. You're better off without him.'

'Yes, I am. It put me off the notion of men alto-gether.'

'And now?'

'I'm coming around to the idea again.' Was it her imagination or were they flirting during this little heart-to-heart? She was afraid to call it that but there was definitely something springing to life between them again.

'I know what you mean. It was different with Renata and I. There was no cheating or Vegas wedding involved but I didn't think there'd be anyone after her.'

'And now?'

'I'm coming around to the idea.' His coy smile was as intoxicating as the wine she was sipping.

'I just couldn't face that kind of pain again. All our hopes for the future had been won and lost with the first pregnancy. After she lost the baby, having another became an obsession. We both wanted a family and it became our sole focus. Our carefree life as a couple was over and all we cared about was seeing another positive pregnancy test. If I'd known I would lose her too I would've done things differently. We should've made the most of every second we had together.'

'How far along was she when you lost the baby?' Sophie's voice was barely a whisper, afraid to appear unsympathetic or obtrusive in the face of Luciano's heartbreak, but she wanted to get to know him and understand his state of mind.

'Only a few weeks the first time. Three months the second time. We'd already had the scan, heard the heartbeat and dared to believe we were going to be a family. Ten days later I'd lost them both. It took a long time for what had happened to sink in.'

'Shock, I suppose. You never expect something like that to happen. I'm so sorry, Luciano. My feckless ex doesn't even compare to what you've lost.'

'We've both suffered but I think the clouds are beginning to clear. I moved on from shock to grief and I think by signing on with the cruise company I moved into denial. Away from home and a life without Renata I was avoiding facing what had happened.'

'How do you feel about things now?' *About me?* she wanted to add, but this wasn't supposed to be about her. Luciano was sharing the very personal details of the worst time in his life. Something he hadn't discussed with anyone else. She was honoured that he was choosing to work through his emotions about that time with her.

He exhaled a long breath that seemed to come from deep within his soul. 'Honestly? I'm not one hundred percent sure. The thought of inviting more potential heartache into my life is terrifying. So is the thought of remaining alone for the rest of my life. Spending time with you has made me realise that.'

'Just take one step at a time. There's no need to rush into anything you're not ready for.'

He nodded. 'This is good. Just hanging out.'

'Do you know what I'm ready for now? Dessert!' It was clear they were both nursing old wounds, unwilling to commit to anything serious that would cause them to reopen old wounds, but at least they were acknowledging that. Sophie didn't want them to dig so deep that they became maudlin when their objective tonight was to have some fun together. They needed to get their date back on track.

'What would you like? I'm sure I could make something.'

'No. You do the dishes and I'll sort dessert.' It was her turn to surprise him, even if she was planning on taking a rather unconventional route.

When Luciano had cleaned up and come to see what

she was doing at the other end of the kitchen, he burst out laughing.

'That's cheating,' he said as she started up the ice-cream machine.

'I didn't know there were rules. If you don't want me to…' She turned away and pretended to put one of the ice-cream cones back in the box.

'I didn't say that. Please may I have an ice-cream cone too?'

Sophie pulled the lever until the nozzle piped a frilly mixture of chocolate and vanilla dairy goodness into both cones. 'Why don't we go up on deck and take these with us?'

She wasn't ready for the night to end and she hoped he felt the same way.

There was an open-air movie screening near the bow of the ship, so Luciano directed Sophie towards the quieter end at the back. He was pleased she'd suggested this, otherwise he would've had to take her to one of the crew bars to continue their evening, and that would have meant sharing her. And, even worse, shouting about their feelings over the loud music within earshot of his crew mates.

He liked it being just the two of them. That was what had prompted him to make dinner himself and keep the evening intimate. He'd wanted quality time with Sophie, time and space to express their fears about what was developing between them. Neither of them was going to jump into something serious and Sophie wasn't pressuring him for anything. He didn't need to be on his guard around her. She had become a symbol of everything that would be available to him in the future.

'It's quiet here. I like it.' Sophie was peering over the side of the ship as she finished her ice cream, watching the wake left in the waves.

Luciano moved over beside her and rested his arms on the rail. 'That's because everything's closed until tomorrow. There's no reason for anyone to come this way. Sometimes I come here at night for a timeout.'

During the day this area was heaving, mostly with children, for use of the climbing wall and the water-slide. For safety reasons they shut down before sunset. He preferred it when the rows of redundant sunbeds were stacked and the sound of the sea replaced the noise of shrieking.

'A timeout from what? Being on your own?' Sophie laughed at her own joke and he decided he preferred that over all other sounds.

'I suppose I have become something of a hermit.' He tossed the last of his cone overboard and watched as it disappeared into the darkness.

'A hermit in plain sight of thousands of passengers and crew. That's quite a feat.'

'Yet you're the only one to notice.' Of all the people he'd met, of all the friends he'd made, Sophie was the only one who'd gotten close enough to see he was essentially alone. It said a lot about her and how much he thought of her to let her in.

'Birds of a feather and all that.' Sometimes an English turn of phrase went beyond his knowledge of the language.

'Pardon?' He looked up at the sky, trying to figure

out what she was talking about, but he couldn't even see any seagulls about.

'Oh, Luciano.' Her giggle was a glorious sound, even if it had come at his expense, but it was the hand lightly resting on his chest that he took most pleasure in. 'It simply means we're very alike. I've spent a lot of time on my own too.'

'Not tonight, though.'

'No. Not tonight. I've enjoyed the company very much.' Sophie faced him and he found he was jealous of the moon putting the silver sparkle in her eyes and the tongue that had licked the last of the ice cream from her lips.

'Me too.' With every word they uttered they were gradually moving closer to each other. No longer fighting the inevitable but fully embracing it.

She tilted her chin up towards him and, convinced this was what he and Sophie both wanted, he captured her mouth with his in a ferocious expression of his desire for her.

Her hand, previously resting on his chest, was clutching the back of his neck. He pulled her forcefully to him, his hands sliding along the cool silk at her back. Everything she'd inspired in him tonight was wrapped up in that kiss. A wish to move on, to live again and enjoy being with someone free from guilt.

Any second now Sophie was sure she'd wake up. This had to be a dream. It was the only explanation as to why she'd found herself here under the moonlight with a gorgeous Italian kissing her as though his life depended on it. All the promises she'd made to herself to steer clear of men launched themselves overboard with the first touch of his lips against hers. There was no sane reason to deny herself this taste of passion.

Luciano couldn't do to her what Ryan had done. He had no intention of marrying anyone and she was the one who'd be doing the leaving in a matter of days. There could be no misunderstanding of their relationship or time to resent each other when every moment together was precious and getting hotter by the second.

The heat of his touch was scorching her skin, sending arousal coursing through her like molten lava. His tongue was rough against hers, and insistent. The firm pressure of his mouth, wrapped up in the warmth of his embrace, was enough to make a girl go weak at the knees. Thankfully, Luciano took the strain, lifting her up against the rail so she could wrap herself around him.

'Go for it, mate!'

'Put her down!'

'Twit-twoo!'

Drunken jeers and wolf whistles ended their clinch all too soon, neither of them wanting to be entertainment for drunken passers-by.

'Let's get out of here.' Luciano took her hand, his face dark and tense whilst she was sure hers was scarlet at being caught smooching in a very public display of affection.

The sound carried down the stairs with them.

'Idiots.' They'd spoiled their evening with their childish taunts because it soon became obvious Luciano was escorting her back to her cabin. Date over.

'I'm sorry if I embarrassed you. I should've known better than to kiss you where people could see.' As they reached her door all his good humour seemed to have dissipated thanks to the interruption.

'You didn't embarrass me. I was just sorry it ended. Do you want to come in and pick up where we left off?' Sophie opened the door as she made the bold invitation. By putting herself out there she knew she was risking rejection but this was what she wanted. There was no way she was going home with regrets. She had enough of those already. Luciano was her new start and that meant being honest with herself.

She recognised the flare of interest darken Luciano's eyes seconds prior to his mouth securely imprisoning hers. She wasn't going to attempt to break free when this was all she'd dreamed of since that last kiss had robbed her of her senses.

Luciano held her face in his hands, kissing her as though it might be for the last time, and backed her farther into her room. She barely had time to register the implication of the move when he kicked the door shut behind them. This was really happening.

'I guess this was a date after all.' She was breathless as she tugged at his shirt, wanting him naked before he had time to change his mind again. He stopped kissing her long enough to strip it off for her then resumed his passionate exploration of her mouth.

She drew her hands over the expanse of his broad chest, exploring the contrast of rough hair and smooth skin beneath her fingertips.

'Unlike any I've ever had before,' he muttered, kissing the skin behind her ear then across her shoulder.

With an impressive sleight of hand, he undid her zip and peeled away her silk layer. Sophie let it fall around her feet and stepped out of it so she was standing before him in only her lingerie.

'What changed your mind about doing this?' Sophie's voice was breathy with anticipation as he undid her bra and brushed his thumbs across her budding nipples.

'We've only got one life. We should live it to the fullest. Squeeze every drop out of it.' He plucked the sensitive nubs between his fingers with a glint in his eye that made her breath catch in her throat all over again. This matched up to every hot dream she'd ever had about Luciano.

She was standing there, exposed and vulnerable, shaking with nerves and need. Luciano didn't have any such qualms as he shifted down her body, his tongue zigzagging across her hyper-sensitive skin until he reached her belly, making her practically convulse with want for him. He hooked his fingers into either side of her panties and slid them infuriatingly slowly down her legs until he was kneeling at her feet and she was completely naked.

Luciano nudged her legs apart so she was open to him, anchored her with his hands at her waist and buried his face between her legs. The instant his tongue darted into her core she had to hold onto his shoulders in case she collapsed, the exquisite sensation rendering the rest of her body immobile. All of her focus was on that one area, proving exactly why Italians had a reputation as excellent lovers. He butterflied in and out of her, drinking her nectar with his fluttering tongue.

Somewhere beyond her closed eyelids and out-of-body feeling she heard the frantic gasps of a woman on the blink of oblivion and realised it was her. Her orgasm came hard and there was no stemming the shudders of ecstasy racking her body.

A determined Luciano didn't deviate in his pursuit of her complete satisfaction until she was breathless with exhaustion and her legs were quivering as she fought to remain upright. It was no wonder the French called it *la petite mort*, comparing the post-orgasm sensation to death. She thought she had died and gone to heaven a million times over.

Her chest was heaving as she fought to get her breathing back to normal, with Luciano kissing his way back up her torso.

'Oh, my. That was…' No words could describe what he'd done to her or how amazing it had been.

'We aren't finished yet.' He popped his fly open and the sound was even sexier than his laugh.

They tumbled onto her bed, with Luciano still nuzzling against her neck, caressing her breasts with his large hands and generally testing her limits.

He was all hard muscle and soft kisses lying on top of her and she wanted to fold him right into her body. Except there was that niggling voice of her conscience refusing to shut up about him not being ready for this. But when he brushed against her inner thigh, she knew he was more than ready.

His hot breath in her ear started another tremor throughout her already satiated body. He entered her quickly, stretching and filling her all at once, and her gasp was drowned out by Luciano's groan. It was good to know she wasn't the only one finding this overwhelming.

He gave her a shaky smile before pressing another kiss on her lips, his eyes filled with a dazed look that showed he was experiencing the same thing she was. When he began moving inside her she knew it was the beginning of something out of this world.

It wasn't long before her exhausted body sprang back to life, greedy for more, urging Luciano to take her back to that heady paradise again. As she tightened around him, the pace between them increased to fever pitch, both desperate to reach that release and the promise of bliss. He was like a drug to her now, every hit pushing reality further away and making her want this to last for ever.

'Sophie.' He cried out her name at the height of his climax, pulling her with him. Together they toppled over the precipice, breathless but happy when they finally came back down to earth.

Despite the air-conditioning, Sophie was perspiring from the heat they'd generated.

'So much for the shower I had.'

Luciano lay beside her, continuing to map her body with his hands and mouth. 'Are you complaining, *mi amore*?'

'Not. At. All.'

He cupped her breast and took her nipple in his mouth, sucking until she was straddling the line that bordered pain and pleasure.

'Luciano… I need a breather.' She giggled, exertion taking its toll after so many years of celibacy.

'Sorry. I just can't get enough of you.' His need was growing steadily against her by the second.

They were the words every woman wanted to hear. Yet Sophie couldn't help but interpret them with some trepidation.

In a matter of days this was all going to be over. It

wasn't simply the euphoria of being post-orgasm, she wanted more of this, more of him. Why did she always fall for the wrong man? Or the right man at the wrong time? If she'd met him during the freedom years she might have joined him on the cruise life and had a series of adventures. As it was, she had a job and a mortgage to return to while Luciano was rediscovering his zest for life. Without her. That made her sadder than anything.

For now, she wanted to stay in this loved-up bubble of a holiday romance where anything was possible. They didn't have much time left together before she had to go back to reality. Like all the best vacations, she never wanted this to end.

'What's stopping you from taking what you want?' Her words came out of the bravado of a woman who wanted a lifetime of memories to take back to England. She was lying naked, coyly batting her eyelashes, whilst her hand was straying down his chest, his taut stomach and towards his solid arousal.

He gave another groan but the expression on his face was one of pure pleasure. 'I thought you needed a breather?'

'I'm breathing. See?' She drew in a few exaggerated breaths delighted in his lustful eyes watching her breasts rise and fall.

With a territorial growl he rolled her onto her back and pinned her hands above her head. Her pulse spiked with anticipation and awareness that he could do anything to her he chose. And that she trusted him not to do anything to hurt her.

'What is this spell you've cast over me, Sophie? You're all I think about. All I want.' There was such genuine confusion in his voice that she felt guilty about distracting him from the grief he'd clung to.

'I'm sorry.' Tears pooled in her eyes. She'd been selfish. Only thinking about herself and her needs when Luciano had told her he wasn't ready for another relationship. No matter how short-lived.

He frowned at her and released her from his hold. 'Don't ever be sorry for who you are. You've done nothing except remind me I'm alive.'

His kiss was sweet and tender and made her cry all the more. When they joined their bodies together once again, making love slowly this time, she knew the tears had been of self-pity. She'd fallen for him, but in only a few days she'd have to let him go and return to her responsibilities. This couldn't be any more than a holiday fling, and that was never going to be enough for her.

Luciano had forgotten what it was to wake up lying in bed beside someone. Disoriented at first, he wondered why he was so warm and why he couldn't move. He opened his eyes to see Sophie's naked body wrapped around his. Rather than pulling away, he snuggled in closer. Her soft breath against his skin and her arm draped possessively around his midriff were things he could get used to. He'd found the peace of mind and joy in his life that he'd been searching for since losing Renata. She was always going to have a special place in his heart, but so was Sophie.

She'd shown him how important it was to receive support as well as give it. Made him see he was allowed to have fun, to explore everything the world had to offer without having to feel guilty about it. Taught him to live the life he was lucky to have. Most of all, she'd taught him to open his heart again. He'd taken the next step with Sophie because he was ready for it, ready to let someone into his life again.

She was sleeping soundly on his chest, unaware of the revelations going on inside him. Sophie had opened up a whole new world to him, one outside his grief and the ship. The problem was she was leaving in a couple of days. That was why it was more important than ever to stop denying himself the right to be happy again. Even if it was only for a short time.

He brushed his fingers through her hair, letting the silky tresses fall onto his chest. She stirred beneath his touch.

'Is everything okay?' she mumbled, her eyes closed, her arm still wrapped around his torso. He didn't want this to end and was tempted to close his eyes again and go back to sleep.

Unfortunately, he couldn't afford to do that just yet. 'I'm going to have to go back to my own cabin, *mia cara*.'

'It's the middle of the night, Luciano.'

'I can't risk anyone seeing me coming out of a passenger's cabin in the morning.'

'I thought I was staff now?' She drew a circle around his nipple with her fingernail, trying to distract him… and succeeding.

'It would look bad for the company. They don't approve of relationships between crew members either.'

'We have a few hours left before dawn. No one's going to see you.' She was dotting feathery kisses across his chest, making it impossible for him to leave now.

'Uh-huh? What have you got planned until then?'

'I can think of a few things.' Sophie shifted across to straddle his hips. She was like a goddess, naked and wanting, and she was all his. For now.

When they were moving together, his hands at her waist as she ground against him, he was in ecstasy. It wasn't only the sex that was great, they had a real connection he'd never thought he'd have with anyone else. There didn't seem to be a logical reason to let her disappear out of his life. Once she stepped off this ship they weren't likely ever to cross paths again. If these past years had taught him anything, it was to savour the good times with loved ones because you never knew when it could all come crashing down. In this instance he knew the date he'd lose Sophie. This time he could do something to prevent his heart from being broken.

It was easy to say 'live in the moment' and accept what they had for now, but the moment was almost over. He was done being passive. Now was the time to be proactive.

She'd told him she wasn't happy with her life in England and he was almost ready to go home again. Given the chance, Sophie would love his part of Italy. She wanted to travel. It was up to him to let her know that was an option because he'd spent so long telling her he wasn't ready to move on again.

They could sort something out if they wanted this to work. After being on his own for so long, he knew he could do a long-distance relationship if it came to it. As long as he knew he'd get to do this with Sophie again, he'd survive.

He'd talk to her tomorrow when they were able to think more clearly. The things she was currently doing to him made Luciano feel as though his brain was about to explode, along with every other part of him. He thrust his hips up, plunging deeper, faster inside her until she was tightening around him, her hands clawing at his chest as she rode to climax with him.

The one thing he was sure of was that he was going to make the most of their time together in case it was their last. He sure as hell wanted to give Sophie reason to remember him, if not come to the same conclusion he had. That what they had together was worth more than a mere fling.

CHAPTER NINE

IT WAS CANNES TODAY. Sophie had never been to France and was looking forward to visiting the most romantic country in the world with her lover. Unlike her, however, Luciano was working. Now they were in port, he'd had to oversee patient transfers to the nearest hospital and was responsible for follow-up appointments for those who had injuries from the rogue wave. She could've undertaken this excursion on her own but had chosen to wait for him to join her. It was strange how quickly she'd become used to being part of a couple.

It wasn't necessarily a good thing when she was going home at the end of the week and this trip was supposed to have been about finding herself again. Getting involved with a man hadn't been part of her plan. Edith's perhaps. She'd be over the moon to discover Sophie had had an affair in her absence.

They'd had only one night together thus far, but one that had left her throat raw from her very vocal orgasms and afraid to run into anyone from the neighbouring suites.

'*Je voudrais*...that one,' she said in her pitiful pidgin French that would have made her high-school French teacher weep.

There were a variety of vendors lined up along the harbour wall to greet disembarking passengers with hats and handbags for sale. She'd chosen a floppy white hat, which should do the job of shielding her from the morning sun and hopefully give her a touch of Riviera glamour appropriate for the trip.

'Let me get it for you,' Luciano insisted, and she was sure he handed over more than it actually cost.

A few euros lighter and one hat heavier, they made their way along the seafront. Wearing her black-and-white swing dress and shades, she liked to think she was channelling her inner Audrey Hepburn to fit in with the sophisticated surroundings. Luciano would make a handsome co-star who would've fitted in perfectly amongst Hollywood leading men like Cary Grant or Gregory Peck.

Last night had surprised her in more ways than she could possibly have imagined. It was so unfair that she couldn't have that passion in her life for ever. After a while it would fade, as she knew all too well, but that didn't stop her hoping it was possible to maintain that level of passion in a relationship. Sadly, life with Ryan had shown her otherwise. He'd decided the only way to recapture that intoxicating desire had been to find it with another woman.

Luciano would have to remain a lovely, sizzling memory because anything more would eventually turn into disappointment. She wasn't going to repeat history. Especially when she knew how much baggage he was carrying with him.

For now, she was an exciting distraction for him. Ultimately, he was a man who would want to settle down, replace the wife he'd lost and probably the family he'd been denied. He wouldn't find that with her.

That was what she was telling herself. She didn't know how she was going to manage to say goodbye. The thought of going home was more depressing than ever. It was hard enough swapping this relatively stress-free life in such a beautiful setting for her hum-drum existence. Because that was all it was: an existence. Out here she was properly living. And a lot of that was down to Luciano's company inside and outside the bedroom.

'It's a whole different world out here, isn't it?' Luciano echoed her thoughts about surroundings she'd only seen on TV before now.

'It doesn't seem like a real place, more like a playground for rich kids and tycoons.' You only had to take a glance up the road to see the souped-up sports cars or hear their modified engines to understand the kind of money that was thrown about here. It was interesting to see how the other half lived and pretend to be part of it for an afternoon.

'We can play here for a little while at least.'

'I wonder what it would be like to live here?'

'Permanently? Financially impossible, I would have thought.'

'I could always live on the beach. I think I could be happy there.'

'I don't doubt it, my little drifter.' He hugged her close, apparently comfortable enough outside the confines of the ship to show his affection towards her. She wasn't complaining and snuggled further into his arms. The nickname he'd given her was apt, she thought. It was more in keeping with the woman she wanted to rediscover—continually moving around without any fixed home or job. She was sure he meant it in the most endearing terms and not with any negative connotations. He got her.

Sophie stopped, stood up on tiptoe and kissed him full on the lips.

'Mmm… What was that for?' He lifted her sunglasses up so he could see into her eyes and kissed her back.

'For being you.' She liked the fact that he didn't shy away from her, even though they were in a public place. As if he no longer cared about the rules when he was with her. Even now there were faces she recognised walking by, the occasional greeting thrown their way. No one seemed to mind in the slightest about what they were doing and she liked to think that they looked so happy together no one would begrudge them this time together.

'We should go exploring. Perhaps we'll stumble onto a movie set somewhere.'

Sophie didn't think she could stand much more excitement today but all the shops and fabulous-looking buildings appeared to be uphill. She could spend all day walking along the shore with Luciano but it did seem a waste to be here and not see something of the sights.

'There's a park across the road. We could cut through there.' She spotted the little oasis of palm trees in the centre of the town and it seemed a good halfway point between the solace of the beach and the rest of the bustling resort.

They dodged through the traffic and entered the park through the black wrought-iron gate. It was like walking into another world. The palm trees lining the pathway provided some much-needed shade and the plots of greenery afforded a different kind of freshness than they'd found the shore.

'It's so peaceful in here.' Even Luciano seemed impressed by it. The gardens made a change from the sea view he was used to.

'We can sit a while if you'd like. There's a bench over in the corner.' They weren't in any rush to go anywhere and it would be nice to rest her feet for a while before they attempted to hike up the steep streets.

'I'd rather do that than join in with the group.' Luciano pointed at the visitors nearby, contorting themselves into shapes on the grass as part of what she assumed was a yoga class. She'd never taken part in one herself because she got all the exercise she needed being on her feet all day in the nursing home. Although she had always thought it did look calming for the soul. Something she would need when the day came that Luciano wasn't available to do the job.

They flopped down onto the bench and it felt natural for Sophie to cuddle up with him. Despite the noise from a few children in the playground nearby, it was peaceful. They could've been anywhere at that moment and she knew she'd feel the same contentment even if they were on a bench in Kent, as long as she was with Luciano.

'Think we could stay here for ever?' he asked, his eyes closed as he lifted his face to the sun.

'It's very tempting.'

Unfortunately, their peace didn't last long as they heard the roar of a supercar, a thud and screams of distress.

They both immediately began running in the direction of the heart-wrenching shrieks. Thoughts of themselves and their oasis of peace were forgotten in the face of someone else's tragedy.

The screech of tyres disappeared into the distance while the crowd congregated around someone lying in the middle of the road, and that told them everything about what had happened.

'Let me through, please. I'm a doctor.' Luciano took charge of the scene, making his way towards the casualty.

'They didn't stop. Just mowed him down.'

'I got the registration.'

'Is he going to be all right?'

The crowd, obviously in shock from what they'd witnessed, were all English tourists Sophie recognised from the ship. A few of the locals came rushing over, mobiles in hand as they phoned for help.

'What's his name?' Luciano was already on the ground, checking the elderly man's pulse.

'Charles.'

'Charles, can you hear me? I'm a doctor. You've been hit by a car. I'm just going to check you over. If you can, let me know where it hurts.' The only response was a series of groans.

'He hit his head hard on the ground when he landed. It sort of bounced.' One of his companions was able to give them enough information to understand there could be a serious head injury involved.

Sophie let Luciano carry on with his assessment whilst she dealt with the man's leg, which had clearly suffered some trauma. His trousers were ripped and although there wasn't any blood visible, the lower right leg was bruised and swollen. The ankle was bent at an odd angle too.

'Does anyone have any blankets or towels? Give me your shoelaces or belts. Anything I can use here.' She was sure the beachgoers would have something she could commandeer to support his leg.

Luciano flicked a glance at her. 'Is everything all right, Sophie?'

She gathered the donated beach towels, using them to pad the affected area, and tied them securely in place with the belts at her disposal, keeping Charles's leg as straight as possible. 'Suspected fracture of the fibula. I've got it.'

The bone hadn't pierced the skin so there was less risk of infection setting in but it would require X-rays to confirm the location and severity of the break.

He nodded and got back to treating the head injury. In the short time they'd known each other they'd worked together sufficiently to trust each other to make the right decisions and it warmed her heart to think of it.

Luciano was glad Sophie was here to help treat the casualty. They made a good team. He didn't have to worry about anything other than treating whatever head injury had been sustained when she was so capable of managing everything else. A high-velocity crash could cause multiple injuries, internal and external. Bones could mend given time but a brain injury could have a life-changing impact.

'Charles, I need to give you an examination to see where you've been hurt.' He was still breathing but he was falling in and out of consciousness. The velocity of the impact would have jarred his brain against his skull but without scans or X-rays there was no way of knowing how much damage had been done.

'There's blood coming from his nose and ears. It's possible he's suffered a skull base fracture. He's got a few lacerations on his scalp but no sign of skull depression.' He kept Sophie up to date with his assessment as she had with the lower limbs. With no apparent palpable dent in the skull he hoped that meant there were no pieces of skull embedded in the brain, which would require surgery to be removed. All they could do was immobilise him until help arrived and prevent any secondary injuries occurring that could arise from moving him carelessly.

'Take a few of these towels to stabilise his neck.' She tossed him a couple of towels, which he folded in half and then rolled up into colourful burrito shapes and placed either side of Charles's head.

'I need to go.' Charles began to come around but was disoriented and kept trying to sit up.

'You need to stay where you are until the ambulance comes.' Luciano pushed firmly on his shoulders, careful not to jolt his neck but determined not to let him sit up.

'I don't need an ambulance. What's going on?' It wasn't unusual for a patient to become confused in these circumstances but it was Luciano's job to keep him still until treatment could be administered.

'You've been in an accident, Charles. I think you might have a broken leg and you've hit your head. We need you to stay still.' Sophie tried her best to reassure him whilst also keeping his leg straight to prevent any further injury.

He kicked out with his other leg, knocking Sophie onto the ground. Although aggression was sometimes part of the job when patients were agitated by their condition, Luciano immediately came to Sophie's defence.

'Hey! You can't lash out like that. I know you're confused and in pain but we're trying to help you. Sophie, are you okay?' If he wasn't so intent on keeping this man stabilised until help arrived, he would've swept Sophie up in his arms and carried her away to safety. The thought of anyone hurting her brought out the protective streak in him he'd thought he'd never have to deal with again. He knew it meant he was in too deep already. Now that he cared so much about her, and her safety, it left him open to getting hurt again too.

'He knocked me off balance, that's all.' She gave him that 'Don't fuss' glare that made him smile.

'If you want to go, I can handle this.' He couldn't bear her to take any more abuse for simply providing assistance.

'I'm okay. You're just a bit confused about what's happening, Charles, aren't you?' Sophie didn't appear to bear the patient any ill will over the incident, which only elevated her in Luciano's esteem.

Thankfully the sound of sirens could be heard not far in the distance. Once the paramedics arrived they could take over and give Charles the best treatment available. Then he and Sophie would be free to enjoy what they had left of their day together.

'Is there anything you'd like to do here before we go back? You didn't really get a chance to see the place.' Once Luciano had passed on the information about Charles's possible brain injury and leg fracture to the paramedics, there was the small matter of contacting the ship to let them know what had happened.

Sophie was left to watch from the sidelines, coming down from the rush of helping to treat their patient at the scene. She had neither the language skills nor contacts to help with the follow-up and was content to let Luciano deal with it. He was good at being in charge—level-headed in a crisis. Yet there was that other spontaneous side of him, which she was sure not many people got to see, the impulsive romantic who would take over a whole kitchen to impress her with his cooking skills. She could do with more of that in her life, given the chance. For now, she had to make do with whatever time they had left together.

'I don't want to go too far. I'm exhausted. How about a walk along the beach? It looks beautiful.' They'd come here to relax and after the drama she could use a little calm as long as she had Luciano to share it with her.

'I think we can manage that.' Luciano helped her down the large step from the promenade onto the shore. The first thing she did was remove her sandals so she could feel the sand beneath her feet. It was so soft she began to sink into it.

'We'll have to start moving before I disappear into this quicksand.' She began walking while Luciano went barefoot too. When he caught up with her at the water's edge she was pleased to see he'd rolled up his sleeves and loosened the top buttons of his shirt, looking more relaxed and off duty now.

'I think you're a real water baby, Sophie. Always drawn to the sea,' he said as she splashed through the soft waves slipping silently onto the beach.

'I find it soothing. The steady rhythm of the waves is like a lullaby to me. It helps me destress.' It was something she'd learned about herself on this trip. Perhaps she should move closer to the coast or buy herself a houseboat when she got back to bring more contentment to her life.

'Destressing is something we both need and I have just the place to do it. Come.' He laced his fingers through hers and lifted her hand to his mouth to kiss it. She didn't care where he was taking her because right now she would follow him to the ends of the earth if he asked her to. This was the perfect holiday romance—if she disregarded the work element and those life-or-death dramas.

To the right they had the beautiful seascape of the Mediterranean glittering in the sun. To the left they passed a strip of luxurious hotels, where she could picture movie stars swarming during film awards season. One even had the red carpet laid out for its exclusive guests. It was fabulous and a long way from her semi-detached in Kent. When Luciano rerouted them off the beach and towards one of the lavish entrances she suddenly felt out of her depth.

'We can't go in there.' She brushed the sand off her feet and shook out her sandals before putting them back on.

'Why not?' He didn't seem at all fazed by the notion of being part of the scene.

'It's a place for movie stars and rich people. They'll take one look at me and send for Security in case I taint the place with my working-class DNA.' Imposter syndrome set in as they got closer to the grand marble staircase leading to the hotel entrance. She was happy where they were and didn't need anyone looking down their nose at her and spoiling the daydream.

'Nonsense. You're beautiful and just as good as anyone else in there. The place can only be improved by having you there.' Luciano had such a confident charm it was easy to believe they could simply stroll in and that's exactly what they did.

She did, however, remain hovering in the doorway while he strode up to Reception so she could make a quick getaway if necessary. He chatted to the concierge at the desk—probably fluently in French to impress the slick fifty-something gatekeeper. He looked the sort who'd be impressed by the chief physician of a ship. Well, who wasn't?

The concierge summoned another junior member of staff, who was soon scurrying off to carry out whatever instructions had been issued. Luciano turned around and beckoned her over.

'Sophie, what are you doing all the way over there?' She took that as a cue they weren't about to be chased out of the building by security dogs chomping at their heels, trained to sniff out the riff-raff.

'Hey.' She slid her arm around his waist and laid her head on his shoulder as though it was the only way she could convince him they were a couple. It only served to have Luciano looking at her as though she'd gone mad but he did drop a kiss on the top of her head.

'*Merci pour votre aide,*' he said to his new friend, and helped himself to the champagne bucket and two glasses presented to him on a silver tray.

'That's for us?' she asked as they followed the junior member of staff through the hotel.

'*Oui. Pour toi, mon amour.*'

'If you're showing off your linguistic skills to impress me, it's working.' Every language he spoke only increased the exotic, erotic nature of the man in her eyes. She couldn't believe her luck that she'd met someone so cultured who was interested in an English Plain Jane like her. She had nothing to offer except her nursing experience and sparkling personality. Thankfully he seemed to have a penchant for mouthy English girls.

'You haven't seen anything yet, *bella donna*,' he whispered seductively into her ear, turning her spine to gelato.

Any thoughts he'd conjured up in her mind of holing up in a luxurious hotel suite for an afternoon of passion vanished as they exited the lobby and continued past the hotel swimming pool.

'Where are we going?' Now they'd left the bar and restaurant behind, she had no idea of their final destination.

Luciano thanked their attendant and slipped a discreet tip into the palm of his hand.

'That's us at the end of the pontoon.' He pointed down the walkway stretching out into the middle of the sea. It reminded her of one of the old-fashioned seaside piers except instead of amusement rides and carnival stalls this one housed several Bedouin-like tents.

They kept walking until they reached the end of the jetty, where the biggest structure sat on its own.

'Seriously? They're letting us use this?'

'Yes. I've paid for it. Sophie, you're as entitled as anyone else to be here. I know your confidence has taken a knock recently but you're a good person who works hard. You deserve a treat now and then.'

She didn't even know what the treat was supposed to

be. From this angle it appeared to be a four-poster bed with three sides encased in a calico material, the front drapes left open and tied to the sides with purple silk rope. The bed, or sun lounger, she wasn't sure which it was, was festooned with satin cushions in opulent deep purples and mulberry colours.

'It's a daybed,' Luciano told her, as if that explained everything. 'I told them we wanted our privacy so no one will bother us.'

'This is amazing. Look at the view.' Standing on the edge of the pontoon, she could see the whole promenade in the distance and the cruise ship farther out to sea.

Luciano adopted his casual look again, removing his shoes and rolling his trouser legs up to his knees before sitting on the edge of the decking. He patted the space next to him for Sophie and she joined him once she was barefoot again too. Dipping her toes into the water was bliss—not as cold as she'd imagined but cool enough to counter the heat of the afternoon sun.

He poured two glasses of champagne and that first hit of bubbles on Sophie's tongue almost did as good a job as Luciano at making her feel fabulous. She leaned back on her elbows, splashing her feet in the water and drinking in the laid-back atmosphere.

'You know, we'd be more comfortable in the bed I hired for the day.'

'Uh-huh? Whose benefit would that be for, mine or yours?' She flicked her foot and splashed water over him to cool his ardour.

'There's no reason why it couldn't be mutually beneficial.' He leaned over and kissed her. It was a long, languid affair that liquefied her bones and organs alike, leaving her a puddle of hormones at his touch.

Eyes closed and revelling in the taste of him, she felt his arm slipping under her knees and a floating sensation as he scooped her up and carried her over to the bed.

'We can't… Not here.' She was breathless from the romance of the setting but she hadn't completely lost her mind.

'No one can see us, Sophie. I want to make love to you.' There was nothing she wanted more, her body throbbing with need for him. It was just the matter of her unwillingness to become an exhibitionist that prevented her from fully giving in to temptation.

He dotted kisses around her neck as he joined her on the soft bed, doing nothing to help her resist. When he slid the straps of her sundress down and exposed more of her skin to his attentions she knew the last vestiges of her willpower would disappear with the rest of her clothes.

'Luciano…' She had to swallow her breathy plea, her mouth as dry as the rest of her was wet.

'Okay. I don't want you to feel inhibited in any way.' Luciano moved away, taking his silky mouth and strong hands with him. For one horrible second Sophie thought he was calling it a day, his spontaneously sexy adventure brought to an abrupt end because she couldn't fully relax.

Instead, he discreetly pulled the drapes closed, leaving them totally obscured from outside view. Apart from the sound of the waves lapping against the pontoon, it was easy to believe they were ensconced in a completely private, luxurious hotel room.

'Happy now?' he asked as he undid his shirt.

Sophie sat up for a better view. 'I will be after the strip show.'

Luciano complied with a sexy smirk and a wiggle of his hips as he unbuttoned his shirt. He gave her a quick flash of his gorgeous chest before covering up again.

'Boo. Get 'em off!' she heckled until her sexy stripper had divested himself of his shirt and tossed it at her, quickly followed by his trousers.

It was so much fun being with him. When he wasn't weighed down with grief and guilt, he was the sort of man she could picture herself being with. There would never be a dull moment when he was constantly surprising her and trying to make her happy. She was a lucky woman and she wished she could hold onto this feeling, this man, for ever.

The thought struck her hard as he bounded onto the bed with that glint in his eye that made her shriek with sheer delight. He would never expect her to change who she was to suit his expectations. He'd known who she was from the first time she'd challenged him in that treatment room. They'd shared their fears and had entered into this fling knowing what scars they both bore from the past.

For now, she had nothing to lose by indulging in this holiday fantasy and everything to gain in confidence and gorgeous memories. Luciano was providing her with a particularly yummy one now, stripping away her clothes to cover her naked body with his. What could be more exciting than making love outdoors and feeling as though they were the only two people in the world?

'Don't hold back,' she gasped, desperate for his body

to join hers and make some more of those memorable moments he'd been so generous with so far.

'Are you sure?' His voice was strained with the restraint he was unnecessarily clinging to on her behalf.

'Love me, Luciano.' She hadn't meant to say those words but it was what she was thinking. For one afternoon she wanted to believe she was the most important person in his world because he was the most important person in hers.

She opened to him, body and soul, and Luciano took possession of everything she offered with a powerful thrust. With him inside her she was complete, whole again, and back to the woman she had been before domesticity and a cheating ex had snuffed out her spark. Luciano had brought her back to herself.

They rocked together, their bodies wrapped tightly around one another, the sheen of sweat glistening on their naked skin. When she reached that peak of total ecstasy she forgot where they were, letting anyone nearby know how much her lover was satisfying her. Luciano echoed her cries soon after.

They collapsed giggling together at their outdoor exploits. Sophie didn't know how she was going to show her face back in the hotel. If the residents and staff hadn't heard exactly what they'd been up to she was sure the great big smile on her face would tell them.

Luciano couldn't remember the last time he'd felt so happy and content. They were hidden away from the rest of the world and experiencing that post-sex euphoria that made everything seem possible. He knew this wasn't real, yet he wanted it all. He wanted Sophie, the walks along the beach, the talking and laughing and making love to last for ever.

He'd never thought he'd feel this way again about anyone but he wanted to be with her all the time. Not in an unhealthy, stifling, toxic relationship but in that loving, couldn't-imagine-being-without-her way. They'd gone into this thinking it couldn't be any more than a fling and they'd go their separate ways when Sophie left to return home. However, with all the signs indicating they were both getting over their past traumas and finding something in each other that made them want to move on, he was reluctant to accept this could be over.

They hadn't discussed anything beyond her trip and he didn't know if being together was even feasible but he knew he wanted to try. He wanted to find a way to keep her in his life. If she didn't yet feel the same way about him then he needed to give her a reason to stay until she did.

CHAPTER TEN

PALMA, ON THE island of Mallorca, was their last port of call before Barcelona, where Sophie would be dis-embarking for the final time before flying back to En-gland. What made the occasion sadder was that she couldn't spend her last day with Luciano because he was working.

Her trip was no longer about exploring new places, as lovely as they were, but about spending time with him. It was him that was bringing out the old Sophie, not the surroundings. When she was with him there was excitement, adventure and all those other things she'd been craving.

Perhaps she could be really impulsive and join him on the ship. After all, she'd already been approved as part of the crew. That way she wouldn't be making a long-term commitment simply to him. It would give them a chance to be together whilst continuing to have some fun and adventure with the pressure off their re-lationship. The only problem was that she'd have to return home to sort things out. But it would be worth it to extend this adventure.

The idea was impetuous and risky...and it was very

Sophie, the old Sophie before she'd compromised herself in the name of love.

She put the idea on the back burner while she did some sightseeing. There were some beautiful cathedrals but it didn't seem right to visit them without Luciano. Instead, she did the typical tourist thing and went shopping. The narrow streets housed dozens of traditional Spanish shops perfect for browsing and marvelling at the local handicrafts. There was also a range of designer retailers occupying some of the most architecturally stunning premises. She only dared window shop in those.

When she'd finished exploring the town, she made her way back towards the marina. She needed coffee to fuel her for the rest of the day and the best place to do that was somewhere with a good view. Carefully choosing a spot that was good for people-watching as well as appreciating the beauty of the city, she took a seat outside and ordered from the nearest waitress.

'*Café con leche, por favor.*' It wasn't much but it was an attempt to ingratiate herself with the locals. Her efforts didn't go unrewarded as her coffee arrived with a complimentary pastry covered with powdered sugar.

'*Muchas gracias.*'

'Is this seat taken?'

She had to tilt her head back to see the face of the man wanting to share her personal space, although her pitter-pattering heart told her exactly who it was attempting to chat her up.

'It is now.' She patted the seat next to her.

Luciano kissed her on the cheek before sitting down. 'I see you're treating yourself. Sorry I wasn't here to do it for you.'

'I think you more than made up for that last night.' She lowered her sunglasses to give him what she hoped was a sultry look. At the mere mention of their night-time shenanigans, arousal was hitting all the same spots Luciano had helped her rediscover. With any luck they'd get a chance to do it all over again tonight.

Her seduction attempt was interrupted by their returning waitress and she was forced to change the subject. 'What are you doing here anyway? I thought you were supposed to be working. It's not a complaint, trust me. It's made my day, seeing you here.'

'You certainly know how to stroke a man's ego. I'm actually on an extended lunch break. I came down hoping to see you.'

'Oh, yeah? I was thinking about you too.' She was strangely touched by the fact that she'd been on his mind. If she was prepared to make some big life changes to join him on his travels, it was reassuring to know she'd be welcome. In his bed, or her bed, she wasn't fussy.

She bounced on the well-upholstered sofa as if to test its durability. 'If you can't wait until tonight, I think this should hold up to the job. But only if you don't mind having an audience.'

It was a ludicrous proposition, with the amount of tourists milling about, but she wanted to keep things light. She didn't want him to think any future plans were based entirely around him. Change had been needed for a long time and her time away had provided the catalyst. There was no way she was giving everything up just for a man again, even if it wouldn't be as much of a sacrifice second time around.

Her antics had the desired effect as the usually smooth Luciano almost snorted coffee up his nose with surprise. He wiped away the drops that had spilled down his shirt with a smirk. 'That's…er…a tempting offer but I'd prefer a little more privacy, thanks. We're in no rush, are we? We've got all night.'

The prospect of that was making her thirstier by the second.

'I've actually been thinking about making it more than just tonight.' She drank her coffee, hoping the caffeine in her system would give her the extra boost she needed to have this conversation.

Luciano's eyes were as wide as saucers and for a moment she thought she'd misread their set-up. It was casual, a fling, but suggesting they extend it beyond this holiday wasn't what they'd agreed.

'I mean, only if you wanted to.'

He grabbed her hand. 'Yes. Sorry. That's sort of what I wanted to talk about. Why I wanted to see you. This doesn't have to be over. I realised we…er…haven't been using any protection. I know it might be too late to ask now but I wondered if you were on any contraceptive?'

Sophie shook her head. Yes, they'd been stupid not to consider the consequences of what they'd been doing. Caught up in the romance and passion, she'd forgotten the reality and possible repercussions of their carelessness. Neither of them was naive and they should've known better, taken precautions. It had been so long since either of them had had casual sex they'd simply got carried away. Unfortunately, hindsight or making excuses wasn't going to change what they'd done. They'd had fun pretending they were invincible but playing with fire could lead to her getting burned. That was the one thing she was trying to avoid.

'You could take the morning-after pill but I wanted you to know that if it came to it, I wouldn't mind at all.'

'What do you mean?'

This wasn't the conversation she'd expected to have. Some flirting, maybe a nod towards their future together but nothing serious. How could she have been so stupid? A pregnancy now would ruin any future plans she had for travelling, snuffing out that last hope she had of ever breaking free from the prison Ryan had created for her.

'I'd like to be a father someday so if you were pregnant I wanted you to know I'd stand by you. It might not be the most conventional start to a relationship but this could be my second chance at a family. A reason for us to stay together.' Luciano was sitting on the edge of the seat as though the prospect of an unplanned pregnancy was something to celebrate.

'Luciano, it's very early days for us to be thinking about that sort of thing. I can't hang about here waiting to find out if I'm pregnant just to ease your conscience. You might want to have a family, but that's not reason enough for me to stay. Besides, I've told you, I want to do some travelling.'

Fear was bubbling up inside her with every hopeful word he uttered. He wanted her to be pregnant so he could be a father, with no consideration of how she'd feel about it. There was no mention of him wanting to be with her because it felt right. Because he loved her. It was the sign of another self-centred man who'd never put her first.

'Only yesterday I was thinking to myself that I'd like to go home and see my family. You could come too. I could set up my own practice out there. You wouldn't have to do anything but rest up and keep our baby safe.'

His excitement would be laughable if it wasn't for the fact that he was mapping out her future for her and taking it to an even more serious level than she could ever have predicted. They'd had a couple of nights together and he was already picking out baby names. Worse than that, he had her bubble-wrapped and securely locked up so nothing happened to their imaginary baby. It was a far cry from the exotic cruise doctor exploring the world who represented no threat to her freedom and far too close to a jailer for her to be comfortable.

Alarm bells were ringing so loudly in her ears they were giving her a headache. This was her worst nightmare come true. She wasn't going to trade a life of domesticity in England for the same in Italy and end up back where she'd started. Meeting his parents would've been a big enough deal for her at present and not in keeping with her idea of adventure, never mind actually setting up home together as well.

She withdrew her hand and sat back, creating some distance and perspective. 'Luciano, I'm sure there are a lot of women who'd love that idea but I haven't planned that far ahead. I'm very much in the moment these days.'

'Sì. I know we've only just met but that's exactly why you're the reason I'm seeing everything so differently now. That's why I think we should be mad and really go for it.'

'What are you talking about?' Her spontaneity had apparently rubbed off on him in the most bizarre fashion.

'Marry me, Sophie.'

'What? No. Stop being ridiculous.' She was on her feet, her blood turning to ice at the horror that was unfolding. A proposal of marriage after a few days together was the opposite of what she wanted. He clearly didn't know her at all. But why should he when this wasn't supposed to have been anything more than a holiday hook-up?

'Hear me out. We're good together, yes? You want to move somewhere new. You can come to Italy with me and we could start a family. Even if you're not pregnant now, it's something we could work on. Losing Renata showed me that life is too short to let the good things slip away. You're the best thing to happen to me in a long time, Sophie.'

'That's not a good reason for me to give up my life and all my future plans.' That fear was closing in around her, suffocating the life out of her the way her last relationship had. Only this time she could end up pregnant and alone in a different country when he decided she wasn't what he wanted after all.

'You said yourself you wanted more and you're the only person I know I'd ever consider marrying again.' She believed he meant what he was saying at that moment but that didn't constitute a good motive for her. He needed a replacement for his wife so he could go back to his old life without too much disruption. That wasn't going to be her.

The reason she'd fallen for Luciano was because of the person he was now, here, with the life she was envious of, not one she'd dread.

'I meant as a work colleague, a travelling companion, good company, an excellent lover. Not a husband.

Not someone I'm tied to for the rest of my days. I'm sorry, Luciano, we should call this what it is—a holiday romance. That's it. Tomorrow I'm going home and we'll leave things as they are now. Goodbye.'

She was shaking as she walked away, gulping back the sob bubbling up from deep inside. Ending things wasn't what she wanted but she couldn't see an alternative. Committing herself for the rest of her life to someone she hardly knew would be a sign of desperation on both their parts, an even bigger trap than buying a house with someone. Especially if she moved what would feel like halfway across the world to somewhere she didn't even know the language, never mind anybody or anything else.

'Why did you have to ruin things, Luciano?' she cried out, much to the surprise of the other passengers she passed on her way back to the ship.

Instead of going home tomorrow excited and full of plans, she would be returning with a heart heavier than ever. She'd fallen for the wrong man again but this time she wasn't going to wait until everything fell apart around her.

Somehow the timing didn't make a difference. Her heart had taken another hammering, irrespective of her new so-called attitude or preventative measures. Love had a whole lot to answer for when it was capable of destroying a person's world once the rose-tinted glasses came off.

Luciano wanted to run after Sophie but she obviously needed space away from him. He paid the bill and walked back towards the ship a lot less enthused than when he'd left. He'd read the situation completely wrong. Thinking she'd appreciate the spontaneity of his proposal, he'd launched into it without proper consideration, carried away by the notion of starting a family with her back home. He'd thought he'd never want to put himself through the heartache again but beginning to imagine it with Sophie had proved he wanted it as much as ever. The idea of having Sophie in his life, along with the chance to become a father, had felt like hitting the jackpot in the casino.

If he'd taken the time to recount the conversation they'd had, the way she'd shrunk away from him at the suggestion of having a baby together, he would've realised he was pushing her too quickly. Instead he'd panicked and thrown the biggest commitment he could at her in the hope she'd realise he was serious—that he was moving on from Renata. He could see now that his actions seemed desperate rather than impulsive, but it didn't have to mean the end for them.

Running out of time to make amends, he gave chase, catching up with her just before she boarded the ship.

'Sophie! Wait!' He saw her hesitation before she stopped, which broke his heart a little more. She'd briefly considered carrying on and pretending not to hear him, without giving him one last chance.

'We can't leave it like this, Sophie. Forget what I said. It was a spur-of-the-moment, idiotic thing to say.'

'Which part? Having a baby with someone I hardly know? Getting married? Giving up everything so you can lock me away until I produce the next in the Montavano line? I can't just forget it, Luciano. I don't want any of that and I won't marry you, now or ever.' She left no room for misunderstanding with the brutal rejection.

'Okay, okay, I'm sorry. Marriage is off the table but

we can still be together. You said you wanted to travel. You could still come out here. We could find a way to make this work.'

As she shook her head she dislodged the tears clinging to her eyelashes. It wasn't a good portent for future plans.

'I don't think so. Not now. You've reminded me how very different we are.'

'Opposites attract,' he said in a last-ditch attempt to convince her.

'No one's doubting there's chemistry between us but I think we're incompatible where it matters. I've been in that kind of relationship before. It doesn't work unless we compromise who we are for the other person. I'm not prepared to do that again for anyone.'

'Tell me what you want me to do to make this right. I'll do whatever it takes to salvage this.'

'Don't you see? Then you're compromising who you are and what you want in order to keep me happy. It's not a recipe for success. It's not being honest. I was attracted to you because I thought it was exciting giving everything up to sail around the world. It's become clear that's not the real you. You ran away from the life you had but deep down you need to admit to yourself it's the one you want back. There's nothing wrong with that but I can't be part of it. If I give up my job and my home it will be to do something amazing, something exciting. I'm afraid settling down again isn't part of that.'

'You don't think what we've shared hasn't been amazing and exciting?'

'You know it was but unless we spend the rest of our days on board this ship, it simply isn't sustainable.

I don't want what you're offering. You need a partner who's going to stick around long term and give you babies. I'm not that girl. Thank you for everything, Luciano. I'm never ever going to forget you, or this trip, but it's over.' She swiped her tears away and forced a smile that made him want to weep too.

'So this is really goodbye?' He couldn't quite believe how this was ending when last night their future had seemed so full of possibilities. This morning when he'd remembered they hadn't used any contraception he'd had that same frisson in his veins, his blood pumping harder around his body, as if she'd shown him a positive pregnancy test. There was a chance of a baby, of becoming a father, having a family again, and that prospect had overridden all the pain that had caused in the past. Even if he couldn't have all that, he still wanted Sophie in his life.

'Yes.' Her tone and body language were firm, but it was Sophie who instigated one last sad, lingering kiss. It only reinforced the enormity of his loss to have her walk out of his life. Grief attacked his body like a swarm of bees stinging him all over, piercing his skin and poisoning his blood until his throat swelled up and he couldn't breathe.

'Goodbye, Luciano. I'll never forget you.'

He was so choked up, so desolate as she left him standing there that he didn't even get to say a last farewell before she was gone.

Though they hadn't known each other long, he knew life was never going to be the same without her. She'd shown him that he couldn't hide for ever. He had a family and a life to return to. He only wished Sophie was going back to it with him.

CHAPTER ELEVEN

IT HAD BEEN five weeks since Sophie had returned home. In some ways it seemed more like five years. Sometimes more like five hours. She'd gone straight back to work as though she'd never left, which hadn't helped her sullen mood.

It was nice to see her patients and colleagues but nothing here was as thrilling as anything she'd left back at the ship: sun, sea and sex with Luciano in exchange for senior citizens and bedpans. It wasn't in her nature to be mean but that was how it felt.

When Edith turned up at her door, unexpectedly, she burst into tears. 'I am so happy to see you.'

'So I see. Now, are you going to invite me in or let me freeze out here on your doorstep?'

'Sorry. Come in.' Sophie stood aside to let her neighbour shuffle inside. She was still trying to get used to the dramatic change in temperature herself, along with everything else. Never mind having to get up in the dark to go to work and cook her own meals, getting used to her own company again was leaving a lot to be desired in the wake of her holiday.

Edith flopped down onto her settee with a soft 'Oof.'

'You look well.' Sophie saw the colour in her cheeks

and the renewed spark about her, probably as a result of being in the bosom of her family again. She knew how it was to thrive in the company of others.

When she'd been with Luciano she'd flourished. She'd actually felt herself blooming like a flower in the sun. Since coming home she'd withered, wilting into the shadows, and not merely because of the inclement weather. Part of her was missing. Her heart. She'd left it back on the ship with Luciano. Coming back had highlighted the contrast between their lives and the one he'd offered her away from here.

It had been too much, too soon. If he'd given her time to get used to sharing her life with someone again, they might have had a different outcome. She would never have married him but she might have been working somewhere more glamorous, living somewhere gorgeous, loving someone fabulous. She might have been happy. At this moment in time she couldn't see how she could be any more miserable than she was now. If things hadn't worked out she could've moved on the way she used to do. A relationship didn't have to be a death sentence to the individual but she'd learned that too late.

'Mmm… I wish I could say the same about you. You look a bit under the weather, not at all how I left you on the ship. Missing your doctor?'

Sophie wasn't sure if it was Edith's on-point perception or her knowing wink that unnerved her more. She'd always been able to see right through her. All the times she'd thought she'd adequately faked her happiness with Ryan, Edith had known all along what had been going on.

'No. Not at all,' she spluttered, her denial too quick

to be plausible. 'I have been a bit peaky. It might be a stomach bug or something.'

Sophie could feel Edith's eyes burning into her soul, seeing the lie for herself, but it wasn't going to make any difference to her situation by telling her the truth. She'd only worry or blame herself for the predicament Sophie currently found herself in.

'Maybe you need a holiday.' Edith's mischievous, twinkly-eyed smile managed to stop her from feeling sorry for herself for a moment.

'Ha-ha.' That was what had got her into this mess in the first place. 'I don't think I'll be travelling again any time soon.'

'That's a shame. I was half expecting you to have eloped with Dr M. by the time I got back.'

She had nothing to say to that.

'There was a definite spark between you two and then he went to all that trouble so I could speak to you.'

There seemed little point in holding back the truth when Edith had it all figured out anyway. 'We might have had a bit of a fling.'

Sophie tried to fake nonchalance but even the mention of it made her blush, her heart pumping all the harder.

'I knew it!' Edith clapped her hands together, clearly delighted by the news. 'I'm so pleased for you.'

Sophie held out a hand before she got so carried away by the idea of their romance that she bounced off the settee and did herself an injury. 'It was a fling, that's all. We haven't stayed in touch but it's not all bad news. That trip made me realise how unhappy I am with my lot. I've handed in my notice at work and I'm thinking of selling up. No idea what I'm doing after that but I have to make a change.'

'Good.'

It wasn't the reaction she'd expected, especially when it had taken Sophie considerably longer to come to the conclusion it would be the best course of action for her.

'I know it must come as a shock to you. You've been such a good neighbour and friend, Edith. I can never thank you enough for the cruise and I'll come and visit you when I can.' Edith was the one thing she'd worried about when making her decision. She'd had so many health problems and with her family living abroad she didn't have anyone else looking out for her.

'Don't you worry about me. I'm glad to see you getting your spark back. Actually, I have some news for you too. That's why I came back. John wants me to go and live with him and the family in Spain. He's gone now to see the estate agent about putting the house up for sale. I said yes, of course. I'm getting on a bit and I don't want to miss whatever time I have left with my family.'

'That's fantastic. I'm so pleased for you.' Sophie went over to give her a hug, tears forming with happiness that Edith wasn't going to be alone any more, but also with sadness at losing her friend.

'You'll come and visit me. John says there's a bed for you whenever you need one. I've told everyone how you've looked after me and I know they're looking forward to meeting you. You will stop by on your travels, won't you?' There was a slight waver in Edith's bravado that almost set Sophie off too. She was worried they might never see each other again and the thought was too horrible to contemplate.

'It will be top of my list of places to visit,' she reassured Edith. Since going to recuperate with her family, she had a new lease of life. Instead of sitting in her front room by the gas fire, watching daytime TV, Sophie could see herself dining al fresco under the Spanish sun.

It brought unbidden images of Luciano, sitting around a table sharing antipasto with his family in the idyllic Italian countryside. Would that really have been so bad? Being part of that couldn't be worse than sitting here at night alone with a TV dinner on her knees.

Edith's fantastic recovery was proof that the power of love could work wonders for a person. At the time she couldn't believe Luciano could have fallen in love with her so quickly, that it was simply the euphoria of a new romance clouding his judgement. Yet deep down she knew he wouldn't have proposed unless he'd meant it when marriage and family had been so important to him. She'd had a lot of time to think since coming back and had come to the conclusion that it was the thought of falling in love with Luciano that had scared her more than anything. It left her feeling vulnerable and she had a right to be wary after the fallout from her last impulsive dive into a relationship. Except she reckoned she was suffering more being so far away from Luciano than if they'd attempted a long-term relationship and failed.

'Earth to Sophie.' Edith interrupted her wandering mind to remind her that they were both sitting in her living room and not lying on the deck of a cruise ship.

'Pardon?'

'Your thoughts are clearly still back there with your dishy doc. Is there no hope of you two getting back together?' The idea of a fling was probably an alien concept to Edith, who'd married her first love and been with him for forty-five years. There hadn't been anyone else. To her generation, when you met 'the one' you never let them go, even after death.

She thought of Luciano and his grief for his wife and unborn children. He'd had the same opinion when she'd first met him. That no one could replace the love he'd lost. By the end of the holiday he'd proposed to her. Perhaps she'd meant more to him than just a mere replacement for what he'd lost. She'd thrown it back in his face and run home. Away from temptation, away from a chance of loving again and away from being loved. Instead, she'd played it safe, or so she'd thought. Now she was alone and more broken-hearted than ever.

She shook her head. 'I said some horrible things I can never take back. I wouldn't even know where to find him.'

'You've thought about it?'

She'd thought of little else over these past weeks and how different her life could have been. They could've found a way to make it work, or at least tried.

'He's crossed my mind on occasion,' she said with a wry smile she knew wouldn't fool Edith.

'I'm sure the cruise company could track him down for you. Trust me, the only things you regret are the things you didn't take a chance on.' Edith got to her feet and Sophie escorted her to the door with the warning ringing in her ears, reinforcing what her gut and her heart were already telling her to do. Take a chance.

'I'll think about it. In the meantime, you take care

of yourself and let me know if there's anything I can do for you.'

'John's sorting everything out for me but I will want to see you before we go back. Hopefully with a plane ticket in your hand and Luciano's itinerary.'

'I'm not making any promises.' She had to admire her soon-to-be ex-neighbour's tenacity. It was that sheer bloody-mindedness that had no doubt saved her life on the holiday and now she was equally as determined to see Sophie and Luciano paired off. If only it was that simple.

Edith patted her on the cheek in that way only a grandmother could get away with. 'Don't live with any regrets.' She started off down the path then turned back. 'Oh, and tell him about the baby. It's only fair. He'd make a great dad.'

Sophie was left standing on the doorstep open-mouthed, wondering how on earth Edith had figured out the secret she'd been slowly coming to terms with herself. She'd come home with something more special than a fridge magnet to remind her of her trip. It was part of the reason she'd been prompted into making those big life changes, knowing that if she stayed as she was she'd be stuck in this rut for ever with a baby to raise. This was her last chance to get away, relocate and start over before she was tasked with the responsibility of raising another human—something that would require a certain level of stability.

She'd considered contacting Luciano. After everything he'd been through she knew how strong his desire was to have a family but confirming her pregnancy would have left her open to further complications. Luciano was currently under no obligation to her for anything, but a child would change that.

He would definitely want to be an integral part of their baby's life and she didn't know how that was going to work out if he was still sailing around the world. That's if he still wanted anything to do with her. They'd been caught in a romantic fantasy and the reality could prove different. He might've even found someone else by now. After all she'd told him, she didn't want anything he was offering. It wasn't true. She'd been scared of what he'd offered. A future. A family. For ever.

She wasn't going to put him under any obligation to do anything in case he had moved on and made different plans. When she told him about the baby she'd make that clear. It would be difficult enough to see him again after her brutal rejection of his proposal, without going back to dump some more life-changing news upon him.

Was she hoping for more than an acknowledgement of impending parenthood? Yes. It was too bad she'd tossed it away so carelessly and now she was afraid it was too late. Even if she knew how to contact him. Which she didn't. She definitely didn't.

CHAPTER TWELVE

'LET ME AT least set the table, *Mamma*,' Luciano pleaded, trying to be useful in some capacity.

'No. Sit. Sit. You are the guest of honour today.' His mother pushed down on his shoulders, forcing him into his seat at the head of the tables shoved together on the porch.

'This is *Papà's* seat. I haven't done anything to deserve it.' He was embarrassed by the fuss, his parents and siblings treating him as though he was a celebrity.

'You came back to us, son. That means more than anything.' Unnervingly, his stoic father was welling up as he shook his hand.

Luciano was forced to sit and watch as his family swarmed around him, filling the tables with enough food to feed an army. He felt like a fraud. A conman who'd benefited from the generosity of vulnerable people under false pretences. He didn't deserve praise and he certainly didn't want to celebrate past, or present, failures. Left to himself, he would have slipped quietly back into his old life as though he'd never run away from it.

'I came home a month ago. You made a big enough fuss then.' The crying, the kissing and hugging when he'd shown up unannounced had convinced him he'd made the right decision, although he hadn't imagined the outpouring of gratitude and affection to extend this long. He just wanted to get back to normal. At least as normal as it got around here without Renata or Sophie.

He hadn't stopped thinking about her. Whatever she'd thought, it had been more than a fling to him. When she'd gone home, the heart had gone out of the cruise life for him. He'd stuck it out for a little while longer, irrationally hoping their tryst had resulted in a pregnancy and she'd have to get in touch with him again. Given the chance to do things over, he'd play things differently and not to come on so strong.

As time had gone on without any word from her, he'd become restless, eager to join the real world again. That was still thanks to Sophie and he'd have preferred to have done it with her by his side. However, that wasn't to be and he'd simply have to get over it the same way he'd had to get used to the idea of living without Renata. This time he'd accept the comfort and support of his family, even though they knew nothing of his most recent heartbreak.

'But this is the first time the whole family has all been together since then.'

'Any excuse for a celebration, eh?' If he believed this was nothing but a ruse for his parents to feed them all up he wouldn't feel so undeserving.

'Do you honestly think they'd let the return of the prodigal son pass without a party?' His youngest sister, Carlotta, nudged him with one hip whilst balancing a toddler on the other. She set a bowl of olives on the table in front of him. It was the kind of sibling teasing he'd grown up with and had missed during his all-too-serious year away.

'I suppose I am the favourite,' he teased back.

'*Were*. There are a lot of younger cuties vying for your crown now.' With that she dumped her chubby cherub accessory into Luciano's lap.

'He's changed so much. They all have. I'm so sorry I stayed away for so long.' He cuddled his nephew, who hardly knew him, and watched the offspring of his brothers and sisters playing in the garden. He didn't know if he was apologising to the baby, his sister or himself. He'd missed a lot.

In his failure to become a father he'd been jealous, bitter at times when his family seemed to reproduce at the drop of a hat. Then his grief had kept him away, a recluse unwilling to engage with anyone. Finally, he'd run away to sea for the better part of a year. The whole time he'd been absorbed in his failure to have a family he'd ignored the one he already had at home. Now that he was back he wasn't going to take any of them for granted. Fate had stolen away his chance to be a husband or parent but he could still be a good son, brother and uncle. He had a life to lead that included so many wonderful people.

'We're just glad you're back, bro, and more like your old self. At least now we can ask you to babysit without worrying that you're going to top yourself.' His brother Sylvestro, as tactful as ever, slapped him on the back.

'Sylvestro!' It was his mother's horrified gasp he heard above all the other noise of cutlery and plates hitting the floor. The eyes of his family were all on his brother, chastising him for his forthright comment.

'What? You know we're all thinking it.' His beefy

older brother held his hands up, apparently surprised he'd offended anyone present, including Luciano.

'You could have worded it better.' Emilia, the eldest of his siblings, threw an olive at him, which bounced off Sylvestro's head without making much impact.

'Sylv's not known for his subtlety, though, is he?'

'Don't worry, I'm available for guilt-free babysitting any time.' He didn't want anyone to feel bad on his account. Especially when his brother was just being honest. It was only now he could see what he'd put his family through. They'd been walking on eggshells, worried about his state of mind, and he'd selfishly shut them out. Goodness knew what they'd thought when he'd gone off to sea. He'd kept contact to a minimum, only phoning sporadically to let them know he was in the land of the living.

'Well, we're all happy you're here, Luciano. *Salute!*' His father raised a glass of wine and the rest of the family joined him in the toast.

He barely managed to lift his glass in response, overwhelmed by the love directed towards him, including from the two-year-old who was now swinging from his neck in an over-enthusiastic hug. 'Glad to be home.'

Perhaps it was his absence that had made his heart grow fonder, or it could be due to Sophie's influence. She'd shown him the difference it made to have someone close again.

'Is that a car coming up the lane?' Everyone followed his father's gaze towards the taxi making its way towards the villa.

Luciano did a quick head count and though he'd lost track of his family for a while he was pretty sure they were all here now. They didn't get many visitors out this way, so the sight of a taxi had everyone straining their necks trying to catch the first glimpse of who was in the back of the car. Unfortunately, his view was impeded by the toddler currently climbing on his head. He did hear the car pull up and the door open as someone got out.

'Who is that?' His sister's whisper was accompanied by his little brother Galen's wolf whistle.

'Ciao, possiamo aiutarti?'

His mother rushed out first to see how they could help the interloper. More out of curiosity than any other reason, he imagined.

'I…um… I'm looking for Luciano.'

There was no denying the owner of that English voice, despite her uncertainty. It had been haunting him for months.

He stood up, peeled off his nephew and handed him back to his mother. His whole body was electrified by the thought of her being here but he needed to see her for himself.

'Sophie?' He could feel the eyes of his family on him filled with questions and astonishment. But his only concern was the woman standing in the driveway, looking as though she was about to duck back into the taxi and make a quick getaway. He wasn't going to let her go a second time.

'I'm sorry. I didn't realise… I should have called ahead.' She gestured to his gathered family and he realised she was carrying a suitcase in her hand.

'No problem. I'm just glad to see you. Surprised, but happy.' Before she changed her mind about being here, he jumped down off the porch, paid the taxi driver and took her case. She wasn't going anywhere until he found out what had brought her here in the first place. 'How did you find me?'

She gave him an uncertain smile before flicking a glance over at their audience. 'You're a hard man to track down. I managed to get hold of Patrice—she's still working for the cruise line. She told me you'd left and I remembered the name of the village you came from. It took a bit more trouble to get information about the family vineyard from the locals with my limited grasp of the language.'

She'd gone to a lot of trouble to find him. He wanted to believe she'd thought him worth it rather than being simply a stop on her grand tour.

'Are you staying for a while?'

'I, er, don't know. That depends on you. I didn't realise you were back living with your parents. I'm sure I can find a hotel nearby.'

'Not at all. My mother would never allow it. I'm here temporarily after selling my house until I find somewhere new.' There was so much he wanted to say, so much he needed to ask her, but it would have to wait until they had some privacy…which could prove difficult at a family dinner hosted in his honour.

'*Buona sera.*'

'A friend of my brother's?'

'Aren't you going to introduce us, Luciano?'

Sophie was inundated with greetings and handshakes, Luciano with questioning looks. How did he even begin to explain this when he didn't know what had brought her here?

'Sophie, meet the family. Family, meet Sophie.' It was a meeting she'd told him not so long ago was too much, too soon and now here she was under her own steam.

He ushered her through the curious throng of family members to the front of the house, where she was ambushed by his father.

'Sit. Sit.' He set a place for her at the table whilst everyone scrambled to sit next to her as though she was some sort of sideshow. 'Galen, take the lady's bag to the spare room.'

'How did you two meet?' Carlotta, the romantic, could probably hear wedding bells already.

Luciano didn't want to embarrass Sophie, or his parents, with the truth of what had happened between them. Neither did he know if that was what had brought her out here or if it was mere curiosity when she'd once expressed interest in seeing his home.

She met his eyes across the table, begging him to help her out.

'We met on the ship. Sophie was a passenger, a nurse, who helped out during that rogue wave.' He had mentioned the incident in passing but nothing about falling for one of the passengers during the crisis.

His mother crossed herself and said a prayer. 'I'm so happy my son is on dry land but tell me, Sophie, what brings you out here, other than my son?' The interrogation to uncover the truth began, assisted by the offer to pour Sophie a glass of lip-loosening wine.

He saw her cheeks go pink as she put her hand across the glass. 'Not for me, thanks.'

'Sophie prefers more exotic drinks. I'm sorry we can't offer you anything blue or with a paper parrot.'

The in joke made them both smile at the memory

of that afternoon but he was aware they both remained the centre of attention.

'I'm fine. I'll be quite happy with a glass of water.'

His brother returned minus Sophie's luggage.

'You can stay as long as you like, Sophie.'

'Thank you. That's very kind, Mr Montavano.'

'Sophie might prefer to share Luciano's room, Pop. It is the twenty-first century. I couldn't figure out what had caused the change in my brother when he came home. Now I know. You're punching above your weight, Luciano, but good luck to you.' It was Sylvestro's wife who chastised his tactlessness this time with an elbow to the ribs.

For the first time since he'd returned, he was regretting selling his own house, simply for the privacy it would have afforded them now. He couldn't bear the hopeful looks in his parents' eyes when there was no guarantee Sophie would stick around, especially if she was going to be confronted by a barrage of personal questions and insinuations by this mob.

He kicked his chair back and went to rescue Sophie before they scared her off altogether. 'I think Sophie and I will go for a walk. I know she's keen to see some of the Italian countryside.' He extended his hand towards her and she seemed grateful to take it.

'Nice to meet you all,' she said graciously, before they walked off hand in hand towards the green fields where they'd have space to breathe. And to talk.

'I'm so sorry about that. If I'd known you were coming I'd have arranged somewhere quieter, minus an audience.'

'It was a spur-of-the-moment decision. I quit my job, sold up and this was the first place that came to mind.'

'You're finally doing the travelling you'd planned?' He'd been hoping it was more about coming to see him but she'd already made it clear there wasn't a future for them.

'I haven't decided anything really.' She began picking some of the wildflowers nearby, concentrating on the posy she was gathering and not on him.

It didn't make any sense to him why she'd pack up her life in England and head out here without any plan. Not when she'd been so against the idea of risking everything when he'd suggested it.

'How's Edith?'

'She's really well. Her son invited her to go and live with him in Seville, so she's moved on too.' That meant Sophie was on her own, although that didn't fully explain why she'd come here.

'Forgive me, *cara mia*, but why are you really here? You didn't want to see me again after I proposed. I admit that was rash but I apologised. I was afraid of losing you or never seeing you again.'

She stopped rummaging in the undergrowth to look at him. 'Do you really mean that?'

He took her hands and turned her round to face him. 'Of course I do. I don't go around proposing to just anyone. I haven't stopped thinking about you, Sophie. If you're not in a hurry to leave I'd really like to spend more time with you.'

He'd do whatever it took to convince her he was serious. If she was giving him a second chance to be with her, he'd grab it with both hands.

'I'd like that too but…er…there's something I have to tell you first.' Her throat bobbed as she swallowed and he could see she was anxious about saying anything more. Whatever it was, he was sure they could get through it if it meant they could start over together.

'You can tell me anything. I'm not going anywhere.' He hoped he could say the same about her.

'I'm pregnant.' She blurted it out, watching for his reaction. Luciano was too stunned to say or do anything whilst he processed that information.

'Say something. Even if it's only to tell me I'm on my own and you don't want anything to do with me or the baby. I came all this way to tell you and I have so I should go.'

'You're pregnant with our baby.' He was really going to be a parent. With Sophie. He almost fell to his knees with gratitude but he didn't think that move would go any better the second time around.

'Yes. I, um, haven't been with anyone else.' She mistook his disbelief for something negative when, in fact, this meant everything to him.

'I didn't mean... I haven't either, just so you know. We weren't very careful.' One could say perhaps subconsciously the lack of contraception had been about his desire for a family but he knew it was more about his desire for Sophie. They'd both been carried away in the heat of the moment and the passion they hadn't been able to escape.

When Sophie didn't seem as thrilled by the consequences as he was, his elation began to subside. She'd made the first move in coming out here to see him, to tell him, something she wouldn't have done if she didn't want to maintain a connection or have him in her life in some capacity. Now it was down to him to convince her to stay.

* * *

Sophie had never really had any doubt Luciano would take the news graciously. He was a gentleman and he wanted to be a father. His hesitation had thrown her so much she was in danger of collapsing. The relief as he accepted equal responsibility for her predicament was overwhelming. As much as she'd told herself she could do this on her own, being here, seeing Luciano, she realised how much she didn't want to.

'Are you okay?' Luciano slipped an arm around her waist to help her stay upright.

'Yeah. A little faint.' It was all she could do not to bury her head in his chest and ask him for a hug.

'Sit down. I'll go back and get you some water once I know you're not going to pass out.' He eased her down onto the grass and sat beside her.

'It's okay. Everything has just been a bit much for me on my own.' Only now had she admitted to herself she was out of her depth alone, pregnant, with no home or job to fall back on. What she'd thought of as a great adventure when she'd started out here had seemed more of a mistake with every passing minute. She'd barely given herself time to think since landing, coming here instead of checking into a hotel.

'You're not on your own any more.' Luciano put his arm around her shoulders and Sophie watched her tears drip onto the grass, clinging to the blades like fresh morning dew and feeling just as cleansing, like the start of a new day full of possibilities she hadn't dared hope for until now.

Then she remembered they hadn't seen each other in weeks. Even then they'd only been together for a few days. She might have been thinking about him this entire time, imagining what could have been and regretting turning him down. That didn't mean they were going to pick up where they'd left off. It was only natural he'd want to be part of his baby's life but she didn't know where she'd fit in. If at all. It wouldn't do to lie to herself that this was something it wasn't.

She shrugged his arm off but lamented the loss as the weight of it lifted from her.

'I don't want you to think you have to take me on too. I'm sure we can work something out between us over child care, once I figure out what I'm going to do for a job or a house.' She was trying not to panic but she hadn't given proper thought to the practicalities of travelling with a baby. It would be completely different as a new mum compared to the young singleton she'd been the last time she'd done it.

He scowled at her. 'Why wouldn't you stay here with me? I told you I'm here for you. Both of you. I know I scared you off by proposing and planning out a life together but I was serious about wanting this to work, Sophie.'

'Are you?' She'd been afraid to believe it had been anything more than a knee-jerk reaction to their time together, or living with the consequences of it, but he'd felt the same.

'I think I fell for you the moment you shouted at me over Edith's treatment,' he said with a grin.

'Mmm, I think it took me a little longer. Perhaps when you threw me out of your clinic like a boss.' She didn't know when exactly it had happened but it had been on the cards since that first meeting.

'I've missed you.' Luciano leaned forward and leaned his forehead against hers.

'Me too.' All the recent uncertainty and worry melted away when Sophie's lips met his in a soft kiss. She wanted this but she'd been so afraid of letting it happen or, worse, discovering Luciano wasn't the man she'd thought; she'd been in denial. Now she could actually express how she felt, it was liberating.

'I know things have moved faster than either of us were prepared for but I want to give us a chance.' He laid his hand gently on her slightly rounded belly.

'That's why I came.' Being with the man she'd fallen for, raising a family of her own was something she was willing to risk everything to get right.

'I don't want to pressure you into anything you're not ready for. Perhaps we could rent a place together and see how it goes. I'm working in the emergency department at the local hospital. Maybe you could get a job there too or we could set up a medical practice of our own. If things work out, who knows where it could lead?'

'You might propose again?'

'If you're lucky.'

'I have some money from the sale of the house that could keep us going for a while too.'

'That's sorted, then. We're moving in together.'

They'd discussed the practicalities of her moving to Italy and raising their baby but she wanted more.

'It's not very romantic, is it?'

'Last time I tried to be romantic you called me ridiculous and left the country.'

'True, but I've had plenty of time to think since then.'

'And if I told you I still wanted to spend the rest of my life with you?'

Sophie screwed up her nose. 'I'm a bit wary of the whole insta-love thing. I think great sex clouds judgement on that score.'

'What if I said I think I *could* fall in love with you and *could* see us growing old together?'

'Better. I think I *could* fall in love with you too.' Who was she kidding? She knew she would. It was only a matter of time since she was halfway there already. Even then it was only her wounded heart preventing her from going all in.

He kissed her again, reigniting the passion she'd only experienced once in her life before. It seemed more intense this time as they expressed their feelings towards one another.

Moving all the way to Italy, pregnant, to be with a man she'd only known for a brief time might seem risky to some, but it was exactly the sort of thing the old Sophie would have done. And that made her so very happy.

EPILOGUE

One year later

'SEI PROPRIA BELLA, CARA.'

'I thought it was bad luck to see the bride before the wedding?' Sophie spun around as Luciano entered the room.

'Since when did we stick to the rules?' He closed the distance between them quickly, took her hand and spun her round to get a full look at her wedding dress. 'You look beautiful.'

'You don't look so bad yourself.' Her heart continued to do that pitter-patter thing every time he came into a room but he looked so handsome in his tuxedo it went into overdrive.

Even though they'd opted for a low-key ceremony in the grounds of his parents' villa, they'd gone for traditional wedding attire. She'd had fun wedding-dress shopping with his sisters in some of the classiest Italian boutiques they could find. In the end, she'd fallen in love with the simple ivory silk gown she was wearing now. It had Luciano's approval too as he pulled her close and nuzzled into the flowers in her hair.

'You know we could skip the ceremony and go

straight to the honeymoon,' he whispered, doing that thing that buckled her knees, almost convincing her to lock the bedroom door on the rest of the world.

'As tempting as that sounds, I don't think our families would approve of us abandoning them. Apart from which, I thought we were honeymooning at home?' She'd been looking forward to a few days together without him having to go to work.

Despite all her worries, the time they'd spent together during her pregnancy had only served to strengthen their bond. More importantly, they'd gotten to know each other properly, their feelings growing as a result. They'd rented an apartment for a few months after Sophie had moved to Italy but with the impending birth of their baby and the growing certainty that they wanted to be together, they'd purchased their own little haven in the country.

With the arrival of baby Alessandro, she'd thought she couldn't be happier, until Luciano had proposed to her again. This time he'd got the proposal exactly right when she knew this was the only place she wanted to be, with her two favourite people in the world. For now he was working hard at the local emergency department and, despite her reservations, she was actually enjoying being a stay-at-home mum, though they had big plans for the future, setting up their own practice for the locals.

Today, getting married, with her mum and son in attendance, was the icing on the wedding cake.

'You haven't travelled in a year. I couldn't have you getting itchy feet.' He produced two tickets from his jacket pocket.

'It's not a cruise, is it?' She didn't really care where

they were going as she hoped not to be leaving their bed for most of the trip, though as much as she loved their son, he had a habit of interrupting their nocturnal activities.

'Ugh. No. I'll never regret meeting you on board the ship, but I have had enough of those. I got us two first-class flights to the Seychelles instead.'

'What? Are you serious?'

'*Sì*. Just you, me and cocktails on the beach.'

'Sounds like paradise. Wait, what about Alessandro?' They couldn't just take off whenever they pleased when they had a baby who took priority over everything.

'Don't worry. You know my parents are dying to babysit and I'm dying to get you alone.'

The idea of spending quality time, preferably naked, with her new husband gave her the same thrill as the first night they'd succumbed to temptation.

'What are we waiting for, then? Let's go and get married.' She tucked the tickets safely back into his pocket and hooked her arm through his.

She couldn't wait to say her vows. Luciano was the only man she wanted to share her life and her dreams with. This time she knew it would be for ever.

* * * * *

FALLING AGAIN
IN EL SALVADOR

JULIE DANVERS

MILLS & BOON

To my best friend, foxhole buddy,
and partner in crime.

CHAPTER ONE

CASSIE ANDOVER HAD been waiting at the Miraflores bus stop for almost two hours before she decided that her ride was not going to show up.

She was on the last leg of an increasingly arduous journey. After a tearful goodbye to her parents at the airport in Manhattan, she'd rushed to make her flight to El Salvador, only to learn that it had been delayed. By the time she arrived in the capital city of San Salvador, she'd missed the first bus to Miraflores, and the second was so crowded that the driver wouldn't allow her to bring her overstuffed hiking backpack on board. The third bus had been blessedly empty, and she'd dozed off for most of the ride, only waking when the bus jerked to a halt.

Now, as she felt the sudden jolt of the bus stopping, she blinked her sleepy eyes open. The bus window revealed a landscape of lush green coffee fields over rolling hills. In the distance, she could see mountains wreathed with blue haze…and nothing else. No buildings, no sign of a town and no other people.

The driver swung the bus door open and waited. When Cassie made no motion to move, he said, "Miraflores," expectantly.

"But that can't be," Cassie said. Six months ago, when she'd accepted her new job as an obstetrician with Medicine International, she'd started intensive refresher courses to improve her Spanish. Her preparation served her well now as she argued with the bus driver that this could not possibly be Miraflores.

"Miraflores is supposed to be a small town," she said. "There's no town here. There's nothing. There's barely even a road."

"Miraflores *is* a small town," the driver replied. "But this is the *bus stop* for Miraflores. You want to go to Miraflores itself, you'll need to walk two miles east or find a ride."

Cassie looked at the patch of grass the driver had referred to as a bus stop. There was a knee-high concrete stump that seemed to be a road marker, but otherwise the dirt road that stretched into the distance appeared no different than it had for the past fifty miles.

"You're sure this is the right bus stop?" she asked again. "If someone said they would meet me at the Miraflores bus stop, then this would be the place?"

"It's the only Miraflores bus stop that I know about," the driver said. "You're welcome to stay on board, but I won't be stopping again until we get to San Alejo."

Cassie glanced at her phone. No bars. She might be able to make a call from San Alejo, but that would mean several more hours on the bus, and after a full day of traveling, she needed a rest. Even if that meant sitting by the side of an unknown road in the middle of nowhere.

She wrestled her giant backpack off the bus and settled down to wait as the driver left in a cloud of dust.

The sky was clear, and the air was still and quiet,

punctuated by occasional notes of birdsong. The road ran along a hill, which deepened into a valley below, revealing coffee fields that stretched all the way to the mountains on the horizon. To the right of the road, tall ferns quickly thickened into a deep tropical forest.

Aside from the neat green rows of the coffee fields, Cassie could see no other signs of civilization. She was completely, utterly alone.

Well, almost alone. A single chicken emerged from the thick jungle foliage, pecking its way through the grass at the roadside.

You wanted to get away from New York, Cassie reminded herself. *You wanted to reconnect with what really mattered to you. Now that it's just you and the chickens, maybe you'll get your chance.*

Cassie had come to El Salvador in desperate need of a change. Being known as the best ob-gyn in New York City came at a price, and years of meeting the demands of New York's society mothers had left Cassie feeling burned-out and disillusioned with medicine.

She'd never imagined that delivering babies could lead to burnout. Cassie had been born with a congenital heart defect, and it meant the world to her to be able to provide infants and mothers with the care they needed, just as Cassie and her family had needed extra care when she was born. But as Cassie's reputation as an obstetrician had grown, her career had taken an unexpected turn, and she found herself increasingly in demand with New York's wealthiest and most well-known families. When she'd started her job, it wasn't unusual for patients to make special requests for mood music and underwater births, but it had become increasingly common for mothers to welcome their infants into the world with live string quartets, and the pools for the underwater births were filled with expensive water filtered through volcanic rock. Cassie's clientele wanted designer maternity care, and the mothers she worked with were not shy about voicing their displeasure when their demands couldn't be met.

"I feel like I don't know who I am anymore," she'd told her best friend, Vanessa, a fellow obstetrician. "All I do is run myself ragged while my patients complain that the walnuts in their macrobiotic salad are unevenly chopped, or that the lactation consultant can't figure out their custom-fitted Louis Vuitton breast pump."

"That's what you get for being the best," Vanessa had replied. "When you're providing maternity care for the wealthy, they think they can have anything as long as they can pay for it. Last week I had a senator's wife yell at me for thirty minutes because I refused to give her baby his first bath using San Pellegrino sparkling water—she got the idea from that pop star who had twins a few months ago. She said I'd be hearing from her if her kid didn't get into Collegiate."

Cassie shook her head. "I always thought that by the time I turned thirty, I'd have a relationship I cared about and a career that meant something to me. But now I wonder if I'm even supposed to be a doctor."

"Maybe you just need a change," Vanessa had proposed. "We get so much pressure from hospital administration to cater to the whims of wealthier patients. Instead of focusing on medicine, we're forced to meet the demands of parents who are acting like babies themselves. That's why you don't feel like yourself anymore—you're not connecting with what really matters to you about medicine. Maybe you just need to work in a different setting."

Vanessa's words had haunted Cassie for weeks. She had to admit that her heart leaped at the idea of leaving Brooklyn General Hospital for something…*more*. The trouble was, she wasn't sure what *something more* might be. She had a steady, secure job at a hospital with the best obstetrics department in the city. If this wasn't the right setting for her, then what was?

Her job at Brooklyn General was safe and dependable. It made no sense to leave. And she might have stayed there forever, if she hadn't been offered the promotion.

They'd asked her to be the head of Brooklyn General's Obstetrics Department. But just before she agreed, a vision of the next ten years flashed before Cassie's eyes. Longer shifts at the hospital, with fewer days off. Endless deliveries of babies born with a higher net worth than she had in student loans. Hours spent soothing the feelings of new parents not because they were afraid or in distress but because their decaf no-foam latte lacked the exact amount of cinnamon they'd requested. Explaining to mothers that they didn't have to keep the placenta and that no matter *what* the latest internet celebrity had done with hers, it was probably against all medical advice.

As Cassie envisioned her future at the hospital, she couldn't deny the sinking feeling in her stomach. Or that nagging little voice in her mind, the one that reminded her of how her heart had soared at the idea of something *more*. That voice wasn't so little anymore. In fact, it was louder than ever.

Her lips had parted to say "yes" to her safe, predictable future…but the words that had come out instead were, "I quit."

She'd used her new abundance of free time to research options for doctors who wanted to work abroad, and she learned about Medicine International, a relief organization that placed health-care professionals into community agencies around the world. They had a need for good obstetricians.

Six months later, she found herself sitting on an unknown road in El Salvador with only a chicken for company. Wondering what she'd gotten herself into.

It had been a long time since Cassie had taken such a risk. Growing up with a heart defect meant that she'd spent her childhood surrounded by well-meaning adults who wanted to protect her. Her parents were constantly telling her to slow down and be more careful, even when she'd wanted to do things as commonplace as playing tag or riding bicycles with other children.

She knew that her parents had good reason to be overprotective, but she couldn't help chafing against all of the rules and restrictions that governed her life. The result was a serious daredevil phase by the time she entered medical school. Her heart was finally as healthy as anyone else's, and for the first time in her life, she was determined to live without fear. In pursuit of this goal, she threw herself into every daring activity she could think of. She bought a motorcycle and explored the countryside surrounding New York. She took a class on rock climbing and rappelling, loving the thrill of pushing off from high places. She visited karaoke bars and belted out terrible songs at the top of her lungs.

She also started dating the surgical resident supervising her clinical rotation.

Residents and medical students weren't supposed to date, but Cassie was fed up with rules. For the first time, she was following what was in her heart rather than obsessing over how to protect it. And it was glorious… right up until she made a terrible mistake.

Her professors had always praised her ability to make quick, bold decisions in clinical situations. A bright and gifted medical student, heady with freedom and confidence for the first time in her life, Cassie never hesitated to argue a point if she believed she was right.

And she'd believed she was right that night to push the surgical team into taking a risk with a patient. She may not have been responsible for the final judgment call—that had been the chief resident's decision—but she was certain that if she hadn't pushed, if she hadn't convinced him to take action, that he would not have made such a risky decision.

Then again, maybe if they hadn't been in a relationship, he simply would have pulled rank and ignored her protests.

And then maybe none of the heartbreak that followed would have happened.

Even though the patient survived, they both faced disciplinary action. He was put on probation and denied a competitive fellowship he'd applied for, while she received nothing more than a stern dressing down from the hospital's training committee. It still made her cheeks burn to think how lightly she'd gotten off, while someone else suffered for her reckless behavior.

Riddled with guilt, she'd broken things off with him.

She'd already put his job at risk and cost him a prestigious fellowship. If anyone found out they were dating, it would be the last straw for him. She couldn't cause any more disruption to his life.

She left him a note, trying and failing to put all she felt into words. She felt a little guilty about sneaking off into the dead of night, but she knew that if she faced him, she'd never be able to go through with the breakup. And she had to go through with the breakup. She could handle her own heartbreak, but she couldn't handle the thought of causing a good man even more pain than she already had.

She took a leave of absence from medical school, and returned home to live with her parents for a while. She resumed her clinical training the next fall. And while she still couldn't let go of her guilt, she could at least vow to be more cautious and careful.

It wasn't difficult to keep that vow. She was at a new hospital, and everyone she'd known had moved on with their lives…including, apparently, the young surgeon she'd fallen for. There was no sign of him anywhere in the New York medical community, and Cassie was determined not to look for him. She'd broken the rules by dating him in the first place. He was part of a reckless phase in her past that she intended to leave behind.

It was the best way to ensure that no one else got hurt, in her love life or in her professional career. She threw herself into her work, devoting herself to her job and to her patients. Instead of going rock climbing and singing at karaoke bars, she worked twelve-hour shifts at the hospital. Her colleagues noticed her dedication and admired her for it, but she never felt she deserved their recognition. She'd only begun working so hard in the first place in order to repair her reputation after making a huge mistake. Nevertheless, her hard work paid off. Five years later, she was the most in demand ob-gyn in New York.

She was successful, respected in her field…and very much alone.

As she let work take over more of her life, she had less time for the things she enjoyed. But that craving for something *more* still nagged at the back of her mind, no matter how often she tried to swat it away.

She was certain that if she had accepted the promotion and stayed in New York, she would have said goodbye to her adventurous side forever. Instead, for the first time since medical school, she'd decided to take a risk. And this time, she was determined to make the most of it. Without anyone else getting hurt.

Now, as she gazed at the mountain in the distance, she couldn't help feeling a thrill, despite her fatigue. She'd read that El Salvador was one of the most beautiful— and dangerous—countries in the world. She could see that everything she'd read and heard about El Salvador's beauty held true, and she could already feel the part of her that craved excitement coming alive again.

But before Cassie could find her adventurous side, she needed to find a way to get to the medical outpost. She frowned at the sun, which was beginning to dip lower toward the horizon.

Where the hell was her ride?

She stood up from the road marker she'd been leaning against and gave her arms an experimental flex. Resting by the road had done her good after so much travel, but she needed to get moving. It was one thing to be enchanted by the thought of rain forests, rugged terrain and wildlife during the daytime, but Cassie didn't relish the idea of waiting out in the open after nightfall.

Her monolithic backpack loomed beside her. She felt a twinge of longing for her motorcycle, which she'd had to sell before leaving New York. Not that she'd ever made time to ride. Her Kawasaki Z650 had sat neglected in a garage while Cassie worked sixty-hour weeks at the hospital.

You wanted to get back to basics, she reminded herself.

And now you're getting what you asked for. At least it's just a two-mile hike. With aching muscles and a touch of sleep deprivation. While carrying a giant backpack that contains all your worldly possessions.

With a sigh, she eased the backpack onto her shoulders and began to hike down the road toward Miraflores.

Bryce Hamlin could see that the baby was breech.

He'd suspected as much. He'd been monitoring Mrs. Martinez's pregnancy closely ever since she'd arrived at the medical outpost several months ago with her family, all of whom had been suffering from malaria. Mr. Martinez had not survived. Mrs. Martinez and her ten-year-old son, Manuel, had recovered, but she had been six-months pregnant at the time and Bryce knew that a hard pregnancy could often mean a dangerous birth.

So he wasn't entirely surprised when the camp medical director, Enrique Garcia, told him that Mrs. Martinez had gone into labor and that the midwife needed his help. Enrique had stopped Bryce just as he was readying his motorcycle for the trip through the rain forest to pick up the new obstetrician, who should be waiting at the Miraflores bus stop and who was probably already wondering where he was.

As Bryce came into the main birthing tent, one of the midwives, Anna, met him with a nod. "We're having a rough start," she said. "She's fully dilated, but labor isn't progressing. I'm still not certain about a natural birth. A C-section could help to avoid complications."

Bryce nodded. A C-section might be necessary, but he wanted to avoid one if at all possible. Without the luxury of equipment such as ultrasound machines or fetal heart monitors, a cesarean birth could create as many risks as it prevented.

Right on cue, a faint, almost imperceptible tremor flared across his hands, reminding him that a lack of modern medical equipment wasn't the only risk factor. He forced himself to ignore the tremor and focused on assessing the position of the baby's head and back. He placed his hands on Mrs. Martinez's abdomen, relieved that she seemed to feel calm.

"You couldn't just wait for me to get back with the new obstetrician, could you, Mrs. Martinez?" he teased.

She smiled back at him. "You've taken such good care of my family since we arrived here. I guess this little one wants you as its doctor, too."

It was all too easy to feel the baby's position through Mrs. Martinez's thin skin: a frank breech position, the baby was ready to make its way into the world buttocks-first. He was needed here. The new doctor, whoever they were, would just have to wait a little longer.

"We'll try a little longer for a natural delivery," he

told Anna and Mrs. Martinez. "But let's all be ready in case we have to do a C-section."

As Mrs. Martinez pushed with each contraction, Bryce patiently waited for the baby's bottom half to emerge. Anna stood at Mrs. Martinez's head, glancing worriedly at Bryce from time to time, but Bryce continued to wait, letting Mrs. Martinez and the baby do most of the work. Despite the risks involved in a breech birth, he knew the baby's best chances lay in practicing immense patience at the start of labor, even when every instinct clamored for him to *do* something. In this baby's case, the best thing he could do was wait.

His trust was rewarded as the baby's hindquarters slowly began to emerge. Bryce gently pulled out the baby's legs and grabbed the towel that Anna handed him.

"It's a girl," Anna whispered to Mrs. Martinez, whose face was a mix of pain, joy and exhaustion.

Bryce wrapped the towel around the baby's body and began to pull gently along with the contractions, first helping the baby's left shoulder be born, then the entire left arm.

Now for the tricky part.

He slowly rotated the baby in a 180-degree circle. With the baby still facing downward, he felt for the baby's cheekbones with his fingers. There—he could just rest his fingers on the baby's cheeks for leverage.

Bryce nodded at Anna. "Now," he said.

Anna placed her hand on Mrs. Martinez's abdomen and pressed down while Bryce pulled, and suddenly a procedure that had been happening very slowly became very fast—the baby's head shot out into the world, Bryce found himself holding a very slippery and squirmy bundle and the baby filled her lungs and gave a full-throated cry, announcing her arrival.

Now for the best part.

Bryce swaddled the baby in the towel he'd used to deliver her and placed her in Mrs. Martinez's waiting arms. It was a sight that never got old—a new life coming into the world, a parent gazing into a newborn's eyes for the first time.

"Congratulations, Mrs. Martinez," he said. "You both did great."

Mrs. Martinez was able to spare him a quick glance and a smile before she turned her gaze back to the bundle in her arms. "I'm so glad you were here, Doctor," she said, though her expression was wholly absorbed in the little one she held. "I knew we were never in any danger the whole time."

Bryce's hands twitched. He'd lost track of time during the labor, and the tremor in his hands was always worse when he was fatigued.

"I'll let you two get to know each other," he said, and stepped outside the birthing tent.

Outside, Bryce sat beneath a sturdy balsa tree and leaned his back against the trunk. He let out a long slow breath. His hands, the traitors, had stopped their trembling. They hardly ever shook now, but the tremors had a way of flaring up at the worst possible moments. He flexed and stretched his fingers. Taking a few minutes to calm himself before and after a procedure always helped to settle things down.

Years ago, Bryce had been a talented surgeon, just one month away from completing his residency. He'd always dreamed of becoming a neurosurgeon, performing operations on the brain and spinal cord. But with one wild swerve from a drunk driver on a highway, his life was changed forever. After the accident, hundreds of hours of physical therapy had allowed him to regain much of the control and flexibility in his fingers. But no amount of treatment could ever give him full recovery of his hands or stop the occasional tremor that flared through them. He'd never be able to work as a surgeon again.

For a while, he'd thought his medical career was over. But then a mentor had recommended that he give up his career in neurosurgery and re-specialize in obstetrics. As an obstetrician, the risk of his hand tremor affecting his patients was negligible.

It wasn't quite as glamourous as neurosurgery. It didn't provide the same excitement or thrill. But it offered other rewards. He'd been surprised to find how much he liked being able to form a connection between his patients and their families. Case in point, the small hands rummaging through the pockets of his white coat now, searching for chocolate.

"There's nothing in there, Manny," he said, meeting the guilty eyes of a ten-year-old who'd been caught red-handed. "But I've brought you something even better today. You have a baby sister."

Manuel Martinez wrinkled his nose. "A sister? What am I supposed to do with a sister? Girls are boring."

"You might not always feel that way," Bryce laughed.

The wrinkle stayed in Manny's nose. "Mother is going to name her Rosibel," he said. "It means kind, sweet and beautiful." The look he gave Bryce was full of disgust. "Can you believe it? The baby's already a girl, and now she's going to get a name that's even girlier."

"It's a pretty name, and very fitting," said Bryce. "Have you seen her yet? She's cute."

"I saw her," said Manny in tones of great despondence. Bryce guessed that it might be some time before Manny let go of his hope for a little brother. "She can't do very much."

"Well, she's only a few minutes old. Your expectations might be a little high. You know, you couldn't do very much, when you were born."

Manny gave Bryce a look indicating that despite his extreme skepticism, he would allow Bryce this illusion due to their deep friendship and mutual respect for one another. The boy had latched onto Bryce from the moment he'd arrived at the camp, and seemed to hero-worship him almost instantly. Bryce suspected that it was because Manny missed his father.

Manny gazed intently at Bryce and said, "Dr. Bryce, I thought that only women doctors delivered babies."

"That's simply not true," said Bryce. "Any kind of doctor with the right training can deliver a baby. It's a very important job."

Manny seemed to ponder this for a moment. "If we all start out as babies, then delivering them must be the most important job, because without doctors to deliver the babies, then there wouldn't be any more people."

"Sounds like a fair argument." Bryce would never admit aloud how much the boy's words bolstered him. It wasn't that he didn't think an obstetrician's work was every bit as important as a surgeon's. It was simply that every so often he had to fight back a small nagging feeling that he wasn't doing what he was meant to be doing. That obstetrics was a wonderful career, but ultimately, it was just a consolation prize. Most of his family and friends were surgeons, and although they had never said so outright, he couldn't escape the feeling that they all secretly pitied his inability to be the exemplary surgeon he'd once been. It was one more reason to get out of New York. In El Salvador, no one cared about who he used to be. No one expected him to be Bryce Hamlin, superstar surgeon. Medicine International had given him a chance for a fresh start.

"Will the new doctor who's coming be a woman?"

Bryce jumped up with a start and uttered something that made Manny bend over with laughter. "You have to put a coin in the camp swear jar, Dr. Bryce!"

In all his concern over Mrs. Martinez, he'd completely forgotten that he'd been about to drive to the Miraflores bus stop to pick up the new doctor. Worse, it had never even occurred to him to tell anyone else that he hadn't left as planned.

And now the sun was dipping low on the horizon. Sunsets in El Salvador came fast. Fortunately, Bryce was pretty fast, too.

He ran across the camp to where Enrique was loading boxes of malaria vaccine onto a small white delivery truck.

"Enrique!" he yelled. "Did anyone pick up the new doc today?"

"I thought you did," Enrique said.

"I was about to, but then Mrs. Martinez went into labor, and I lost track of time."

Enrique stopped loading the vaccines. "Then you'd better take the milk truck. You'll never get back before dark, and you'll need some cover after nightfall."

"I can get there faster on my bike."

Enrique shook his head. "You and that bike. I know it's fast, but you seem to think it can perform miracles. Take the milk truck. We're supposed to get rain tonight."

But Bryce was already rummaging through one of the camp's outdoor storage trunks for a spare helmet. "The mountain villages need those vaccines," he said. "You said yesterday they're almost a week overdue."

"Then they can wait another day."

"Not an option," Bryce replied as they headed toward his motorcycle, parked just a few feet away. "No reason to do one task when we can do both. What's this new doctor's name?"

"I can't remember. I took a look at her file this morning, but our internet's been down all day and I can't log into the system. Are you *sure* you won't take the truck? It's slow, but it's reliable."

"My bike's reliable!" Bryce said, mildly offended. The motorcycle was his pride and joy, and he maintained it with loving care. It had never broken down, exactly, but he did have to be careful of hidden stones and tree roots whenever he tore along the unmarked jungle road that led from the camp to wider civilization. "She's already had to wait long enough. The least I can do is get there quickly."

Enrique looked at the sky, dubious. "And if it rains?"

"Don't worry. I'll get back here before you know it. Meanwhile, you can take the truck out to the mountain towns and come back in the morning." Bryce hopped astride the bike and snapped on a pair of heavy goggles in anticipation of the muddy road ahead. He started the engine and felt the thrill of anticipation that al-

ways came whenever he felt the motor thundering beneath him.

"You'll never make it back before nightfall," Enrique shouted above the noise of the engine. He was
still shouting as Bryce gunned the engine of his motorcycle and took off at top speed.

Cassie trudged along the road, trying to find a positive
side to her situation. The long walk gave her a chance
to stretch her cramped legs after so many hours of
travel. And the cool breeze against her face felt en-
ergizing. It would have been easier to focus on the
positive if the straps of her backpack weren't digging
into her shoulders quite so much, or if her feet weren't
quite so sore.

Embrace the moment, she kept telling herself.

But it was hard to embrace the soreness in her feet.
She tried to focus on the birdsong in the air, but was
quickly distracted by another noise: an engine.

It sounded like a motorcycle engine. Even though it
had been a long time since she'd ridden her own bike,
she hadn't lost her ear for engines. This one sounded
very well maintained. Whoever was riding it knew
something about motorcycles.

The noise grew deafening as the driver burst from
the rain forest on a very nice motorcycle, indeed. He
was riding a Suzuki V-Strom 650, if she wasn't mistaken. One of the best bikes for rugged, unpredict-
able terrain.

As the rider pulled up beside her, his half-shaven
face hidden by splattered mud and thick goggles, she
allowed herself a moment to appreciate the aesthetics
of such a beautiful machine. The body was power-

fully built, gracefully compact and radiating an almost magnetic heat.

The bike was nice, too.

The rider simply sat next to her for a moment. Cassie felt as though he were staring, but she couldn't read his expression—the goggles completely covered his eyes. Was this the ride she'd been waiting for?

He cut the engine and eased his body off his motorcycle. He was six feet of lean, angular muscle. He wore a leather bomber jacket and jeans that hugged his thighs. And his clothes were streaked in mud. A shock of brown hair flopped over his forehead, which he pushed up as he casually lifted the goggles to the crown of his head, revealing deep-set brown eyes.

Eyes that Cassie recognized: pools of tenderness in an angular face.

Eyes she hadn't seen in five years. Not since medical school.

Eyes that belonged to…

"Bryce?" she said, not prepared for the well of emotion that sprang to her voice.

"Hey, Cass," he said. "Sorry I'm late."

CHAPTER TWO

CASSIE LOOKED THE SAME. The thought reverberated in Bryce's mind as he tried to absorb the shock. Five years had passed since he'd seen her, and yet she looked exactly the same. Her blond wavy hair was chopped into a short bob, and there were faint thin lines around her blue eyes. But they were unmistakably *Cassie's* blue eyes, and seeing them for the first time in five years sent the same jolt of electricity through him that he'd felt when they first met.

Recovering from the accident that damaged his hands had been hard, but recovering from Cassie had felt almost impossible.

And yet, somehow, he'd done it.

When he'd found her brief note on his nightstand, he couldn't believe she'd actually left. She was the first woman, the only woman, he'd ever been able to imagine a serious future with. He'd thought she wanted the same things he did: a life together, with the possibility of a family someday. Accepting that she hadn't wanted that was like trying to accept a knife wound to the heart.

At first he'd thought it was because of a decision they'd made that had led to disciplinary action for him at the hospital. She'd pushed him to perform a risky surgery, and even though he'd known he would face censure from the hospital, he ultimately agreed with Cassie that the risk was worth it. Unfortunately, the hospital board didn't see it that way, and he'd been denied his prestigious fellowship and placed on probation afterward. He'd known Cassie felt guilty about that, even though he had been the one to make the final decision. But the way she'd left—without even discussing it with him, just leaving a *note* and disappearing—made him realize that she wasn't simply feeling guilty about a risk they'd taken together. No, it had to be more than that.

Most likely, he'd been kidding himself about the depth of their relationship. Seeing what he wanted to see instead of what was actually there.

The more he'd thought about it, the more that had made sense. Cassie's boldness, the fearlessness with which she approached life, had been what attracted him to her at first. His own parents, both surgeons themselves, had been extremely overprotective. They'd seen countless trauma cases in the ER, and were always warning him of ways he could get hurt. Cassie, adventurous and unafraid of taking risks, had been a breath of fresh air. But the way she left had made him wonder if she'd ever really cared about him at all. Or if she was simply attracted to the excitement of their clandestine affair. Dating between medical students and residents was forbidden, after all. Their whole relationship had probably just been another thrill for her.

Her note had asked him not to call. And so he hadn't. Not even when, a few months later he'd been hit by that drunk driver. He'd spent years trying to put the accident and the breakup behind him. In El Salvador, he'd finally been able to piece together a life that wasn't overshadowed by anyone's expectations of who he used to be.

With Cassie standing in front of him now, a ghost from his past, he wanted to turn his motorcycle in the opposite direction and drive away. But he also found himself gripped by a perverse desire to gather her into his arms and feel the crush of her lips against his again.

Since neither of those choices were viable options, he simply sat on his bike and stared at her.

He didn't think she could have raised her eyebrows any higher than they already were, but at his casual greeting, they somehow managed to gain another inch on her forehead.

"But how… What…"

He waited, trying to give her time to adjust to information that must surely be just as surprising to her as it was to him. He couldn't blame her for needing a moment to collect herself. At least he'd had a few extra seconds to prepare.

At last, she seemed to find her words. "Sorry you're *late*? Does that mean what I think it does?"

"If you're thinking that I'm here to pick you up, and that we're both going to be working together at the Medicine International outpost, then…yes."

She shook her head. "But that can't be. It just can't."

He would have loved to agree with her about the impossibility of the situation. But if there was one thing the past five years had taught him, it was how to accept situations that he couldn't change.

All he could do was move forward.

He tried to look as relaxed as possible, hoping Cassie wouldn't be able to see beyond his facade. Their situation was already difficult enough without her picking up on the conflicting emotions that were roiling in his chest. He didn't feel calm, but he tried to sound casual as he said, "I hope it's not the case that we *can't* work together. Otherwise, it looks like one of us is about to be out of a job."

For a moment, he thought she might be about to argue with him, and to his surprise, he almost wished she would. The blaze that flared up in her eyes stirred memories of all the things he'd liked the most about Cassie: her passion, her determination, her refusal to back down. But then, just as suddenly, her fiery expression changed into something he wasn't used to seeing on her face: caution, and even uncertainty.

Was Cassie Andover, the headstrong daredevil, actually hesitating? It wasn't the kind of reaction he'd ever expect from her. Typically, she'd act first and think later, trusting her gut and her instincts to guide her decisions. In the past, he'd envied her resoluteness. Of course, in the past, that resoluteness had left him heartbroken.

But she didn't need to know that.

He flipped the ignition switch on his bike, and the engine roared to life.

"The sun's going down," he said. "Are we going to stand here talking or are you going to get on this motorcycle so that I can take you back to camp?"

Cassie really wanted to get on his motorcycle.

Part of her was aching to do it. More than anything, she wanted to throw a leg over the bike and feel it thundering beneath her. Feel the wind against her face, the sensation of flying over the road.

But another part of her was remembering that the last time she'd rebelled against the rules of safety and caution she'd been taught as a child, Bryce was the one who had gotten hurt.

And now Bryce was in front of her.

She'd finally chosen to reconnect with her adventurous side, and right on cue, here he was. A reminder of everything that could go wrong when she threw caution to the winds.

Yet Bryce seemed different than he had five years ago. He certainly *looked* different. She wondered when he'd started working out. The white T-shirt underneath his open leather jacket didn't leave much to the imagination. He'd been fit when they'd dated, but now the outline of every muscle was visible through the shirt that stretched tightly across his chest. One of his triceps flexed as he rested his hand on the motorcycle's handgrip. Despite herself, she swallowed as the tan skin of his arms rippled with the movement.

The changes weren't merely physical. She couldn't put her finger on it, but his posture seemed more relaxed, more carefree. The old version of Bryce Hamlin had been sweet and funny. She'd often felt protective of him. This new version was someone she wanted to sink her teeth into.

She tried to steer herself away from such thoughts. It had been hard enough to find a way to live without Bryce for five years—*five years, three months and six days*, her brain helpfully reminded her—and she had no business thinking about Bryce's tanned skin now. Or his deep brown eyes. Or his hair. He'd always had great hair.

She shook her head. If they were going to be working together, she needed to keep her mind from going down this track.

For example, she really shouldn't be thinking about how it might feel to wrap her arms around Bryce's torso and press her body against his as they sped off into the forest together. That was exactly the kind of thought she didn't need to deal with right now.

But she did need to get on his motorcycle. There was no other way to get to the medical camp, and Bryce was already handing her a helmet that he'd produced from the storage compartment of his bike. She was so tired that she almost dropped it, and she couldn't help swaying where she stood.

"Hey." Bryce left the bike to idle on its kickstand and was at her side immediately. "Let's get this pack off you. That way you can sit down while I strap it to the bike."

The relief in her shoulders was glorious as he eased the giant backpack off her. It felt almost as good as the sensation of Bryce Hamlin's fingers brushing against her body for the first time in five years. Almost.

He took the helmet from her as well and tried to put it on her head. She leaned back from him, annoyed. "I can do it myself," she snapped, grabbing the helmet from him and adjusting the straps. Bryce's protectiveness reminded her of how people had once treated her as though she were made of glass. She didn't want that from Bryce, of all people. Especially right now.

Also, she'd had about as much physical contact with Bryce as she could handle for the moment.

In her fatigued state, she thought that she was doing an admirable job of dealing with the shock of seeing

Bryce, and the closeness of his physical presence, until he took off his leather jacket and handed it to her.

"Put this on," he said.

"Why?"

He gave her a fierce look. "Because you won't be safe riding without it. If you fall off, you'll need something to protect your skin. I've seen bikers come in to the ER with half the skin torn off their arms, and it isn't pretty."

This reminded her of the Bryce she knew. Cautious, planning ahead for every situation. Safety always came first with him.

As Cassie put on Bryce's jacket and the familiar masculine scent washed over her, she found herself inundated with memories. In a way, the good memories were just as painful as the bad ones. What might her life be like now, if she hadn't broken things off with Bryce? If she hadn't put his career and everything he cared about at risk?

It was a question that answered itself. Leaving him had been the only option. She could never ever have allowed Bryce to put his career at risk for her. There was nothing he loved more in the world than being a surgeon. She'd already cost him a prestigious fellowship, and she would never have been able to forgive herself if any further harm came to his career because of her.

But what was a surgeon as talented as Bryce doing working at an obstetrics clinic in El Salvador?

She wanted to ask him, but she wasn't sure if she was ready for the answer.

She eased herself onto the motorcycle behind Bryce and put her arms firmly around him. She'd come here to reconnect with her adventurous side, and she wasn't going to let the surprise of seeing Bryce again derail her from that plan. She was determined to find the excitement she'd come for.

"Ready to go?" he yelled over the engine, looking back at her.

She certainly didn't feel *ready*, but the sun was only getting lower in the sky.

"Let's do it," she said, and gripped him tightly as they sped into the jungle.

Bryce's thoughts felt as tangled as the roots and vines of the foliage that surrounded them as they sped through the trees. He was grateful that the unmarked road through the forest required his full attention. It spared his mind from being overrun by feelings he hadn't had to deal with for the past five years.

He felt Cassie's grip tighten around his waist, and he realized that he might be going just a little faster than he needed to. Still, he didn't slow down. The sooner they got back to camp, the better. Feeling Cassie holding tightly to his body brought back all the memories he'd come here to escape.

It had been a long time since he'd felt her arms around him. Anyone's arms, for that matter.

He needed to get the trip over with quickly. The sooner he didn't feel her body against his, the sooner they could shift into professional mode. They were two coworkers who happened to have a past, and nothing more. He needed to forget about everything they'd had together. After all, she probably had. It wouldn't be realistic or fair to expect that she'd spent the past five years ever thinking about him.

He gunned the bike faster, racing against the setting sun.

But as dusk fell, it became harder to see the road, as well as the treacherous roots and stones that lay in their path. Despite Bryce's desire to get their journey over with as quickly as possible, he knew he needed to slow down.

"What is it?" Cassie asked as he slowed to a crawl.

"I can barely see the road," he replied. "I don't want to—dammit."

The bike sputtered and choked.

"Come on, baby," he said to the bike. "Don't do this now."

But as he tried to press onward, the bike hit a loose stone, leading it to bounce and twist in the air. He heard Cassie shout and felt her body sliding behind him, and he braked hard and leaned back to prevent her from falling off the bike. She held on, but barely. Bryce cut the engine and parked the bike. He turned back to Cassie. "Are you all right?"

She'd pulled one leg up onto the bike's seat and was rubbing her ankle. "I'm fine, just jarred my ankle a little when we stopped."

"Let me see."

She jerked away from his touch with a fierceness that surprised him. "It's fine. It's just a little sore." She took off her helmet. "What's our situation?"

He frowned at the bike. "We hit that stone pretty hard. I think the engine's flooded." He tried to start the bike, to no avail. "I might need to take a look at the spark plugs." Cassie slipped off the bike and helped Bryce to remove her pack. He opened up the motorcycle's storage compartment, bringing out a small tool kit.

Cassie looked at the sun, low in the sky. "There's not much light to work by. How far is it from here to the medical outpost?"

"About five miles. The camp's fairly deep within the forest. It's close enough to town that we can get there easily to restock on supplies, but being in the forest gives us easier access to roads to the mountain villages. It's too far for us to walk tonight unfortunately. The trail's hard enough to see by day. We could get seriously lost in the forest. Not to mention the danger of running into animals or wandering into territory controlled by gangs. It's not worth the risk."

Although the light was dim, he could see by her expression that she had the same sinking feeling in her stomach that he did. "So if we can't get it fixed by nightfall…"

"We'll have to spend the night out here," he confirmed. "I've got a pop-up tent and a sleeping bag." *But only one of each*, he thought, but didn't say.

"What about those animals you mentioned? And gang members?"

"There's little chance of running into any danger as long as we stay near the trail. Most animals will ignore us as long as we leave them alone. And we're close enough to the medical camp that I doubt we'll run into anyone who's not with our team… Although if we do, I should be able to talk us out of any trouble." He smiled, remembering Cassie's fondness for adventure. "Of course, I'm sure none of that would phase you."

Cassie took a few steps away, into the darkness. He guessed that she wanted a couple minutes to compose herself. He couldn't blame her. An hour ago, he'd never dreamed he'd be working with Cassie again, let alone facing the prospect of spending a night alone with her in the woods.

He turned back to the bike. "I think I can fix it. The only trouble is that it looks like it might—"

But before he could even finish his sentence, a fat raindrop plummeted from the sky onto his nose. Followed by several more. And then the sound of many more, hitting the tree leaves high overhead. Bryce estimated they had about two minutes to pitch the tent before they were both completely soaked. He was fast, but he wasn't that fast. He turned to Cassie, wondering how to break the news to her.

She said it for him. "We're going to have to spend the night out here, aren't we?"

"I'm afraid so. There's no way I can fix anything in this rain. I can barely see the engine."

She gave a curt nod and tucked the ends of her hair behind her ears as the rain began to plaster it to her head. *Funny*, he thought. At first, he'd felt a pang of regret that she'd cut her long hair, but as she tucked her locks behind her ears, he could see how the short bob suited the angles of her face.

"Bryce?" Cassie broke him out of his reverie. "If there's a tent, we'd better get it up now."

"Right." He retrieved the tent from the storage compartment, where it was bound into a compact square. It was large, but not that large. Two people would fit quite snugly, if they didn't mind sleeping close together. Very close.

Enrique was right, he thought. *I should have taken the milk truck.*

* * *

Cassie shivered inside the tent, cold and damp and fairly miserable.

Bryce had insisted that she take the sleeping bag. He was stretched out beside her, using his arm as a pillow. She, at least, had the luxury of burrowing down into the sleeping bag and bunching up the fabric beneath her head. It wasn't comfortable, but it was better than sleeping on the ground.

"You're shivering," he said. Damn. She'd hoped he wouldn't notice. But then, crammed inside the tent as they were, it was probably impossible to ignore even the slightest movement.

"I'm fine," she lied.

"You're not fine. Just being in the sleeping bag isn't enough. You need to get out of those wet clothes."

She would have loved nothing more than to get out of her wet clothes. In privacy. With some clean, dry pajamas to change into. And without her ex nestled firmly beside her in a small tent.

As long as you're wishing for things, you might as well add a million dollars and a pony to the list, she thought.

"What do you suggest?" she asked. "There's barely any room to move around in here. One of us can't go outside while the other changes." As if to prove her point, a clap of thunder broke overhead and the pattering of the rain on the canvas tent grew harder.

"Easy. I'll turn away, and you just sort of shimmy out of whatever you need to from underneath that sleeping bag."

She frowned, skeptical. "I'm not sure there's enough room."

"I'll keep my back turned. Use the sleeping bag for

cover. It'll be just like changing clothes at summer camp as a kid."

She wouldn't know. Summer camp, with all of its outdoor activities, had been deemed too risky for Cassie as a child. But she understood the gist of what Bryce was saying. There was just one problem.

"What about you?" she said. "You're soaking wet, and you don't even have a sleeping bag or a blanket."

"I can deal with it. I have before. Believe me, just having the tent is a luxury compared to some of the situations I've had to sleep in since coming here."

"I have a feeling that no matter what you've been through, *this* sleeping situation is one of the strangest."

A small smile crossed his face. "I have to admit that meeting you here, learning we'll be working together, and then sleeping together in close quarters on your very first night was not exactly how I thought the day would go."

She was glad to see that he felt the situation was as absurd as she did. But she couldn't let him shiver on the ground all night. She wouldn't be able to sleep, knowing that he was so uncomfortable.

There was only one thing she could do. "Bryce, I can't let you sleep on the ground in wet clothes while I'm dry in a sleeping bag. We're both adults. Just… strip down to your boxers, or whatever, and we can open up the sleeping bag like a blanket and share it."

He hesitated.

She mentally kicked herself. Less than an hour ago, she'd hopped onto the back of his motorcycle and promised herself that she'd still find her adventurous side, even with this new complication of seeing Bryce for the first time in years. But that wasn't meant to include convincing him to strip off his clothes and huddle next to her for warmth, without giving a second thought to how he might feel about it. She'd certainly spoken before thinking about how *she* might feel with him so close to her.

To her surprise, after a moment, he said, "Okay. I'll turn around, and we'll both do what we have to do. At least this way we'll have a chance of having dry clothes by morning."

Ten minutes later, Cassie found herself stripped down to her underwear, with Bryce in the sleeping bag behind her. The bag could fit them both, but just barely. They had to lie on their sides, and Bryce's arm was draped over her.

It felt surreal to be so close to him again. Still, Cassie had to admit that she was far more comfortable than she'd been a moment ago. It was a relief to be out of her wet clothes, and she was sure Bryce felt the same. As the warmth of their bodies heated the small space, it was almost pleasant to lie together, listening to the rain drumming on the canvas tent.

In such close proximity to Bryce, it was impossible not to notice that she was once again enveloped by the cedar spice scent of him. She took a deep inhalation as quietly as she could.

And then, in spite of herself, she started giggling.

She couldn't help it. Somewhere, far in the back of her mind, her physician self was running a mental self-diagnostic. *Sleep deprivation accompanied by fits of hysterics*, she thought. *Diagnosis—you've probably run into an ex while in the middle of nowhere.*

"Something funny, Cass?"

"It's just that earlier today I was talking to a chicken,

and now…" She couldn't finish, erupting into paroxysms of laughter again.

"I know," he said. He rubbed his hand briskly along her arm, comradely. "Weird day, right?"

"Yeah. Super weird." Her laughter fading. "Sorry. It's just that I haven't slept in twenty-four hours, and then when you showed up on that motorcycle…it was just so unexpected."

"I wasn't expecting to see you, either," he admitted. "I was just heading out to pick up the new doctor for the camp. I had no idea it'd be you."

His breath tickled her ear, and she felt another wave of worry. So much had happened, and they weren't even at the camp yet. There'd been no time for either of them to adjust to the shock of seeing each other again or to process the situation at all.

"Are we going to be okay working together?" she said.

"As I recall, we always worked well together."

"Until we didn't."

He groaned. "Cassie…it's in the past. We made the decision we made. And a lot has changed in five years. Can't we just focus on how to move forward?"

His breath tickled her ear, ever so slightly. He was so close she could almost feel his lips brush her skin. How long had it been since Bryce had held her this close?

Five years, three months and six days.

The whole point of breaking up with Bryce via note five years ago was that it had allowed her to flee his apartment without confronting him. Because she'd known that if she had to face him, he would convince her to stay. She wasn't proud of what she'd done. It had simply been what was required, in order for her to follow through with the breakup. The one thing she couldn't steel her resolve against was seeing Bryce in pain. And it was the thought that staying with him could result in even *more* pain that had spurred her onward all those years ago. She didn't know how he could look at her and not see the woman who had cost him a prestigious fellowship, and who had almost cost him his job. Who might *still* have cost him his job if anyone had found out they were dating. And so she'd left, knowing that she wouldn't be able to see him again without betraying both herself and him.

And now here he was, asking if they could move forward.

His body was so warm next to hers. His arm settled so naturally around her waist. As though no time had passed since the last night she lay curled beside him.

Did she *want* to move forward? She supposed they didn't have a choice. Lying next to him and sneaking surreptitious inhalations of his scent was nice, but it didn't get them anywhere. They'd never be able to work together if she was still holding on to the past.

"You're right," she said. "We did work well together. And in spite of everything that's happened between us, the fact that you're here speaks well of the organization. They must be a very committed group of doctors to have you on the team."

"Very kindly said, Dr. Andover," he replied. "See? Just because we have a past doesn't mean we can't be professional."

"I agree," she said. "Although…maybe we don't need to tell our professional colleagues about tonight's sleeping arrangements."

"You read my mind."

After several minutes more, Cassie began to hear slow gentle snores from Bryce. She was glad he'd been able to get to sleep. She, however, was having more trouble.

Because it had been a long time since she'd been nestled in someone's arms. And…it had been a while since she'd had sex…

Five years, three months and six days, in fact.

As she felt Bryce's body shift in his sleep, his arm tightened around her and pulled her closer to him.

Staying professional wasn't going to be easy.

No, it wasn't going to be easy at all.

CHAPTER THREE

THERE WAS A small commotion the next morning when Cassie and Bryce arrived back at the medical camp. Bryce's motorcycle had taken more damage than expected, and they'd had to walk the rest of the way with Bryce pushing the bike along. The ankle that Cassie had jarred when the bike had broken down still felt a bit tender, but she told Bryce she was simply footsore from walking so much the previous day. She knew if she mentioned her ankle to Bryce, he'd be concerned, and there was nothing she hated more than someone fussing over her. The last thing she wanted was for that person to be Bryce.

Dr. Enrique Garcia, the camp's director, met them at the entrance.

"I told you there'd be trouble with that motorcycle," he said, shaking his head at Bryce.

"It made more sense to take the bike than the milk truck. The bike's faster," Bryce replied.

"Faster! Right, so much faster that you arrived twelve hours later than you planned. I can't imagine what kind of ramshackle operation our new doctor thinks we're running here." He turned to Cassie. "I can't tell you how glad we are to have you here, Dr. Andover."

Cassie shook his proffered hand. "Pleased to meet you."

"Cassie and I are actually…old friends," said Bryce.

If Enrique caught the hesitation in Bryce's voice, he didn't show it. "Let's get you settled in," he said. "I can assure you that despite the rustic appearance of our camp—" he waved an arm to indicate the cinder block walls and portable canvas medical tents in the forest clearing behind him "—we do have access to some decent amenities and technology. It's just that yesterday our internet happened to be down, and we were hit by a number of emergencies all at once, including a complicated breech delivery that Bryce got caught up in."

"Why would Bryce get caught up in a complicated delivery?" Cassie asked. "He's a surgeon, not an obstetrician." She turned around to look for Bryce, who was already striding across the camp.

"Need to check on Mrs. Martinez!" he called over his shoulder as he sauntered away.

He didn't have to leave so fast, Cassie thought. But then maybe he was just that eager to get away from her. Even after all their discussion of keeping things professional the night before, maybe Bryce still didn't know exactly how to get through the awkwardness of working together again. To be honest, she didn't know, either.

Enrique looked a bit taken aback. "Well, with Bryce otherwise occupied, I suppose I'll be the one to show you around."

"I could show her around." A boy of about ten had come to see what all the commotion was about.

"Not right now, Manny," said Enrique. "But why don't you run Dr. Andover's pack over to her living quarters for her? She's in block seven." Before Cassie could blink, the small boy flung her giant backpack over his shoulders and took off at full speed.

"Are there many children here?" asked Cassie as Enrique led her toward the nearest cluster of cinder block buildings.

"A handful. Manny seems to be their self-appointed leader for now. He's very curious, gets into everything—don't be afraid to be firm if he pesters you too much for chocolate, Dr. Andover."

"Duly noted. And please, call me Cassie."

As the tour continued, Cassie remembered that no one had answered her question earlier. "You said that Bryce was helping with a breech birth. Was there something so unusual about the case?"

Enrique looked at her quizzically. "No. Why do you ask?"

"Because you said that Bryce was called in," said Cassie, still wondering why they'd called a surgeon in to help.

"Yes, of course. Our midwives are incredibly skilled, but it's nice to be able to have an obstetrician on hand for complex cases."

"Bryce…is an obstetrician?"

"Of course. Almost all the doctors here are."

Her mind was spinning. She'd known the medical camp focused on providing services to new mothers and women giving birth, but somehow, when Bryce had picked her up on his motorcycle, she hadn't put the pieces together. She'd been so overwhelmed by seeing him again, by everything that had happened since she'd left home, that she hadn't bothered to think carefully about what Bryce's presence here might mean. He wasn't a surgeon anymore. He was an obstetrician.

Why wasn't he a surgeon anymore? Had he lost his job after she'd left him, after all? She couldn't think of anything on earth that would have led Bryce Hamlin to voluntarily give up surgery. Even Cassie, who had only been a medical student when they'd met, could see that Bryce was an artist in the operating room. And the passion had been evident on his face whenever he talked about his profession.

But even if he'd lost his job, why would he change specialties? Surely, he could have gotten a job as a surgeon somewhere else.

Was he no longer a surgeon because of her? Had she cost him everything, just as she'd feared she would?

She had to find out.

"Back when Bryce and I used to work together, he was a talented surgeon," she said. "Why would he change specialties?"

Enrique hesitated. "Bryce mentioned the two of you are old friends."

"Yes. We used to know each other well but…that was a long time ago. I haven't seen him in five years."

"Ah." The confusion lifted from Enrique's face, but he still seemed to be choosing his words carefully. "Then I suppose all I can say is that Bryce reached a point in his life where he needed a change."

That was probably true, but it was also frustratingly vague. Bryce had been a rising star in surgery. Why would anyone need a change from that? From Enrique's hesitant response, she had a feeling that if she wanted to find out, she was going to have to ask Bryce.

"I'm sure you and Bryce will have a great deal of catching up to do," Enrique continued, confirming her suspicions that she wouldn't get much information from him. "Personally, I'm just glad he's here. I don't think we've ever had a better obstetrician than in the three years he's been here."

Three years. No wonder it had been so easy to avoid news of Bryce. Early on, after the breakup, she'd tried not to hear any news of him through the medical community grapevine. But after a while, it seemed as though he'd disappeared completely. Now she knew why.

She pulled her focus back to the tour as Enrique pointed out the various buildings and features of the camp, though it was difficult to keep her thoughts from returning to Bryce.

"What kind of obstetrics cases come in?" she asked.

"We see a lot of Zika virus, but many of our patients are simply mothers who are undernourished, or who've been through enough harrowing experiences during their pregnancy that the fetus is at risk. It's hard to work without as much modern equipment as we'd like, but our medical team is great at improvising."

It sounded as different from Brooklyn General as she could possibly have asked for. Cassie felt a surge of excitement. *This* was medicine.

Enrique pointed out the shower unit somewhat apologetically. Six outdoor wooden shower stalls stood in the open air. A hose was rigged above each stall to approximate a showerhead. Cassie couldn't help feeling a twinge of longing for the luxurious steam-filled staff showers at Brooklyn General, with their organic jasmine soap and tea-tree-oil-infused shampoo.

"There's hot water," said Enrique encouragingly. "Although you'll want to shower early if you can, because it runs out pretty quickly. And you've really got to watch out for the door. It can swing open unexpect-edly if the wood gets jostled even the tiniest little bit."

He showed her the dispensary, where staff received any necessary medical care and daily doses of antima-larials. She made a mental note to return for a bandage and some pain relievers for her throbbing ankle as soon as the tour was over.

As they continued, she realized the camp was larger than she'd expected. It was fairly deep within the forest. Earlier that morning, as she and Bryce had been walk-ing and pushing the motorcycle the last five miles to the camp, she'd barely been able to discern the road lead-ing to the front gate. Enrique explained that the camp's relatively hidden location had a tactical advantage.

"We can travel wherever we need to in El Salvador, but it's best if the camp itself is in a location that's fairly out of the way, so that it won't become the target of a gang dispute," he said. "Plenty of the women and fami-lies here are escaping domestic violence situations or are seeking refuge because they're caught in the cross fire of territorial disputes. We're not exactly hiding, but we also don't want to be easily found."

"I've heard that gangs are a significant problem," Cassie said.

"One of the most challenging parts of our work in-volves dealing with the artificial borders created by gang activity," he said. "Different factions claim terri-tory in the forest and in the mountains, and that makes it hard to deliver medicine and treatments to some of the people most in need. Of course, Bryce has been incredibly crucial in negotiating agreements so that our docs can travel where they need to, no matter who controls the territory."

Cassie wasn't certain she was hearing him correctly. Enrique made it sound as though Bryce negotiated with gang leaders on a regular basis.

"He has a surprising success rate," Enrique continued. "And for the mountain areas we absolutely can't get to, we can always do helicopter drops of medical supplies. Sometimes we'll have medical personnel drop down as well to perform a procedure. There are women who would have died if we hadn't been able to send anyone to help deliver the baby."

"You do helicopter drops here?" said Cassie.

"Oh, don't worry," said Enrique, mistaking her reaction for fear. "Bryce does most of those. We have a few other physicians who will do them, but most prefer keeping their feet firmly on the ground to jumping out of a helicopter. But you know Bryce. He loves that adrenaline rush."

"Right," said Cassie softly.

Gang negotiations? Helicopter jumps? Who the hell are we talking about? Because it's definitely not Bryce Hamlin.

Clearly, there was even more to the mystery of Bryce than she'd originally thought. Whatever he'd been doing over the past five years, it had involved a lot more than going to the gym. And she was determined to find out what it was.

The moment they'd arrived at camp, Bryce had welcomed the opportunity to head directly to the obstetrics tent, claiming the need to check on Mrs. Martinez. He needed space to think. Ever since he'd driven to the Miraflores bus stop yesterday and laid eyes on Cassie, he'd fought against the tension of two conflicting impulses.

He wanted to put as much distance as possible between himself and her.

He wanted to wrap his arms around her, hold her and never let go.

Sleeping next to her, practically naked in the cramped tent, hadn't exactly helped to resolve either of those impulses.

It had felt both sweet and frustrating to be so close to her. There were so many things he remembered that hadn't changed and yet felt completely new. The way his arm notched perfectly into the curve of her waist as he lay on his side, arm draped over her. The tiny divot in the nape of her neck.

But they'd both agreed to move forward, and thoughts like this would only serve to keep him stuck in the past.

Moving on hadn't come easily for Bryce, especially in the early days after the accident. When that drunk driver had swerved into his car, his life had changed forever. The physical recovery was hard, but giving up his career as a surgeon had been devastating.

His parents, grandparents and sister were all surgeons. They made jokes about surgery being the family business. Bryce hadn't always been certain he wanted to follow in their footsteps, but from the moment he first picked up a scalpel, he knew the operating room was where he belonged. Early on in his residency, he developed a reputation for being able to handle especially difficult cases that required singular patience and dexterity. Other doctors didn't merely praise his work, they described it with words such as *gifted* and *exceptional*.

Once, his father had sat in the operating theater and observed him working. "Son," he'd said afterward, "there are some people who are good surgeons. But you were *born* to be a surgeon."

At the time, his father's words had meant the world to him. But after the accident, the memory of that day was like a weight around his neck. If he was born to be a surgeon, and his hands had been permanently injured, then who was he supposed to be now?

His family and friends didn't seem to know how to support him. They made well-meaning comments about what a talented surgeon he'd been, but their words only served to remind him of everything he had lost.

Although no one said it outright, he could tell that some people from his past felt pity for him. Instead of being impressed by the new life he'd built for himself, they lamented the old life that he'd lost.

If Bryce were being truthful with himself, he missed that old life, too. He missed the life-and-death intensity of the operating room, the pride his family showed in him and the feeling of beginning an operation and knowing exactly what to do next. He missed being the person trusted with the most difficult, delicate cases. Surgery had provided all the excitement he needed in his life—or so he'd thought, until he met Cassie.

And now, she was in his life again. Here to remind him of a version of himself that he hadn't been in five years. A version of himself that he was sick of competing with, and had done his best to escape.

He'd worked hard to build a new life in El Salvador. He took pride in being a good obstetrician, and he'd mostly managed to move beyond any longing he'd once had for his past.

Mostly.

Cassie's return had brought back so many memories of their time together, as well as the person that he used to be. But that's all they were: memories. He was tired of competing with his past self. The old Bryce needed to stay in the past, where he belonged.

Just as his relationship with Cassie needed to stay in the past, where *it* belonged. He felt again the tension of those two conflicting urges: to run from her and to hold her close. He couldn't run from her, so he'd simply have to ignore the desire to hold her the way he'd held her for warmth the night before. *That* certainly wouldn't be happening again. He would make sure of it.

Cassie had been brusque and businesslike when they'd woken in the morning to don their clothes. He still couldn't believe he'd agreed to strip down at Cassie's insistence. He had just been so cold after his dousing in the rain that he couldn't resist the prospect of getting warm. At least huddling together naked had given their clothes a chance to dry.

They'd have to be careful to avoid situations like that in the future. Especially if they were going to keep things professional, as they'd agreed.

But did he want to keep things professional?

He tried to tell himself the same thing he'd told Cassie last night: they needed to focus on moving forward. But it was hard to think about moving forward while he was being tantalized by the recent memory of her skin, dappled with raindrops, drying in the warmth of the sleeping bag.

It's just a physical attraction, he told himself. *She's always been a beautiful woman. There's no denying that.*

He could handle a physical attraction. He'd just give it a few weeks, and it would pass. Since the breakup with Cassie, Bryce hadn't been seriously interested in anyone. There had been a few casual encounters, but nothing that went far below the surface.

When he and Cassie had met, he'd been attracted to how daring she was. Growing up in a family of surgeons, Bryce had constantly been subjected to his parents' stories about patients who'd suffered serious injuries from accidents. From an early age, he'd learned to practice immense caution in order to prevent himself from becoming one of the victims in his family's stories. Then, when he'd finally become a surgeon, his family had repeatedly stressed the importance of avoiding any kind of injury to his hands. His hands were his living, his father had said. Any injury to them meant an end to his career. And his father had certainly been proven right about that.

Cassie's carefree nature had been a welcome contrast to his overprotective family. At first, he hadn't been certain of what to make of the headstrong woman who always seemed to be at the top of her medical cohort, eager to answer questions and ready to volunteer for any procedure. He'd noticed his attraction to her from the beginning, and he'd done his best to hide it. As a medical student, she was off-limits as a dating option, and he wasn't sure if she was even interested in him.

But then she'd invited him to meet her for coffee in the commissary. A simple cup of coffee seemed harmless enough. They'd talked about how they liked to spend the weekends. At the time, he'd preferred reading and listening to music. Safe indoor activities that kept his feet firmly on the ground.

Cassie, on the other hand, enjoyed rappelling. She

headed to a state park every weekend to push herself off the cliffs.

Bryce had expressed his amazement at her willingness to drop off a cliff, only a rope between herself and certain death. "I could never do anything like that," he'd said.

"Sure you could," she'd replied. "I'll take you there some weekend on my motorcycle."

He'd sputtered a bit over his coffee. "Your *motorcycle*?"

Motorcycles were commonly referred to as *death traps* within the Hamlin family. His parents, both ER trauma surgeons, had shared many stories of motorcycle riders badly injured in accidents. He was pretty sure no Hamlin in three generations had ever ridden a motorcycle. And yet Cassie spoke of them as nothing more than an exciting mode of transportation.

"If there's one thing I could never see myself doing, it's riding a motorcycle," he'd said.

And yet, somehow, the next weekend found him tentatively getting onto a motorcycle behind her. To his surprise, the ride was freeing. With nothing surrounding him but the wind, and the road, and the closeness of Cassie, he felt much of his caution and worry drifting away.

He'd been exhilarated by the ride, but he was even more exhilarated afterward, when they'd gotten off the bike and she'd turned around and kissed him.

It had been a nervous, quick brush of a kiss, and he knew that she'd taken a risk by doing it. She hadn't been sure how he would respond. And he couldn't help himself. Despite the rules, he pulled her to him, and a kiss that had begun as tentative deepened into something much more.

After that, he spent much more time doing the kinds of things his family would have deemed too dangerous. There were many more trips on her motorcycle, as well as days spent riding roller coasters and rollerblading at skate parks. Things that he'd once found terrifying became thrilling when Cassie was there. There was an element of adventure she brought into his life that he hadn't known was missing.

She'd even talked him into doing karaoke. Never mind that he couldn't carry a tune. As it happened, neither could she. But he loved the way she belted out songs as though she meant them from the depth of her heart and soul—no matter how her audience might react.

Shortly after their last karaoke outing, he'd bought the ring. He'd spent the night in tears of laughter, watching her give her hammiest performance of classic love songs in front of an obstreperous crowd. He'd been having so much fun, and then he'd realized that he never wanted to stop having fun with her. Or to be apart from her at all, really. And so he'd kept the ring close at hand, thinking that after she finished medical school, he might propose. But then the incident had happened.

Bryce and Cassie had been several hours into an ER shift. As senior resident, he was in charge; he was almost finished with the final year of his five-year residency as a surgeon. A patient had come in with an abdominal aortic aneurysm, a complicated procedure that only senior attending physicians at the hospital were allowed to perform. But by midnight, the attending physicians had all gone home. Bryce had put in a call for a senior surgeon, but with the terrible weather, several main roads were blocked and there was no telling when help would arrive.

"You have to do something," Cassie had said. "You know how to do the surgery. The aneurysm could burst any minute."

"It's against the rules," he'd replied. "What if something goes wrong? What if the patient dies because I took a risk?"

"He's guaranteed to die if you don't."

In the end, he'd compromised. Bryce informed the surgical nurses that instead of performing the full surgery, he would simply make an incision into the patient's abdomen large enough to expose the aorta. By starting the surgery, he could keep the patient alive until the attending physician reached the hospital. It was a bold plan, but it meant the patient was more likely to survive if the aneurysm ruptured while they waited for the attending physician.

The patient did survive, but the hospital board still felt it was necessary to take stern disciplinary measures. They attributed the patient's survival to luck rather than to Bryce's skill. As a medical student, Cassie had only received a warning, but as the resident in charge, Bryce had taken full responsibility for the decision and had been put on probation. If he made one more mistake, he would be fired immediately.

Bryce had told Cassie that it wasn't her fault. Ultimately, it was his decision, and even though they had broken the rules, they had also saved the patient's life.

He knew she felt guilty about pushing him to make the decision. But he had been the one to make the final call, and in spite of everything that had happened, he didn't regret it. The patient had survived and that was what mattered. If being put on probation was a consequence he had to live with, then he could handle that. He had a spotless record otherwise.

Cassie, however, was devastated that he was on probation. He was somewhat concerned, too, but he was reasonably sure that as long as they continued to keep their relationship a secret for a few more months, he wouldn't be fired. But to his great surprise, Cassie the daredevil, the fearless woman he thought he'd fallen in love with, was afraid to take the risk.

When she expressed her worries to him, he'd thought she simply wanted to lay low for a few months. Perhaps see each other less often until she graduated, just to play it safe for a while. But then he'd learned he lost a fellowship he'd applied for due to his probationary status. He couldn't hide his disappointment from Cassie.

Three days later, he found the note on his nightstand.

Sometimes he wondered if things between the two of them would have turned out differently if he hadn't been hit by a drunk driver six weeks later. His recovery had kept him from calling anyone at first. Only his immediate family had known what had happened, and he'd asked them to keep the news private. If Cassie knew about the accident, she might want to be there to support him. But he didn't want to have to deal with his feelings about her while he was also recovering from his injuries. And he definitely didn't want her pity.

And worse, what if she didn't come at all?

Then he'd know for sure that the appeal of their relationship had never been that she was with him. Instead, it had been about the secrecy, the excitement and the danger of getting caught. A way to flaunt the rules, to get a thrill. That's what she'd been attracted to.

He'd held on to the ring for a while—longer than he thought he would—and then eventually sold it to pay for the Suzuki 650. A ring for a motorcycle. Not a bad trade, all things considered.

He'd been in El Salvador for three years, and in that time, he'd managed to build a life he could be proud of. He might not be a superstar surgeon, but he was a damned good obstetrician. And as for relationships… there had been a few flings, here and there, but no one serious since Cassie. He told himself that he preferred it that way. Life in El Salvador was complicated enough without romantic feelings getting in the way. Hell, practicing medicine was complicated enough without all that nonsense.

Which was why it was so important that he be able to accept that he and Cassie were two professionals with a past, and nothing more. Whatever physical attraction he might feel for her, it didn't change the fact that the two of them hadn't worked out, wouldn't work out and were never getting back together.

Realizing that he hadn't yet stopped by the dispensary for his daily antimalarial dose, he headed to the small cinder block building at the center of the camp. To his surprise, he found Cassie alone inside, struggling to wrap a bandage around her ankle.

"Are you okay?" he asked, alarmed. "What happened?"

She shrugged, dismissive. "It's no big deal. I just jarred my ankle a little when the bike jerked on that stone last night."

"Why didn't you let me look at your ankle? Why didn't you tell me something was wrong?"

She scowled at him. "Because nothing *was* wrong. It's not even a sprain. It's just a little tender and swollen. I'm only taping it up so it has a little support."

He looked at her ankle. It did indeed look a little red and swollen, but not serious. Nothing that a little rest, support and pain relievers wouldn't cure. Cassie, however, had spent half the morning hiking back to camp. Why hadn't she said anything? Did she really feel the need to be so guarded that she couldn't even tell him when she was hurt?

Also, she was making a complete mess of the bandage. He'd had plenty of experience with sprained and stressed ankles, and he could think of at least three better ways to bind her foot that would offer more support.

"I would have appreciated you letting me know that you'd been hurt," he said. "Especially with all the walking we did this morning. I could have helped you."

She rubbed her ankle and undid the bandage again. "I don't need help."

He looked at where the bandage lay unspooled around her foot. Despite his frustration at her for not telling him about her injury, he couldn't help smiling at her clear difficulty with the bandage.

"Is that so? Because I've seen first-year medical students provide better first aid than this. Are you sure you're a doctor?"

Her eyes sparked. "I'm an ob-gyn, not a physical therapist. I haven't needed to tape up an ankle in years."

He sat beside her. "Come on, let me take a look. I've had to take care of plenty of my own bumps and bruises since I got here. You develop a knack for it after a while."

Grudgingly, she handed him the bandage. He probed her ankle, looking for tender spots. After he'd ascertained for himself that Cassie's injury wasn't serious, he wrapped the bandage around her ankle and her foot, creating a makeshift splint.

She flexed her foot, testing. "That actually feels a lot better. Thank you." Then she looked rather shamefaced. "Look... I'm sorry if I was giving you a hard time. The truth is, I absolutely hate being fussed over."

He knew the feeling. It was often hard, as a doctor, to be in the patient role. Bryce always felt slightly uncomfortable whenever he needed any sort of medical attention of his own. He smiled at her. "Fiercely independent, as ever." And then, although he tried to stop himself, he couldn't help adding, "Is it worth it?"

"Is what worth it?"

"Proving that you don't need any help. From anyone." *Especially not from me*, he didn't say, although the words hung unspoken in the air.

She thought for a moment, and he cursed himself for letting his words slip out. Why couldn't he have simply accepted her thanks, instead of making the moment so awkward? What could he possibly expect her to say?

She took a deep breath. "There's something about me that I've never told you."

Something in her tone made him pause. Whatever it was she was working up to, it seemed as though it were difficult to get out. He regretted his sharp words from a moment ago. Cassie was the one with the hurt ankle, and he'd just made the situation worse.

And yet he did want to know why she was so determined to prove that she didn't need anyone's help. It certainly wasn't getting her anywhere—look at what a mess she'd made of that bandage.

He recalled his physical therapy after the accident. There had been so many times when he'd wanted to be independent. He'd hated having to admit that he was at his limit, and that he needed to ask for help from someone else.

But he'd learned to do it. What was keeping her from doing the same?

Her next words took him by complete surprise.

"I was born with a heart defect. I had three surgeries before I was sixteen."

It was not the turn he'd expected the conversation to take. Not by a long shot. "Why didn't you ever tell me?"

"I hardly tell anyone. It's the kind of thing that can make people think differently about me once they know it. And I didn't want that to happen with you. It might sound silly, but…I didn't want you to see me as weak."

"Weak? Why on earth would I think that?"

"Sometimes people react that way. Even though I'm healthy now, sometimes people start treating me as though I'm excessively fragile when they find out." Her eyes met his, and he saw their familiar blue blaze burning. "I never wanted *you* to see me that way. As someone who needed extra protection or as this dainty, fragile object, always a moment away from breaking. I never wanted you to see me as anything less than capable."

"No one who knows you could ever think that." He held her gaze for a moment longer than he meant to.

Could she really think that he would ever see her as weak? Nothing could be further from the truth.

He'd seen the same fire in her eyes in the past. It blazed whenever she was arguing a point or advocating for a patient…or whenever she was at her most passionate. He looked away and cleared his throat. "So that's why you need to show you can do everything on your own. You need to prove that you're more than your diagnosis."

"I've always wanted to be. But ever since I was born, my diagnosis ruled my life. When I was in school, my nickname was Heart Defect Girl. My entire identity was reduced to my heart condition."

He winced. "Children aren't always good at making sure everyone feels included."

"You'd be surprised at how adults aren't all that different."

He nodded slowly. Cassie's news was unexpected, but it also made certain things click into place. He remembered how she'd snapped at him yesterday in the forest when he'd offered to look at her ankle. He'd only meant it as a thoughtful gesture, but Cassie had probably chafed against what she'd perceived as overprotectiveness.

Other things were clicking into place, as well. He remembered how she had always jumped into things with both feet, whether it was a complicated birthing procedure or the longest, loudest song at a karaoke bar. Had all the risks she'd taken during their relationship been her way of proving that she wasn't fragile?

He thought about how his own childhood had been full of activity. He'd leaped off swings, jumped on trampolines, played sports. All things that children with healthy hearts could do without a second thought. He couldn't imagine what it would feel like to have to constantly sit on the sidelines, watching everyone else have a normal, active childhood.

"It must have been hard to miss out on so much."

She sighed. "Missing out was bad enough, but my parents treated me as though I were made of glass. Everyone was constantly telling me what *not* to do so that I wouldn't put a strain on my heart. Even things that were normal for other kids were deemed too dangerous for me. You mentioned summer camp last night. I've never been to summer camp in my life. I couldn't climb trees. I couldn't ride bikes. Hell, after I had my last surgery, there were a few weeks where I was so weak I couldn't even tie my own shoes."

"I bet all of the rules and restrictions were suffocating."

"Actually, all of that overprotectiveness backfired. I promised myself that as soon as I was strong enough, I'd never let anyone tell me anything was too dangerous ever again." She smiled ruefully. "And then I went to medical school and got my big chance. My heart was finally completely healthy. I was living on my own for the first time in my life."

"And you wanted to seize the day." All of this explained a lot. But it also made him consider Cassie in a new light. He'd always thought her fearlessness was an inherent part of her personality. But the information about her heart defect put everything in a different context. Now he found himself wondering if she wasn't such a natural risk-taker, after all. Instead, she'd been pushing herself to take risks. Somehow, thinking about her in this way gave him an unexpected pang of warmth for her. For the small girl Cassie had been and the young woman who had been trying so hard to prove herself.

Her next words confirmed his hunch.

"Carpe diem, indeed. Half the reason I argued so much with the other residents and attending physicians was because the feeling of going against authority was so new to me. From the outside, I looked like a med student advocating for her patients, but inside I was basically a teenager who saw rules as something to be broken."

He couldn't stop himself from asking. "Was our relationship another opportunity to break the rules?"

She looked as though he'd slapped her. "Wait a minute. Is that what you think? That our relationship was just about me getting a thrill?"

He shrugged. "I get it. You'd been sheltered your whole life and were chafing against the rules, understandably so. And you decided to use me as one more way to rebel."

For a moment, her eyes blazed, but then she grew thoughtful. "That was part of the appeal at first," she admitted. "But only at the very beginning."

What did she mean by *only at the very beginning*? Did she mean that she'd eventually developed deeper feelings for him later on? Or that the appeal had faded and she'd ultimately viewed their relationship as a mistake? He wasn't sure he wanted to know.

She was staring at him as though she expected him to say something. But his mind was spinning with questions, and his heart was full of a feeling he couldn't name. All he could manage to say was, "Everybody has regrets."

"Well, I regret the way I left. I shouldn't have left a note. I should have talked things over with you, ended it face-to-face. For all the risks I took that year, I should have at least been able to handle that. But I couldn't and…I'm sorry."

She was trying to move on, he realized. She was trying to do exactly what they'd talked about last night: find a way to move forward, as professionals. Maybe even as friends.

He realized she was still watching him for some response. He decided that if she could move forward, then he could, too.

"Apology accepted," he said, and he found that the words did leave him feeling as though a weight had been lifted from his chest.

But any relief he felt was short-lived. Because the moment the tension in his chest eased, he found himself confronting a new problem.

He no longer struggled with the two conflicting impulses that had been tearing him apart since she first arrived. That problem was solved. Because the urge to run from her was gone.

But the impulse to gather her into his arms was stronger than ever.

Apparently, moving on was going to be harder than he'd thought.

CHAPTER FOUR

CASSIE SPENT THE next few weeks adjusting to life at the camp. Because her patients came from such varied situations, each day was different, and she never really knew what was in store for her when she began her work in the morning.

The camp was unlike any setting she had ever worked in. It was difficult not to have modern medical equipment, but she also found that the limitations she faced made her rise to the occasion and work harder than ever before. During each delivery, she had to keep her attention focused in numerous directions. Without a monitor to alert her of when a fetal heart rate was dropping or a pulse oximeter to measure oxygen levels in a patient's blood, she had to rely on her training and her observational skills, and she couldn't afford to lose focus for a second.

Delivering babies had always held its share of drama. If something went wrong, it meant tragedy for everyone involved. The despair of losing a new life or of a mother being at risk, all of it was the price Cassie paid for the other side of obstetrics: the side filled with celebration and joy. But practicing in El Salvador raised the stakes to a whole new level. The more Cassie saw of the struggles that her patients faced, the more she felt that she was in the right place. Her patients wanted what any parent wanted: to give birth in a safe place, with the best care available. Cassie was determined to offer them that in any way she could.

She found herself rediscovering some of her most deeply held beliefs as a physician. She'd started her career in medicine with the dream of showing each patient the same kind of personalized care her family had received when she was a child. Each doctor who'd operated on her heart had taken the time to get to know her family and had closely followed Cassie's recovery afterward. But by the time she'd graduated medical school, the landscape had changed. Many of the hospitals with the most resources were private hospitals, where the administration's focus was on the bottom line. That meant less time spent with patients and more pressure to complete as many billable procedures as she could each month. She'd chosen to work at a private hospital so that she could provide her patients with the best care possible, but she wasn't sure, now, if it really was the best care. There was so much focus on profits that she'd felt more like a baby delivery service than a real doctor.

And for a long time, she'd accepted that as the way of things. She hadn't started out that way. Back when she'd been a medical student who pushed herself to be fearless, she was a fierce advocate for her patients. If she felt that one of her patients needed extra time or care or a risky procedure, she wouldn't hesitate to fight on her patient's behalf. But she'd buried that part of herself behind after she'd left Bryce, blaming her outspoken, adventurous side for causing so much trouble.

Working at the camp was making her wonder how she could have gone for so long without challenging the status quo. That young rebellious version of herself hadn't been afraid to go against the system or take unorthodox steps if she felt she needed to advocate for the well-being of her patients. At some point, she'd lost sight of that person, but as she spent more time working at the camp, she realized that this was a setting in which risk and improvisation were far from discouraged. In fact, they were viewed as a necessary part of providing care. She was reconnecting with her passion for medicine, just as she'd hoped she would.

She also found that she was reconnecting with Bryce. It was impossible for them to avoid running into one another in such a small camp, and they often worked on the same cases together.

It was so easy to fall back into a steady rhythm of working with him. She'd forgotten how well they'd collaborated, but as they shared more cases, they resumed their natural tempo as though the years hadn't passed. They worked together seamlessly, especially during difficult or complex cases that required taking medically necessary risks, as well as exercising extreme caution with the same patient. The patients who needed more risky procedures were often the most fragile, and Cassie noticed that she and Bryce balanced each other out especially well with these cases.

She still hadn't found out why he'd become an obstetrician. Somehow, she couldn't get up the nerve to ask him outright. There was so much she didn't know about what had happened to Bryce over the past five years. Had he ultimately lost his job after she left? Even if he had, why would he give up surgery?

And the conversation she'd had with Bryce as he'd bandaged her ankle continued to reverberate in her mind. His words had cut her to the bone.

Was our relationship another opportunity to break the rules?

At first, she couldn't believe he'd think that of her. He made it sound as though to her the relationship had just been some meaningless fling, a chance for her to rebel. But as their conversation continued, she'd realized, horrified, that he did see it that way. And worse, she could understand why.

She'd left her short, terse little note because by giving up Bryce, she felt as though she were giving up everything. She couldn't find the words she needed to say to him, and she knew she wouldn't be able to go through with it if she saw the pain on his face. But when he'd lost his fellowship…she couldn't stand to hurt his career anymore. Leaving him was the hardest decision she'd ever made.

But she realized now that Bryce hadn't understood that at all. He thought she'd left because she didn't care about him. He thought, now that she'd had the fun of a secret relationship, she'd dashed off the note and left because the relationship had never been that important to her in the first place.

And now she didn't know if there was any way she could convince him to see things differently. To make him know just how much she cared.

In order to go through with the breakup, she'd tried to convince herself that giving up Bryce was the right thing. The brave thing. But after hearing Bryce accuse her of taking their relationship lightly, after learning that he believed she'd just been enjoying a fling, she had to admit that the way she'd handled the breakup hadn't been brave at all. Instead, she'd just been afraid.

As far as she could tell from Enrique and their other colleagues, fear was not an emotion that Bryce struggled with. Apparently, he volunteered for daring missions into the mountain territory as often as possible. That was something unexpected about him, as well. The Bryce she remembered had been exceptionally cautious, careful and measured. Why had he changed?

Manny Martinez, the child who'd carried her backpack to her room on the day she arrived, held a wealth of information about Bryce. The boy seemed to hero-worship Bryce and followed him everywhere, although he often tagged along with Cassie and ran errands for her when she made her morning rounds. He enjoyed regaling her with stories of Bryce's exploits, many of which had clearly been enhanced by Manny's imagination. For example, she didn't believe that while traveling miles to deliver medicine to a remote village, Bryce and Manny had crossed a river by stepping on the backs of crocodiles, only to be accosted by a nest of snakes when they reached the other side. She expressed her doubts to Manny, with the result that he doubled down and implied that jaguars may have been involved, as well.

He'd proudly shown her Rosibel, his newborn sister, at the first opportunity. Apparently, Bryce had delivered the baby on the day Cassie arrived in El Salvador.

"I wanted a brother, but girls aren't all bad," Manny said. "Mama is so busy taking care of Rosibel that she never even notices how many pieces of chocolate I have." The grin on his face suggested he was making the most of his mother's distraction, and Cassie noticed that his pockets bulged with sweets pilfered or begged from other doctors.

Cassie held her finger out to little Rosibel now as she checked in on the mother and baby. The baby instantly closed her tiny hand in a firm grip. So Bryce had brought this sweet baby into the world. Bryce the obstetrician, not Bryce the surgeon. There was something about a newborn that always made her feel hopeful. A new life with so much possibility ahead. When Cassie had been born, everyone had been afraid for her. But in spite of everything, she'd focused on pursuing life as vigorously as she could. For her, that was what delivering babies was all about: focusing on life. And now Bryce was delivering babies, too.

Who was this mysterious man who apparently delivered babies one day and jumped onto the backs of crocodiles the next?

There was so much she didn't know about him.

Over the past five years, whenever she'd thought about Bryce, she always pictured the man she'd known in the past. She'd never thought that he might change.

But of course he had, and she knew that she shouldn't be surprised. They were both different people than they used to be.

She'd always been drawn to his tenderness. She recognized it in the solicitous way he'd helped her bandage her ankle and the patience he exercised with Manny. But now there was also a toughness to him that she'd never expected. She noticed it whenever she saw him tearing away from the camp on his motorcycle or shouting orders to medical teams as they prepared for a new influx of refugees. The same tenderness she'd always seen in him was still there, but now it was balanced with a rugged determination to do whatever it took to get a job done.

She found it damned attractive, if she were honest with herself.

She'd seen glimpses of that determination when she'd watched him work as a surgeon.

She wondered again why he'd ever given up surgery. It was such a vastly different process from obstetrics. In surgery, patients were usually anesthetized, and the skill lay entirely in the doctor's hands. But delivering babies was a team effort. The patient's role was every bit as active as the doctor's, often more so. Building trust between the patient and medical personnel was crucial, especially if the patient was scared or if things weren't going as expected.

Why would Bryce, a masterful surgeon, seek out such a different experience? What had made him change?

It could have been anything. Five years was a long time. Perhaps he'd met someone else who'd inspired him to switch to obstetrics?

Another thought settled into her stomach like a block of ice. What if switching specialties hadn't been Bryce's choice at all?

Changing specialties was no small feat. He would have had to redo his residency, probably at a completely different hospital.

She could think of only one reason why Bryce might have needed to move to a different hospital and redo his residency. Thanks to her, he'd been on probation when she'd left the hospital. Another mistake could have cost him his job.

For example, if anyone had found out that he'd dated a medical student, it might have been the final straw for Bryce. That was why she'd left—to avoid causing him any more pain.

But what if someone had found out? What if, despite everything she'd given up by leaving him, Bryce had been fired because of her, after all?

But if he had been fired, wouldn't he have been able to finish his residency somewhere else? He'd been such a talented surgeon. Any hospital would have been lucky to have him. Surely, she couldn't have ruined his career that much... Could she?

She needed to know. Even if she didn't like the answer, she absolutely needed to know if Bryce had lost his job and put himself through the ordeal of changing specialties because of her. Because despite what Bryce might think, their relationship had been important to her. She'd left him in order to protect him, hoping not to cause any more damage to his career than she already had. And even if there was nothing she could do about it now, she needed to know if she'd ruined his career. And if she had, she'd find a way to make it up to him. Somehow.

Bryce was surprised when Cassie showed up at the front door of his quarters, asking if he wanted to join her in the mess hall for a morning coffee. He was even more surprised when he found himself saying yes.

Slipping back into professional mode with Cassie had turned out to be far easier than he'd thought. He found he enjoyed working with her as much as ever. In fact, all the things he'd missed about working with her had come rushing back. The banter over patients and the ease with which they anticipated one another's decisions was refreshing after the years they'd spent apart. And he had to admit that despite himself, his curiosity had continued to burn after their conversation in the dispensary. He'd never known that Cassie had a heart defect. She had kept that information from him all that time.

Before the accident, he might not have understood her choice to keep the secret. But he could understand all too clearly now. For so long, his family had seen him only as the superstar surgeon. They'd focused on that one single part of him so much that when his life changed, they could only see what he'd lost. Sometimes it was still hard for Bryce himself to see that he was more than his past.

Cassie wanted to keep her heart condition private for the same reasons he wanted to keep the accident and his former career as a surgeon private. Once people knew something so serious, there was a chance they might only view you through that lens. He didn't want to be known as a person who used to be a gifted surgeon. That wasn't his identity anymore. He'd fought hard to become more than an accident victim, more than someone who *used* to be something.

It sounded as though Cassie had also been fighting to be seen as a whole person and not just one thing.

He remembered what she said her childhood nickname had been—*Heart Defect Girl*. What must it have been like for her to constantly feel singled out like that?

He wondered what else she hadn't told him.

When they reached the mess hall, he got their cups of coffee while she waited. When she put her cup to her lips, she smiled. "You remembered just how I like it."

"Black, with two sugars. There are some things about Cassie Andover that you don't forget. How she takes her coffee is one of them. Not if you know what's good for you."

"We've got a lot of memories, don't we, Bryce?"

He returned her smile. "We do. And I'll even go as far as to say that most of them are good ones."

She was silent for a moment, then cocked an eyebrow over her cup of coffee. "Agreed. But I didn't ask you here this morning to talk over old memories. I want to solve a mystery."

He waited, wondering what she was getting at. "As you may remember, I do love a good mystery."

She set her cup down. "That's the thing, Bryce. I *do* remember that about you. And you remember how I like my coffee. So clearly you are the same Bryce I dated five years ago."

"Who else would I be?"

"That's the mystery we're here to solve. The Bryce I remember had to be begged to get on my motorcycle back in New York. He didn't have one of his own, and if he did, he'd *never* have driven it the way you drove yours when you picked me up a few weeks ago. The Bryce I knew loved being a surgeon and couldn't imagine any other career. He didn't jump out of helicopters or negotiate with gang leaders. And he sure as hell never wrestled any crocodiles in any sort of man versus reptile death match."

"Ah, I see you've been talking with Manny." Bryce wondered if Cassie had been seeking out information about him from the boy or perhaps even from some of their other colleagues. Did that mean he'd been on her mind? Just like she'd been on his.

"Manny's cute. Don't change the subject. Who are

you and what have you done with the Bryce I used to know?"

Bryce slowly stirred his coffee, wondering how to answer. Of course, his life had changed since the accident and since giving up his career as a surgeon. But he hadn't thought that he had changed that much as a person, until now. He supposed Cassie had a point. He *had* been reluctant to do anything risky back when they'd dated. One of his favorite things about her had been her ability to pull out his adventurous side from wherever it was hidden.

It had also been one of the reasons he was so devastated when she left.

As he wasn't quite sure how to answer her, he stalled for time instead. "It's been five years, Cass. That's a pretty big question."

"Then start at the beginning. No, actually, start with what I really want to know. How the *hell* could you afford such a beautiful bike on a Medicine International salary?"

Typical Cassie. Cutting straight to the heart of things without even realizing it. He'd been enjoying their renewed connection over the past few weeks, but he wasn't sure he was ready for this conversation. In fact, it might be because of their renewed connection that he didn't want to simply blurt out the full story of how he'd come by his motorcycle—that he'd bought it by selling the ring he'd meant to propose to her with.

The trouble was, he'd never been a very good liar. And since their breakup, he'd gotten even worse at it. His hand tremor flared any time he lost control of his emotions. Cassie wouldn't know to look for it, but if his hands wavered, if she noticed and asked him about it…he had no idea how he'd respond.

He decided to offer up half the truth.

"I was dating someone a while back and saved up for an engagement ring. But it didn't work out. Sold the ring, bought the bike. Not much else to tell." He shrugged, trying to keep his body posture casual. It was all true. He was simply neglecting to mention that the ring had been meant for Cassie. A small extraneous detail.

She choked on her coffee. "You almost got engaged? Then you weren't just dating—it must have been serious."

"I thought so, but I guess she didn't."

"What was her name? What was she like?"

Bryce paused. He hadn't intended to tell Cassie any outright lies. He'd been hoping he could get away with simply omitting certain truths. He was relieved when she continued, "Actually, scratch that. You don't have to tell me anything you don't feel like talking about. Whatever happened, I'm probably the last person you'd want to rehash all of it with. I only invited you to meet here because I wanted the two of us to have a chance to talk about *us*, about our…" She seemed to be struggling to find the right words.

"Our friendship?"

"Yeah," she said. "Our friendship. It's such a small camp, and we see each other every day. And aside from the initial shock of seeing you on my first day, now that I've had some time to adjust… I really like it here. The only thing that could possibly make life better would be if the two of us could be friends. But in order to do that, we'd have to get to know each other again, don't you think?"

She was right. They'd both changed. He probably was a bit more reckless than he used to be, especially as he didn't have to obsess over protecting his hands anymore. And he'd always thought of her as bold, adventurous. But now he'd learned that those qualities didn't come naturally for her. She'd had to work to find them. He wondered if she'd been able to keep in touch with her adventurous side over the years since they'd been apart.

She was right. They needed a chance to get to know each other.

"You're not the only one with questions, you know," he said.

"I'll answer yours if you answer mine."

"Okay. I'll go first. What's the best ob-gyn in New York City doing in El Salvador?"

Her burst of laughter surprised him. "Did I say something funny?"

Her eyes sparkled. "I think I laughed because your question answered itself. My job in New York is what drove me straight here. And I don't know that I was the *best* ob-gyn."

"Come on, don't be modest. My friend Marcus's wife said she couldn't even get an appointment with you. The scuttlebutt is that you have to know someone who knows someone if you want to get an appointment with Cassie Andover."

She rolled her eyes. "Ugh, that's exactly why I came here. I never meant for it to be that way."

"But there has to be some truth to it, otherwise you wouldn't have earned that reputation."

"Maybe. But honestly, sometimes I think my entire reputation is a fluke. I was just in the right place at a significant time in someone's life."

"How so?"

"A few years ago, there was a car crash off the interstate. One of the survivors was a pregnant mother who started going into premature labor. She also happened to be a very famous singer. I delivered the baby, word got around and suddenly I was working more and delivering some very wealthy babies into the world. Which meant dealing with some of the most demanding parents I've ever met. And the more money they have, the more demands they have. They treated me and my nursing staff like servants."

"Sounds like you needed a change."

"Exactly. And so—" she spread her arms out to indicate the mess hall and the rest of the medical camp "—here we are."

Suddenly, her eyes flickered in recognition. "Did you say *Marcus's* wife wanted to get in to see me? Marcus, from the old hospital? God, I haven't seen Marcus since—" her face broke into a grin "—since the last day of his surgical rotation, when you dared him to drink from that phlebotomy sample cup."

"I did not *dare* him… I kindly *offered* him fifty dollars to drink whatever I might have happened to put in the cup."

"Which happened to be a pale yellow liquid."

"As I recall, you were the one who walked away with the fifty dollars."

Cassie scoffed. "It was obviously apple juice."

"But you had no way of being sure."

She smirked at him. "I trusted you. For the most

part. I'm surprised Marcus didn't. He could have made a quick fifty bucks."

"The face he made when he saw you drinking what he thought was a urine sample was pretty priceless. Well worth fifty dollars."

"Poor Marcus. We were pretty relentless with the pranks."

"We all were," he said. "Marcus got back at me by putting surgical lube on my stethoscope ear tips. That was just delightful to put into my ears, let me tell you. And I remember a time when it wasn't safe to fall asleep in the staff room because you'd wake up finding that someone had put a plaster cast on one of your arms or legs."

They'd had a lot of fun, roping one another into hijinks back when they'd worked together. Bryce had always felt passionate about medicine, but it was also something he'd approached very seriously. Cassie had added something to his passion. She'd made working at the hospital fun.

"I miss things being so easygoing," she said. "Brooklyn General's a lot more uptight than our old hospital. There's no tolerance for pranks. With our clientele, all of the focus is on meeting their demands. No one has the time or energy to let loose."

"So you haven't pulled any death-defying stunts lately? I thought for sure I'd hear about you delivering a baby while white-water rafting by now."

"Only if it becomes the next celebrity birthing craze. Which wouldn't entirely surprise me. In fact, keep that thought to yourself—don't give my patients any ideas."

"That bad, huh?"

She shook her head. "I was working so much that

I could barely tell my days apart anymore. I wanted something that would let me slow down and get in touch with what really mattered. Whatever that might be."

Now it was his turn to raise an eyebrow. "Only you would come to a country with twenty active volcanoes to slow down."

"Hey, that's not fair! I've actually become fairly responsible over the years."

He snorted. "I'll believe that when I see it."

"But you've changed, too. Tell me about this new Bryce who jumps out of helicopters."

"It doesn't happen that often. Maybe four times over the past year."

"Even *once* a year is just very…different from the Bryce I used to know. But it's not just the idea of you jumping into danger that surprises me. You changed specialties. Why on earth would you do that? That's huge, that's not something one does on a whim. Especially as you were such a talented surgeon."

He cringed inwardly. There they were, the words he dreaded most: you *were* talented. The words he'd come to El Salvador to avoid ever hearing again.

He reminded himself that Cassie didn't know about the accident. She couldn't know how much of the past was a sore spot for him.

For a moment, he thought about coming out with the whole story. The crash, the tremor it had left in his hands and how he didn't have to worry about preventing injuries anymore because protecting his hands didn't matter as much as it used to. But something stopped him. Cassie had clearly heard some stories about some of the more dangerous things he'd done since coming to El Salvador. There was a familiar light in her eyes, an eagerness he remembered from the old days. He'd seen a flicker of it when he'd picked her up and insisted she get on his bike.

He couldn't quite bring himself to tell her that he hadn't turned into some sort of adventurous medical version of Indiana Jones. He didn't take on the camp's more dangerous duties because he craved excitement. He did it because it simply didn't matter if he got injured anymore. He wasn't brave; he just didn't care if he got hurt.

But even though years had passed, even though the way she felt about him shouldn't matter anymore…for some reason, he didn't want her to stop looking at him the way she was right now. As though he were someone who was fearless.

He told himself he was being ridiculous. The way Cassie looked at him shouldn't matter. It *hadn't* mattered for years, and he'd gotten along just fine without giving a moment's notice to what she might think of him. So there was no reason for him to hesitate in giving her the truth now.

He opened his mouth, about to explain, when the doors of the mess hall burst open and Anna, the midwife, rushed in. "We've got a complicated delivery in tent three," she said. Bryce noticed she was somewhat breathless. She must have run across the camp. "We need you both right now."

As Bryce and Cassie rushed to their feet, he realized that the moment to explain the changes in his life over the past few years was gone. But that was all right, he told himself. He'd simply explain things later. If the subject happened to come up.

* * *

They dashed across the camp to the birthing tent, Cassie and Anna struggling to keep up with Bryce's long strides.

As they entered the birthing tent, Cassie recognized the patient. Elena Hernandez lived in a village nearby. Cassie knew Elena had had several miscarriages and desperately wanted a child. She also knew that the baby was far too early, as Elena was only a little more than halfway through her third trimester.

"What's the situation?" said Bryce.

"She's fully dilated," said Anna. "But she's labored for three hours with no progress. At first I thought maybe the baby's shoulder was stuck, but it's been so long that there might be something else going on that we can't see."

Cassie was still getting used to the challenge of working without a fetal heart monitor. But as she gently ran her hands over Elena's abdomen, she had a feeling that she didn't need modern medical equipment to guess at one piece of this puzzle.

"We might be looking at twins," she said. Elena's build was slight, and Cassie surmised that malnourishment combined with premature labor was likely to make it look from the outside as though she carried one baby rather than two. She hoped there were no more than two.

"Let's cross that bridge when we come to it," said Bryce. "For now, we need to prepare for a cesarean section. We should move her to the operating tent."

In addition to working without a fetal heart monitor, there were other adjustments Cassie was making as she learned to adapt to the equipment at the medical camp. About half of the hospital beds in use had been made without wheels. In every hospital Cassie had ever worked at, she'd typically transferred patients by wheelchair or by rolling a gurney down a hall—but wheelchairs and beds with wheels were luxuries she no longer had easy access to. Transferring Elena to the operating tent's table would require some ingenuity.

Cassie watched as Bryce and Anna began unfolding a large swath of canvas. Bryce handed one end to her. She stared at it, confused.

"We're going to make a makeshift stretcher to slide her onto for transport," he explained.

Oh. Of course. Without wheels on the hospital bed or a gurney to transport Mrs. Hernandez, they'd have to be creative. Sheepishly, she grabbed one end of the canvas.

She and Bryce held the canvas taut from end to end while Anna eased Mrs. Hernandez onto it. They transported the canvas to the OR tent with small hurried steps and placed Mrs. Hernandez onto the operating table.

As they got Elena on the table, Cassie saw something that made her stomach drop. In the few minutes it had taken to transfer their patient to the operating tent, the situation had changed dramatically. Elena's abdomen had contorted into an hourglass shape, indicating that something was obstructing the birth canal. Elena was at risk of immediate uterine rupture, and possibly death, if they didn't act fast.

"Anesthetize the patient as best you can," Cassie said to the operating room nurse. "We need to start immediately. What equipment do we have available for neonatal resuscitation?"

"Just our breath and thumbs," said Bryce.

"Great," said Cassie through gritted teeth. It was life or death. If the baby was born in distress, there would be no equipment to assist—she'd have to perform neonatal CPR. If it came to that. She decided she wouldn't let it come to that.

Bryce began to make the incision for the cesarean. But inexplicably, almost as soon as he had begun, he stopped.

"What is it?" she said. "Bryce, we have to act now. There's not a moment to spare."

He handed the scalpel to her. "You do it."

"But you've already started."

"Doesn't matter. This is a complicated procedure. You should be the one to do it. You're the best ob-gyn in Brooklyn."

She took the scalpel, unwilling to quibble further while the seconds ticked away. She tried to control her intense irritation. Bryce had already started the operation. There was absolutely no reason for him to hand the scalpel over to her. What did it matter whether she or Bryce did the surgery? They were both competent doctors, and Elena and her baby needed help quickly. As she concentrated on the procedure, the thought flashed through her mind that Bryce seemed to have been *nervous* to start the C-section. But surely that couldn't be true. She'd seen Bryce deliver a few babies over the past few days, and he'd been more than competent. He was a skilled obstetrician. True, she hadn't seen him do any C-sections, but if anything, an obstetrician with Bryce's background as a surgeon should feel even *more* confident during C-sections.

But there was no time to figure out what on earth

he was thinking now. Cassie carefully completed the incision. Like so many of her patients here who suffered from malnutrition, there was no fat tissue to put aside, only a thin layer of skin to protect the uterus. She made another careful incision, knowing that she had to get the baby out quickly. A clearer view showed her what had been obstructing labor: the baby's head was just a little too big. It was also a bit too far down the birth canal for her to cup and deliver.

Bryce immediately saw the problem and came to assist. With a few skilled maneuvers, Cassie was able to reach the baby's feet and deliver it bottom-first. A wave of relief washed over her as she heard the tiny cry of a newborn girl fill the room.

The others in the tent cheered as she handed the baby to one of the midwives for cleaning. She had stepped away from Elena and was letting her breath out in relief when Bryce nodded toward their patient. "Don't relax too much," he said. "You were right the first time. She had company in there."

For a moment, Cassie wasn't sure what he was talking about, but as she took another look at her patient, she saw it—the faintest flicker of motion inside the abdomen. She drew closer and saw a tiny hand.

Twins.

"I'd have missed it if it hadn't been moving just a bit," said Bryce. "You want to do the honors?"

In response, Cassie gently placed her fingers inside the abdomen, reaching for that tiny hand. She removed the second twin, a boy, and passed him to the midwife, as well.

Bryce started working on closing Elena's abdomen while two thin cries began to fill the room. For Cassie, it was the sound of victory. There would be no neonatal CPR today.

She stripped off her gloves, exhausted. Bryce gave her a huge grin and a nod. So he was impressed? Good. He should be. She was still baffled by his hesitation earlier. In a situation where every second counted, what could possibly have led Bryce to stop an emergency surgical procedure and hand the scalpel to her? She couldn't fathom what would lead him to hesitate at such a crucial moment.

She could only come to one conclusion: despite all the reports she'd heard of his daring exploits, he was just as cautious as ever. But that still didn't make sense.

Cassie knew that if she'd taken charge of the OR, she would never have stopped to question whether she or Bryce should perform the surgery. She'd simply have taken a scalpel into her hand and started, and dealt with any problems as they arose.

Then she was overcome with a wave of contrition. Despite Bryce's hesitation, they'd saved three lives that day. She smiled, knowing how much Elena had wanted to be a mother. Well, now she was, twice over.

Bryce squeezed her shoulder as he left the tent. She was determined to ask him why he'd hesitated. But before she could say more than, "Bryce, why—" he'd rushed past her.

Why would Bryce Hamlin, of all people, hesitate to do a surgery? And why did it seem as though he didn't want to talk to her about it?

CHAPTER FIVE

BRYCE SAT BENEATH his usual balsa tree, exhausted. The complicated delivery that he and Cassie had performed that morning had been the first of a day full of challenging cases, and his mind was aching for some peace. He'd worked a twelve-hour shift, but it felt like twelve years since he and Cassie had shared coffee together in the mess hall.

Now dusk was falling, and he could finally have a moment to breathe. He leaned his back against the tree's broad trunk and tried to let the tension drain from his body. The camp was surrounded on most sides by thick forest. But the trees fell away on the west side, and he could gaze at the rolling hills leading up to the mountains miles away. The sun had almost set but still cast a golden glow over the mountaintops, and underneath the balsa tree, a few early fireflies were beginning to make their appearance.

As he sat in the quiet, his stomach rumbled. He hadn't had any time to eat since breakfast. Despite the stress of the day, it had been a relief to be so busy. The rush of deliveries had meant that he hadn't been able to have a moment alone with Cassie, which meant the two of them hadn't been able to talk since that morning. He wasn't trying to avoid her, exactly. He was just certain that she'd have some questions on her mind after his noticeable hesitation during the procedure that morning, and he didn't think he was ready to answer them.

Bryce knew on an intellectual level that his tremor wasn't severe enough to prevent him from performing C-sections. Still, he was anxious whenever they were necessary. Knowing that he could do something wasn't the same thing as feeling confident about it. It was as though he'd been asked to relearn how to ride a bicycle. He could know that sitting astride a bicycle and pedaling should move him forward, but that wouldn't make him feel any more certain about keeping his balance.

Usually, if his hands started to tremble, a few deep breaths were enough to calm their twitching and allow him to continue. But this time, they hadn't stopped, and he had a feeling he knew the reason why. It was because Cassie had been there.

He wasn't sure why Cassie's presence would affect him so much, but he thought he could make a reasonable guess. Cassie was the first person he'd met in El Salvador who knew the old version of himself that he'd been in New York. When he'd first arrived in El Salvador, it had been such a relief to finally be free of everyone's expectations. His family, in their attempts to be supportive, had always spoken about what a talented surgeon Bryce *used* to be. But in El Salvador, everyone only cared about who he was now. He didn't have to live up to any expectations about who he'd been in the past. Instead, all he had to do was be the best doctor he could be right now. But Cassie would expect to see the great Bryce Hamlin in action. She would expect things to go smoothly. She wouldn't understand if he got nervous, or if he needed extra time with a procedure, or if the patient's stitches didn't look like they'd been completed by a master when he closed.

Their relationship had undergone a strange reversal. When they'd dated, he'd been an up-and-coming surgeon. He'd taken pride in his talents, and his reputation was growing. He was especially adept at maneuvers that required extra dexterity and precision. He supposed that he'd gotten used to others looking up to him. But now he found himself admiring Cassie's skills. He'd been struck by her quick action in the delivery tent, her ability to soothe Mrs. Hernandez's nerves while deftly navigating the difficult delivery. When they'd dated, she'd been a promising medical student, but she'd grown into a dedicated physician.

He, on the other hand, was no longer the star surgeon he'd been five years ago. He'd noticed her confusion as he handed her the scalpel. And he was sure she would want an explanation.

A rustling of the trees startled him for a moment, and then Cassie emerged, holding a white paper lunch bag. "Care for some company?"

He leaned his head back against the tree. "I don't know if I can be the best conversationalist right now. It's been a long day."

"I know," she said, sitting down beside him and opening the paper bag. "That's why I brought some snacks."

"Pupusas!" he cried, a smile breaking over his face. The bag contained fluffy pieces of flatbread, each stuffed with different fillings of cheese, chicken and beans. He bit into one with gusto.

"Mmm," he said. "Chili cheese…my favorite." Only, it came out sounding like, *Hilee eese, um havorite.*

"Glad you approve. Now, I haven't been in El Salvador long, but I don't think you're supposed to eat the entire thing in one bite. At least leave yourself some room to breathe. And don't hog those. I brought them for us to share."

He slowed his chewing and passed the bag back to her. They sat on the forest floor, companionably munching their flatbread as the twilight faded.

He could only see a faint outline of her face. She sat close beside him so that she would have enough room to lean back against the balsa tree. Maybe it was because he was unable to see her face clearly, or maybe it was because of the food she'd brought him—he had been very hungry—but Bryce found himself feeling glad of her presence. Usually he preferred to be by himself after a long day. But Cassie didn't barrage him with questions or try to pull him into a conversation. Instead, they just sat together, watching the fireflies.

After they'd been silent together for a while, she said, "This is a nice spot."

"It's my favorite spot in the camp. I come here to unwind after a tough delivery, or a tough day."

"Like this morning?"

He rubbed his temples. "This morning was scary. I wasn't sure the patient was going to make it."

"But she did. They all did. There was one complication after another, but we saved three lives. I felt like I was holding my breath through the whole procedure. I still can't believe we pulled it off."

"It was mostly *you* who pulled it off," he said, wanting to give credit where it was due.

"It was a team effort, and you know it."

Well, Cassie certainly seemed to be thriving in the camp's intense atmosphere. He supposed he shouldn't be surprised. Despite how she'd changed, in many ways, she was still the Cassie he'd known five years ago. He wondered how long she would stay. Some of the camp's staff were *lifers*, returning year after year. They considered Medicine International to be their professional home. Others only joined for occasional yearlong stints. Bryce had stayed for three years, and could easily see himself staying longer. He could also see Cassie staying for a long time. To his surprise, he realized that the idea of Cassie staying at the camp for a long-term assignment held some appeal.

"It's been just over a month since you got here," he said. "Think you'll plan on sticking around for a while?"

She gave him a sidelong glance. "Trying to figure out how long you have until you'll be rid of me?"

Quite the opposite, he thought. If he were being honest with himself, he had to admit that he liked seeing her every day. But he wasn't about to tell her that. He didn't want to say anything that would lead them to revisit a host of complications.

"It's not that. It's just that it takes some people a while to adjust. You wouldn't have to deliver babies in situations like this without modern equipment back in New York."

"Are you kidding? This is exactly what I came here for. Yes, that was a stressful delivery this morning. And it was also awesome. And amazing. And incredible."

"That sounds like the Cassie I remember. You never did let a few challenges scare you off."

Even in the darkness, he could see her smile. "I'm glad to hear that you think that part of my personality hasn't changed. Before I came here, I was starting to worry that my life would be all about making sure celebrity moms got their preferred brand of organic granola, or helping some internet influencer set up cameras in the delivery room so she could livestream the moment she gave birth. But this morning was as different from my old life as I could possibly imagine. It's some of the most rewarding work I've ever done. I think I'm going to stay for a long time."

He noticed that even though her tone was casual, she seemed to be watching his face intently, trying to gauge his reaction.

Over the past few weeks, he'd grown far more comfortable with the idea of working with her than he'd been when she first arrived. He often found himself looking forward to running into her, whether it was to consult on a case or just to chat.

"I'm glad to hear you're enjoying it here," he said. "And I think…that I might be enjoying it, too."

Her eyes widened in surprise, and he quickly clarified, "I mean, I'm enjoying working together again. It's like old times."

"Old times with some new twists?"

"Exactly."

She tilted her head to one side, causing her hair to swing past her face. He often found himself wondering what it would feel like to wrap a strand of hair around one finger. He'd noticed himself banishing such thoughts from his mind more and more frequently in his attempts to respect their professional working relationship.

"I'm so glad to hear that you feel okay about working together," she said. "I was shocked to see you here, that first day, but we've done pretty well so far, haven't we?"

Her body was close enough to his that he could feel the warmth radiating from her. He mustered all of his professionalism and said, "I think so."

"And I think I figured something out this morning."

His body tensed. Had she noticed his shaking hands during the procedure?

"I finally get how you fit in to all this. Until this morning, I've been trying my hardest to solve the mystery of how cautious, mild-mannered surgeon Bryce Hamlin ended up at a medical outpost in El Salvador. But after this morning, it all makes sense. The challenges, the excitement, the adrenaline rush. How could you want to work anywhere else?"

He relaxed, relieved that she hadn't brought up his hands. "It's not always like this. Sometimes things even go pretty smoothly."

"I'll believe that when I see it. Ever since I've gotten here, each case has had its own unique chaos."

"And you love it."

Even in the dim light, he could see that her eyes sparkled. "You know I do."

"I wouldn't expect anything less from you."

"Speaking of expectations, we didn't really get a chance to talk about your new career this morning. The last time we worked together, you were a surgeon."

"Yeah. That would be one of those new twists we were talking about."

"What happened? The Bryce I remember loved his work more than anything. But that's not the only thing that's changed. All those stories about you wrestling crocodiles, negotiating with gang members… I don't know what to make of them."

"As much as I wish the story about wrestling crocodiles were true, I'm afraid that one's the result of an overactive imagination."

"Still. You've changed. You're not a surgeon anymore. You started the C-section this morning, but then stopped and handed me the scalpel during a critical moment. You used to be obsessively protective of your hands, but now apparently you tear around on your motorcycle and jump out of helicopters without a second thought. There's something you're not telling me. Spill it."

It should have been so simple to tell her about the accident. And yet somehow, he couldn't.

He didn't want to go through explaining about the accident, everything it had taken from him and the long recovery afterward. But even more than that, he didn't want her to stop looking at him the way she was now. She seemed to think he'd grown braver and more adventurous over the years. If she knew how devastated he'd been after the accident, how it had taken away his identity, his calling, she might not look at him the same way. If she knew how he'd had to cobble a new life together out of broken pieces of his past, she might pity him. He didn't want pity from anyone, but especially not from her.

"It's true that I've been through some changes," he said. "I switched specialties. I've been living here in El Salvador for three years, and I suppose that would change anyone. But does it really matter why? Maybe I just needed something different, like you did."

"It matters if it's my fault."

"Your fault? What are you talking about?"

"You lost your fellowship because of me."

Now he remembered. The Beaumont Fellowship. Weeks before the accident, he'd learned he had been removed from consideration for the fellowship because he was on probation. At the time, the news had been terribly disappointing. But then being hit by a drunk driver several weeks later had put things in perspective.

But Cassie hadn't known about the accident. And now she sounded absolutely wretched. She felt guilty, he realized. She thought that his change of careers had something to do with her.

"First of all, I lost the fellowship because I was on probation," he said. "And I was on probation because of a decision that we made, together. And even though the hospital administrators disagreed, I still think we made the right decision."

"But starting the operation was my idea. If I hadn't convinced you, you never would have followed through with it."

It was true that when they'd dated, he'd been known for being cautious, always leaning toward the safest option. Had she thought that just because he was reserved he didn't have a mind of his own?

"That's simply not true. Despite what you may believe, it is possible to stand up to Cassie Andover. The final judgment call was mine, and I'd make the same call again today. So I'm not sure why you're feeling so guilty about it."

"Because I got off so lightly!" she cried. "They blamed you for everything. I should have been suspended at the very least. But instead, I got a stern warning and a talking-to, and before I knew it everything was back to normal. I worked so hard to repair my reputation. In fact, I worked too hard. I gave up everything that made me feel like myself, because I didn't like who I was. I don't deserve to be known as the best obstetrician in New York. I don't deserve any of it. I didn't deserve you."

He could see that tears were streaming quietly down her face. He put his arm around her, rather gingerly at first, but then he held her closer. The whole time he was recovering from the accident, he'd known nothing about the guilt Cassie was holding on to. How could he?

As he held Cassie, he wondered if he should have handled things differently. He'd told himself that his anger and hurt over the way she'd left had prevented him from trying to reach out to her, to talk things over, but now he wondered if his own pride had gotten in his way.

She's the one who left me, his anger had retorted. He'd spent years clinging to that anger, painting himself as the victim in their breakup because anger was easier to deal with than pain.

Except it was one thing to blame her for the breakup from afar. But now, holding her in his arms in the darkness while she cried, somehow it didn't seem to matter whose fault the breakup had been. All that mattered was that it was in the past. Here, in the present, he just didn't want Cassie to hurt anymore.

"I had no idea you felt this way," he said. "But for what it's worth, you are not the reason I stopped being a surgeon. And when I finally did stop, it was freeing. It opened up a whole new world for me that I never would have considered otherwise."

"Really?" she said, drying her eyes on the sleeve of her coat.

He hesitated. He'd meant to tell a small white lie designed to make Cassie feel better. After the accident, nothing had felt freeing at all. He'd been heartbroken when he realized that no matter how much work he put into physical therapy, his hands were never going to be steady enough to be a surgeon's hands again. But if he told Cassie about the accident now, it would only add to her guilt.

And so he told her a different part of the story, a part that was mostly true, even if it left out the accident and all the fallout from it.

"You know how you said your parents were overprotective? Well, mine were just as bad."

She laughed through the last traces of her tears. "I'm not sure that's possible."

"Okay, maybe mine weren't quite as bad as yours. I was never forbidden from riding my bicycle or going to the playground. But both my parents were trauma surgeons. They would come home from work and scare my sister and I with stories of patients who'd hurt themselves by doing things that were dangerous or careless. I think their intentions were good. They were trying to get us to think and be cautious. But they may have gone a little overboard."

"It sounds like my parents would approve of their methods. Maybe we should get them all in a room together so they can exchange child-rearing tips." She shuddered. "Actually, that's probably a terrible idea."

He couldn't help smiling. "Let's make sure they never meet. You'd think they would have become more relaxed after I became a surgeon, but instead, they got worse. They were always warning me to protect my hands at all costs. My hands were my career, they always said."

"No wonder you were always so obsessive about hand injuries."

"I know. I didn't have a rebellious phase like you did. Surgery was kind of my thrill. It was life-and-death enough for me."

"But then why would you ever stop?"

"I guess after we broke up… I realized I needed to find out who I was. All of my plans for my life have always been wrapped up in other people. My career was what it was because I came from a family of surgeons. I never had a chance to consider anything else." He swallowed.

"Anyway, I realized I was living a life based on other people's hopes and dreams for me," he continued. "And other people's worries, too. All those stories my parents told about patients who'd been horribly injured in accidents, all of my father's lectures about protecting my hands, because God forbid I should twist a finger and not be able to perform surgery for a few weeks… All of it made me way too cautious. It kept me from living my real life."

She nodded slowly. "You needed to get away from everyone else's expectations in order to find yourself."

He was surprised to find that her words seemed so exactly right, even though he hadn't shared the whole truth with her. Even though he'd never wanted to give up surgery, life *had* become more exciting after his surgical career was over. He'd never needed to seek out excitement before, because surgery had been exciting enough. But without having it in his life, he'd had to open himself up to new things, sometimes taking new risks. It had been freeing after all, he realized, to give up surgery and all the pressure of it, and find a whole new side of himself in El Salvador.

She shook her head slowly. "All this time, I was blaming myself for putting your career at risk."

"I hope you don't feel guilty anymore," he said, meaning it. As he spoke, he realized that he himself didn't feel angry anymore. It was strange, he thought, that after harboring that anger for so long, it could simply drift away. Yet as he saw Cassie's face, half lit in the shadows, he knew that he never wanted her to feel guilty when she thought about him. And he didn't want to be angry with her.

In fact, when he looked at her now, he felt an entirely different range of emotions. He wondered if she could ever possibly feel the same about him.

She blotted her eyes with her sleeve. He knew he should take his arm from around her shoulders, but he couldn't bring himself to do it.

"Just think," he said. "If I were still a surgeon, I wouldn't have been there today to watch the best ob-gyn in New York help a mom from a rural mountain village in El Salvador bring her twins into the world. I wouldn't have been here to help save three lives."

"Thanks," she said. "I'm glad that our ability to work together hasn't changed. And I think I'm actually glad that we're both here together."

"And I'm glad you're no longer horrified at the thought of working with me."

"Oh, it was never horrifying. Just very, very surprising. It's funny… I came here because I thought I needed to get away from my past, but I never thought I needed this."

"Needed what?" he asked.

"To see you again."

She looked up at him. They were enveloped in shadow, and yet the moon was bright enough that he could see her face. Her eyes were still wet with the last drops of tears, and they shimmered in the moonlight. On impulse, he reached a finger to her cheek and brushed a single tear away.

As he felt her skin beneath his fingertips, he realized that this was the first time he'd touched her since the day she'd arrived at the camp.

He rested his hand against her cheek for a moment longer than he meant to. Her hair brushed his fingertips and he was gripped by an irrational desire to smooth the stray locks around her forehead.

She held his gaze, and he realized their faces were only inches apart.

He knew he should move away, as much as he didn't want to.

He mustered every last bit of resolve he could find and started to pull away from her. But as he started to pull back and began to say, "I'm sorry," she leaned in and stopped his words with a light kiss. And then both his arms were around her and he was holding her even tighter, close to his chest. Their lips met again, not lightly at all this time, but a deep kiss in which his mouth pressed against hers, demanding entry, pouring five years of yearning into a single moment. Her mouth yielded readily to his, inviting him to revisit familiar ground and to explore new territory. There was a new taste of wild berries, but underneath it the familiar taste of sweetness and *her*. As her lips opened beneath his, he found he could no longer discern what was familiar and what was new, because he was lost in the heat and warmth of Cassie as he crushed his lips against hers.

As he leaned in closer, pressing her back against the tree trunk, she made a small squeak. He broke away from her instantly.

"It's just…the trunk was poking into my back," she said.

And just as abruptly as it had begun, the moment was over.

He felt thoroughly embarrassed. He couldn't believe he'd allowed himself to get so caught up in the moment that he'd kissed her.

He could still taste the faint sweetness of berries on his lips.

He was playing with fire, and he knew it. He'd already been hurt by Cassie once before. He'd assumed she wanted more of a life together than she did, and he'd paid the price for that assumption. He had no idea, now, what she wanted out of a relationship, but five years ago, he'd had the experience of being one of her thrills, easily disposed of. He didn't want to put himself through that again, no matter how much he wanted to continue holding her in his arms.

And so he disentangled himself from her and stood, brushing himself off. She stood, too.

"I'm sorry," he said, just as she blurted out the same words.

"It's okay," she said. "I know you want to keep things professional."

"Right," he said. "I think with all this talk of old

memories, and with it being such a long day for both of us, maybe we both got a little bit tired and…confused."

"Of course," she said. "It's been a very long day. I'm sure once we both get some sleep, we can start over again in the morning."

"Nothing would make me happier."

"Well, then. We're agreed. I think it's long past time I went back to my quarters and got some sleep. Hand me that last *pupusa* for the road?"

He gave her the flatbread and watched her retreat into the darkness.

He told himself that he was glad he'd stopped the kiss when he did. But he noticed that he had to work awfully hard to convince himself that *not* kissing her could ever be the right thing.

And yet, he'd been hurt by Cassie in the past, and he knew what that felt like. He wasn't interested in something that would turn out to be just another meaningless fling to her. He was tired of wasting time on heartbreak, and if he were to get involved with anyone again, he would want that person to be looking for a serious future. But he had no idea if that's what Cassie was looking for, and he'd been wrong once before. Getting involved with Cassie again would be moving backward, and if there was one thing Bryce had learned over the past five years, it was how to move forward, even if the circumstances weren't ideal. Even if he cared for someone who didn't feel the same way about him.

Cassie went back to her quarters, but she failed to get any sleep. Instead, she gazed up at the mosquito netting that protected her bed, replaying the moments that had led up to the kiss over and over in her mind.

She could still feel the warmth and pressure of where he'd held her on her body. It had felt every bit as good to be wrapped in those arms as she'd imagined.

She hadn't expected the kiss to happen. And yet when it did, it felt so right. Like coming home.

When Bryce explained that she wasn't at fault for his career change, she'd felt so relieved. She'd meant what she said: she *had* needed to see him again. All this time, she'd thought she needed to stay away from him as much as possible. But now, knowing that Bryce had found it freeing to give up surgery, knowing that he'd dealt with high expectations and overprotective-ness from his parents, just as she had, made all the difference.

With a pang, she wondered if they could have talked about all of this five years ago. But there was no use looking back. Five years ago, Bryce hadn't given up surgery, and she hadn't given up blaming herself for all his troubles. But now it seemed that Bryce had never blamed her at all…and apparently there was no reason for her to blame herself.

But if he'd forgiven her, why had he been so brusque after the kiss?

Just because he'd forgiven her didn't mean he wanted her. Maybe he'd merely been feeling nostalgic. He'd es-sentially said as much. *I think with all this talk of old memories, and with it being such a long day for both of us, maybe we both got a little bit tired and…confused.*

So he'd been *confused* when he kissed her. And yet during the kiss, he hadn't seemed confused at all. She shivered, remembering his arms pressing her to his chest, the masculine warmth of his lips on hers. Far from confused, he'd seemed to know exactly what he wanted, for a moment.

But just for a moment. As soon as they'd broken apart, he'd become businesslike. Still, for all their talk of staying professional, Bryce hadn't kissed her as though he wanted to stay professional. He'd kissed her as though he meant it. As though he wanted more.

It amazed her how their kiss had felt so natural, but seconds later they'd been so awkward with one another. She wished she knew how Bryce really felt. Did he think the kiss was a mistake or had he simply been caught up in the heat of the moment?

Or perhaps, just possibly, the kiss meant something... more.

She'd practically fled the scene afterward, afraid that she might say something terribly wrong and completely botch the moment. Or that she'd hear him say more about being—she rolled her eyes—*confused.*

She hadn't wanted to stop the kiss, but she wondered if Bryce had felt as though he had to. Five years ago, he thought she had left him without a care in the world. He'd never realized how guilty she felt. Or just how hard it had been for her to leave. He still didn't realize all that he had meant to her.

She wondered if there was any way to show him just how wrong he was about that.

So much had changed since they'd last known each other. She'd almost lost her adventurous side forever, and he'd almost gotten engaged. He'd done what people were supposed to do after breakups: try to move on. She just wished that he hadn't gone through it all believing that he was nothing more than a fling to her.

After everything that had passed between the two of them, the chances of she and Bryce becoming anything more than friends to one another were smaller than the tiny mosquitoes trapped in the netting above her bed.

Which was a problem. Because she refused to accept that that kiss under the balsa tree was the last kiss she would share with Bryce.

Somehow, she was going to show him that their relationship wasn't just a thrill to her, and never had been. She just needed to think of a way to do it.

CHAPTER SIX

OVER THE NEXT few days, the medical camp was busier than Cassie had ever seen it. A series of landslides in the mountains had displaced the residents of a number of rural villages, and more families were arriving at the camp every day.

The extra work meant that she had barely any time to herself, let alone to speak with Bryce. As desperate as she was to speak with him, she also felt nervous about what she would learn if she did.

After their talk under the balsa tree, it was nice to feel as though they were friends again. But as Cassie considered their kiss, she was faced with a growing realization that friendship wasn't going to be enough. She wanted more. Much more.

And there was no time to find out whether Bryce felt the same way.

She couldn't stop thinking about the kiss. Her sleep was terrible, to the point where one of the midwives commented on the dark circles under her eyes. Cassie had gotten flustered and said something about the long shifts getting to her. She hadn't wanted to admit that each night she fought for sleep but was kept awake by the memory of Bryce's lips on hers. And, of course, thinking about that led to all the other memories she had of times when Bryce's lips had been on hers. And that left her wanting more.

She tried to tell herself that there were countless reasons she should let all of the memories go, including the memory of their most recent kiss. She ticked the reasons off in her mind. They'd agreed to be professional. Bryce had probably only kissed her out of nostalgia. It would probably be incredibly hard for him to trust his heart with her again.

She wanted so badly to show him that he could. But she didn't know how. She didn't even know if Bryce felt anything more than friendship for her.

But as the days passed, she couldn't deny that she wanted more than friendship from him.

At first, she tried to cope with her feelings by ignoring them. She threw herself into her work, just as she had in New York. Back then, she'd been trying to forget that Bryce existed.

Now, she was trying to forget how his kiss had made her feel. As well as the jolt of electricity she felt when his arm brushed against hers in passing. And the flutter of butterfly wings in her stomach when she caught him glancing in her direction.

Her strategy was about as effective now as it had been back then. Which was to say, not very effective at all.

When she'd first arrived at the camp, it had been hard enough adjusting to seeing Bryce every day while she worked. Now she had to deal with seeing him every time she closed her eyes in her quarters at night.

Despite her fears about what Bryce might say, she

knew they needed a chance to speak alone. She had to know how he felt.

Especially because there were moments where she could swear she'd caught Bryce staring at her. His glances were discreet, but they were definitely there. And they were intense enough to make her wonder if he was thinking about their kiss under the balsa tree every bit as much as she was. And perhaps experiencing some rekindled desire of his own.

But she couldn't know unless they talked. And as each day at the camp became busier than the last, she wasn't sure when she'd be able to speak with him.

Then, inspiration struck. She'd been reviewing patient charts and listening to little Manny chatter away about a jaguar with cubs that he and Bryce had supposedly come upon in the forest when Bryce took him along on a medical mission. Manny's story reminded her that Bryce and some of the other doctors went on medical missions all the time. Usually they delivered vaccines, transported refugees away from dangerous mountain areas vulnerable to volcanic eruptions and rockfalls or helped with difficult births when women couldn't reach the camp. Cassie had been hoping for a chance to join such a mission herself as soon as she could, but she'd been absorbed in adjusting to life at the camp.

Now, she realized that joining a mission might be the perfect opportunity to get some alone time with Bryce. Enrique had told her that Bryce did most of the off-camp missions. He'd said that he often wanted to send another doctor along with Bryce for backup, but the camp lacked the manpower.

Cassie was more than eager to help. The camp was

so busy that it was the only way that she and Bryce would ever be able to get some time to themselves. Hopefully, they'd have a chance to talk about what was going on between the two of them.

Even if he only wanted to be friends, she needed to know. Because nothing was worse than not knowing if he would ever kiss her like that again.

As she'd predicted, Enrique was thrilled when she volunteered to be available for any upcoming off-camp missions.

"It'll be good to have more people who can go off-camp besides Bryce, especially because it's best to send people in pairs," he'd said. "I'll keep you in mind for the next mission that comes up."

But as the days passed, nothing out of the ordinary happened, other than one of the camp's rickety wooden shower stall doors falling in on her as she rinsed her hair.

She took her showers early in the morning, for both the hot water and the privacy. For the most part, she was impressed with how well the camp managed to provide protection from the elements in the middle of the wilderness. The cinder block buildings and canvas tents might not be pleasing to the eye, but they were safe and sterile. But the showers left much to be desired. They were relics of an earlier era, the only buildings in the camp made of wood rather than concrete. The showerheads were little more than hoses jury-rigged to the walls so that water cascaded from above. The wood doors almost hung off their posts, and extreme care had to be taken to make sure they didn't come apart upon opening or closing.

I just wanted some excitement, she thought, grumpily making her way from the shower stall back to her quarters. *I didn't think that would involve taking my own life in my hands every time I shower.*

She was still muttering under her breath in frustration a few minutes later, after she'd thrown on a khaki field shirt and made her way to the mess hall for her morning coffee. Enrique and Bryce were already there, and Cassie forgot her frustration as she heard their conversation.

"It shouldn't take more than a couple of days," she heard Enrique saying. "I don't want to take you away from your patients, but the farthest town is only a day's drive from camp."

As she approached, both men turned toward her, and Enrique said, "Ah, Cassie! Just the person I'd hoped to see!"

"Why's that?" said Cassie and Bryce at once, and Cassie noticed that Bryce's tone had a suspicious edge.

"I need two doctors to deliver a load of vaccines to Juayua and to a couple of other towns outside the camp."

"Why-*what*-a?" she asked.

"Why-*yoo*-wah," he enunciated. "Juayua. It's a lovely town."

"Now wait a minute," said Bryce. "I thought that you and I were going to go."

Enrique bit his lip with apprehension. "That's why I was hoping to see you, Cassie. Originally, the plan was for Bryce and me to make the trip together. But I have the chance to start some furlough a little bit earlier than planned if I leave tomorrow. I know it's short notice, but if you go, I can spend a couple of extra days with my wife in San Salvador."

"Of course!" she said at once. "I've wanted to see more of the countryside, and I'm happy to help you out."

Bryce's frown deepened. "Cassie's only been here for a few weeks. She's not ready for a field mission."

Cassie opened her mouth to protest, but Enrique was already rolling his eyes at Bryce. "Don't listen to him," he said to Cassie. "You've been here for over a month—just as long as Bryce, when he started accompanying me on missions. Of course, I'd never ask you to go if you were uncomfortable."

"Not at all," she said, ignoring Bryce's scowl.

"Excellent. It's more than a matter of simply dropping off the meds at each village. You'll need to do brief demonstrations of how and when to administer each one, and spend some time explaining what the vaccines will do. Some of them are antimalarial, so you'll need to make it especially clear which ones are safe for pregnant mothers and which are not."

"Count me in," she said.

"Shouldn't Cassie have at least a few months to settle in before you start sending her tearing off through the countryside?"

"Oh, come on," said Enrique. "A trip to Juayua isn't exactly the same as trip through gang territory up in the mountains. In fact, it'd be a great way to introduce her to the wider world of El Salvador." He turned toward Cassie. "If you go, you're in for a treat. The road you'd be traveling is one of our most famous—it's called the Ruta de Las Flores, because of all the wildflowers that grow like a carpet on either side of the highway. It's definitely one of the most beautiful parts of the country. There are tons of places to stop for the best coffee you've ever had along the way, as well as some lovely murals to take in at each town. And there are some beautiful hiking areas and waterfalls around Juayua. The trip will take at least two days, and your first furlough won't be coming up for a while, so you should take advantage of it."

"Cassie should stay in the camp, where it's safe," Bryce said.

Cassie bristled. Bryce's caution brought out the familiar urge to rebel. She knew that El Salvador had its dangers, but she hardly blinked at the idea of leaving the safe familiarity of the camp. She had a feeling that she knew what was really bothering Bryce. They hadn't been alone together since their kiss, and now they were about to go on an overnight mission—that she'd had a minor hand in orchestrating. But he didn't need to know that.

"Bryce," she said calmly. "Might I have a word with you, for a second?"

She pulled him aside from Enrique. "Look, just be honest with me. Should we talk about why you don't want me going on this mission with you?"

"I already explained. You're still adjusting to life here."

"Would you be putting up this much of a fight if any of our other coworkers wanted to go with you?"

"No," he admitted. "But no one else here knows you like I do. And I was also trying to give you a way out, in case you didn't want to go with me, after what happened a few nights ago."

She was relieved that his reluctance seemed to stem from his desire to make sure she felt comfortable. She wondered if his avoidance of her lately had been because he thought she was the one who didn't want to talk. At least it wasn't that he didn't want her company on the mission.

"I'm excited to go," she said. "I really am. Look, we both agreed to be professional, and the two of us going on missions together is going to have to be part of that."

He nodded, conceding her point. They turned back to Enrique.

"All right," Bryce said. "We'll head out first thing tomorrow."

"Great!" said Enrique. "That means I can leave tomorrow to meet my wife in San Salvador. She'll be thrilled that I have an extra day of furlough. I can't tell you how much I appreciate this, Cassie." He clapped a frowning Bryce on the shoulder. "And I'm going to need the milk truck, so you'll be able to take that blasted motorcycle of yours instead. That should cheer you up."

Bryce still looked somewhat reluctant. "Be ready at dawn tomorrow," he said to Cassie. "We'll need to be on the road before 6:00 a.m."

Bryce kicked the large boulder that marked the entrance to Enrique's administrative tent. Immediately, his foot began to throb. The boulder, for its part, remained unaffected.

He wasn't frustrated because he didn't want Cassie to come with him to Juayua. He was frustrated because he wasn't sure he'd be able to handle an overnight trip with Cassie.

He'd already shown that he couldn't trust himself to control his feelings when he'd kissed Cassie several days ago. How the hell was he going to get through an overnight trip alone with her?

His attraction to her was just an attraction, and nothing more.

But despite his intentions, he kept thinking about that kiss. How good it had felt, and if there might be some way to make it happen again. Since he couldn't keep his mind off those thoughts, trying to keep his distance from Cassie was the least he could do.

He decided that this was all Enrique's fault. Why had he specifically asked Cassie to take his place on the mission?

"What the hell was that all about?" he asked his boss, who looked back at him with wide-eyed innocence.

"I'm not sure what you mean."

"That whole thing back there, pressuring Cassie into venturing outside camp before she's ready!"

"Pressuring her? If you must know, she asked to be put on a few off-camp missions. I thought she was ready, and I knew she was interested, so I wanted to ask her to take my place."

This was news. He hadn't realized that Cassie had volunteered for any missions. For a moment, he wondered if she'd volunteered because she knew that he did most of the off-camp missions, and she wanted a chance to be alone with him. But then he remembered who he was thinking about. Cassie had always had a thirst for adventure. He was part of the adventure this time.

"I thought she seemed pretty eager to go," Enrique continued. "If anything, you were pressuring her to stay at the camp. Do you honestly think she'll be in danger on the Ruta de Las Flores? Especially with you there? She'll be fine. You'll both be fine. Personally, I thought that sending Cassie out on a mission in one of the more serene parts of the country would be a good way to get her feet wet."

"Did you? Because it sounded an awful lot more like you were setting us up on a date."

Enrique raised his eyebrows. "I was merely trying to describe the situation accurately."

Bryce snorted. "Really. *Tons of coffee places to stop at?* A *carpet* of wildflowers?"

Enrique shrugged. "I can't help that the road happens to be very beautiful."

"And what's this about you needing the milk truck all of a sudden?"

"I need it to run a few errands on my way to San Salvador. I have to say, I'm surprised by your reaction. I did think you'd be thrilled. I thought you'd be here in my tent saying, *Thank you, boss, for sending me on an easy mission through one of the loveliest parts of the country.* And yet somehow it seems to me that you aren't pleased." He paused thoughtfully. "It seems to me that it's not exactly the mission but the company that concerns you. I get the impression that there's more to your relationship with Cassie than you've let on?"

"We used to date."

"I knew it! Dr. Andover is a delightful, intelligent, beautiful woman—so of *course* you dated. Did you screw it up? Do I need to move you two to separate schedules? Wait, you're not going to transfer, are you? You can't leave, Bryce. We need you here."

"No, no." Bryce waved his hands. "We don't hate each other at all. We're fine. Nobody's transferring.

And I didn't screw it up—she left me, if you must know, although I'd rather not get into all of it. It was a long time ago, and it's…complicated."

"With you, my friend, it always is."

"I'm just saying that while it's been fine working with Cassie…I'm not sure about going on a trip together."

"Because?"

Bryce hesitated, and Enrique said, "Oh, I get it. You still have feelings for her."

"Absolutely not. That's in the past, and even if it were true, it wouldn't matter, because she just wants friendship."

"Uh-huh. So does your *friend* know that you still have feelings for her?"

"Enrique. All of that was over a long time ago."

"Exactly! You've both had a long time to change. Maybe her feelings toward you have changed, too. She wanted to go on this trip with you, didn't she?"

"That doesn't mean anything. Cassie's always loved a thrill. She's probably just bored with the camp and wants a little excitement."

"And this is the perfect time for you to offer her exactly that!"

"That was the problem before. She liked to get swept up in the thrill. And that's all I was to her—a thrill. We dated back in my surgery days…back when I was the up-and-coming superstar who was always asked to scrub in on the complex cases. She and I weren't even supposed to date, because I was a resident and she was a med student. But after it was all over, I realized that that was the appeal for her. It wasn't me she liked. It was that she was secretly dating the superstar surgeon. That's who she was attracted to."

"Hmm. Maybe. But have you ever thought that it might have been *you* who was attracted to the superstar surgeon?"

"Excuse me?"

"Being a surgeon fit all your dreams, and your family's dreams. And you were good at it. You got a lot of recognition for a talent that you had. You got to be a superstar. But did you ever spend time just being plain old Bryce?"

Bryce thought for a moment. "Not until after the accident. Even then, everyone seemed more interested in the memory of who I used to be, rather than who I'd become. I don't think I felt like myself again until I came here."

"Exactly. Most people start out as plain old versions of themselves, and have to work to become a star. You started out a star, and now you have to be okay with being just the regular you. Fortunately for everyone here, the regular you is the person this camp needs. There are no rock star surgeons here. Just good docs who do good work. And who are willing to tame jaguars once in a while."

Bryce chuckled. "Manny again. That kid."

"He says you have a pet jaguar in a cave in the forest."

"Hmm, I'll bet that's his excuse for sneaking extra snack rations—that he needs to go and feed it."

Enrique grew thoughtful. "So you and Cassie dated back when you were a surgeon. But when she first arrived here at the camp, she asked me why you'd changed your specialty to obstetrics. She doesn't know about the accident, does she? She doesn't know that you quit surgery because of the tremor in your hands."

Bryce rubbed the back of his neck. "The accident happened so soon after the breakup. I wasn't ready to talk to her. And most of all—" he swallowed, trying to keep his voice steady "—I didn't want her pity."

"Okay, but why not just tell her about it now?"

Bryce sighed. "Growing up in a family full of surgeons I used to be completely overcautious about my hands, with myself. She was always so…fearless. And now she's hearing about me going on all the missions here, and I can tell she sees me differently. I want her to think I've actually changed. Not that I was just some… victim of circumstance. I want her to think that I really have become braver."

"But haven't you? Last I checked, you do like motorcycles, and probably roller coasters, too. It seems to me that the person she believes you are is…you."

"Yes…but I like that she sees me as someone who changed because he…I don't know, grew as a person, I guess. Not someone who was a victim of an unfortunate accident and had to change his life because it was the only way to move forward."

Enrique let out a low whistle as he shook his head. "Yeah, you *definitely* don't have feelings for her. None at all."

"Look, even if I did have feelings, they would just make things more complicated. So it's best to just leave things alone."

"Great idea. Let me know how that goes. Meantime, I'm going to go video chat with my wife. For some reason, hearing all this from you has made me especially appreciative to have the love of a good woman."

* * *

The next morning, Cassie woke just before dawn, flushed with excitement at the prospect of seeing more of El Salvador. She dressed hastily, remembering Bryce's request that they leave as early as possible. As she threw a spare set of clothes and other necessities into a small backpack, she realized that she was about to spend two days with someone who she'd once thought was out of her life forever. Just six weeks ago, if someone had told her she'd be working with Bryce Hamlin again, she wouldn't have believed it.

It was amazing how dramatically things could change in such a short amount of time. She'd never thought she would see Bryce again, let alone become friends with him. Yet here they were, going on a medical mission together.

Maybe, she thought, this could be her chance to prove that she had valued their relationship. That he'd meant more to her back then than he realized. And now…she wasn't sure if there was any possibility of things going beyond friendship. But if there was any hope of Bryce kissing her again the way he had the other night, he'd need to know that she had never meant to hurt him.

She stepped out of her quarters to see Bryce waiting just outside, strapping a cargo box to the back of his motorcycle. Little Manny was helping, running back and forth for various items for Bryce to add to his storage compartment.

"So we're taking the bike?" she said, barely able to hide the excitement in her voice. Her heart lifted at the idea of taking to the open road.

"Don't worry," he said, mistaking the excitement

in her voice for apprehension. "I've given it a thorough tune-up since our last excursion. It's not going to break down this time. And the road we'll be on is well-traveled, so we're unlikely to hit any rocks or roots like we did before."

Far from worried, she was thrilled. She'd been dying for a chance to get back on that motorcycle since her first day in El Salvador.

"Can't I come?" Manny begged. "I could fit right on top of the cargo box. Please, please, please?"

"Not this time," said Bryce. "It's too far away, and even the safer parts of El Salvador aren't exactly safe. It's certainly too dangerous for a kid."

Manny looked crestfallen. Cassie thought she knew how the boy felt; after all, she'd spent most of her childhood surrounded by adults who told her that everything she wanted to do was too dangerous.

"It's also too much time to spend away from your family," she told the boy. "You have a baby sister to look after. Where would she be without her big brother? You stay here and protect Rosibel, keep her safe until we get back."

Manny gave a begrudging nod, indicating that for the sake of his sister's welfare, he was willing to forego an adventure with Bryce.

Bryce switched on the ignition, and as Cassie eased her body onto the bike behind him, she couldn't help feel her heart begin to soar. She put her arms around Bryce's waist and nodded when he asked if she was ready.

Once again, he held out his leather jacket to her. She did a small internal fist pump of excitement as she put it on. She hadn't thought she'd get to wear the jacket again. But, of course, she didn't have one of her own, and Bryce wouldn't want her to go unprotected.

She wrapped her arms around his torso, noticing once again how firm his body had become.

You're on a medical mission, remember? she thought. *Try to maintain some self-control.*

She nuzzled her nose into the collar to smell the warm spicy notes of Bryce's jacket. Self-control wasn't going to be easy. But she'd never backed away from a challenge. Bryce had said so the other night. Just a few moments before he'd kissed her.

She held on tight as the bike took off with a thundering roar.

CHAPTER SEVEN

IT FELT AMAZING to be back on a motorcycle again.

Cassie's trip with Bryce several weeks ago, when she'd first arrived in El Salvador, had given her just a small taste of how much she'd missed the freedom of the road. More than that, she'd missed the sense of glorious possibility that accompanied the sensation of speeding along stretches of wide-open highway. The feeling of adventure was intoxicating.

The road was every bit as beautiful as it was rumored to be. They were driving along the Ruta de las Flores—the Road of Flowers—and Cassie could see that it was aptly named. The roadside was thick with purple, pink and yellow wildflowers. In the distance, a volcanic mountain range towered over the horizon. Cassie knew that many of El Salvador's volcanoes were active, but the peaks of the range were unexpectedly lush and green, contrasting nicely with the blue of a cloudless sky. As the miles of road dropped away behind them, Cassie felt the sensation of flying, as though she were a bird skimming the road with its wings.

She chalked up most of her excitement to the thrill of being back on a motorcycle.

But as amazing as it was to be back on a motorcycle, it was even more amazing to be next to Bryce again.

His jacket enveloped her in his scent, just as it had on their earlier ride. She knew he'd only lent it to her because it was in his nature to be protective. But sitting behind him, with her arms wrapped around his torso and the warmth of his body close to hers, it was hard not to get swept up in the emotions that washed over her.

She felt tears forming at the corners of her eyes that had nothing to do with the wind. It had been far too long since she'd had such a sensation of pure joy, she thought. Overworked and burned-out, she hadn't realized how long it had been since she'd simply let herself enjoy the moment. Whatever this feeling was, she didn't want to let go of it ever again. She let out a whoop, unable to stop herself, and not caring whether Bryce heard. But he must have, because at her cry, he went even faster, and she let out another shout of delight. This, she thought, was how life was meant to be.

They rode steadily for most of the morning. The road wound through coffee plantations and towns with brightly colored houses, where they stopped every so often for breaks. The plan, Bryce explained, was to stop at three different towns to give vaccines and educational presentations to the residents, and then spend the night in Juayua before returning the next day.

Their first stop was Apaneca, where Cassie was charmed by the cobbled streets and adobe houses. After they'd delivered a batch of vaccines, they stopped for coffee at a small roadside shop. One wall of the shop had been painted with an elaborate mural of flowers and butterflies, and Cassie and Bryce sat outside, sipping their coffee and discussing their plan of attack for the next two towns. A lifelong caffeine addict, Cassie considered herself something of a connoisseur when it came to coffee. El Salvadoran blends were fuller and bolder than she was used to, with a somewhat floral aroma. She inhaled deeply, savoring the scent.

Bryce was drinking coffee, too, but he seemed to be drinking it rather hastily, and Cassie noticed that he kept looking at his watch.

"Slow down!" she protested as he finished his remaining coffee in one big gulp. "It's a crime to drink coffee this good so fast!"

"You think this coffee is good? Well, just wait until we get to Juayua. The coffee there puts this stuff to shame."

"Nonsense. This is one of the best cups of coffee I've ever had. Why are you really hurrying?"

"Well. Here's the thing. Every weekend there's a food festival in Juayua, called the Feria Gastronomica."

"Hmm, a food festival. Why do I suddenly have the feeling that we're not just on this trip to deliver vaccines?"

Bryce checked his watch again. "If we make it quick, we can wrap things up in Salcoatitán in about an hour, and then hit Juayua by early afternoon. Just in time to have some of the best street food El Salvador has to offer."

She cocked an eyebrow at him. "You just might be speaking the language of my heart, Bryce Hamlin. What kind of food are we talking about?"

"Everything under the sun, and trust me, it's all delicious."

"I don't know, Bryce. You are asking me to rush

through a pretty damn good cup of coffee just on faith alone."

"I promise it's worth it. I make a trip to drop off medical supplies to Juayua every few months, and the food festival's the main reason I always volunteer to make the run."

She gasped in mock indignation. "Wait a minute. This festival's the *main* reason? What about your passion for providing medical care? What about building ties among the communities we serve?"

"Those are all nice perks, but the real reason I got into this doctoring business was so I could indulge in local cuisine."

Cassie drank the rest of her own coffee in a final gulp. "Then it sounds like we'd better get a move on."

His eyes danced. "There's the Cassie I remember. Always up for new things."

She smiled at his enthusiasm. Where had this care-free version of Bryce been when they were dating? Five years ago, if they'd gone on a trip like this together, she'd have expected him to maintain their schedule with meticulous care. And he'd have driven something much more practical than a motorcycle. But now, he seemed relaxed. He even seemed as though he were having fun.

She'd never known he could be like this. But then, clearly, she hadn't known him as well as she'd thought.

A short time later, they arrived at the town of Sal-coatitán, where they demonstrated how to administer the vaccines to town officials in a beautiful nineteenth-century church. Before getting back onto the road, they stretched their legs under a giant tree that loomed over the town square.

"Couldn't we just stay here for the rest of the day and do Juayua tomorrow?" she asked, stretching her arms overhead. The afternoon sunlight was luxurious, and she was beginning to feel sleepy.

"Nope," he said firmly. "The food festival's only on weekends, so we have to keep to a tight schedule. It'll be worth it, I promise."

She gave him a skeptical look.

"All right, here's something I know you won't be able to resist. There's a huge waterfall that's about a twenty-minute hike outside Juayua."

A waterfall? Her eyes gleamed. She'd been aching to see a waterfall since the day she arrived.

"Let's get a move on," she said, snapping her helmet back on. "We don't want to stand around here and lose the rest of the day."

It was midafternoon when they finally arrived in Juayua. They were greeted enthusiastically by a woman with a kind face and graying hair. Bryce introduced the woman as Gina Lopez, one of the town's most senior midwives and their medical liaison to the local health community.

"Mrs. Lopez is one of the best midwives in the country," said Bryce. "We'd get nowhere in Juayua without her."

"Nonsense," said Mrs. Lopez, giving Bryce a fond smile. "I've birthed most of the babies in this town. But every so often there's something that's more than what a midwife can handle. There are mothers and children who wouldn't be here today if there weren't a Medicine International outpost within driving distance."

They discussed the vaccines with Mrs. Lopez, and she invited them to stay for dinner. "Not this time," said Bryce. "It's Cassie's first time in Juayua, and she was really hoping to go to the Feria Gastronomica."

Cassie rolled her eyes. "*I* was really hoping to go?" she muttered to Bryce as Mrs. Lopez led them back outside.

"You haven't lived until you've had the prawn sticks," he muttered back.

Outside the house, Mrs. Lopez's teenage son and two of his friends were discussing Bryce's motorcycle with frank admiration.

"Is there any chance you'd let us try it, Dr. Bryce?" Fernando Lopez wheedled. "We'll be careful, I promise. Just around town a few times."

"Not today, Nando," Bryce said. "But tell you what, tomorrow there might be time for me to take you on a ride around town for a bit."

Fernando scowled, and Cassie had a feeling that the boy had been entertaining images of himself impressing girls while driving the motorcycle all by himself. "It takes a while to learn to ride a motorcycle," she said, hoping to help Fernando understand that he most likely would not have been able to race off down the road even if Bryce had said yes. "But sitting on one while someone else drives can help you learn."

"Enough!" Mrs. Lopez scolded the boys. "Stop bothering the doctors this instant." To Bryce, she said, "You can leave your bike here. No harm will come to it. I'll keep a close eye on it and put these boys to work. They've got better things to do than ogle a motorcycle." She was still shooing the boys away from it as Cassie and Bryce ambled toward town.

The Feria Gastronomica was everything Bryce had

promised. The town center was bustling with people milling about food stalls and eating at colorful tables and chairs. Bryce couldn't seem to resist plying her with food, and she couldn't seem to resist eating of it.

"Start with this," he said, handing her an *elote loco*—corn on the cob on a stick, covered with cheese and a tangy sauce. "That way you can still walk around while you're eating and decide what you want to snack on next."

There truly did seem to be every sort of food under the sun available. The smell of grilled meat was irresistible, and she and Bryce munched on shrimp sticks while they chose their next course. They finally sat down at one of the brightly colored tables with a huge plate of beef and chicken alongside rice, salad and tortillas.

Cassie loaded meat and vegetables onto a tortilla and pinched it into a taco. She took a bite and sighed. "Okay, you were right. It was worth rushing to get here so we could do this. This is some of the best food I've had since I got here."

"Surely not better than the food at the camp mess hall!"

She winced. "Don't tell anybody back at the camp, but after trying the *pupusas* here, I'm not sure I can face the ones back at the mess hall. Does saying that make me a terrible person? Our cooks work so hard for us."

"Don't worry," he said. "It'll never get back to camp. I won't tell a soul."

She smiled and gazed into his eyes. "I knew I could

trust you." They held each other's gaze for a moment. Cassie had forgotten how warm his eyes could be.

She cleared her throat. "Now what about this waterfall?" she said.

The waterfall was only a short hike from town. The path was visible, but only just; thick overgrown foliage threatened to eliminate it.

"It's a good thing we're here in the late afternoon," said Bryce. "Enough tourists have come through here today that the path is fairly clear. If we'd come earlier, I probably would have had to borrow a machete from Mrs. Lopez to clear our way."

A machete. She pictured Bryce swinging a machete to clear away the tall grass. There was still a lot about El Salvador that she was getting used to.

Pushing the jungle foliage back from the path was hot exhausting work. Bryce traveled in front of Cassie so that he could bear the brunt of the labor. Within moments, both of their shirts were soaked with sweat. Cassie couldn't help but notice the way the muscles tightened under Bryce's white T-shirt as he pushed back the grass and ferns. Then, as if her resolve hadn't been challenged enough for one day, Bryce removed his T-shirt and tied it around his forehead to keep the sweat out of his eyes.

Lord have mercy, Cassie thought. Bryce was perfectly tanned underneath his shirt. Beads of sweat formed along his chest and back, and his jeans hung low on his hips.

The image of a half-naked Bryce leading her through the jungle was going to be with her for a long time. "How far away is it now?" she asked, wondering just how long she was going to be tortured.

"About ten minutes," he replied.

You can handle anything for just ten minutes, she thought.

Finally, they arrived, hot and exhausted.

"Here it is," said Bryce. "Los Chorros de la Calera."

The waterfall consisted of several crystal streams; some strong and thundering, others quiet and fast. Each stream cascaded down a rock face covered with moss and vines, and they all fed into the same pool at the bottom. The sun dappled the surface of the water, and all around her was the fresh smell of the forest: wood and vegetation. It reminded her of the visits she'd made to greenhouses and conservatories in New York, but there, she'd always been aware of the traffic and the throngs of people just outside. Now, she was completely surrounded by greenery, and the mist rising from the waterfall was the only source of coolness in the heat.

"It's beautiful," she breathed, and for a moment she and Bryce simply stood together in the silence. Then she turned toward him, and there it was again—that feeling of old emotions being stirred.

It's just nostalgia, she thought. But as the sounds of the waterfall rushed in her ears, she knew her feelings were about more than just the past. They were about this moment with Bryce, too.

She turned toward him, looking into the warmth of his brown eyes.

And then, in spite of herself, she started to giggle.

"What's amusing you now?" he murmured.

"It's just that it's so beautiful here…with the light reflecting off the pool and the forest surrounding us…"

"And natural beauty is…funny, somehow?"

"No, natural beauty is breathtaking. What's funny

is that amid all of it, you've got a T-shirt tied around your head. With the jungle backdrop, you look like a kid playing Rambo."

"Oh, so you're laughing at *me*. Why don't you take a picture of my amusing headgear so you can show everyone back at the camp?"

"I would, but I left my phone back at Mrs. Lopez's."

"Excellent. Then you won't mind if I do this." He pushed her straight into the pool beneath the falls.

"Bryce!" she shrieked, laughing as her head broke the surface. "That was *completely* uncalled for!" Also shocking and completely unexpected. She'd never been pushed into a body of water in her life. Overprotected and sheltered as she was, no child or adult would ever have dared to do something as unsafe as shove her into a pool. She hadn't even been allowed to swim until she went to college. She remembered going to pool parties on rare occasions as a child, watching sadly from a patio as other children splashed and screamed, pushing each other into the water with reckless abandon.

And now Bryce had just shoved her in. As though she weren't breakable. As though she were just an ordinary person.

"I disagree," he called from the shore. "You looked hot. I helped you cool down. You're welcome."

"We just ate!" she said, with mock annoyance. "What if I got a cramp?"

"Then I guess I'd have to come in after you." And with that, he dove into the pool himself.

He broke the surface beside her. They held on to each other for a moment, gasping for air as they found one another in the water. Her head spun, and she wasn't sure whether it was with excitement or confusion.

Maybe it was a mix of both. He'd become so much more carefree, and she loved it.

Without realizing it, she tilted her face toward his and then suddenly, they were kissing.

It was everything she remembered; it was *better* than she remembered. It was even better than the moment under the balsa tree, because this time his arms were wrapped around her and she could feel the full length of his body against hers. And this time, there was no mistaking the kiss for an accident. They hadn't just gotten caught up in the moment. He was kissing her as though he meant to kiss her. She knew it, and she was letting him know in every way she could that she meant to kiss him right back. His lips were heat and salt against hers; his arms wrapped about her and pulled her close with a firmness that felt more right than anything she'd experienced in years.

And then they heard voices coming from the path ahead. They pulled apart just as a group of tourists emerged from the foliage.

Cassie's breath was fast and ragged. She fought for control as she tried to compose herself. "Well. That was certainly something," she said, trying and failing to keep the emotion out of her voice.

"Here, let me help you out of the water."

Was his voice quavering, too? His breath seemed uneven, but that might just be the exertion of swimming to the side of the pool and helping her climb up onto the grass. "We should get back to Mrs. Lopez's," he said. "She's probably getting worried about us."

He was still holding her hand, even though she was already back on dry land. She gave no indication that he needed to let go.

Their eyes met. She had absolutely no idea what to say.

Fortunately, he did.

"I know we've been talking a lot about moving forward," he said. "And if you don't want that to happen again, I completely understand. I won't put you in that position ever again. But I had to take the chance. I needed to make damn sure I left that waterfall without any regrets."

She stepped close to him. "I'm glad," she said.

"That I kissed you?"

"That you took the risk."

Bryce's lips burned as they hacked their way through the foliage back to Mrs. Lopez's house.

He'd known the moment he was going to kiss her again. It had been the moment she'd emerged from the water, laughing. He'd pushed her in completely on impulse, unable to resist her playfulness. And when he'd seen her head break the water, eyes sparkling and face filled with excitement, he'd known that nothing was going to stop him from kissing her again.

And she'd wanted the kiss every bit as much as he did.

But they still had to work together. How would things go once they got back to camp, resumed their daily lives? A kiss by a waterfall made for a pleasant moment, but ultimately, he and Cassie might not be looking for the same things. He'd been down that road with her before, and he didn't want to make the same mistake again. He wanted someone who was serious.

The trouble was, he also wanted someone who kissed him the way Cassie had kissed him just a moment ago. Completely, wholeheartedly, without holding back.

No, he didn't want *someone* who kissed him that way. He wanted it to be Cassie.

He'd meant what he had said. He didn't regret that kiss, not for an instant. But where did it leave the two of them now?

I'm glad that you took the risk, she'd said. But that didn't tell him anything about how she wanted to proceed.

And no matter how they did proceed, there was no way that things could return to the way they had been going at the medical outpost.

Any semblance they'd had of maintaining a professional relationship was slipping away, and fast. He didn't think he could return to being just colleagues with her. And he didn't think that she wanted to take a step back, either.

Her words reverberated in his head again. *I'm glad that you took the risk.* So was he. But the kiss had been a single moment, outside of their normal lives at the camp. Once they returned to their usual daily routines and went back to the daily routine of being colleagues, would she still be interested in a relationship? The familiar worry that she only wanted a fling cropped up.

A kiss was one thing. But neither of them had really talked about what they wanted.

What Bryce wanted was time. Time to see things unfold, see how they felt about one another. Without putting any pressure on either of them, or on the relationship.

But they had to return to camp soon. He wished there were some way that they could delay returning, to give themselves more time to see what happened between the two of them, without forcing anything. And to have the chance to find out what she wanted. How she felt. If she wanted a fling, or if she wanted him.

Or maybe it would be best to simply return to the camp as soon as possible. Maybe they should just see about going back tonight. They were tired, but the moon would be full and bright. He didn't want to get back to the camp anytime soon, but at least, once they did, he'd have a better idea of where they stood.

But when they returned to Mrs. Lopez's, they learned that it would be impossible to return that night.

Tragedy had struck. They were met by a scowling Mrs. Lopez, three shamefaced teenage boys and a heap of mangled metal that was barely recognizable as a motorcycle.

Apparently, all three boys had been riding the bike at once and had lost control while heading toward a ravine. No one had been hurt, but the motorcycle was unsalvageable. The boys had collected the rubble from the ravine and placed it on a blanket in the front lawn. Bryce sifted through the mess of pulverized motorcycle parts, trying to find some way to wrap his mind around what had happened.

Cassie put a hand on his shoulder. "It's okay to be upset."

"I'm not upset."

"No—maybe devastated would be a more apt description. Come on, Bryce. It's obvious how you feel. That bike was your pride and joy."

"It's just a little dented," he said through gritted teeth.

"In twenty places. And the front wheel's bent. And

it's been smashed into multiple pieces." She nudged the debris with her foot. "I guess you could salvage the engine and try to build a new motorcycle around it, but at that point…wouldn't it be less expensive to just buy a new bike?"

He felt his stomach roil at her suggestion, even though he knew that what she said was logical. The bike was beyond repair. But he couldn't fathom leaving it behind. Over the past few years, the bike had become a part of him. It had been with him on every mission outside the camp. Riding the bike around the countryside had been his main source of freedom and joy outside of work. He felt as though he were leaving a fellow fallen soldier behind in the field.

"I can't leave it," he said. "You can take a bus back to camp if you like, but I'm staying with the bike." He knew he sounded absurd, but he didn't care.

She knelt beside him. "I know it was more than just a bike to you. I know what it represents. You bought it with the money from the engagement ring you sold. I'm sure that whomever that ring was for, she was someone special. But if she was someone who couldn't see everything you are, all that you have to offer, then she didn't deserve you. And now that it's over, you've got to let it go…just like you've got to let your motorcycle go."

The words came out before he could stop them. "I bought the engagement ring for you." He hadn't ever meant to say it. The words just slipped out. And there was no unsaying them now. He held his breath, waiting for her reaction.

Her eyes widened. Her mouth was set, her jaw determined. He'd seen that look on her face before. It showed up when someone tried to tell her that a patient couldn't be saved or that her treatment plan wouldn't work.

"We've got to save this bike," she said. "We've got to get it to a shop right now."

He shook his head. "No. Cassie, you were right the first time. The bike is done for. The only thing I can do is let it go."

"No, *you* were right. Like you said, it's just got a few dents here and there. Come on, if we gather the corners of the blanket together, I think we can get all the pieces to a shop." She began gathering broken motorcycle parts into her arms.

"Cassie." He took her hands to stop her from picking up more pieces. Her hands were so delicate and soft. She'd have made a great surgeon, if she'd wanted to be one. "There's no saving this bike. It's been with me for years, and now it's time to say goodbye. If there's one thing I've learned, it's that we can't keep living in the past. Let's just focus on what comes next."

With much reluctance, she dropped the armful of parts she'd been holding.

Of all the reactions she could have had to learning that the engagement ring he'd bought had been for her, this was one he'd never imagined. And yet it felt right, somehow. As sad as he was to lose the bike, Cassie's strong reaction had a calming effect on him. She seemed almost as devastated as he was. He wondered if she might be able to understand just how much the bike meant to him.

"I'll arrange for a scrap truck to pick it up tomorrow," he said to Mrs. Lopez.

"I'm so sorry," she said again. "I can't believe those

boys would disobey me. I told them they'll be grounded for the rest of their lives."

"I shouldn't have left the keys here," Bryce said. "I should have realized it would be too tempting. The important thing is that no one was hurt."

"How will we get back to camp?" Cassie asked.

"Let's head to the hotel and start fresh in the morning," said Bryce. "We'll probably have to take a chicken bus to get back."

"That doesn't sound quite as glamorous as the way we got here," said Cassie.

He managed a small chuckle. "No, a chicken bus is exactly what it sounds like." They began to walk toward the hotel when Bryce thought of something. "Wait!"

He ran back toward the heap of rubble on the blanket and began sifting through it.

"What are you looking for?" asked Cassie.

"This." He picked up the bike's ignition switch and removed the ring that held the copper casing together. "I want to keep something to remember it by." He pocketed the ignition switch ring and stood up. "I'm ready. Let's get to our hotel."

After the harsh conditions of the medical camp, the luxury of the hotel was a little overwhelming for Cassie. They were staying at a cozy bed-and-breakfast in Juayua, away from the bustle of the central streets. The building was secluded among a grove of palm trees, with a perfectly manicured lawn that was striking after so much untamed jungle foliage. Rocking chairs beckoned invitingly from the front porch, and water bubbled merrily from concrete fountains with statues covered in soft moss.

Cassie was still trying to absorb what she'd learned at the scene of the motorcycle crash. *That engagement ring was for me. He bought the ring for me, which means he was going to propose. And then I broke up with him.*

Everything about the past five years could have been different. She'd never known he'd bought a ring. Never even known he'd been thinking about marriage. If he'd asked her, back then, would she have said yes? She couldn't say, but she saw how a future with him could have been possible. And she saw, for the first time, just how much she'd given up. She'd known, at the time, that she was giving up the most important relationship she'd ever had. But she hadn't really thought about the future she was giving up, as well.

An alternative life flashed through her mind. She and Bryce could have been married by now. Maybe even started a family together. She pushed away thoughts of sandy-haired children with Bryce's warm brown eyes.

It wasn't meant to be, she thought. She and Bryce had both had things they needed to learn. Bryce had had to find himself, away from his family's high expectations, just as she'd needed to learn who she was, away from her family's overprotectiveness.

Another thought occurred to her. *He bought the bike with money from the ring that he got for me. So it's like I've been with him all this time.*

Bryce had looked so sad as he stared at the wreckage of the bike. Was it because of the motorcycle itself or because of what it represented?

She only knew that the second she'd heard the ring was meant for her, she'd wanted to save the bike at all costs. But Bryce was right. It was completely pulverized. There was no saving it now.

If the bike represented their relationship, and now it was completely destroyed, what did that mean for the two of them? She could probably make herself crazy by trying to read something into that.

She would have done anything to fix the motorcycle, if there had only been hope. But it was too badly damaged. She wondered if it was the same for her and Bryce. Yesterday, she had worried that there'd been so much damage that the two of them could never be anything more than friends. But today, there had been that kiss at the waterfall. She could still hear the roar of the waterfall in her ears, the heat and the feeling of Bryce so close to her again. She could still feel exactly how her body had responded.

The concierge seemed to be taking an awfully long time getting them checked in.

Cassie marveled at the beauty of the hotel lobby. How did she and Bryce keep finding themselves in such romantic settings? The road full of wildflowers, the waterfall and now this secluded hotel.

Just watch. The way this day has been going, they'll probably tell us that there's only one room available, and then I'll have to deal with sleeping in the same room as Bryce on top of everything else.

Finally, the concierge placed a set of keys on the counter. "I'm afraid there are only two rooms available, and they're quite a way down the hall from one another," he said.

"That's perfect," Cassie replied, laughing inwardly with relief. It seemed that at least for tonight, she and Bryce would not be sleeping tantalizingly close to one another.

"In fact, they're on separate floors," the concierge continued. "If you'd like, I could try to see if we can ask a guest to move…"

"Separate floors is fine," Bryce said hastily, grabbing the keys and giving one to Cassie. "Looks like you're on one, and I'm on three." They gave one another an awkward wave goodbye, and Cassie watched as Bryce headed toward the third floor.

Her room was bright and cozy. She showered, reveling in the seemingly limitless supply of hot water.

It was almost impossible to get her mind off the ring. *Why didn't he tell me?* she thought again, wrapping herself in one towel and using another on her hair.

Had he thought she would say no? Had he been afraid to take the risk? She wasn't sure there was any way she'd ever be able to know for sure.

She heard a knock on the door.

She tucked the towel around her body a little tighter, and gave her hair one last tumble with the other towel before tossing it aside. She looked through the peephole in the door and saw that it was Bryce.

What did he want with her?

From the way he'd responded to her during that kiss, she had a feeling she knew. She wasn't certain, but she thought—she hoped—that Bryce was about to take another risk. And if he was, then this time she was determined not to pass up her chance to show him exactly how she felt.

She let the door swing open, and Bryce walked in. A second later, she was in his arms. The towel barely made a sound as it fell to the floor.

CHAPTER EIGHT

HE PRESSED HER into his arms, slamming the door shut behind him with his foot as he pulled her body into his. As her towel fell from her body, she felt the roughness of his clothes against her naked skin. An electric heat crackled between them as he bent to kiss her again.

For weeks, her mind had swirled with *what-ifs*. What if Bryce thought she was just out for a thrill? What if that first kiss had only been about nostalgia? What if they were only getting caught up in the moment, influenced by their romantic settings?

But there was nothing uncertain about what was happening now. He kissed her in a way that claimed her. He held her body close as he entered the hotel room and leaned her against the wall, his tongue exploring every corner of her mouth.

And she kissed him back just as ardently, hoping to make her intentions clear. For days, she'd been looking for a chance to show him exactly how she felt. Now that chance was here, and she wasn't going to waste it.

Bryce's kisses began to move down to her jawline. He made his way down her neck, and the crook of her shoulder, and then lower, to the first rise of her breast.

She leaned her head back and moaned in response to the heat of his mouth against her skin.

A yearning had been stirring in her body for weeks. That yearning was fully awake now, and for the first time, she didn't feel she had to hold it back.

And then his mouth was on hers again, and as his hands found her breasts she couldn't think anymore. She was lost in sensation. The traces of cedar and spice that had teased her since her arrival covered her body now. The fabric of his shirt, rough against her bare skin, both chafed and tantalized. Her fingers trembled as she reached to undo the buttons. She slid the shirt from his back, *finally* able to touch his naked chest after weeks of burning to feel his skin against hers. The room was quiet except for the rustle of their bodies moving together, but the roar of her pulse in her ears drowned out everything except the small voice inside her that screamed, *Don't stop!*

She wholeheartedly agreed with that voice. She didn't want to stop. Except for one thing.

She wrenched herself away from Bryce's kiss. "There's something I need to tell you," she said.

"What?" His breathing was heavy, ragged.

"It's been…a long time, since I've done this."

"How long?"

Five years, four months and twenty-two days. She hesitated. She didn't want to tell him. It was embarrassing. And yet…

Show him how you feel, the voice inside her urged. If she was going to get her chance, this was it.

His eyes bored into hers. "How long, Cassie?"

"About five years."

Something in his face changed. If he'd been eager

before, now he almost looked hungry. As though her words, far from slowing him down, had sparked renewed desire. He kissed her with renewed urgency, and her mouth opened to his as she desperately tried to give him all the unspoken words and pent-up emotions that she hadn't known how to express.

They were still leaning against the wall. He held her body against his, hands pressed against the small of her back as they advanced farther into the room. He walked her back until her thighs touched the edge of the four-poster bed, and then he toppled her onto it with a gentle push. He kicked off his shoes, then pulled a small packet from his pocket. Ah. Protection. She was glad to see that this was at least one way in which Bryce hadn't changed. He was still looking out for them both.

He shoved his jeans off and stood before her in his boxers. She took in everything she'd wanted to see since her first day here. Well, almost everything. His body was familiar, but different in all the ways she'd anticipated it to be. His thighs were smooth and muscled, his torso defined. His tan covered his whole body.

And if there had been any doubt up to this point about the way he felt about her, it fell away as she saw the full evidence of his attraction beneath his boxers. He eased those off now, and let her look her fill. He stood before her, vulnerable, exposed…and wanting her.

"I missed this view," she said.

"You're not the only one," he replied. He stepped forward, slipping onto the bed with her, his body alongside hers.

"There were some other things I missed, too."

"Oh? Like this?" He leaned forward and kissed her.

"Yes."

"And this?" He stroked her breast and planted a slow kiss on one nipple.

"Yes."

"How about this?" He slipped his hand away from her breast, down the length of her body and to the top of her thigh. Her legs fell apart as she felt his hand between them, searching for the sensitive little nub between her legs. His thumb glided back and forth with slow, smooth strokes, and she began to melt with pleasure.

He lifted his body atop hers, and she could feel him hard and ready at her entrance. "Now," she whispered, and he eased himself into her, in one long slow thrust. He gathered her hair into his fingers and pressed her lips toward his, and on instinct she wrapped her legs around his waist, pulling him in even deeper.

Their hips rocked together in a dance that was time-less, familiar and yet somehow entirely new. As his strokes increased in their intensity, she felt her body responding to his, a heat rising within her core. Her mouth yielded to his, over and over, and her body hovered on the brink of ecstasy. Finally, unable to resist the sensation of her body moving with his, she let herself go, her mind spinning past a place where thought existed. He continued thrusting into her for a moment longer and then shuddered before he sank beside her onto the bed.

Her body was nerveless, replete with satisfaction. She could barely move, but as his lips sought hers once more, she lifted her head to his before resting it against his chest.

They lay with their arms and legs tangled together.

She neither knew nor cared where he ended and she began. She felt him tracing one of her shoulders lightly with his finger, and despite her best efforts, the soothing caress began to lull her into sleep.

As she drifted off, she felt Bryce pull her closer against his chest. Her last thought before she fell asleep was that she'd never have had the courage to show up at Bryce's hotel room.

But she was so glad he'd taken the risk of coming to hers.

Bryce woke first early the next morning. He'd always been an early riser. It was a good quality for a surgeon. In his residency days, he'd sometimes had to wake at 5:00 a.m. or even earlier to begin his day. He'd never been able to break the habit of waking up just before dawn, even now, when his surgical career was long over. Now, with the exception of the occasional emergency, he could usually count on sleeping through the night and enjoying a leisurely morning.

He hoped that he and Cassie would be able to spend this leisurely morning together. There was no hurry to get back to the camp, and after last night, they needed some time to get their bearings with one another. Everything had happened so fast.

After their kiss at the waterfall, Bryce had known that he wasn't going to be able to set his growing attraction for Cassie aside. But he hadn't expected himself to act on it, at least not so quickly. But then he'd seen her reaction after he'd told her about the engagement ring. She had looked at the crashed motorcycle and understood exactly how he felt about it.

He hadn't wanted to admit it, but for five years, he'd

carried Cassie with him in one way or another. First by holding on to the engagement ring, then by pawning the ring and using the money for his motorcycle. And also by holding on to the anger and resentment he'd felt for so long. It had been all he had left of her, and he had been unwilling to let it go. Until she came back into his life, and he realized just how simple it could be to let it go.

He'd wrestled with his thoughts in his own hotel room for less than ten minutes before running down to Cassie's. He didn't know for sure if she wanted any more than the kiss they'd shared. But nothing could stop him from finding out.

In the heat of the moment, he hadn't cared that he was once again putting himself in a vulnerable position with her. It was one thing to act on physical feelings. It was quite another to take the risk of telling her how he felt. Or of asking how she felt. She'd certainly responded enthusiastically…but sex, he supposed, could mean anything. It didn't mean she wanted a relationship.

Had it really been five years since Cassie had had sex? That he was the last person she'd been intimate with. Although he hadn't thought about it much, he'd assumed that Cassie had probably had other partners over the years. But apparently not.

Ever since Cassie had come to El Salvador, it seemed that so many of his assumptions about her were untrue. He'd always thought of her as a bit reckless, a bit of a daredevil, but he knew now that was only one side of her.

Unlike him, Cassie was not an early riser and never had been. He watched her sleep, the sun peeking in through the blinds and casting shadows on her face. He ran his hands through her short hair, gently, careful not to wake her. He still wanted her. He'd been trying so hard to push his feelings away because he wasn't sure what she wanted. But last night, his desire had taken over.

But giving in to one night of desire didn't change the fact that he and Cassie might want very different things. No matter how he felt about Cassie, he still wanted a committed relationship. He'd had his share of flings, as well as his share of heartbreak. The next time he got emotionally involved with someone, he wanted it to be with someone interested in the long term, who might even want to start a family someday. He had no idea if that was what Cassie wanted. From everything they'd discussed about what had brought her to El Salvador, he had the distinct impression that she'd come here to escape predictability and routine. She may not be the same reckless daredevil he remembered, but he knew that she liked thrills and excitement just as much as ever. She'd told him about how much she needed to get out of the routine of her daily life in New York. What if her night with him was about nothing more than reconnecting with that adventurous side of herself?

He did not regret their night together for an instant. But he also didn't want to set himself up for more pain. He'd misunderstood Cassie's feelings for him in the past, and so he'd need to guard his heart now. Which meant telling her, as soon as possible, that he was looking for more in a relationship than she might be willing to pursue at this point in her life.

They'd have to have The Talk about how they were

going to figure out continuing to work together. The sooner they had The Talk, the better.

He'd been trying to keep quiet next to her, but suddenly both of their phones began to vibrate. Hers was across the room, inside her open travel bag, while his was next to the nightstand. Cassie opened bleary eyes at the noise. "Whuzzit?" she mumbled.

Bryce grabbed his phone from beside the bed. "It's a text from the camp," he said.

Cassie sat up, wide-awake. "What's it say?"

"There's an emergency. They need all doctors who are off base to return to the camp as soon as possible. There've been more rockfalls up in the mountains. They need all hands on deck to cope with the influx of injuries coming in. We've got to get back as soon as we can."

They looked at one another in dismay.

"I was hoping we'd have time this morning to talk about…things," said Cassie.

"Me, too. We'll have to save our conversation for the bus. Speaking of which, we should start making arrangements to get back right away." He got out of the bed and stretched. "I'll take our stuff down to the lobby and figure out our transportation home. You can meet me there when you're ready."

She nodded. He wanted to lean in for a kiss, but wasn't sure if it was a good idea. After all, they hadn't had The Talk yet. In the end, he gave her an awkward kiss on the forehead and rushed out the door.

Cassie brushed her teeth with haste. She knew the bus trip back to camp would take several hours, but that was all the more reason to leave as soon as they could.

Unfortunately, it meant that there might not be much time to talk with Bryce about what had happened.

Sex is what happened. You had sex for the first time in five years, four months—oh, who cares. The point is, it's time to reset the counter.

Indeed it was.

She'd felt vulnerable telling Bryce about her five-year dry spell, but she'd wanted him to know. Especially after he'd told her about the engagement ring. He'd kept that a secret from her for such a long time, clearly nervous about how she might respond. But telling her about the ring had changed everything. Until that moment, she'd been determined to show Bryce how she'd felt about him. But, of course, the way he felt about her was just as important.

She hoped that Bryce understood how she felt. She wasn't sure what to make of his brief kiss—on the forehead, of all places—as he'd left to make their travel arrangements. He'd been so brusque. Not unkind, but not exactly melting with emotion, either.

She wondered if he were worried about how they were going to handle working together and being in a relationship at the same time. In a way, it had been simpler five years ago, when their relationship had been a secret. They didn't have to sort out any workplace complications, because they'd simply tried their best to pretend they weren't dating while they were at work. Now, they'd probably have some complexities to work out, and she could imagine that Bryce was as worried as she was about potential pitfalls and how to avoid them.

Or so she assumed. They hadn't had time to discuss much of anything. Certainly not something as complicated as their relationship status. They hadn't

even had time to talk about whether they were in a relationship at all.

She headed to the lobby, where Bryce had arranged
their passage on a bus that would take them back to
Miraflores. When she found him, he was talking with
Enrique over the phone about the emergency. Enrique
was planning to come back from San Salvador to help
out with the victims of the rockfall. He would pick
them up in Miraflores, and they'd all head back to
camp together. Cassie felt a preemptive twinge of awkwardness as she thought about adding another person
to their party so soon after her intimate night with
Bryce. She wished they could have more time away
from the camp so that she and Bryce could have some
space to figure out what they were to each other, as
well as what they wanted to tell other people. But as
things were, it looked as though they would have to
do most of their talking on the bus. If they were even
going to talk at all.

The chicken buses of El Salvador weren't exactly
modern, but they were convenient. Although Cassie
would have preferred to travel by motorcycle, she'd
been interested in trying out the chicken buses since
she'd arrived. She'd noticed them everywhere on the
road to Juayua; their bright colors were hard to miss.
The name "chicken bus" referred to the occasional
practice of passengers bringing on chickens or other
livestock. As she boarded the bus that morning, there
wasn't a chicken in sight, although she did hear faint
clucking noises from the back of the bus.

"I know it's probably different from what you're
used to, but it's one of the most practical ways to get
around," Bryce said.

"It's perfect," said Cassie. "And it sounds like it's the fastest option we have for getting back to the camp to help out."

"The driver says the trip will take about two hours," said Bryce. "We're lucky to get on early in the morning. The buses can get pretty crowded later in the day, but we should miss the worst of it."

"Two hours," said Cassie. "It sounds like we'll have some time to talk, you and I."

He settled down beside her as the bus took off with a lurch. "I suppose it does. Look, last night…" He faltered.

She felt her stomach plummet. What was it that was so hard for him to say? Did he think last night was a mistake? Her head spun at the thought. She'd been determined not to let go of him again, but if Bryce didn't feel the same way she did, she might not have any choice in the matter.

"What is it?" she said. "Don't you think we should talk about it? Especially given that we work together? We need to figure out what we're going to tell everyone else."

"But we need to figure out what we're telling ourselves first."

It was the way she felt, too, but somehow, the way he said it filled her with trepidation.

"Look," he continued, "last night was fun. But I'll understand if you don't want anything like that to happen again."

She stared at him, aghast.

"Why do you keep saying things like that?" she said. "First after the waterfall in Juayua and now, after this? Why would you assume I wouldn't want this to happen again?"

"Because I don't know what you want," he said.

She couldn't believe it. "I thought I made it pretty clear last night that I wanted you."

"You did. For last night. But I'm not sure what that means for the future."

Hadn't she made it clear, last night, that he meant something to her? That sleeping with him meant something, just as their relationship had meant something?

Apparently not.

They both stared at each other. She realized that they were at a stalemate. One of them was going to have to take a risk and share their feelings. She was just about to speak when he did.

"Didn't you have fun, as well?" he said.

Fun? Well, she supposed she'd had fun, too. It just wasn't the first word she would have chosen to describe their evening.

Words like *intimate* or *special* or *earth-shattering* would be her preferred adjectives.

"I didn't *not* have fun," she said.

He instantly looked hurt.

"What I mean is that it was more than fun for me," she continued quickly. "This was something that I've been hoping would happen from the moment I arrived in El Salvador."

"Me, too," he said, his voice tinged with emotion.

Relief flooded through her. "It's just been so long since I've had any real excitement in my life. For the past few years, it's all been about work and about making sure other people have what they need. People who have everything they need, but who can still manage to be pretty demanding. But yesterday, I finally felt like myself again, after trying to be someone else for so long. It was like the adventurous person I used to be was still there, just waiting for me to let her out. And you helped me do that, Bryce."

He looked as though she had slapped him. "I see," he said. "So, just to be clear, last night was all about you kind of getting back in touch with your old self?"

How had she managed to say the wrong thing? She tried to reassure him.

"I just meant that I couldn't have done that without you. I was trying to explain what last night meant to me. And I'd really like to know what it meant to you."

He was silent for a long moment, and then he said, "This is what I was afraid of. All this time, you've been trying to get back to your old self. But I remember who you were, too. You're someone who's always in search of excitement, and being here gives you a chance to find it. Being *with me* gives you a chance to find it."

Cassie was horrified. Did Bryce still think that for her, last night was just about finding a thrill? Even after everything they'd been through in the last twenty-four hours, all the ways in which she had tried to express how much he meant to her, she couldn't believe that that was still how he thought about her.

"Bryce, after last night, didn't it feel to you as though something had changed between us? Didn't it feel *at all* as though something new was happening?"

He was quiet for a long time. Then his brown eyes pierced her heart as he said, "I thought that last night was about us. But it seems like it was about you. I'm glad you found yourself, I really am. But I'm looking for something more."

"Wait. Just let me explain. My words didn't come out right the first time. Will you please just listen?"

He leaned back in his seat. "I'm not going anywhere for a while."

"Ever since I was born, my diagnosis ruled my life. People were constantly telling me what I couldn't do. And so once my heart was healthy, I was determined to do everything that I couldn't do before. And I know that right at the height of my rebellious phase, I met you. You got caught up in my determination to prove myself. And that wasn't fair to you, because it probably felt like I put our relationship second to maybe… wanting an adventure or a thrill. But I don't know if anyone's ever really been able to understand what that means to me. For me, being adventurous is about living life to the last drop. It's about affirming that I actually am alive. Because I couldn't really live for the first years of my life. I was just surviving."

He nodded thoughtfully. "So last night was one of those life-affirming experiences?"

"Yes. But it was also special, because it was with you."

He seemed more relaxed now, and she took that as a good sign. "Maybe we shouldn't put too much pressure or expectations on ourselves, and just see where things go," she said.

"Fair enough," he replied. "But what do we tell people back at the camp?"

She thought for a moment. "Do we…have to tell them anything? Maybe we could keep things just between ourselves for a while. Get a sense of how we feel before we go telling other people about how we feel."

He nodded, but she wasn't sure how to read his expression. For a while, last night, Bryce had surprised her with his willingness to take chances. But at this moment, he seemed as guarded as ever.

The chicken bus lurched from side to side as it lumbered down the road. Cassie had fallen asleep, and her head dropped against Bryce's shoulder. He didn't mind it there. But their conversation had left him with a sense of unease.

He wasn't sure exactly how they were defining their relationship after their talk. He liked the idea of staying open to see where things would go, but he wasn't certain he wanted to forgo telling their colleagues anything at all. He'd done the secret relationship thing with Cassie before.

She just wants the excitement, a nagging voice said in the back of his mind.

That wasn't fair, though. It made sense not to tell their colleagues at the camp about their relationship while they were waiting to understand it themselves.

And he'd been touched by how Cassie had explained her search for excitement. How she'd spent her childhood feeling not as though she were living but merely surviving. What must it have been like, for a young, ambitious Cassie, to be cooped up in a recovery room for months on end? To be prevented from going out and exploring the world? He could certainly relate to the frustration of a long, slow recovery, constantly being told what he could or could not do. His hands trembled a bit as he recalled the early days of his recovery after the accident. Everyone had told him to take things slow, but he'd been desperate to push his recovery as far as possible, to prove what he could do, instead of wallowing in grief over what he'd lost. Finding the patience to take things slow had been one of the hardest parts of his recovery.

He realized that he had just missed the perfect opportunity to tell Cassie about the accident. Except he couldn't. What had she said? *It's about living life to the last drop.*

What would she think if she knew that coming to El Salvador wasn't about living his life but about hiding from it? Here, he was safe from the sympathetic looks of former friends who knew everything he'd lost. He was safe from anyone who might compare him to the gifted surgeon he used to be and find he didn't measure up. He was safe from family gatherings where everyone was a surgeon except for him, sharing a bond that he no longer had access to.

Cassie had said that he had helped her to find her old self. How would she feel if she knew it was all a sham? That no matter how many risks he took here, no matter how many daring things he did, none of it felt more frightening to him than going back to New York and being faced with the expectations that everyone held there. He gave a short laugh. Cassie had wanted to find her old self, while Bryce wanted nothing more than to get away from the past. From Bryce Hamlin, superstar surgeon, and all of the pressure that went with living up to that reputation.

He was glad to know that for Cassie, last night had been about more than just excitement. And he could understand that to her, being a thrill-seeker meant something more than it did to most. But what about what the two of them meant to each other?

He couldn't forget that he'd misread her before. He

reminded himself that he couldn't expect to form a long-term relationship with someone who didn't feel the same way. He needed to guard his heart until he learned what Cassie wanted: an adventure or him? Or perhaps both?

He wondered if Cassie even knew the answer.

CHAPTER NINE

THEY ARRIVED BACK at the camp in the late afternoon, and jumped right into work. They had no time to rest or get their bearings—the camp was in chaos. Bryce left their luggage next to the main office building, surprised that little Manny hadn't run up to greet them or take their things back to their cabins for them.

Medical workers were moving quickly through the camp. Bryce saw Anna, the midwife, racing toward a tent with some bandages, and he asked her how they could help.

"Everything happened so fast," Anna said. "At first there was a huge influx of patients all at once, but then the flow started to slow to a trickle about an hour ago. We think everyone who sustained injuries is here at the camp now. We're trying to triage and take them one at a time. The best thing you could do would be to grab a patient and get moving."

Bryce moved through the camp, assisting with triage so that the worst injured patients would get help first. As he continued to work his way through the wounded, he became increasingly aware of the absence of his ten-year-old shadow. Usually the boy was the first to greet him when he got back to the camp and was constantly underfoot with questions, even during emergencies. He was helpful, too, as he could often be sent to run messages between the camp doctors. His worry began to grow, until he saw something that confirmed his worst fear: Mrs. Martinez standing outside one of the medical tents holding Rosibel, tears streaming down her face.

He gripped her arm in reassurance as he headed into a tent, where Manny lay on a camp cot. A nasty gash was evident on the boy's forehead, but as Bryce examined him, he became increasingly concerned about injuries he couldn't see.

Manny tried to sit up, and Bryce put his hand on the boy's too-thin shoulder to keep him lying down.

"Do you know who I am, Manny?"

The boy seemed to be fighting to stay awake. "They told me to wait here," he responded. "But I can't stay. I have to look after Rosibel." The baby gave a cry that Mrs. Martinez quickly hushed.

As Bryce continued his examination, he was aware that Cassie had quietly entered the tent. Manny asked for his mother a few more times, but didn't seem to hear when Mrs. Martinez tried to reassure him. After a few more moments, he didn't respond at all as Bryce tried to rouse him.

"Subdural hematoma," murmured Cassie.

"We don't know for sure," he said. "Not without a CT scan."

"And we're not going to get a CT scan out here. A hospital in San Salvador might have one, but there's no time to get him there. The confusion, the loss of consciousness—it all points to subdural hematoma. We need to relieve the pressure on his brain, fast."

He knew she was right. Manny's symptoms indicated that he had suffered a blow to the head, possibly multiple blows. The trauma had resulted in a buildup of blood between the brain and skull. Each passing second put Manny at increased risk as the pressure on the brain from the bleeding increased. They needed to operate as quickly as possible.

"Is my son going to die?" asked Mrs. Martinez.

"We'll do everything we can," said Cassie. "There's bleeding that is putting pressure on his brain. We need to drill a small hole into his skull, and we might have to put in something called a shunt in order to drain the pressure. I know it sounds scary, but if we don't do it, Manny might never wake up."

Mrs. Martinez looked terrified, but she nodded. "Do whatever you need to do. I trust you, Doctor."

"The good news is that you're in very safe hands," Cassie said. "Bryce used to be one of the best surgeons in New York, before he got into obstetrics and started delivering babies. Manny couldn't ask for a better doctor to do this operation than Bryce."

Dread settled like a block of ice into Bryce's stomach. If they didn't relieve the pressure on Manny's brain quickly, he could die. But to do such a procedure here, without the benefit of modern equipment and a full staff, was daunting. Worst of all, he knew that the greatest need at this moment wasn't for modern equipment or a staff of doctors with impressive credentials.

What they needed most of all was a pair of steady hands.

"Cassie," he murmured, "can I have a word?"

She stepped away from Mrs. Martinez. "What is it?"

"I don't think I can do this."

She put her hand on his arm. "I can understand why you're nervous. It's been a while since you practiced. But there's no one else here who has more experience than you with a procedure like this, even if it's been a few years since you performed one."

"It's not that. I just don't think I can drill into Manny's skull."

"I know you care about him. The camp wouldn't be the same without him. But you can't let your feelings interfere with the operation. I don't like the thought of drilling into the cranium, either. It terrifies me. But at least you've done it before. And even though it's a dangerous procedure…even though he might die if you do it…"

"He'll definitely die if I don't," he finished for her. He knew the line. Her face was a mirror image of what it had been five years ago, when she'd said almost those exact words, and convinced him to perform an operation that had impacted their relationship and his career.

But she'd said them because she was convinced that there was no alternative. And just as he had then, he agreed with her. There was certainly no alternative now. The longer they did nothing, the more likely the subdural hematoma was to increase its pressure on Manny's brain.

"All right," he said. His voice was firm, decisive. "Let's get him prepped with anesthesia."

Maybe his tremor wouldn't flare up, he thought. As long as he kept calm, the chances of it flaring were small. And the procedure would be brief. He'd drill for a few seconds at most, just enough to open a hole in the cranium and relieve the pressure on the brain. As long as he stayed relaxed and focused, everything would be fine. The faster he worked, the less chance there would be of any complications.

For a moment, as the nurses prepped Manny for surgery, Bryce almost felt like his old self again. It was just like the days of his surgical residency. Once again, he was the one expected to step up to handle a dangerous, difficult case. And once again, Cassie was looking at him as though she relied on him. As though she trusted him.

Ultimately, it was her look of trust that stopped him.

Cassie had faith in him. Not to perform surgery, but to do the right thing. And he knew that he couldn't operate on Manny just because he wanted to feel like a surgeon again. The risk of his hands trembling at the wrong moment was simply too great.

He couldn't put someone in danger. Especially not someone he cared about.

He lowered the drill. "I can't do it," he said. He saw the surprise in her eyes above her surgical mask. He knew he needed to explain quickly, in a way that would brook no argument. Every second counted. "I have a hand tremor. I can usually control it, but I can't always predict when it will flare up. I can't do this operation. It's too risky."

He put the drill into Cassie's hands and closed her fingers around it.

To her credit, Cassie didn't hesitate, although she must have been shocked to find herself to be the one holding the drill. But if she did feel shocked, she didn't show it. She simply took Bryce's place at Manny's head.

"Show me exactly where to drill and for how long," she said.

Bryce was relieved that she hadn't stopped him with any further questions. He knew that Cassie would always put her patient's well-being above her curiosity, but he was sure that he would have questions to answer the moment the surgery was over.

He showed Cassie where to place the drill. With luck, they would be able to suction the blood out through the hole.

Cassie's hands were perfectly steady as she drilled the hole, stopping exactly when Bryce gave the word. Bryce was relieved as he saw that blood immediately began to drain from the hole. There would be no need for a shunt—Cassie had performed the procedure beautifully, and they could close as soon as the blood had finished draining.

"You're doing great," he said to Cassie. Her face was white as a sheet.

"Glad to hear it," she breathed. He could almost feel how still she was trying to be as the fluid drained from Manny's head. "I have to say, this is a first. When you deliver babies, you typically don't require the use of a drill."

"Just keep your hands steady. We're almost there."

Finally, enough fluid had drained that they could close the scalp. He showed Cassie where to stitch the scalp, but she was already starting to press the edges of the incision together as he spoke. He straightened his back and went outside to where Mrs. Martinez was waiting.

"Manny came through the procedure just fine," he said as she cried tears of relief. "He should start coming round in a few hours. We'll monitor him for at least seventy-two hours, but the procedure went smoothly.

He'll need to keep still for a long time, but he should be feeling better soon."

"Oh, thank you," said Mrs. Martinez. She rushed inside the tent to be near her son.

It was starting to rain. Bryce could feel a few drops at first, and then a stronger, steady patter. He couldn't bring himself to move back inside the tent. He wanted just a moment to breathe, to feel relieved that Manny's procedure had gone well.

But his relief was short-lived. As Mrs. Martinez went into the tent, Cassie came out, her eyes blazing.

"What the hell just happened, Bryce?"

"You saved a child's life."

"Bullshit! You know that's not what I'm talking about. You hesitated. You handed the reins over to me at a crucial moment, just like you did with that complicated C-section. What's going on? Why aren't you doing surgical procedures?"

"I told you why, in there." He held up his hands. The tremor was faint, but it was visible. "Can you see it?"

"My god, Bryce, how long has that been going on?"

"Since a few weeks after we broke up."

He saw the realization dawn on her face.

"I was in a car accident, just after you left. Hit on the expressway by a drunk driver. The physical therapy helped quite a bit afterward, but I was never able to recover the full use of my hands."

"So that was the reason you lost your job. That was why you changed specialties. You couldn't be a surgeon anymore. Not with a hand tremor." She gave a low dark laugh. "And to think that when I first got here, I was worried that it might have had something to do with me."

She was still slowly shaking her head. The expression on her face was incredulous. "I can't imagine what the recovery must have been like."

Her continued silence was making him anxious, and he spoke nervously to fill the gap. "There's still a lot I can do," he said. "For a while, I thought I'd never be able to be a physician again. But then one of my mentors recommended obstetrics. There's a lot I can do that doesn't involve surgery. Most of the procedures that come my way are pretty low risk."

"How could you not tell me this?"

"It was five years ago. Does it really matter anymore?"

"Yes! Yes, it matters! Why didn't you call me, why didn't you say anything? You were in a major life-changing accident. No matter what happened between us, if you'd called me, I would have been there for you."

His jaw tightened. "I didn't want your pity."

"I wouldn't have offered you pity. I would have offered you support. I would have been there for you. I didn't know. I wish you had called me. I wish you hadn't had to go through your recovery alone."

"You left a note that indicated you didn't want any calls from me."

"And that was a mistake. It was a stupid mistake! But I couldn't have known you were going to be in an accident. I didn't know you were going to lose your profession. You loved being a surgeon. It was everything to you. And you were so gifted."

There, he could see it in her eyes. Pity. The exact response that he didn't want from her.

He'd spent the past three years in El Salvador trying to escape from the shadow of Bryce Hamlin, genius surgeon. He'd tried to carve out a life for himself in New York, and it hadn't worked. Everywhere he turned, everyone—whether they were colleagues, family or friends—wanted to talk about the doctor he *used* to be. The person he used to be. No one seemed to be able to talk to him without comparing him to his past, pre-accident self.

But he wasn't that person anymore. Even though everyone seemed to regret that that version of him was gone. Even though Cassie now stood before him, expressing her pity that he was no longer the surgeon he had been.

He realized that she'd done the same thing she'd done when she came into his life five years ago. Back then, she opened his life to more excitement. She pushed him to take more risks. Just as she unwittingly had today. Even though she hadn't known about his hands, she'd still pushed him to do the procedure on Manny. That was who Cassie was. She pushed him, challenged him, made him take risks he hadn't even known were there.

But letting her back into his heart was a risk he couldn't take. Because along with all the memories of how she pushed him, came all the feelings of heartbreak after things had gone too far.

He'd already survived that heartbreak once. He knew he would never be able to survive it again.

"Cassie," he said. "We need to end this."

"What do you mean?"

"I mean us. We need to stop, the two of us. We aren't going to be able to make it work."

Tears mixed with rainwater streamed down her face.

"I don't understand," she said.

"Because I'm not the rock star surgeon anymore. More than that, I'm not the *person* I used to be. But I think you might still need that person in your life. Everything you said today on the bus made me realize that you want an adventure. And I think that's a wonderful thing. It's even something I want, a lot of the time. But it's not something I want from a relationship."

Her lips barely moved, and he had to strain to hear her against the rainfall as she said, "Is that all you think I want from a relationship?"

He didn't know. But he didn't think he could handle the disappointment of finding out.

Not again.

"Let's just call it what it was," he said. "A trip down memory lane. The sooner we stop holding on to the people we used to know, the sooner we can both focus on our futures."

Her chin trembled, and he could hear her trying to keep her voice steady. "I'm not holding on to anyone I used to know. Because I don't think I ever really knew you. I sure as hell don't know you now."

She turned and left, leaving him standing there in the rain.

Strange, he thought, as she walked away. Right after the breakup, he had fantasized about what it would feel like if he had been the one to initiate the breakup. He'd nursed his hurt and his anger, and he'd thought he wanted a chance to show her how it felt, to hurt her the way she'd hurt him. But as he watched her walk into the darkness, he knew that turning the tables wasn't satisfying at all.

* * *

Cassie bunched her pillow into a ball. She'd tried a hundred different pillow positions and multiple corners of her mattress, but she couldn't get comfortable enough to sleep. The rain pounded on the roof of her quarters. She was exhausted from a long day of travel and treating patients injured by the mountain rockfall. But sleep would not come. She'd been tossing and turning for hours with little success. She checked the time on the cell phone next to her bed. Three in the morning. If she was going to get any rest before her shift started in four hours, she needed to drift off soon.

The trouble was, it was hard to sleep when you were heartbroken and furious with someone at the same time.

She turned onto her other side, trying to block out the noise of the rain with her extra pillow. Stupid raindrops. There was no way she was ever going to fall asleep with it pounding on the roof, insistent as a drum.

Oh, who are you kidding? she thought. Her sleeplessness had nothing to do with the rain, and everything to do with Bryce and what he'd said earlier that evening.

She had thought he'd be willing to give their relationship a chance. Instead, he'd cut things off abruptly. Before they'd even gotten off the ground. What was he thinking?

Just twenty-four hours before, they'd made love. And now, she wasn't sure he ever wanted to look at her again.

What did you expect? she asked herself. *He put his*

heart on the line for you once, and got it broken. You should have known he wouldn't be able to do it now.

He'd told her that he thought she wanted an adventure. It confirmed everything she had feared. Despite her best efforts, despite everything she'd tried to show him, she had failed. She had hurt him too badly five years ago. He was never going to believe that he'd been more to her than an exciting thrill.

And now things were over between them, almost before they'd begun.

She wondered, for the millionth time, why he hadn't called and told her about the accident. No matter what had happened between them, he should have known that she would have been there to support him through something like that.

But maybe he hadn't wanted her support at that particular time. And if he thought that he'd been nothing more than a fling to her, then it made sense that he wouldn't call.

At the very least, he could have told her about his hand tremor when she arrived at the camp. But he'd kept that a secret, as well. She thought about how Bryce had claimed that it had been freeing to give up surgery. To her, it didn't sound as though he felt it had been freeing. It sounded as though the pain of the breakup had been compounded by the pain of the accident.

When he'd told her that she would be the one to drill into Manny's skull, she'd almost wondered if he'd lost his mind. She couldn't believe that he would turn such an important procedure over to her. And she trusted him. She'd been so confident that he would be able to help. The situation was dire, but she'd known that Bryce, of all people, was the perfect person to handle it. His natural caution and his surgical expertise had been crucial at that moment.

For a split second, she'd been unable to comprehend his hesitation. Oh, she could understand why it would be a hard moment for him. She could tell he cared for Manny deeply, and treating a subdural hematoma was not without its dangers, even though trepanation and drainage often led to dramatic improvements in patients. It was a crude procedure, but it was effective. Even if they'd had time to bring Manny to a hospital in San Salvador, his treatment would have been much the same. The boy would most likely be on the mend within days.

At least that was one thing to be relieved about on a difficult day such as this. When everything else was going wrong.

Bryce had said he didn't want her pity. She thought about when he'd bandaged her ankle, and she'd told him about her heart defect. How she'd become known as Heart Defect Girl in school. She had never wanted to be seen just as someone with a heart defect. There was so much more to her than that. Just as Bryce probably didn't want to be seen as just an accident victim, a former surgeon with the best days of his career behind him.

She wondered if that's what he'd heard when she'd expressed her shock that he hadn't called her for help during such a difficult time in her life. It wasn't what she had meant. But then maybe he'd only heard what he was afraid of hearing.

If he had called, would they still be together now?

The question stopped her racing thoughts. Maybe that was the point. After the breakup, she'd felt so guilty about getting Bryce into trouble. She'd left him out of guilt. If he had called her, or if someone had told her that Bryce had been terribly injured in a life-altering car accident, she might have felt even guiltier because of his injuries. Perhaps even to the extent that she would have felt compelled to stay with him.

As much as she hated to admit it, maybe Bryce had been right not to contact her. He did know her, after all. He knew that if she found out about the accident, she would have come rushing to his side. But then Bryce would have had to deal with her presence while he was recovering, and she would have had to deal with her own feelings while also supporting him. It would have been very hard for both of them. If Bryce had reached out to her, then maybe they would still be together now. But it would be for all of the wrong reasons.

They'd both needed some space to grow in the past five years. He might not have been honest with her about everything, but the changes she saw in him were things he couldn't lie about. He was more easygoing, more carefree than he'd ever been when she had known him. Those changes were real. She thought again of their night in Juayua. Her response had been real.

She wondered who she would be today if she hadn't left Bryce all that time ago. As painful as the breakup had been, the last five years had helped her to know who she was in a way she could never have imagined. She wasn't the wild child she used to be, nor was she the straitlaced, buttoned-up Dr. Andover who did noth-ing but work, cook meals and then go to work again the next day.

She thought back to what she'd told Bryce on the bus. She'd tried to explain that for her, having adventures and taking risks were life-affirming. She'd meant it, from the bottom of her heart. But would she ever have realized that about herself if it hadn't been for that conversation with Bryce? She hadn't really thought about what it meant to her to be daring until she was confronted with the possibility of losing him again.

She would never have had that conversation with Bryce, or even with herself, if she hadn't come to El Salvador. For years, she'd told herself that she'd given up her daredevil personality because of what happened with Bryce. But she'd found that part of herself again because of him, too.

She'd done what she came here to do: she'd reconnected with her adventurous side. She had hoped she'd be able to do it without anyone getting hurt this time, but history, it seemed, was doomed to repeat itself.

At least this time, she knew what she needed to do next.

Bryce wasn't sure what it would be like to work with Cassie after their trip to Juayua, especially after he'd told her that he didn't see things working out between them. He was worried that their mutual discomfort would probably be distracting for both of them. But his concerns about working with her turned out to be unfounded. He barely ever saw her anymore. On the rare occasions when they did cross paths, she was excruciatingly polite. They kept their conversations short and professional. He missed the easy friendship that had built between them, but he didn't see any way for those times to return.

He considered asking Enrique if the two of them could be placed on opposite schedules, even though their awkward run-ins were already few and far between. But as he and Anna were talking together after a tough delivery, Anna mentioned how much she missed seeing Cassie during the day.

"What?" said Bryce. "Are you not seeing much of her, either?"

"She asked to be switched to night shift two weeks ago," Anna replied. "I guess maybe she needed a change. But it means we're not able to work together very often anymore. It's too bad. She's got such a reassuring way with patients."

It seemed there was no need to request a schedule change, as Cassie had beaten him to it. He didn't know if he should feel grateful that he wouldn't have to work the night shift or annoyed that Cassie had requested the change before he did. He supposed the important thing to focus on was that he didn't see Cassie very often at all.

It was a small consolation. He missed her terribly. He missed her banter, her laughter, their occasional squabbles over patients. He missed her, but it would have hurt more to see her.

Little Manny's recovery was going well. The biggest obstacle the medical team faced was trying to keep the boy still. He was curious as a squirrel, constantly being reminded that he couldn't run after the doctors to see what they were up to. Bryce tried to ease his restlessness by visiting frequently.

He was glad when a shipment of donated books and toys came in from San Salvador. He headed to the pediatric recovery tent, hoping that bringing a few of the new items to Manny would help to relieve his boredom. He was surprised to find the normally cheerful boy looking despondent.

"What's wrong?" Bryce asked as Manny sorted list-lessly through the bundle Bryce had brought him.

"I miss Dr. Cassie," he said.

He felt a jolt through his stomach at Cassie's name.

"I understand," he said. "You don't get to see her as much anymore now that she's on night shift."

"No, I don't get to see her as much because she's *gone*," Manny said.

Bryce froze. "What do you mean *gone*?"

"She left a few days ago," said Manny, mournfully. "She woke me up to say goodbye and said she wasn't sure when she was coming back." His teary eyes met Bryce's. "But she will come back, won't she?"

Bryce tried to conceal his shock. "I hope so," he said. And the moment he spoke the words aloud, he realized they were true.

For five years, he'd lived without Cassie in his life. And as difficult and painful as the last few weeks had been, he realized that nothing was more painful than the possibility that she might be gone from his life forever.

He had to find out if she were really gone. And if she was, then he wouldn't rest until he found a way to get her back.

CHAPTER TEN

BRYCE COULDN'T STAND another moment of uncertainty. He went directly to Enrique's tent. "Is it true?" he said, striding in.

"Hold on," said Enrique, who was wrapping up a conference call. He finished, and then turned to Bryce. "I could sit here and pretend to be naive, but I have a feeling I know what you're asking about. Or *whom* you're asking about."

"Is she really gone?"

"If you're talking about the best ob-gyn this camp has ever had, then yes, Dr. Andover is gone. She went back to New York. She said something about a job at her old hospital that sounded very interesting."

Bryce waved a hand dismissively. He didn't care about whether Cassie had her old job back. He cared that she was gone. "When did she leave?"

"A couple of days ago. She asked me to be discreet about it."

She'd been gone for days, and he hadn't noticed? His heart plummeted.

"In fact, I'll be blunt. She asked me specifically not to mention it to you when she left. But she did leave you a note." Enrique handed him an envelope.

A note. How appropriate. Would it always be notes with the two of them? He could see the outline of her writing from within the envelope. Clearly, she'd had much more to say this time than she had five years ago.

He opened the note.

Dear Bryce,

I wanted to leave you a better note this time. One that would force me to say everything our relationship deserves, no matter how hard it is to put the words down on paper. I used to think it was so important to live without fear, but thanks to you I know that it's even more important to live without regrets. And if I left El Salvador without you knowing how much our time together has meant to me…well, that would be a huge regret.

We've both talked about how we grew up in overprotective families. We probably both know, more than anyone, that sometimes you have to have some distance from the people you care for the most in order to grow. And so I'm leaving now, in order to give us both that distance and in the hope that we're both stronger, better people for it.

We've said some wonderful things about moving forward, but I guess Juayua showed us that we'd never be able to follow through. I have to admit that there were many, many times that I didn't want to follow through. Holding on to the past felt so good that I didn't really want to think about the future.

But we both need to move on, because we both deserve good futures. You, Bryce, deserve

an amazing future. And I can't bear to stand in your way.
Cassie

He blinked back tears.

He'd messed up. He knew it. He'd been so worried about protecting his heart that he hadn't realized he was preventing himself from seeing what was right in front of him. He really was his parents' son. He'd grown up to be just as overprotective and obsessive as they were, except for him, his overprotectiveness was all directed toward his emotions. And now it had cost him everything. Unless there was a chance he could get it all back.

He knew, now, that he'd been foolish to ever think that he was just a thrill to her. She'd shown him that repeatedly. And if she also happened to be someone who needed excitement in her life...well, he'd learned that so did he. He'd never want to quell that adventurous side of her. It was an integral part of her...a part of her that he wanted in his life more than ever.

He folded the note into a small square and put it into his wallet. "I've got to find her."

Enrique sighed. "Why do I have a feeling I'm about to lose yet another one of my best doctors?"

"Just for a little while. I'll come back, I promise."

"Anything to help you figure out your love life," said Enrique. "Actually, it's fine. You've got more vacation days saved up than any of us. But...don't stay away too long, Bryce. We need you here. Come home soon. And bring her with you, if you can."

He felt that he'd have to be very, very lucky to come back with Cassie. Still, he had to try. He might not be able to find her in New York. And then even if he did, she might not even want to see him.

It was just a risk he'd have to take.

It felt incredibly strange for Cassie to be back at Brooklyn General Hospital.

After just a couple months in El Salvador, it felt surreal to set foot in a New York hospital again. The rooms and hallways were immaculate and full of state-of-the-art equipment. The hospital was set up to take care of anything a patient needed, as well as some things they didn't. Cassie remembered all too well the requests many of her patients had made for specialty spa treatments as part of their birthing "packages." If a patient were wealthy enough, the hospital would provide anything that money could buy.

Despite all of the wealth on display, she was also struck by how impersonal the hospital was. She watched doctors and nurses reviewing charts and transporting patients, and she realized that she barely recognized any of the faces. When she'd worked here, she'd been so focused on her job that she hadn't had much time to form relationships with many of her team members. It was different at the medical camp, where everyone knew everyone else on sight. The small size of the camp made it easy to discern who did and didn't belong there. But here, even though she knew the entire layout of the hospital like the back of her hand, the people themselves were strangers. Even though she'd spent more time at work than at home over the past few years, these people didn't know her and she didn't know them.

But the impersonality of her surroundings was a small price to pay for the position and salary she'd just negotiated. Cassie had returned to her old hospital with a proposal. Brooklyn General, with its wealth of resources, was in an ideal position to form a liaison office with Medicine International. Doctors at Brooklyn General would be able to volunteer in El Salvador as well as other countries, and physicians from around the world would be able to consider Brooklyn General a home base to use for research, medical supplies and equipment. And Cassie would oversee it all.

The hospital administrators had been thrilled with the idea. It would make the hospital look good—a private hospital with a strong philanthropic outlook—and it would allow physicians to volunteer without having to leave their jobs as Cassie had. They were concerned, however, that overseeing the department would mean extensive amounts of travel to El Salvador and probably to many other countries, as well. Would Cassie be able to handle that?

She smiled and said that she thought she could make it work.

She walked out of the hospital's large double doors and took a deep breath, reveling in the warm sunshine. In a single afternoon, she'd set up a job that could provide all the adventure and excitement she would ever need.

The only thing to overshadow her happiness was the occasional thought of Bryce.

She knew she'd done the right thing by leaving, but that didn't make it any less painful.

Forward motion, she thought. She had left so that she and Bryce could move on. And for the past few days, she'd been doing exactly that. She had an exciting new job to look forward to, and as for her love life…maybe, someday, that would sort itself out. Until then, she was going keep trying to let go of the past and move forward.

To celebrate the good news about the job, she headed to her favorite coffee shop just across the street from the hospital.

She was standing in line to order when she felt a tap at her elbow. She looked down at a coffee cup. And the hand that was holding it belonged to Bryce.

"Black, with two sugars," he said.

"Bryce!" she cried. "What are you doing here?"

He gave her a lopsided smile. "Do you really have to ask? I got your note."

"But how did you know I was here?"

"A little social media detective work. Also it's a coffee shop. Any given coffee shop, on any given day, has a fifty-fifty chance of you being inside it. The odds were increased for this one, though, because I heard through a friend of a friend that you had a job interview at your old hospital today. It wasn't too hard to predict that you'd stop for coffee afterward."

Her eyes didn't leave his. Why had he come all this way?

She had a feeling it wasn't just to buy her a cup of coffee.

Although she did gratefully accept the cup. They headed outside into the sunshine.

As she sipped her coffee, he explained. "I did come because of your note. Because everything you said in it was right. And because it made me realize, finally, that you weren't leaving because you didn't care. You were willing to give up everything for both of our sakes, all over again. And I was so afraid of the past repeating itself that I couldn't even see the future that was unfolding right in front of me."

She smiled. "If I'd known this would be your reaction, I'd have left a better note five years ago."

He winced. "I should have called you after the accident. I should have known you would want to know. I was such an idiot."

She put a finger to his lips. "Neither of us made the brightest moves five years ago," she said.

"But I should have at least told you about it when you got to El Salvador," he said. "I guess I didn't because it felt as though you were looking at me in a way that you never used to. I wanted you to think that I was this brave person, someone who took risks and went on dangerous medical missions because I had courage. Not because I was someone who'd been through an accident, lost his chosen profession and didn't feel he needed to be as careful as he used to be."

"Oh, Bryce. You were so worried about what you lost. Didn't you notice what you'd built for yourself? Didn't you think I'd see that?"

"I wanted you to see that. I hoped you would. But I was worried you'd compare me to who I used to be."

"Well, you were right about one thing."

"What's that?"

She smiled. "I *was* looking at you quite a bit."

He laughed.

"I can understand why you didn't tell me, but I wish you had," she said. "If only for the sake of being honest with each other."

"Honesty is always a good idea," he agreed.

"In the interest of total honesty, I should say that I'm glad you're here."

"Am I too late, though? It sounds like you've already got your old job back. If you're settling into your old life here, I'll understand."

She swatted his shoulder playfully. "My old job? Are you kidding me? That's not what I'm here for." She told him about the Medicine International liaison office she would be heading.

She carefully emphasized that the job would involve lots of travel, especially back and forth to Central American countries. In fact, there might even be a chance to build a strong relationship between the hospital and an El Salvador office.

"Wow," he said. "With all of that excitement in your life, I wonder if you might have room for someone who's just...ordinary."

She looked him square in the eye. "I don't know anyone who is *just* ordinary."

"But you do. You know me. And I've worked very hard to be okay with being ordinary."

"Bryce, you are *not* ordinary."

"I am, though. For years, I've been trying to be okay with the idea that I'm not gifted anymore. I'm not the person who handles all the challenging cases. I'm not the person who pulls off miracles in the operating room. I'm just a normal person who tries hard to be a good doctor. And it's taken me a long time to be okay with just being a normal person, because for so much of that time, I was competing with my past self. Instead of just trying to be me."

"And so you needed to get away from everyone else who was comparing you to your past self."

"Exactly. Because I had to accept that instead of being talented and admired and a star in the operating room, I was just plain old Bryce Hamlin. And being around other people who knew me in the old days made it so hard. Because if we're being honest, what's really so great about being plain old Bryce Hamlin?"

"For one thing, I'm in love with him."

The words had sprung from her lips, unbidden. She hadn't meant to say them. She hadn't planned it at all. But from the moment she'd seen Bryce at the coffee shop, she'd known it was true, even if she hadn't yet formed the words consciously in her mind.

She loved him. And no matter how he felt, she wanted him to know. She'd spent five years of her life without Bryce.

Five years, five months and twenty-three days, her brain supplied helpfully. The time that had passed, to the day, since she'd left that horrible note for him.

But she didn't want to spend another minute apart.

If writing the first note had been like tearing her heart out, writing the second had been like stomping it into the ground. But just like last time, she couldn't see any other way out of the situation.

Fortunately, Bryce could. She still wasn't sure what she'd written in that note to compel him to seek her out, but she supposed it didn't matter. He was here now. It was still hard to believe that he'd actually come all this way, that he'd found her. As they walked together, she slipped her arm into his. Partly to be companionable and partly to prove to herself that he was really there.

Her words still hung in the air between them. She'd taken a risk. But even though she didn't know what he would say, she didn't wish her words unsaid. Bryce had talked about the future. If they were going to have a future together, they'd need to be completely honest with each other, starting now. And the honest truth was, she loved him. And even if he didn't feel the same way, she needed him to know.

He took her hand, his brown eyes dark and wet. "You're in love with plain old Bryce Hamlin, huh?" His voice sounded rather dazed.

"Total honesty, remember?" She was still nervous, because he hadn't yet told her how he felt, but she gained confidence from knowing that her words reflected what she really, truly wanted to say to him. "You said that I've been looking at you in a different way. And maybe you're right. But it has nothing to do with the fact that you were riding a motorcycle, or negotiating with gang leaders, or going on midnight rides through the mountains to deliver vaccines. It never had anything to do with that.

"I fell in love with your kindness, Bryce. I fell in love with the look on your face when you hand a baby to a new mother. I fell in love with your determination to protect everyone in your care. And none of that has anything to do with you being a gifted surgeon. It has to do with you being a committed doctor and a compassionate human. That's who plain old Bryce is."

"Wow," said Bryce. "He sounds like a pretty swell guy."

"I think so. When he's not being a complete lunkhead."

"This ordinary Bryce…he sounds like he has a lot of people depending on him."

"Oh, yes. There are colleagues back in El Salvador who are counting on him to return as soon as possible. There are patients who need his help. And there's a ten-year-old boy whose heart is aching for him to return."

"Well—" he took the arm that was entwined with hers and pulled her close to him "—it sounds like plain old Bryce has a pretty amazing life. Awesome job, great friends and colleagues, and…someone who loves him." He put his arms around her, touched his forehead to hers. "And he loves her right back."

He kissed her then, his lips demanding that her mouth open, and she yielded readily to the touch of his mouth on hers. For a moment, she was completely lost, the sensation of his kiss invading her senses. And there again was that cedar spice smell, tingling at her nose.

Suddenly, she had an idea. She wasn't sure how Bryce would react but…*total honesty*, she thought.

"Wait," she said, pulling away from him. She got down on one knee, still holding his hand in hers. His eyes widened. She definitely hadn't planned on doing this today, but now that they were here, she knew it felt right. Five years ago, Bryce had wanted to propose to her, but he'd been rejected before he even got the chance. She wasn't going to put him through that again. At that time, she'd led him to believe that she wasn't serious about their relationship. She wanted him to know, here and now, that she was ready for commitment.

As she took his hand and knelt before him, a flutter of nerves overtook her stomach. *Damn, this really is nerve-racking. What if it's not the right time? What if he says no? No wonder it's hard for so many men to get up the nerve to do this.*

Anxiety washed over her. She could feel Bryce's hand shake a little, but she held it steady in hers. If there was ever a time to jump in with both feet, this was it.

"I want to ask you something."

"Cassie."

"Just let me finish. I want to do this properly. Five years ago, you were going to put your heart on the line for me. And now I'm going to put mine on the line for you."

"Cassie."

"I don't have a ring, or anything. But we can—"

"Would you look at your hand?"

She looked at her hand, the one he was holding. The copper spark of the motorcycle ignition ring winked back from her from where it rested around her ring finger. Her mind seemed to be working very slowly. She kept looking back and forth from his face to her hand, trying to absorb what had just happened. Then she stood up with a start.

Finally, she managed to croak out a question. "How long have I been wearing this?"

"I'm not exactly sure, but I think it was somewhere around the words *total honesty.*"

"That long? I can't believe I didn't notice!"

His smile went from ear to ear. "Then it must feel pretty natural for you to wear it."

She was still staring at the ring in amazement. He put both arms around her. She leaned into him and he nuzzled her hair.

"If our goal is to be totally honest, then I want to start by being honest about how I feel." He tilted her chin up toward his. "I love you, Cassie. I love everything about you, but most of all, I love your adventurous side. I love the part of you that pushes me past my limits. I don't know how I've managed to get through the last five years of my life without you, and I don't want to waste another minute anywhere other than by your side. I love you, and now that I've finally got you back, I'm going to hold on to you with both hands."

He kissed her deeply, but after a moment she had to break away. She was smiling too hard to hold his kiss. There were tears in her eyes, which he brushed away. "Happy tears, I hope?" he said.

"You know they are."

He kissed her again. "Now, I don't want to be presumptuous. But given that you got down on one knee just a moment ago…can I assume the answer is yes?"

"That would be a safe assumption."

He buried his nose in her hair again. "We can get you a real engagement ring. I've been holding on to this as a good luck charm. I just used it because I happened to have it handy. The moment I saw you, I knew I had to take the chance. We'll head to a jewelry store tomorrow and you can pick out something beautiful."

"Oh, no," she said. "This one is perfect. It's already beautiful. Besides, we don't have time to go ring shopping. We'll need to get started on wedding planning soon if we want to get married before we head back to El Salvador."

The smile on his face told her everything she needed to know about his desire for a quick wedding. "It sounds like a plain old New York City Hall wedding might be in order for plain old Bryce Hamlin."

She kissed him. "Sounds perfect."

"Are you sure that's okay? You don't want a big wedding?"

She poked him in the side. "I want a fast wedding.

I've spent the past five years not being married to you, and I don't think I can take it for another minute longer than I absolutely have to. Besides, people are waiting for us in El Salvador."

"My poor motorcycle. At least it gets a chance to live on with us."

"It's the perfect ring. It tells our story. I wouldn't want anything else. Unless you want to keep it for luck?"

"It's brought me all the luck I need," he said. And they were quiet for quite some time after that.

When they did stop kissing, Cassie wanted to know how Bryce had had the courage to slip the ring on her finger. "How did you know I'd say yes?"

"I didn't! I knew that it might all end in disaster. But I had to take the risk. I remembered what you said about living rather than just surviving. I wanted to live, so I decided to put the ring on your finger and see what happened. I knew that even if you didn't say yes, it was the right thing to do."

"How come?"

He snuggled closer to her. "Because I've realized that bravery has nothing to do with the danger you're facing and everything to do with what's in your own heart."

She wrapped her arms around him and considered her own heart. Broken and repaired, a hundred times over. But for all the trouble her heart had caused her, it was hers, and it was the kind of heart that showed who she was. Maybe her heart hadn't started life in the strongest shape, but with enough love and care, it had healed. And that made sense to her. Learning to love, she knew now, wasn't about guarding your heart or trying desperately to keep it from getting broken. Love wasn't about protecting your heart from getting hurt. It was about trusting that it would heal when it did.

* * * * *

MILLS & BOON

Coming next month

A PUP TO RESCUE THEIR HEARTS
Alison Roberts

'Off the sofa, Lucky,' he commanded. 'We've talked about this before, haven't we?'

Lucky jumping down was enough to break that stillness for Stevie. She was moving further away from him – towards the fireplace.

'This mantlepiece…' She stepped onto the flagstone hearth to reach up and touch the massive beam of wood that was embedded in the wall. 'It looks like a whole tree trunk. It's incredible. How old *is* your house?'

'Dates to about mid-eighteenth century I believe. The wood burner doesn't look too out of place, though, does it?'

'It's gorgeous. And I love how you can stack the logs on either side like that. Did the flue from the log burner just go inside the original chimney?'

She was leaning in, to peer up into the space and Josh didn't think to warn her not to touch the inside of the chimney. It hadn't occurred to him that there could still be some ancient soot clinging to stonework until Stevie straightened and pushed that curl back off her face, leaving a huge, black streak in its place.

'Oh, no…'

'What? Have I got something on my face?' Stevie was touching her nose now, and then her cheek and then she saw her fingers and laughed.

'Don't move…' Josh walked past the fireplace to where the living room led into his kitchen. He grabbed a clean tea towel, ran it under the tap and went back to Stevie who used it to wipe her hands and then her face.

'Have I got it all?'

'Almost.'

Without thinking, Josh reached out and used the pad of his thumb to wipe a remnant of smudge from her cheek. Close to her mouth. So close, he could feel the corners of her lips. And how incredibly soft her skin was… It was his turn to stop in his tracks, suddenly overwhelmed with what he could feel. And see. The way Stevie's gaze was locked on his, the way those gloriously tawny eyes darkened and…oh, man… the way her lips had parted again. And this time, he just knew that she *was* waiting to be kissed.

That she *wanted* to be kissed.

Continue reading
A PUP TO RESCUE THEIR HEARTS
Alison Roberts

Available next month
www.millsandboon.co.uk

COMING SOON!

We really hope you enjoyed reading this book.
If you're looking for more romance, be sure to
head to the shops when new books are
available on

Thursday 21st January

To see which titles are coming soon, please visit
millsandboon.co.uk/nextmonth

MILLS & BOON

THE HEART OF ROMANCE

A ROMANCE FOR EVERY KIND OF READER

MODERN

Prepare to be swept off your feet by sophisticated, sexy and seductive heroes, in some of the world's most glamourous and romantic locations, where power and passion collide.
8 stories per month.

HISTORICAL

Escape with historical heroes from time gone by. Whether your passion is for wicked Regency Rakes, muscled Vikings or rugged Highlanders, awaken the romance of the past.
6 stories per month.

MEDICAL

Set your pulse racing with dedicated, delectable doctors in the high-pressure world of medicine, where emotions run high and passion, comfort and love are the best medicine.
6 stories per month.

True Love

Celebrate true love with tender stories of heartfelt romance, from the rush of falling in love to the joy a new baby can bring, and a focus on the emotional heart of a relationship.
8 stories per month.

Desire

Indulge in secrets and scandal, intense drama and plenty of sizzling hot action with powerful and passionate heroes who have it all: wealth, status, good looks…everything but the right woman.
6 stories per month.

HEROES

Experience all the excitement of a gripping thriller, with an intense romance at its heart. Resourceful, true-to-life women and strong, fearless men face danger and desire - a killer combination!
8 stories per month.

DARE

Sensual love stories featuring smart, sassy heroines you'd want as a best friend, and compelling intense heroes who are worthy of them.
4 stories per month.

To see which titles are coming soon, please visit

millsandboon.co.uk/nextmonth